Finn Rhodes Forever

Finn Rhodes Forever

Stephanie Archer

ORION

Stephanie Archer writes spicy laugh-out-loud romance. She believes in the power of best friends, stubborn women, a fresh haircut, and love. She lives in Vancouver with a man and a dog.

For spicy bonus scenes, news about upcoming books, and book recs, sign up for her newsletter at:
https://www.stephaniearcherauthor.com/newsletter

Instagram: @stephaniearcherauthor
Tiktok: @stephaniearcherbooks

To check content warnings for any of Stephanie's books, visit www.stephaniearcherauthor.com/content-warnings

An Orion paperback

This edition first published in Great Britain in 2024 by Orion Fiction
an imprint of The Orion Publishing Group Ltd
Carmelite House, 50 Victoria Embankment
London EC4Y 0DZ

An Hachette UK company

1 3 5 7 9 10 8 6 4 2

A CIP catalogue record for this book is
available from the British Library.

ISBN (Mass Market Paperback) 9781398724501
eBook ISBN 9781398724518

Printed in UK Clays Ltd, Elcograf, S.p.A.

www.orionbooks.co.uk

Finn

LIV MORGAN'S biological father didn't recognize me.

He sat two stools down from me. In the six months I'd lived here in Whistler, I'd seen him around a few times—in the grocery store, in his work van, but mostly here in this bar, knocking back booze. Back home in Queen's Cove, Liv's stepdad, Joe, was the only real dad she'd ever known.

I wondered if she knew Cole lived here.

My chest ached as I remembered her at my brother Holden's wedding to Sadie back in January. Seeing Liv for the first time in over a decade had hit me like a freight train. I hadn't been able to say a word. I had just stood there, staring at her, taking her in.

Fucking hell, I missed her.

Grown up, she was so beautiful it hurt. I had scrambled to memorize her. The soft, wavy pink hair cascading around her shoulders. Her pretty brown eyes, rimmed in dark lashes. The slope of her nose, sprinkled with freckles even in winter. Her eyes had widened in shock before a cold glare slid into place.

In the bar, Cole and I made eye contact, and my insides froze into a block of ice. The look in his eyes—shame, loneliness, misery—filled me with disgust. He had more wrinkles now, and gray hair at his temples, but there was no doubt in my mind. It was him.

Now, looking at him, I felt rage. Liv had his eyes, which pissed me off more. My hands made fists as my blood rattled in my veins. The words were in my mouth, ready to go.

You hurt Liv. You left her and Jen. Your misery is your own fault.

Something stabbed in my chest, and I rubbed my sternum. When I looked back at him, I saw myself. It was *me* spending every night at the bar alone. It was *me* regretting my fuckups.

My stomach plummeted as it clicked into place in my head. For most of my life, I'd been madly, stupidly in love with her. It wasn't going away, and I needed to fix the mess I made twelve years ago.

Liv and I were soulmates.

Leaving was the biggest mistake of my life.

I needed to make her fall back in love with me, or I'd regret it forever.

I was about to make a fucking fool of myself over Liv Morgan.

Olivia

Sadie and I stood in the bar, arms crossed and staring up at the enormous alien dildo mounted on the wall beside the TV.

"I can't get it down," I told her.

Sadie chewed her lip, studying it hanging there. It had been sent to her by mistake last year and I had put it up to make her laugh, but now the fucker wouldn't detach from the wall.

"Pull harder on it," Sadie suggested.

Behind us, sitting at the counter, Sadie's husband Holden choked on his beer.

My expression turned horrified. "*You* pull on it."

Her snort turned into a full-out laugh. "Let's just leave it up."

My dad walked out of the storeroom carrying a case of beer. His eyes went straight to the alien dong and he winced. "Still can't get it down?"

I shook my head at him and he laughed.

"Sorry, Joe," Sadie said.

"Yeah, sorry, Dad," I added.

He waved us off, shaking his head and grinning. "If that's the most trouble you got into while we were away last year, we're good."

Last year, while my parents went traveling, I ran the bar while working on my PhD dissertation. That's how I became friends with Sadie—she needed a job while she and Holden fixed up the inn they'd inherited.

"Are you okay to close up?" he asked me, standing and dusting his hands off.

I nodded. My apartment was over the bar, so I usually closed. "I've got it under control."

"Sounds good. Goodnight, honey." He dropped a quick kiss on the top of my head before he headed out, something he had been doing since he married my mom when I was five years old.

Joe wasn't my biological father, but he was my dad. He'd raised me, he loved me and my mom more than anything, and I couldn't imagine a life without him. He taught me how to ride a bike, how to make a whiskey sour, and how to make pancakes. Where it mattered, he was my dad. The guy who knocked my mom up at twenty and slowly faded from my life? I didn't call that guy Dad. I didn't call him anything because I hadn't heard from him in years.

As Sadie and I cleaned and prepared to close, I glanced around my dad's bar at the regulars finishing up their drinks, at the old wood floors, the mismatched collection of photos and artwork. I'd been working here on and off since university, over a decade. Every year while I was in school I'd come home to Queen's Cove, a small town on the coast of Vancouver Island, to help my dad with the summer tourist rush, and in the fall, I'd return to school.

I'd been back in town full time for almost two years working on my dissertation, and after the conversation I had with my advisor this morning, a new sense of urgency weighed in my gut.

"What's up with you?" Sadie asked beside me at the bar. "You're quiet tonight. Quieter than usual."

I flattened my lips into a tight line. "I spoke to my advisor this afternoon."

Sadie leaned in. "Okay, and?" She knew I'd been dodging my advisor's calls and emails all week.

"She's not dropping me like I thought." I rubbed the bridge of my nose, replaying the conversation in my head before I winced. "She took a position at the University of Toronto." She currently held a position at the University of British Columbia in Vancouver. "It starts in September but she can delay my deadline until October."

"What does this mean for you?"

"It means that I need to find the flower by October or I'm dropped from the program."

For years, I'd been trying to prove that certain plants could adapt to climate change, and that the pink sand verbena from the Queen's Cove area, rumored to be extinct, had changed location because of the increasing coastal temperatures.

A memory popped into my head—the only memory I had of the flower. It was floating down a creek in the woods, its pink petals standing out against the dark stones as it meandered downstream before it disappeared.

I saw that flower. No one believed me, but I did. I knew it was still out there, but now I was running out of time to prove it.

Sadie reared back, frowning. "They can't do that."

I winced. Fuck, this was so embarrassing. "Yes, they can. I've been 'finishing my research' for two years." I used air quotes around the words. "Most people finish their dissertation in one year, maximum."

"Can you switch to another advisor, someone staying at the university?"

Shame twisted in my gut and I could barely meet her gaze.

"I asked, and she said no one else wanted to take my work on."

Meaning everyone else thought I was on a wild goose chase. My face heated in embarrassment, thinking about all the advisors in a meeting, discussing my work.

"She said the longer I take on my dissertation, the lower my chances of finishing are."

Sadie blinked. "Shit. That's harsh."

I shrugged. "She's right. I've been working on it for two years." And three years of school and lab research before that. My stomach rolled as I remembered the tentative tone my advisor had used on the call. "I think she thinks I'm wasting my time."

Sadie shifted, crossing her arms and leaning against the counter. "You're out in the mountains looking for the flower all the time."

"And I still haven't found it."

We stood in silence, listening to the music and quiet chatter in the bar.

"What are you going to do?" Sadie asked, studying my face.

A knot formed in my throat and I frowned down at my hands clasped on the countertop. It was May, and based on data from the flower in other parts of the world, it should be in bloom from now until the end of August.

"I have one last summer to find it before I get kicked out of my program." I shrugged and looked at her. "So I'm going to get out there as much as I can and find it." I straightened up, trying to brush the bad vibes away. "I'm going on a hike tomorrow. I'll send you my route before I leave."

She didn't like that I hiked alone in the back country, especially because the terrain wasn't for beginners and cell service was spotty, so to keep her from worrying, I always sent her my itinerary and route—even though between school and growing up here, I'd spent countless hours in the mountains. I knew what I was doing.

Sadie tapped her nails on the bar counter and chewed her lip, glancing at me.

I frowned. "What?"

Her mouth twisted to the side and I stared at her. I knew that look. That was the same look she had when she explained that the person I hated more than anyone on the planet would be at her and Holden's wedding a few months ago.

My gut flipped.

"What?" I asked again, leaning in. "Spit it out, please."

She blew out a long breath. "He's moving back."

I froze before shaking my head. "Nope." I wiped the spotless counter.

"Olivia."

"He's not." I was practically rubbing the varnish off.

She sighed. "He left Whistler a couple days ago."

Fuck. This was bad. My stomach dropped.

Finn Rhodes and I had an unspoken agreement. In the summers, Holden's youngest brother left Queen's Cove to fight wildfires around the province, and I worked in my dad's bar. In the fall, I returned to school and he came home until he inevitably got bored and left for the summer.

And then last year, my dad needed help running the bar while he and my mom went on their dream trip around Europe, Finn moved permanently to Whistler, a ski town in BC, and I figured my problem was solved.

As kids, we were best friends. We grew up next door to each other, and we did everything together. We even had the same birthday. When most kids hit puberty, they thought the opposite sex was gross, but not us. We were inseparable all the way up to the night of our high school graduation.

He was everything to me, and he ditched me. My stomach dropped with the memories of that night before I pushed them away.

Finn Rhodes was a cruel joke from the universe. He had smashed my heart into a thousand pieces without a second thought, and I would never, *ever* let it happen again.

That day I saw the pink sand verbena in the forest? Finn had been standing right beside me, watching the flower disappear down the creek.

I adopted an apathetic expression, shrugging at Sadie. "Here's the thing about Finn," I said in a low voice so Holden wouldn't overhear. "He's an adrenaline junkie. Compared to fighting raging wildfires, our town isn't interesting enough for him, so even if he does come home, I don't expect him to stay."

Sadie lifted one eyebrow, looking uncertain.

"Trust me," I told her. "I know him."

He *said* he was coming back to town, but if I knew one thing about Finn after growing up with him? It was that I couldn't trust a fucking *word* he said.

"It's been a long time," Sadie offered.

I remembered the way he had looked at me at Sadie and Holden's wedding, and the zap of electricity down my spine when our eyes had met. I hadn't seen the guy since we were teenagers, and seeing him standing there in his suit, with his unruly dark hair looking perfectly rumpled, his sharp gray eyes assessing me in my dress—my heart had nearly stopped.

God, he had looked so good. His frame had filled out, probably from the physical demands of his firefighting job. His tattoos had poked out beneath his collar and the hems of his sleeves, and the way his gaze had raked over me with a mix of longing and heat?

A shiver rolled down my back at the memory.

He hadn't changed. Not one bit. Same cocky, reckless, thrill-seeking Finn.

Rage flooded my blood and I scowled.

Asshole.

Sadie yawned and her eyes watered.

"Go home," I told her, grateful to end this conversation.

She shook her head. "I'm good," she warbled through another jaw-breaking yawn.

Holden glared at me and I threw my hands up. "I told her to go home."

"Just because I'm pregnant doesn't mean I can't hear you," Sadie said, walking around the counter to sit beside Holden. She was only two months along, not even showing yet. His arm automatically came around her waist, and when she smiled at him, the corner of his mouth ticked up.

Before Sadie, some people would call Holden *grumpy*. Now? I saw him smile at least once a day.

"Stop," I told them.

Sadie laughed. "What?"

I gestured between them. "Gazing. Quit it."

Holden turned back to the game on the TV above the bar with a little smile on his face, his hand lingering on her knee, and Sadie shook her head, still grinning.

It was sweet how much they loved each other, but sometimes being around people who were madly in love got old.

When they headed out moments later, I waved goodbye then I closed up the tabs on my other tables.

Something weird rolled in my stomach. I was happy for my friends. They'd fallen for each other in this very bar last year, right in front of me. Sadie was one of my best friends, and I was relieved she chose to make Queen's Cove her home. She moved here almost two years ago when she inherited her aunt's inn. She and Holden had had this weird arrangement for her to find him a wife, but it turned out differently than they expected.

Well, differently than *she* expected. Holden always had a thing for her. It was only a matter of time.

I was just stuck after the call with my advisor. Twenty-nine years old and in the same place as five years ago, while all my friends fell in love, progressed in their careers, and started families.

My last tables finished up and left, and I headed to the front door to lock up after them.

He's moving back, Sadie had said.

I dragged in a deep breath to calm myself down. No, he wasn't. What the hell would Finn want here?

Besides, it didn't matter. I didn't care about Finn Rhodes anymore.

3

Olivia

MY HIKING BOOTS crunched on the forest floor as I made my way down the side of the mountain, surrounded by towering emerald trees. Sunset was in two hours, and it had been pouring since noon. My boots were still dry, my raincoat had held up, and the wet forest smelled earthy and fresh and incredible, but my hands were frozen and all I could think about was sinking into a hot bath as soon as I got home.

Another day in the forest with no trace of the flower. Disappointment rose up my throat but I shoved it down. I paused for a break, pulling my map out of my pack. While I sipped water, I studied the route back to my car. Another hour of hiking. I traced my thumb over the route—down the mountainside, over a creek, through a sloped, rocky area, and then around the base of the mountain to where I had parked at the end of the old logging road.

At the top right corner of my map, I had taped an image of the flower. My stomach twinged as I stared at it, and I remembered what my advisor had said yesterday.

I had the whole summer to find it, I told myself.

I made my way down the side of the mountain, balancing against a nearby tree on a slippery section.

An entire summer out here, hiking among the trees, breathing in the fresh air with blue sky stretching overhead. The corners of my mouth ticked up, picturing the family of beavers I had spotted last year. Maybe they'd return to the same spot. Even though I worked for my dad's bar back in town, the forest was where I belonged. It was where I spent most of my free time as a kid and teenager, and now that I was wrapping up my PhD, it was where I'd spend my career.

I hiked around a group of big trees and picked my way down the side of a hill that led to the creek, but the second it came into view, I stopped short.

"Shit," I muttered, brows creasing.

Two weeks ago, it was a creek, a little trickle of water down the mountain. Today, the water rushed, fast and loud. If it wasn't raining, I would have heard the river up higher in the mountain. I couldn't even see the rocks I had used last time to step through the creek.

It had been pouring rain for a week, I realized, closing my eyes at the rookie mistake. I should have known it would affect water levels.

I weighed my options, climbing down the slope to get a better look at the river. Water roared over the rocks. I pictured myself slipping and hitting my head. Getting swept away, unconscious. Best case, I got through the river soaking wet and had an hour to hike, shivering. I'd be risking hypothermia.

No fucking way was I getting into that river.

I glanced downstream. If the river split further down, it might be safe for me to cross. I chewed my lip. There was no guarantee that would happen, and I had no idea how far I'd have to follow the river. I didn't have service out here, and although I had enough food and water for tonight, I wasn't prepared to spend a couple days out here.

The sun was starting to set, and the sky was dimming quickly. There was another route back to the car that would take about four hours. Hiking in the dark was both dangerous and miserable, so my best option was to wait out the night here and hike back at sunrise.

In my head, I heard the rules we had been taught in school for spending time out in the back country.

Bring extra water, food, and socks. Tell someone your route and your expected return time. Always give yourself enough time to get home.

My pack was stocked and Sadie knew my itinerary, but I should have known better about the stream. I ignored the frustration in my gut as I pulled out the tarp in my pack and strung it up to keep the rain off me.

———

THREE HOURS LATER, rain tapped on my tarp as I shivered and tried to fall asleep. I didn't bother trying to light a fire—the wet wood wouldn't light.

A rhythmic beating noise cut through the sound of the rain and I frowned, lifting my head to listen.

The noise got louder.

"Oh, fuck," I whispered, eyes going wide.

Not again.

The beat of a helicopter grew louder as it approached and I closed my eyes, frustrated. I was supposed to check in with Sadie when I got back to my car, and when I didn't, she did what she told me she would do.

She called Search and Rescue.

Through the trees and rain, I watched the helicopter land in a clearing about two hundred feet away. I fought the urge to turn off my lamp and hide, and began untying my tarp.

An ugly chill wavered through me. Being rescued like this added to the feeling of incompetence that already rested on my shoulders every day.

Headlamps bobbed through the trees as the responders approached. I folded my tarp into a square and was shoving it into my bag when I turned and—

My stomach dropped through to the core of the earth.

Finn Rhodes stood tall, decked out in his emergency responder gear, wearing a cocky, wicked grin. His gray eyes met mine, and every muscle in my body tensed.

"Hey, Liv."

4

Finn

SHE WOULDN'T EVEN LOOK at me.

It was one in the morning at the Queen's Cove hospital, but I was wide awake, knee bouncing up and down, pulse skittering around, my stomach flip-flopping. It took everything in me not to blurt out what I had figured out in the past few weeks. Picking her up in the helicopter wasn't how I planned to see her for the first time.

I didn't have a plan. I was just winging this.

We were supposed to fill out the Search and Rescue paperwork before her medical exam, and I didn't know where to look. Her wavy, pale pink hair, tied up in a cute ponytail? The freckles scattered across her nose and cheekbones? Or her warm brown eyes, eyes that wouldn't meet my gaze for more than a few seconds?

In the chair across from me, she shifted, crossing her arms.

I opened my mouth to say something, but her gaze flicked to mine and the words got stuck in my throat.

Olivia Morgan had always tripped me up.

"What, no kiss hello?" I asked. The helicopter had been so loud, and there were two other people with us, watching and listening, so we couldn't talk.

Her lip curled as she stared at me in disgust. "Can we finish up the paperwork so I can go home?"

I crossed my arms, mirroring her body position, leaning back in my chair to study her. "You're cranky tonight."

Her nostrils flared, and behind her eyes, I saw rage. Amusement pitched in my chest.

"If you're cold, I can put a blanket around your shoulders," I continued. Her jaw tightened, and it took everything I had not to smile.

"Finn." Her voice was sharp and her glare could melt my skin off.

The way she said my name made the back of my neck prickle.

I raised my eyebrows at her and patted my lap, because around her, I couldn't help myself. "You can sit on my lap for warmth."

She looked like her head was about to explode, and I tried not to laugh. This rage? This was good. Rage was better than indifference, because indifference meant she was over me. Rage meant she still cared—which meant there was hope for us.

Olivia's eyes flashed. "You have three seconds to start asking me the questions on your form before I leave."

"Are you seeing anyone?"

She stood. "I'm out of here."

I jumped up, hands in the air in surrender. "Okay, okay. I'm just teasing you. Let's fill out the form."

She regarded me for a moment before taking her seat again, and I sat down across from her. I glanced over the form.

"What were you doing out there?"

She glanced away, crossing her arms. "Hiking."

"Just hiking?"

Over the years since I left Queen's Cove, I'd never outright asked about Olivia, but any scrap of information, any overheard gossip or updates, I was listening. I knew she was finishing up her PhD in forestry sciences, and that she was looking for a flower she and I had spotted as kids.

Since she was a kid, Olivia's dream was to work in forestry science. She had always been curious about plants and ecosystems in school. Two decades later, I still remembered how her whole being transformed in the forest, how she smiled and laughed more.

I leaned in. "You were looking for the flower, right?"

Her gaze lingered on mine, wary and uncertain, but she didn't answer me.

"Sadie had your route, which was helpful. That was smart of you," I told her, "to give her that information."

She snorted. "I'm *thrilled* to have your approval."

"We would've had a tough time finding you if not for that map. The Search and Rescue crew picked up a group of hikers last week from that area as well."

I watched her face, hoping this information would make her feel better about being rescued. Olivia hated being helped.

She was safe, though. She was the most qualified person in this town to be hiking out there by herself, but the idea of her stuck alone all night in the pouring rain? I'd hike out there by myself to rescue her if I had to.

Her gaze swung to the forms in front of me. "What other information do you need? I have to be up early."

I pulled the forms closer to me so she couldn't see them. Most of the information I could fill out myself. Location of rescue, reason for rescue, time and date, name of person rescued. She didn't need to know that, though. I had a feeling that finding moments like this, just me and her, would be tough.

"You need to find the flower to finish your studies, right?" I asked her.

"That's not a question on the form."

The corner of my mouth ticked up. "Just trying to get a full picture of what happened tonight."

She stared at me. Fucking hell, she was so pretty. I couldn't help but smile wider.

In my head, I replayed images from that night years ago. The way her soft, smooth skin looked in the dim lighting. The way her hair looked fanned out across her pillow. The sweet sound of her gasps as her back arched.

She must've seen something in my expression because she stiffened. "What are you doing here?"

I held her gaze, ignoring my heart beating in my chest like a drum. I could smell her shampoo from this distance, light and floral, and I had the urge to pull her into my chest and bury my face in her hair.

She'd bite me if I did that.

"I moved home," I told her.

Her eyes narrowed. "For how long." She didn't say it like a question, she said it like a statement. Like it was inevitable that I'd leave again.

My entire life, I had had a reputation. When I left, I cemented that reputation in Liv's head.

"For good," I told her, holding her gaze. "I'm not leaving this time."

She gave me a look like *who are you fooling?* and my chest pulled tight. I didn't blame her, but that didn't mean I liked it.

"Okay," she said. "Sure. I won't hold my breath."

Her gaze flicked to someone behind me and I turned.

Beck Kingston, a doctor at the Queen's Cove Hospital and my older brother Wyatt's friend from school, leaned against the doorframe.

"Hey," he greeted me with a smile. "I heard you were back in town."

I beamed back at him. "You heard right. How's it going?"

He shrugged, gesturing around us at the hospital. "Good. Keeping busy here. You know how it is."

The town's fire department worked closely with the medical staff at the hospital, and I knew the demands of Beck's job in a small town where resources weren't always available.

When he wasn't working insane hours at our small-town hospital, he was out on his boat. I think a few years ago he had a crush on Wyatt's now-wife, Hannah, but Wyatt put a stop to that. Beck was the kind of guy who moms mooned over. His dark hair was always combed like he was on his way to church, for Christ's sake. He answered his phone at all hours of the night, hardly ever took time off, and remembered everyone's medical history off the top of his head. Beck Kingston, Queen's Cove most reliable guy.

My complete opposite.

Beck crooked a grin at me. "First day back and you're here already, huh?"

I'd lost count of the number of times I'd been admitted to this hospital with injuries. A broken arm from climbing a fence, an ankle on backwards from falling out of a tree, a head injury from falling out of the same tree, a broken collarbone from falling off my bike.

I forced a smile. "Dr. Kingston, I have no idea what you're talking about. I'm the perfect picture of responsible reliability."

I used to revel in the troublemaker role, but now, it left a bad taste in my mouth.

He laughed before turning to Olivia. "Your checkup will only take a few minutes, and you can come back and finish the questions later if you need to." He gave her an apologetic look. "It's procedure."

"I know. We've been through this before." Olivia jumped up, and guilt stabbed me in the gut at how quickly she wanted to get away from me. "We're done, anyway."

I watched her disappear out the door before meeting Beck's curious gaze.

Olivia's hatred toward me was no secret around town. No one knew what happened, but everyone knew we had been best friends until we weren't.

He raised an eyebrow, glancing between me and the door. "So," he prompted.

I let out a long breath. "Yeah."

"I guess that didn't go as expected."

I didn't know *what* I had expected. Liv sure as shit wasn't going to jump into my arms and cover me in kisses. The thought made me huff a laugh and rake a hand back through my hair.

"Nope," I told him with a lopsided grin, ignoring my sinking stomach. "No, it did not."

He said goodbye and left, and I sat there in the empty room, hearing Liv's mom Jen's words from years ago in my head. The same words that had been playing over and over for years.

I wasn't that guy anymore. Doubt rose up inside me but I shoved it away. If I wanted Olivia back, I *couldn't* be that guy anymore. I had to prove her and everyone else wrong.

Olivia hated me, but this summer, I was going to change that.

5

Finn

THE NEXT EVENING, I caught a flash of her pink hair as I slipped into the back of the meeting room at town hall, nodding hello at the people around me before I took my seat. Town hall meetings weren't my thing but the conversation I'd heard at the fire hall this morning stuck in my mind all day like a thorn.

At the front of the room, my oldest brother, Emmett, took his seat among the rest of the town council.

He gave everyone a friendly, confident smile. "Let's start, shall we?"

Emmett looked good up there. Natural, like he was in his element. He had always been a leader, but seeing him as mayor felt right. Back in school, he was class president, captain of the soccer team, and Mr. Popular. The guy had an MBA in finance, and he and Holden had built a successful construction company here in Queen's Cove from the ground up.

On the other side of the room, Holden sat with Sadie. Holden was the *responsible* brother. The guy took care of everyone in his life. I usually stayed at his place if I was in town for only a weekend, mostly because before Sadie, he was a grumpy asshole and I loved to get on his nerves.

Beside them sat Wyatt and Hannah. Wyatt was a professional surfer. Part of Queen's Cove's appeal as a tourist destination was the cold-water surfing off our coast, and growing up, Wyatt spent most of his free time out on the ocean. He and Hannah had a one-year-old daughter, Cora, the cutest kid I'd ever known. Although he had slowed down since Cora came along, Wyatt still competed, winning tournaments and sponsorships.

And then there was me, the youngest Rhodes brother. The troublemaker. I held the record for number of trips to the principal's office at both the elementary and high school in town. My own mom joked that I was the devil.

Self-doubt crept up my throat, but I shoved it away.

Emmett started talking about the next town festival—raccoon-themed, this season—as I watched Liv. Her pink hair glowed and there was something about her in that soft-looking plaid shirt that was so fucking cute.

"Next up," Emmett continued, scanning his notes. "Chief Bell with the Queen's Cove Fire Department has a concern. Chief Bell, you have the floor."

Chief Bell, my boss, was in her early fifties and had the most intense *don't fuck with me* energy of anyone I'd ever met. She gestured to Miri Yang, who nodded and woke up the computer. The projector lit up and a PowerPoint slide appeared on the wall.

Olivia Morgan: Misuse of Search and Rescue Funds

In the front row, Liv sat up taller. I couldn't see her expression from the back of the room.

"Are you serious?" she hissed at the council.

Chief Bell nodded to Miri, who clicked to the next slide. The projector flipped to a picture of Liv being helped into a helicopter. It had been taken when she was mid-blink, looking over her shoulder.

"September 18, last year. Olivia Morgan twisted her ankle and limped down the mountain until she had cell service. This was her first Search and Rescue call."

Liv's ears were turning pink.

"By the time we picked her up," my firefighter colleague, Jay, added from a few rows back, "her ankle was the size of a grapefruit."

Liv turned and glared at him. He withered in his seat, not making eye contact.

"Thank you, Jay," Chief Bell added before nodding to Miri, who flipped to the next slide, a picture of Liv with her arms crossed in the hospital waiting room, scowling at the camera.

I bit back a laugh.

"April 27, last month. Olivia Morgan failed to return to home base by two hours after the estimated time of arrival."

"I was a kilometer from the car," Liv told her, shaking her head.

Chief Bell turned her hard gaze to Liv. "You were hiking in the dark. That's dangerous."

"I know what I'm doing."

Chief Bell's eyebrows lifted. "After yesterday, we don't want to take any more risks."

The room fell silent.

"What does this mean?" Liv asked, blinking. "You're saying I can't go anymore?"

She flipped to the next slide of two stick figures holding hands, smiling.

Liv stared and I put a hand over my mouth to hold in a laugh. This was the conversation I had overheard this morning at the fire hall.

Emmett cleared his throat. "Thank you, Chief Bell. I'll take over before Olivia throws a chair." The captain took her seat as Emmett turned his focus to Liv. "We can't tell you to stay out of the back country, but we're encouraging you to bring someone."

Liv's jaw dropped. "Are you kidding me?"

Emmett winced. "It's getting expensive, Olivia, and we don't know how long it's going to go on for."

Liv stared at him for a moment. "Oh." She scoffed. "You don't think it exists."

"I didn't say that." Emmett looked torn.

"You didn't have to," Liv shot back. "You think the flower's extinct, and I'm never going to find it."

She laughed in disbelief, looking at the council beside him. "I didn't ask to be rescued. I didn't even *need* to be rescued. I always plan for being stuck overnight. I'd have been fine on my own."

Chief Bell shook her head. "We can't let you fend for yourself out there. Besides, it's good practice to go with a buddy."

Liv blinked at her. "You want me to pay a guide? I can't afford that." She hugged herself tighter, brow creasing, and my heart squeezed in empathy. For a moment, she looked lost and I hated seeing that look on her face.

That was why I was here.

Chief Bell folded her hands in front of her, not giving an inch. "Your safety is important."

Liv's nostrils flared, like last night in the helicopter when she wouldn't even look at me. "Who's going to spend their entire summer trekking around the back country with me?"

I cleared my throat. "I'll do it."

Every set of eyes in the room glanced between Liv and me with interest.

She didn't even look at me. "No." Her gaze searched the room before she spotted someone. "Randeep?" Her eyes pleaded.

Randeep Singh ran a local tour company, leading back-packing trips through the mountains.

He winced at her and shook his head. "I'm sorry, Olivia. We can go once or twice, but with all the tours I have booked and the kids, it's tough for me to be away more than I already am."

Liv chewed her lip, brow furrowed with worry. "Yep, I understand. It's a big ask."

I shifted in my seat, crossing my arms over my chest. "I saw it," I told the room before meeting Liv's eyes. "I saw the flower, and I want to help you find it."

"No," Liv snapped.

Emmett's gaze flicked to me, considering my offer. "Finn has experience in the back country from firefighting."

Emmett had a bottle of whiskey coming his way.

Chief Bell nodded once. "Rhodes would be an excellent chaperone."

Liv choked. "Chaperone?"

"Buddy," Emmett cut in quickly. "Not chaperone. Just consider it. You don't have to make any decisions right now."

Liv's gaze came to mine. Cold, biting fury flashed across her face. A spike of panic and excitement shot through me.

Fucking hell, she was cute. Even when she was mad at me. Even when she hated me. She had this tiny nose and when she was super mad, it twitched, like she was trying not to scrunch it up.

Fucking adorable.

A memory flashed into my head of us as teenagers, riding our bikes through the forest. Her hair was her natural brunette back then, long and wavy, flying in the wind. When she turned back to look at me, laughing with bright eyes, my heart had leaped into my throat.

Fuck, I missed her. I had missed her every day for twelve years, but seeing her in front of me ratcheted that longing ache up tenfold.

I stared back at her, lifting one eyebrow, holding back the grin. The grin would piss her off and then she'd say no, but I really, really wanted her to say yes. Besides, she needed me. She just had to be the one to make the decision.

She turned back to Emmett, pointing at me. "You planned this. You both did."

"I swear," Emmett told her, "we didn't."

The entire room held their breaths. I could see her chest rising and falling as she considered her options.

"I believe you," I told her in front of everyone. "I know it's out there."

She closed her eyes a moment, defeated, and my stomach dipped. "Fine," she muttered.

"Great." Emmett nodded to Miri, taking notes. "Let's move on."

Before she sat down, Liv shot me a look so pissed it could have melted the skin from my bones. Her look said *you planned this*. I rubbed a hand over my mouth, hiding my smile while my heart did somersaults in my chest.

After town hall was over, Holden pulled me aside.

"What's up?" I asked him, watching over his shoulder as Liv slipped out. I had been hoping I could try to chat with her for a few minutes.

"I want to make sure you're up for it, helping Olivia like this."

Holden and Olivia were friends because he hung out at her bar a lot, and now he was married to her best friend.

"Of course I am."

He studied me. "Alright. It's important to her."

Again, Jen's words from years ago replayed in my head, and anxiety pinched between my ribs.

No one thought I was good enough for her. No one thought I'd follow through.

I got it. I did. I had a history of fucking up, running wild, and leaving. I loved an adrenaline rush. Trouble found me, and most of the time it was because I went looking for it.

I clapped a hand on Holden's shoulder. "I'm not going to bail on her."

Holden arched an eyebrow like he didn't believe me. "Okay."

Sadie appeared behind him, smiling at us. "Hey, Finn."

"Hey, Sadie."

"Ready to go?" she asked Holden, and he nodded as his arm snaked around her waist.

My heart twisted, watching them smile at each other as they said goodbye and headed off.

I wanted what they had, but it seemed so far out of reach.

Down the street, I watched as Liv strode toward the bar. She lived in an apartment upstairs.

She had said *yes*. A grin stretched wide across my face. My original plan for this summer was to follow her around like a dog until she gave me the time of day. This was so, so much better.

Maybe what Holden and Sadie had wasn't so far out of reach.

6

Olivia

A COUPLE MORNINGS LATER, I stepped outside the back door of the bar to meet Finn, and came face to face with him leaning against an emerald-green vintage sports car. His eyes met mine and a mix of panic and excitement shot down my spine as a cocky grin grew on his mouth.

I let out a *ha!* "Absolutely fucking not," I said, stopping short at the door, glancing between him and the car with disgust on my face. "No. No way."

He tilted his head at the car, smiling wider. "Come on. I'll drive." He winked.

Sam Rhodes' green car had become a strange tradition among his sons. When the Rhodes boys knew they had found the person they wanted to be with forever, they took her out in the vintage Porsche 911, a deep emerald green like the forests surrounding our town. Avery, Hannah, and Sadie had all been picked up in the car.

There was no way I was getting in that car.

I rubbed the bridge of my nose. This was a mistake. I knew he'd pull this shit. My stomach rolled forward, and when I looked up at him, I couldn't tear my gaze from his. God, his eyes were so pretty.

No. I mentally slapped myself. I didn't care that Finn had pretty eyes and thick lashes. I didn't care that when the corner of his mouth kicked up and his eyes lit up like that, all amused and mischievous like he was up to something, my heart beat harder.

I fucking *hated* Finn Rhodes.

This summer, I was going to find that stupid little flower as fast as I could. The faster I found it, the less time I had to spend with Finn. I'd finish my PhD, he'd get bored and leave town, and we'd all move on.

"I'm not getting in that car." I strode over to my own car, parked beside his, and hauled my pack into the trunk.

Finn pushed off the car and tossed his pack in beside mine. "Alright, next time, then."

"No. Never." I slipped into the driver's side, turned on the engine, and threw it into reverse.

Finn opened the passenger door and got in just as the car started moving. A laugh burst out of his chest.

"This is going to be fun," he told me as I pulled the car out onto the street. His fingers drummed on the car door as he smiled out the window, up at the clear blue morning sky.

———

A COUPLE HOURS LATER, we were both breathing hard as we stopped at the top of the hill we had hiked, and his scent breezed past me. My stomach fluttered and I ignored it.

I swung my pack down and pulled out my notebook, studying my map. Half the map had been hatched with red lines, indicating areas I had already searched.

Beside me, Finn dropped his bag and took a deep breath, inhaling the forest. "God, it's fucking gorgeous out here."

I ignored him, pulling out my printed images of the pink sand verbena. The pictures were burned into my brain.

Finn leaned over my shoulder to study them, and my

stomach dipped at the heat of him against my back. His smell invaded my space and I stepped away, tucking my papers back into my bag.

"You can't ignore me forever, Liv," he said, a teasing note in his voice.

When our eyes met, my pulse picked up.

I'd never admit this out loud, but fucking hell, he was hot.

My gaze lingered on the tattoos circling his right forearm, disappearing beneath the hem of his sleeve. On the other arm, stars spilled down his arm, constellations of pinpricks. Finn had always been my kryptonite, but as an adult? With the tattoos, his filled-out form, and the sparkle in his eye?

If I didn't hate him so much, he'd be irresistible.

"I'm surprised you're not bored." I shrugged, keeping my face blank. I whirled around and walked away, eyes scanning the ground, cataloguing every plant.

"Bored? No way. Out here, with you?" He winked at me and a spark traveled down my spine. "This is heaven." The grin hitched higher on his mouth.

Yeah, this bantery bullshit? I wasn't doing this. "It's quiet time," I told him. "I'm working."

My gaze swung back to the ground, scanning the surrounding area. *Sword fern. Pacific oak fern. Western hemlock.*

My mind wandered to the old house at the edge of town we had passed on our drive into the mountains this morning. As teenagers, we used to ride our bikes to it. It was an older couple who lived there, and since the house was deep in the forest, they didn't get many people coming by. They used to keep popsicles on hand in the summer for us. They passed away in the years since, and their adult son owned the property but didn't live there. The yard was overgrown and the house looked like it needed more upkeep.

My heart twisted. This town was full of memories of Finn and me.

"Rocky Mountain juniper," Finn said at my side, pointing off to our right.

"That's a common juniper."

He narrowed his eyes. "Are you sure?"

"Yes." I stared at him as his expression broke into a roguish grin. He knew it was the common juniper. "It's still quiet time."

"Sadie said the bar is busy. You work there a lot?"

I gritted my teeth, keeping my eyes on the ground.

"My shifts at the fire hall are four days on, four days off," he continued. "I was thinking we could do a few overnight trips if it works out with your bar shifts, now that your parents are back."

My skin prickled at him citing things I hadn't told him. Had he been asking about me? What else did he know?

"We're not doing overnight trips," I said. "I don't need you crawling into my tent pretending you're cold."

He laughed. The sound was low, warm, and rich, and it sent a thrill through my stomach.

That was why Finn was so dangerous. Around him, my brain melted. I used to love making him laugh. I was addicted to the sound.

"If we camp, we can cover more ground instead of having to go home each night."

He had a point. I thought about my conversation with my advisor. I had until the fall to find this flower. It made sense to cover as much ground as we could.

I'd have to talk to my dad about coverage at the bar. The summer season was starting soon and our town thrived on tourism. With only two thousand residents, Queen's Cove saw over a million tourists a year. People flocked from all over the world to enjoy our cold-water surfing, lush emerald forests, and sparkling Pacific Ocean waters. In the evenings, they packed the bar. He had hired a full staff for the summer, so could handle me working fewer shifts than usual.

I stared at Finn, with his trademark cheeky smile.

When we were hiking and I didn't have to talk to him, it was manageable, but what about at night when we had to eat dinner and sit by the fire? We couldn't just sit in silence.

"No overnight trips," I told him.

He shot me a smug, knowing smile. "By the end of the summer, Livvy, we're going to be best friends again."

My stomach clenched. "Don't call me that."

Livvy. He used to call me that when we were teenagers. Only when we were alone, only for my ears.

I turned around and continued traipsing through the forest, eyes on the ground.

Our boots thumped on the soft ground, and something poked in my brain. Twelve years we had circled each other, leaving town when the other was about to come home.

I stopped and turned to him. "Why now?"

His eyes widened for a brief moment. "What?"

"Why now?" My brow creased and I swallowed. "You've had twelve years and now you come back and want to be besties again. Why?"

I caught a flash of insecurity across his face. "I, uh." He lifted a hand and ran it over the back of his neck, breaking eye contact before his gaze came back to mine. Gray eyes like his brothers, but his irises were darker than theirs. "I realized I made a mistake." His gaze roamed my face, like he was memorizing my features.

Did he think I looked different than before? Did he hate my pink hair?

I don't care, I reminded myself.

Finn dragged in a deep breath, like he was steeling himself. "Liv, I know you hate me, I know I fucked up and deserve to rot for how badly I fucked up, but—" He took another deep breath. "I love you, you're my soulmate, and we're destined to be together." He swallowed, and his broad chest rose and fell with another deep breath. "And I'm going to do everything I can to change your mind about hating me."

Well, then.

My stomach fluttered with a flock of butterflies. My pulse pounded in my ears. This was a weird dream, and any second I'd wake up and laugh at the fucking bizarro world where Finn and I were soulmates.

We weren't soulmates.

Fuck that shit.

I opened my mouth to tell Finn to go fuck himself. I'd tell him it would be a bitterly cold day in hell before we got back together. If he was waiting for me to run back into his arms, he'd be waiting until the day he died.

Something occurred to me and I paused.

I knew Finn. It had been over a decade but I *knew* this guy. Finn would get an idea in his head and he wouldn't let it go. He didn't care how dangerous something was, or whether it was illegal or not.

My stomach bottomed out. It was just like graduation night. He had wanted to go cliff jumping, so he did. Drunk. Even when he said he wouldn't.

Finn wouldn't stop until I gave in, and a tiny part of me wanted to give in, even though he hurt me. Even though I knew he'd do it again.

I couldn't have my heart broken again by Finn. I'd never put it back together again.

I had to convince Finn that he was wrong, that he didn't want me. That we weren't soulmates. That I wasn't the same person as I was twelve years ago.

It had to be his idea, though.

Finn stood there, watching my reaction. I could see in his features—the lifted eyebrow, the cruel mouth curled into an amused smirk—he was ready for me to shoot him down. To tell him to go fuck himself and go bleed out in a ditch.

"I don't hate you," I lied.

He blinked, frozen. "What?"

I shook my head. "I don't hate you. I agree with you."

"With what part?" I nearly laughed at the surprised look on his face.

"The, um." I cleared my throat and crossed my arms. "That word you said. We're, um, that."

"Soulmates?"

"Yep."

His eyes narrowed. "You think we're soulmates," he repeated in a flat tone loaded with disbelief.

"Uh-huh." I nodded.

"Really."

"Yes," I hissed before I put on a small smile. "We are."

"Say it, then." The corner of his mouth curled up and his eyes danced.

"Say… that word?"

"Soulmates. If you think we're soulmates, say it out loud."

My mouth went dry. "Soulmates." The word tasted like chalk.

He flattened his lips and glanced away with a smile before looking back at me. "And you forgive me for leaving?"

"Mhm." It came out higher pitched than I expected. I swallowed, smiled, and nodded. "I forgive you for leaving."

"And you're ready to be together again?"

"Yep." My heart slammed in my chest and my stomach did flips as nerves poured through me. Every cell in my body screamed *this is a bad idea*.

He stared at me for a moment, blinking, before his face broke into a huge smile.

My heart fluttered.

That *smile*. My underwear practically disintegrated. The way his eyes lit up, the way his grin stretched across his face, lifting a little higher on one side, it had always disarmed me. Finn could always talk me into doing things with that lopsided smile.

This was a bad idea.

Ha. No. Finn loved a thrill, and he'd get tired of Queen's Cove soon enough.

Guys like Finn and my biological dad, they got bored and moved on. They'd both done it before, and it was only a matter of time before Finn lost interest in me and the town.

He stepped forward and wrapped his arms around me in a warm, tight hug. His mouth pressed to the top of my head in a firm kiss and he inhaled my hair. His warmth surrounded me, his scent whooshed up my nose, and my brain stuttered.

Fuuuuuuuck. This felt good.

"Knew you'd come around," he whispered against my forehead as I stood with wide eyes, heart beating wildly.

Finn and I were back together, but not for long. I was going to make Finn Rhodes dump me.

7

Olivia

AVERY SWUNG the front door open with a big grin. "Hello, sunshine. You're the first one here."

I held the wine bottle up. "I hope you have your own because I'm drinking this whole thing. Your husband is evil and I hate him."

She laughed and stepped back to let me in. Emmett popped his head out of the kitchen and waved.

"Hi, Olivia."

I shook my head at him. "No. Don't talk to me."

Emmett's face fell. "Are you actually mad?"

Avery and I walked down the hall into the large, open kitchen, where he stirred pasta sauce on the stove. Sliding glass doors led to the outdoor deck, and their property backed onto the forest. Early evening light spilled into the kitchen from the windows and skylights.

"Yes." I slipped onto a barstool. "I'm going to cut all your boxers into thongs tonight. And you're not allowed to drink in my bar until you've apologized for sticking me with your brother all summer."

Avery took the stool beside me, grinning. "Oooh. Bummer, Emmett. Guess you can wait outside if I go in for a drink."

He turned from the stove and gave her an incredulous look. "You're supposed to support me in sickness and in health."

She put her hands up. "I'm with Olivia on this one."

He lifted his eyebrows at her, an amused grin quirking on his mouth, so similar to his youngest brother, before he narrowed his eyes at me. "I heard a rumour you two were back together, but I didn't believe it."

Avery snorted. "Yeah, why is Finn telling half the town you two are soulmates?"

I fought an eye roll. Jeez, that guy worked fast. I let a breath out of my nose before I nodded at them, jaw tight.

"We are," I told them lightly.

Avery studied me with a small grin, like she was trying to read my thoughts. I stared back at her in challenge.

"Really?" Emmett asked, setting the wooden spoon down.

"Yep."

Avery rolled her lips to hide her smile.

Emmett turned slowly, frowning. "But you hate each other."

Irritation sizzled down my spine and I glared at him.

"Emmett, get your gossip from somewhere else," Avery told him. "Olivia is our guest."

I shot her a grateful look. I had always liked Avery. She owned The Arbutus, a restaurant in town, and she and Emmett had been married three years. I vaguely remembered her hating him, him having a massive crush on her, and suddenly they were trying to convince the town they were madly in love, despite their engagement being fake.

But we weren't supposed to talk about that. It became real in the end.

Avery shot me a look that said *you'll spill once he's gone*.

"You're not actually upset, right?" Emmett turned back to the stove and sent me a concerned glance over his shoulder. "I know you can fend for yourself. You're the most experienced hiker in this town, but I couldn't forgive myself if you got hurt."

I let out a long breath. "No, I see it from your perspective." The low-boiling fury in my gut was because the universe had shoved Finn in my face.

This would just be more motivation to find the flower as fast as possible.

Emmett turned the stove off and covered the pasta sauce as we heard a knock on the door.

"It's open," Avery called.

The door opened. "Is it safe?" Sadie called.

Avery rolled her eyes, laughing. "I said *it's open*. That means it's safe."

Moments later, Sadie and Hannah walked into the kitchen carrying bags of snacks and drinks.

"Hello." Sadie wrapped me in a hug from behind. "Uh, cannot *wait* to get into the latest town gossip tonight." She shook her head, long brown hair swinging in her usual high ponytail. "Holden won't tell me anything, it's so annoying." She squeezed me tighter, binding my arms at my sides.

"You can let go of me now," I told her.

"Not yet."

I huffed a laugh. Sadie and I were complete opposites—she was bubbly, friendly, cheerful, and spontaneous, whereas I was more like Holden—quiet, a little cranky, antisocial, and didn't love surprises.

Hannah gave me a wave and a smile. "Hey, Olivia."

"Hey, Hannah. How's Cora?"

Hannah owned Pemberley Books, a romance bookstore in town. Growing up, I had known Hannah as shy and quiet, but a couple years ago, she blackmailed laid-back Wyatt into helping her find a boyfriend. They were married now with an adorable baby girl, Cora.

She smiled wider and tucked a lock of pale blonde hair behind her ear. "She's great. She's with Elizabeth and Sam tonight so I'm sure they're spoiling her rotten. She loves your parents' dog."

I smiled. My parents still lived next door to Elizabeth and Sam Rhodes in the same house I'd grown up in. They'd gotten Evelyn, a chocolate Lab, when they returned from traveling last year. She was big, goofy, and incredibly sweet. "Evelyn loves kids."

Hannah's expression melted. "It's so cute. Cora can't say her name so she calls her Ellen."

"It's the cutest," Sadie said before turning a chiding but amused look to Emmett and Avery. "Nice to see you two with clothes on this time."

Avery buried her face in her hands. "I'm going to pass away now."

Hannah winced. "We love you two but…"

"You don't want to see us hooking up again?" Emmett provided, smirking.

"Oh my god." Avery's face was going red. "I already apologized for that. We don't usually—" She cut herself off. "—on the back patio."

Emmett glanced outside while he filled a pot with water. "I don't know. Weather's warming up."

She shot him a hard look. "Emmett."

His eyes danced with amusement as he set the pot on the stove. He picked up the bag of fresh pasta. "Three minutes in boiling water. Sauce is ready to go." He made his way around the island and wrapped his arms around Avery. She leaned back into his chest with a blissed-out smile on her face. "If you all want to have a few drinks," he told us, "I can drive you home. Just send me a text."

"Thanks, baby," Avery said, tilting her face up.

"I love you," he told her, dropping his mouth to hers for a quick kiss.

"Love you, too," she murmured.

My heart squeezed. That looked nice, what they had.

He winked at her, pressed another kiss to her cheek.

"Oh." He straightened up. "The Thompsons cornered me again."

Avery groaned. "They're relentless. What did you say this time?"

"That I'm training for a marathon and have to go to bed at seven thirty every night." To the rest of us, he explained, "They've been hounding us to go on a double date."

Shannon and Jackson Thompson were a couple in their late thirties. They didn't come into the bar much because they frequented the more upscale places in the Queen's Cove hotels, and when I saw them, I usually avoided them. In public, they were either dry humping each other or at each other's throats, threatening divorce.

Avery leaned toward us with a hard look. "The Thompsons are the reason I have a firm no-double-dating rule. They're the *worst*."

"I'm well aware," Sadie said in a dry tone before shuddering. "Never again." She laughed and cringed. "Holden's face, oh my god. He was so irritated."

Hannah chuckled. "I use Cora as an excuse." She shrugged. "I don't think they like kids, so we're home free."

"Smart." Emmett tilted his chin at Sadie. "Use your pregnancy as an excuse next time."

"I'll do that," Sadie told us, and we all laughed.

Emmett said a quick goodbye and the second the front door closed, Sadie whirled on me with bright eyes.

"Okay, what the actual fuck is going on?" she demanded. "Rule three of working at the bar is that Finn Rhodes is evil and we never, ever let him inside, and now you two are back together?"

I nodded, blowing a long breath out. "I can explain."

8

Olivia

"WE DON'T KNOW *why* we hate him," Avery said with eyes narrowed at me as we moved into the living room, "but we do."

My mouth twisted as I held back a smile. These women, they were so fucking cool. They always had my back. I hoped they knew that.

Hannah shot me a tentative look. "You don't have to explain anything to us, Olivia."

"Yes, I do," I said.

"Yes, she does." Sadie poked my foot with hers. "What's going on?"

I dragged in another breath. "I need Finn Rhodes to dump me."

The women were silent.

"He thinks we're soulmates," I continued, rolling my eyes. Soulmates. Like that was even real. There was no chance in hell that Finn was my *soulmate*. "And he'll never stop thinking that unless it's his idea, so I agreed to get back together with him, and now I'm going to make him regret that."

Sadie's eyes lit up with excitement. "Oh my god. Olivia. You're a genius."

I shot her a wry smile.

Avery grinned. "This is going to be fun."

"I don't know." Hannah wrinkled her nose.

I stared at her. "You blackmailed Wyatt with a European music video where he was dressed as a merman. He wore silver body paint."

"I wasn't going to do anything with the video." She winced. "Okay, I see your point. And Finn *is* really stubborn."

Avery nodded with a small smile. "Yeah, we can help with that."

Sadie jumped up and returned moments later with a pen and notepad, and the four of us came up with ideas to get Finn to lose interest in me.

"You should hit on other guys," Hannah added half-way through the list, smiling shyly as we all gawked at her. Her smile turned cat-like. "Wyatt got really jealous when I went out with Beck."

"Oh, yeah," Avery said, narrowing her eyes as she remembered. "I forgot about that. Beck is so sweet, you should ask him out."

"That guy's like my brother." I thought about what Finn's face would look like watching me flirt with another guy, and a thrill ran through me. "And that wouldn't work on Finn."

Hannah nodded. "Probably not. It would make him super possessive."

Sadie tilted her head, watching me. "Which we… *don't* want?"

"Right," I emphasized. "We want to gross Finn out. We want him to look at me and lose his lunch. We want him to get bored and lose interest. We want him to walk away and say, *phew, bullet dodged*."

"Are you ever going to tell us what happened?" Sadie asked, tucking her feet under her legs on the floor.

Their gazes swung to me while I sat there, squirming. The words locked up in my throat, and tension twisted through my entire body as my mind flashed back to graduation night. In my lap, my hands made fists.

"Did he cheat on you?" Avery asked quietly.

"No," I said quickly, frowning at my hands. "Nothing like that. He, um."

The room was quiet as they waited. I took a deep breath.

"We went to grad together," I started, swallowing past the knots in my throat. "We were still just friends but we obviously liked each other."

An image of my notebook from high school appeared in my mind. He'd draw a bird cartoon for me, little scenarios with the bird eating ice cream or flying around in the sky or reading a book. Sometimes he'd leave little sticky notes of the bird in my bedroom or locker.

"But I knew something was going to happen that night. All year, we'd been circling it. I knew he liked me. You know when you have that feeling about someone?"

They all nodded.

"And there were a few times that year, when we were saying goodbye or something to each other, I knew he wanted to kiss me."

A memory struck me—me leaning on my bedroom windowsill, window up while Finn sat at his own bedroom window, whispering goodnight to each other across the distance between our houses. We used to do that almost every night.

"We were dancing at grad, and he got this look on his face." In my mind, I was back there—the low lighting, the music, my hands around the back of Finn's neck while he gazed down at me. Our high school had held a grad event similar to prom after classes and exams were over. "He pulled me out into the lobby and told me everything."

I paused. "This is weird. I don't talk about this stuff." I took another deep breath. "He said he loved me, that I was his best friend, and he wanted to be with me." Finn had always been so cocky, so sure of himself, but in that moment, my heart had melted at the vulnerable look on his face.

I lifted a shoulder. "And then I kissed him."

Sadie made a strangled, gurgling noise. "And then?"

"And then we left." I shrugged again.

Avery sighed. "And *then*?"

My face burned harder. "And then he snuck into my bedroom and we had sex."

Hannah's eyes were saucers as she did an excited little wiggle.

"This was twelve years ago," I told her. "Don't get too excited." My stomach dipped. I didn't like thinking about the next part. "A bunch of guys from school were going cliff jumping that night out at the canyon."

Hannah winced. She was a few years ahead of Finn and me in high school, but she knew the story.

"A guy in my grad class died there," she explained to the others. "I think he jumped too close to the rocks?" she asked me, and I nodded.

"He was drunk and he wasn't running fast enough before he jumped. It's this shitty tradition where a bunch of dumb kids get wasted and go swimming, and it's really fucking dangerous." My hands twisted in my lap. "I didn't want Finn to go. He said he wouldn't. He wanted to, I knew he fucking wanted to. He loves that stuff, you know?" I frowned. "Finn loves all the dangerous stuff. He's made a career out of it. But he promised he wouldn't go."

My stomach churned at the memory. "We had this amazing night and we finally told each other the truth. It turned out he had wanted to say those things for so long. Like, *years*." I tucked my hands in the sleeves of my shirt. "He snuck back out to go home, and as I was falling asleep, I heard a car pull up outside." In the dim street lighting, I had watched him get into a guy from school's car and drive off. I felt sick, remembering it. "He went cliff jumping, and when he got home, he was drunk."

Sadie's mouth fell open.

"Yikes," Avery muttered.

Even Hannah frowned.

I clenched my hands and shook my head. "I couldn't sleep because I was freaking out, but *finally*, I heard him get home." The car door slamming replayed in my head, and I remembered how he staggered up the front steps.

"Did he see you?" Hannah breathed.

I nodded, rolling my eyes. "I was fucking furious, so I went outside while he fumbled with his keys." He'd seen me marching across the front lawns and his face fell, but there had been something else in his expression.

Acceptance, like he had been waiting for this moment.

"He was super weird and defensive." I shrugged. "Kind of brushed me off, said it wasn't a big deal and asked me what I expected."

"Asshole." Sadie glared at me. "What a fucking asshole."

"Yeah. I thought we'd talk about it the next morning but he was already gone." I hadn't seen him again until Sadie's wedding. The backs of my eyes burned but I blinked furiously, clearing it away. I would not cry over that guy. "Finn thinks about himself. The guy is chaos. He goes looking for trouble and finds it." I folded my arms over my chest. "I'm done with him. He just needs to be done with me."

"He was just a kid, though," Sadie said with doubt. "That was a long time ago."

I shook my head adamantly. "No. He knew better, and *I* know better. Finn will get bored the way he did before." The way Cole did. My heart twisted at the lingering rejection.

This was safer. Falling for Finn again… When he inevitably left again, I'd be right where I started. Devastated.

On the table, Sadie smoothed out the list we had brainstormed, ways to turn Finn off and bore him to death.

"Okay," Sadie said, a coy smile curving onto her mouth. "Let's convince Finn to dump you."

"Let's do a cheers." Avery lifted her glass and we followed.

I sat up straight, strength coursing through my veins with the power of my friends behind me. For the first time in a long time, I had a plan.

"Fuck you, Finn Rhodes," I said.

"Fuck you, Finn Rhodes," they chorused and we clinked glasses.

9

Olivia

I RETURNED HOME THAT EVENING, optimistic about life. I had a plan to get rid of Finn, and it was only a matter of time until I found the flower. My heart squeezed with gratitude for my girls.

In the hallway upstairs from the bar, my key was in my front door lock when I heard a noise.

A rustling noise came from the wall on the other side of the hall. A sliding, scraping noise, and then a thump. My pulse picked up as adrenaline dripped into my blood.

There were two apartments above the bar, but the other one was empty. My dad used it as storage, and since it was after eleven at night, I doubted he was rustling through old photos in there.

Another scrape of something against the floor. The walls were thin. I swallowed, head tilted, staring at the door across from mine.

Maybe it was an animal. Maybe a raccoon got in and was causing chaos in there.

Footsteps thumped across the floor. Loud, clunky, and heavy. My stomach dropped. It wasn't a raccoon. Someone was in there.

Fuck.

I glanced between my door and the staircase back down to the bar, flipping between my instinct to run inside my apartment, lock the door, and call the police, or hightail it down the stairs and get out of here. Before I could decide, the other door swung open.

Finn stood in the doorway, a devilish grin growing on his features as he crossed his arms and leaned on the frame. His black t-shirt from a local brewery stretched across his broad shoulders. My gaze snagged on his tattoos, inked over the lean, defined muscles of his arms. I recognized a few of those birds from the forest. His gray sweatpants hung low on his hips.

When my gaze returned to his, his grin widened. "Like what you see?"

Um. *Yes.* "No." Shit, I was supposed to be his soulmate. "I mean, *yes.*"

He eyes glittered with amusement.

"What are you doing here?"

He tilted his head behind him. "I'm moving in."

I strode over and peered past him. Boxes filled the apartment. "Like fuck you are."

His smirk lifted higher on his lips. "My dad mentioned to your dad that I was looking for a place, and since it's summer, there's nothing left. I told Joe I'd be happy to clean the place up for him and do any repairs."

Oh, fuck no. "What? No. Can't you live in a shared house with a bunch of twenty-year-old surfers?"

He shrugged, smug gaze on me. "I think he liked the idea of someone being here in case of break-ins."

I scoffed, blinking at him in disbelief. Our town was so safe. No one was going to break in. I loved my dad, I did, but sometimes, he was so clueless. He had no idea what happened with Finn because I didn't talk to my parents about that kind of stuff. My mom would know better than to let him live across the hall, though.

"Besides," Finn added, gaze raking down my body, sending shivers up my spine, "we're together now, so it shouldn't be a problem, right?"

My mouth opened to protest but my brain held a hand up to stop me. Right. Together. Getting him to dump me.

Our eyes met and his eyebrows lifted, daring me, and something excited fizzed through my chest.

"Right." I cleared my throat and offered him my own smirk. "Together."

"Great." His eyes glittered.

"Mhm." I nodded, holding his gaze. "So great. Having you live here across the hall from me is going to be so great... *boyfriend.*"

The word almost made me gag. His mouth twitched and his eyes gleamed like he was holding back a laugh.

"Goodnight." I whirled around, unlocked the door, and stepped inside.

"Goodnight, Liv," he called as I slammed the door closed.

I leaned my back against it, breathing deep as I listened to him close his own door. His low laugh rumbled through the walls.

Fuck.

Across the *hall*? Not only did I have to see the dickhead all summer while we scoured the back country, I was going to run into him *every day*?

We're soulmates. Say it.

A rock landed in my stomach. This was going to be so much harder than I expected. Finn wasn't playing around. He was throwing everything he had at me.

I thought about one of the items I had scribbled on my list of ways to get Finn to dump me, and a smile curled onto my mouth.

Ten minutes later, I stood in front of the bathroom mirror, kitchen scissors in hand, a handful of my hair pulled taut in front of me. A crazed look flashed through my eyes and I smiled.

Sadie was going to scream when she saw this, but it would be worth it.

I hacked through the section of hair, shearing off a chunk of my pink waves. They fell into the sink and I stared at them, my blood rushing with delirious energy. I looked up at my reflection and let out a bark of laughter.

I looked terrible.

I snatched up another lock and began to chop.

When I was done, I studied my reflection, beaming back at myself with a look most people would describe as 'unhinged'. Choppy, uneven bangs framed my cheeks, making my face look both too round and too long at the same time.

It was perfect.

"Hideous," I whispered at my reflection. Delight fluttered in my chest like butterflies.

Finn wasn't going to make this easy on me, but two could play at that game. I'd spent a long time stewing in anger over what he did. He was stubborn, but so was I.

Let the games begin.

10

Finn

"HEARD you and Olivia got back together," Holden said, eyes on the TV above the bar.

I ran my thumb up and down the condensation on my beer, glancing at the hallway to the apartments upstairs. A grin spread across my face.

"Yep," I told him. "We're soulmates."

He raised an eyebrow at me. "That was fast."

I shrugged, grin widening as I watched the TV. "I'm charming and irresistible."

I replayed the other day when I had blurted my intentions to Liv. Even I could see that her flipping from hating my guts to being my girlfriend was too good to be true. She was up to something, and I was happy to sit back and watch things unfold. I thought about the way her gaze had roamed my body last night as we stood in the hallway, heat flashing behind her eyes.

She wanted me, she just wasn't ready to give in. That was fine. I'd wait. I could be patient. I'd earn it.

Holden snorted, gaze returning to the game. On the wall below the TV hung a painting Sadie had done of him last year. She had painted him sitting in this bar, staring at the TV and crying. I think he had done something to piss her off, and she had created a collection of retaliation paintings. My parents had one in their house. Emmett's hung in his office at town hall.

"Hey," Emmett said, taking the seat on my other side. He glanced at the score and swore. "Jesus."

Wyatt was right behind him. He gave me and Holden a nod hello before slipping into the seat beside Emmett.

"So what's this about Finn and Olivia back together?" Emmett asked us with an incredulous expression. "She did that glaring thing when I asked her about it."

I beamed at Emmett, picturing her squirming like she did last night in the hall.

"The rumors are true," I told him. "Liv and I are an item."

Wyatt leaned forward, looking at me with disbelief. "I don't believe it."

"Me neither," Emmett added.

I shook my head at them, laughing. "Wow. What a welcome home."

Holden paused with his beer an inch from his mouth, giving me a look. "She hates you."

I ignored the pinch in my stomach and sipped my beer. A flash of pink caught my eye and my head whipped to where Liv strode into the bar, tying her apron, eyes on me.

I choked on the mouthful of beer, sputtering as she moved behind the bar counter.

"Hi." A little smile played at her lips.

"Um." I rolled my mouth to hide a laugh. "What happened to your hair?"

Behind the chunks of hair, her brows rose. She lifted a hand to brush a jagged lock aside. "I thought it was time for a new look."

Beside me, Holden kept his gaze trained on the TV and

Emmett covered his mouth with his hand. Wyatt shook his head with a lazy, amused grin.

Liv leaned in, smiling at me in challenge. Her hair looked terrible, like she had run a wig through a blender before pulling it on.

"Do you like it?" she asked, mouth still quirking.

Was she *blind*? I stared at her in shock, pushing down the laughter that bubbled up my throat.

And then it hit me. Ohhhhkay. That hunch I had that Liv was up to something? I was bang on.

She was trying to drive me away. Of course. Ignoring me and keeping me at a distance hadn't worked so now she was trying a new route.

I stared at her hair. It was really, *really* bad. People around the bar were glancing at her, either wincing or staring with slack jaws.

I studied the grisly mess on her head. It looked like she had head butted a Weedwacker.

She totally still loved me. If she didn't, she wouldn't care. She'd find me annoying, but she'd never chop her gorgeous hair like this. She was hacking it to bits to protect herself because the feelings I had for her, she felt them right back, and that was terrifying to her.

Her plan wasn't going to work, but I was still curious where this was going.

I cleared the laugh from my throat. "Yes, I do like it."

She blinked. "You do."

I nodded, leaning forward, holding her gaze. Her eyes widened a fraction as my hand came out and I toyed with a jagged lock, running it through my fingers. Her nostrils flared and her throat worked, and the smile on my face was all natural.

"You look really hot," I told her in a low murmur, running my finger up her jawline.

She looked like when a kid cuts their own hair, or like one of those shelter dogs whose haircut is so sad, you pity them.

"To me, baby," I murmured, "you're the most gorgeous woman in the world."

And that was the truth.

Irritation flashed in her eyes and she jerked away. "Great." She tried to smile but it looked like she was baring her teeth. Emmett flinched.

After she had taken our drink orders and disappeared, Emmett shifted to face me.

"So…" he started, watching Liv move around the bar as people stared at her hair. "That was weird."

I leaned back, folding my arms over my chest. "She's trying to drive me away."

Holden snorted. "Smart."

"Thanks a lot."

He stared at me. "You obviously did something to hurt her."

A flicker of guilt pinched in my gut, and I knew that was the truth.

"What's your plan?" Emmett asked.

"Plan?"

He nodded. "How are you going to fix things?"

"I'm hiking with her in the back country until we find the flower."

Emmett nodded. "What else?"

"I moved in upstairs."

Wyatt shot me an incredulous look. "No."

"I moved in across the hall from her so we can have like, snuggle parties and stuff." Naked stuff, hopefully. Just the memory of Liv's smooth skin and the way she gasped when she—

Holden shook his head. "You can't be serious."

I glanced between the guys. "What?"

Emmett laughed. "You are so fucked. This isn't going to work. You're going to drive her away faster."

Wyatt's eyebrows bobbed in agreement as he took a drink of his beer.

"That's because you guys are married and boring."

I thought about Olivia's biological father in Whistler, alone in the bar every night, and rubbed a hand down my face. I couldn't turn into him. I had to make things right with Liv.

I also had no clue how to bring up with her that I knew what her dad was up to. Last I heard, he stopped phoning and showing up when she was fourteen, not that he was very present before that.

"I need uninterrupted alone time with her," I said, nodding to myself. "I can blindfold her and take her to an Airbnb in the woods for a few days. Somewhere without cell service where we can disconnect—"

"That's kidnapping," Holden cut in.

"It's not kidnapping, it's hanging out."

Emmett looked like I'd suggested Liv and I rob a bank as a fun bonding experience. "*No*," he emphasized. "No kidnapping. Ever."

I threw my hands up. "If you assholes are so smart about relationships, tell me what to do."

11

Finn

"LOOK." Emmett shifted in his seat at the bar counter, staring at me straight on. "Finn? I love you, man, but you have a reputation for being trouble. Even Mom jokes that you're the devil."

I glanced over at Liv taking a customer's order on the other side of the bar. "Liv likes that about me."

Even as I said the words, I didn't believe them.

"She did when you were sixteen," Emmett continued. "You know what grown women like?"

"True crime documentaries."

Emmett paused before nodding. "Yeah, I think a lot of women do like those, but no, that's not what I'm getting at. Stability. Responsibility. A reliable guy." He gestured at himself. "Look at me, Finn. What do I look like?"

I surveyed his Oxford shirt and neatly combed hair. "A dork."

Holden and Wyatt laughed, and Emmett shook his head at them. "Can I get some help here?" he asked them.

Holden cleared his throat. "He's right," he admitted.

"You've got a reputation," Emmett went on.

"I don't have a reputation," I laughed. "Come on."

Wyatt made a *ha!* noise over the rim of his beer. "Remember the ladybugs?"

"Oh my god." Emmett cringed, laughing. "The fucking ladybugs. Mom almost killed you. She was so embarrassed."

I winced. Okay, yeah, I forgot about the ladybugs. I was twelve years old. The gardens outside our school had aphids, so they brought in ladybugs to eat them. The ladybugs arrived frozen in plastic bags, hundreds of them in each bag. The gardener had left them in the bed of his truck to thaw out before he released them in the gardens.

I'd seen those bags of frozen ladybugs, tucked two bags under each arm, and opened them inside the school. For weeks, ladybugs swarmed the windows in every classroom, flying into teachers' mouths or kids' food during lunch.

God, I had been such a little shit.

I sighed. "I was figuring out I had a thing for Liv, and it made me do weird things."

"It wasn't just that time," Holden added. "Remember when you fell out of the tree?"

My stomach tightened. Another bad one. I was ten and cracked my skull falling out of the tree in our backyard. Holden had been a wreck because he was supposed to be watching me, but it wasn't his fault. I was the one who climbed the tree after he told me to stay inside.

Wyatt snapped his fingers as he remembered. "The grocery store windows."

Emmett hooted with laughter and Holden put his head in his hands.

"*Right.*" Emmett leaned back, laughing. "Glass everywhere."

I had been sixteen, sprinting down Main Street in the rain. The soles of my skate shoes had zero traction left, and when I tried to turn the corner, I slid across the slippery sidewalk, straight through the grocery store's front windows. I walked away with just a tiny white scar on the back of my head.

A weird heaviness settled in my gut. When they laid it all out like this, especially compared to their accomplishments and where they all were in life, I saw myself in a new light.

I didn't like it.

The last thing Olivia needs is a guy like you dragging her down, her mom had said to me after Liv and I got in trouble for skipping class.

She had been right, and I *knew* she was right. That's why I left. That's why I said the things I did on the front porch when I got home on graduation night. *I'm bored with this town. Bored with you.*

It was only a matter of time until Liv figured out she was too good for me. Her mom saw right through me.

My stomach sank even lower. Fuck. No wonder Liv didn't trust me. My entire life, I'd shown her that I couldn't be trusted, and then I bailed on her the same night I told her I loved her.

Fucking hell, I was an asshole.

My brothers must have seen the anguish written all over my face, because Emmett clapped a hand on my shoulder. "Show her you're not that guy anymore."

What if I am that guy, though? I glanced at Liv with her terrible haircut. Her eyes met mine, and my stomach flipped.

For Liv, I could change.

I swallowed. "Yeah. Okay."

"First thing you have to do is tell her you want to be friends, nothing more," Emmett said.

I shook my head at him. "I don't want to be just friends with her."

Holden let out a long-suffering sigh and Emmett raised an eyebrow at him.

"It wasn't long ago that you were in a similar position," he told Holden.

Holden rolled his eyes and turned back to the game.

"I've already told her I'm going to make her fall back in love with me," I explained, feeling dumber by the second.

Why did I show my hand like that?

She breezed past behind the bar, tray in hand, and my gaze stuck to her like glue. My heart twisted, sharp and sweet, and I swallowed past a tight throat.

Because it was Liv. Because I had never been able to keep secrets from her. She made me say everything in my head. Around her, I got dumb.

"Forget the friends thing, then." Emmett crossed his arms and rubbed his jaw, thinking. "Focus on showing her how you've changed. Put on a nice shirt. Comb your hair. Cover up the tattoos. Get a responsible car."

A strangled laugh slipped out of my throat. "What? No."

My car was my baby. A black 1969 Mustang I had bought in my early twenties. When I was away, I paid a friend to keep it in his garage at the edge of town, covered by a protective sheet. I had it detailed regularly, only used premium gas, and brought it in for maintenance more than I needed to.

I loved that car. My happy place was driving it along the coast with the windows down, wind in my hair and music roaring through the stereo. Gripping the shifter in my hand, the way it felt to change gears on the open road.

"I can't get rid of my car." I shook my head. "No fucking way."

"You need to get something responsible," Emmett said, "like my car."

"I'm not getting a loser car."

He blanched. "My car isn't a *loser* car." Emmett drove one of those sporty crossovers made for families.

"It's one step below minivan."

Holden and Wyatt chuckled.

Emmett's jaw clenched. "Don't you *dare* make fun of minivans."

I made a jerking off motion. "Hey look, it's me, Emmett, thinking about minivans."

Holden and Wyatt started laughing and Emmett looped his elbow around my neck, trying to put me in a headlock while I fought him off, laughing.

"He has a point," Holden added when we sat back down. "About looking responsible." He spared a glance at me, frowning. "But you have to do it the right way. A way that'll matter to Olivia. She won't give a shit about you combing your hair."

I gestured at him. "Yes, that's what I'm saying."

"If she's worried you're going to leave, you need to put down roots here." Emmett's eyes were bright as he gesticulated. "Get involved in the community. Find a place to live long-term. Make it clear that you're staying and committed. Stop doing dumb shit for the adrenaline rush because that'll freak her out."

My mind wandered to the old house at the edge of town Liv and I used to ride our bikes past as kids. We had driven past it the other day.

"Get a car that can fit a car seat," Emmett added.

I picked up his beer and poured it into mine before turning back to Holden. "Go on."

His gaze flicked up to the game and we watched our team lose before he turned back to me. "Find out what she needs and then give that to her, or help her get it for herself."

I thought about the flower, how she'd been working on her thesis for almost two years.

She used to laugh so easily around me. She used to be right behind me, sprinting down a hill or climbing trees to race to the top.

I spotted her ringing an order through on the side of the bar, her eyebrows knitted together. She never used to be so serious and guarded like this. Now she seemed... stuck.

I chewed my lip, thinking.

"Yeah," I said. "I can work with that."

I'd be the guy Liv needed, because the alternative was too fucking sad to even consider.

———

"YOU'RE STILL HERE," she said later, appearing in front of me, drumming her fingers on the counter. Her expression was indiscernible as her warm brown eyes roamed my face.

I leaned forward, resting my chin on my palm, smiling. "Thought I'd keep you company for a while."

I waited for her to tell me she didn't need company.

She lifted an eyebrow. "We should go on a date," she said instead, ignoring my brothers' glances.

My mind stuttered.

"Since we're, you know," she shrugged, "*together* and all."

I sat up straighter. "Yes. Fuck, yes." My mind ran wild with a thousand images of the things we used to do— stargazing on the roof outside my bedroom window, riding bikes with the wind in our hair, exploring the coastline, collecting shells. "I'll plan it."

"No," she blurted out before catching herself and smiling quickly at me. "I want to take you out. Let me plan it." Something that looked like mischief flashed behind her eyes.

Okay, so she was up to something, but damn if I wasn't curious as hell. If I wanted Liv back, I needed to show her that no matter how hard she pushed me away, no matter how fucked up her hair looked, I wasn't going anywhere.

A beaming smile stretched across my face. "Alright. It's a date." I glanced at the time. "Are you okay down here if I leave? I have an overnight shift tomorrow and I want to get enough sleep. I never sleep well at the fire hall."

She rolled her eyes. "Yes, Finn, I will manage to run the bar if you're not sitting here."

Even in a flat tone like that, I loved the way she said my

name. I stood, tucking my stool under the counter. "Alright, I'll say goodnight then, *baby*."

She stiffened. She didn't like that nickname. "Bye."

"How about a goodnight kiss?" I said, because playing with fire made my blood whistle.

"Finn." Emmett's eyes widened. Holden and Wyatt watched in amusement.

My gaze stayed on Liv's face as I made my way around the bar behind the counter. When I stopped a foot from her, her eyes dropped to my mouth once, then came back up to my eyes. Energy rushed through my blood. She blinked at me, swallowing, as a flush crept up her throat.

"You're not supposed to be back here," she managed.

I gave her a soft smile, tucking a lock of her hair behind her ear. "Can't I give my *girlfriend* a kiss goodbye?"

"Girlfriend." Her chest rose and fell.

"Mhm. Or is it too soon? Because it's not too soon for me, Liv. I know what I want."

Come on, play with me.

She snorted. "Fine."

My eyebrows lifted in delight. "Yeah?"

She shrugged. "Sure. Whatever. I don't care."

"Alright." I took a step toward her, aware of everyone in the vicinity staring at us. "Here I come."

She swallowed again. The flush crept up to her cheeks and she looked so fucking adorable, blushing with her freckles like that. "Ready whenever you are."

I paused an inch from her mouth, waiting for her to meet me the rest of the way. Up close, her eyes were flecked with honey. Her chest rose and fell, and her breath tickled my lips.

My eyes said *I dare you.* Her gaze dropped to my lips before she dropped a quick peck on my mouth. Before I could even register what happened, she was hustling to the other end of the bar.

"Goodnight," she called in a strangled voice.

I grinned after her. "Goodnight, baby," I called back.

"This is going to be a fucking disaster," Holden muttered, shaking his head at me.

I beamed at him. A renewed sense of resolve flooded my veins.

Liv still had feelings for me, and I was going to do everything I could to show her I wasn't the same guy who broke her heart.

12

Olivia

FINN'S front door swung open and he stepped back, eyes going wide as he took in my shirt.

"Wow," he said, rolling his mouth into a thin line, eyes bright. "That is a *shirt*."

"Oh, this?" I looked down at myself, pinching the fabric of my oversized polyester button-up and holding it out. It was from my dad's Halloween costume last year, when he dressed as Guy Fieri, Mayor of Flavortown. "Do you like it?"

I looked up, daring him to say he didn't.

His mouth curled up as he met my gaze. "I love it."

My eyebrows lifted. "Really? You love it?"

His gaze raked down my shapeless form. The shirt hung past my butt, it was so long. "Oh, yeah. You look cute."

"I'm wearing it on our date."

"I hoped you would."

We stared at each other. My eyes narrowed and his smile lifted even higher.

Oh my god. Did he *know*?

He winked at me, grinning, and my chest simmered with nerves, irritation, and bottled-up laughter.

Alarm bells rang in my head. He knew what I was doing.

"It'll fit you, so you can borrow it. Actually, you can have it." I stared at him. "And I would *love* for you to wear it to the bar."

He shrugged, still smiling that stupid fucking smile. "Sure. Can't wait."

Ugh.

The frustrating thing about Finn was that he was totally shameless.

I used to like that about him, but now it was complicating my whole *make Finn dump me* plan.

Which was why I had planned the worst date possible for today.

My gaze dropped to his mouth and I remembered our weird kiss the other night in the bar. All night, I'd felt his eyes on me, despite my hair looking all fucked up. By the end of the night, I was so wound up, I was itching to get out of there. It had taken me hours to fall asleep because I kept replaying the evening.

I'd never admit this, but I wanted to kiss him. A real kiss. Like we did on graduation night. A kiss like we wanted each other.

Finn used to be a very, very good kisser.

I wondered what kind of kisser he was now.

I needed to get rid of him, fast, before I got attached. Before I was disappointed again.

"Let's go," I said, eager to get this over with.

"THE DOILY MUSEUM?" Finn read the sign hanging in front of the little house, hands on his hips. "The doily museum. You want to go here."

I smoothed out the polyester masterpiece that, along with

my hair, was attracting some strange looks from the street. On the way here, everyone had gawked at us. Finn had insisted on holding my hand, and whispers rose up all around us while I tried to act normal.

"I've always wanted to go."

He narrowed his eyes. "Haven't we been here before? Grade two, right? Mrs. Phung's class. I feel like she took us here as a punishment."

Oh, I remembered. It was the most boring field trip we ever went on. This was going to be the worst date *ever*. My mouth twisted as I tried not to grin. Finn would die of boredom in this dull museum. If I was lucky, he'd slip out the back door within ten minutes.

"I don't remember that," I told him, shrugging. "Look, Finn, this is the kind of thing I like to do in my spare time, but if you don't want to go, I completely understand. Some people aren't suited for—"

He wrapped an arm around my shoulder and his intoxicating smell filled my nose. God damnit, he smelled amazing. His arm brushed mine and my breath caught.

"Oh," he laughed. "I want to go. I absolutely want to go to the doily museum with you."

My teeth gritted.

We climbed the steps to the house and knocked. The door swung open immediately, and our gazes dropped to the tiny, ancient woman in front of us.

Her small, wrinkly face broke into a big smile. "Welcome to the number one doily museum in Queen's Cove."

Dot, the museum curator and owner of the home, led us inside, clearing her throat and gesturing to a scrap of garbled white yarn stitched onto white fabric.

"This collection's first piece is from 1927, and was gifted to my mother when my family lived in Saskatoon. The Miller family lived two farms over and were moving to the West Coast because Mr. James Miller wanted to relocate them to a warmer climate, and so they gifted this piece to my mother, Mrs. Margaret Adams. As you can see by the delicate weave, this doily has been crocheted with a size eight thread, which is more rare than the typical size three or size five threads, which the North American Doily Society cites as the most common during that time. If you're interested in this style, I'm teaching a seminar on the twelfth on how to…"

My eyes drooped as her soft voice went on and on about doilies.

Dot pointed to the next doily and Finn's hand wrapped around mine and gently pulled me along. I ignored how nice his hand felt around mine.

"That's a nice one, Dot," he said, leaning in to study the doily under the glass case, spotlights on it like it was an Academy Award.

"It's my favorite in the whole museum," she said, beaming.

My heart squeezed. Finn being nice to old people should not have been this endearing.

She preened. "I found this one at an antiques sale in Prince George in the seventies. Although it was done with yarn, the delicate pattern lends itself to a very refined style. This type of doily would be placed as decoration on a table or across the back of a Chesterfield…"

I glanced at the clock. We'd been here twenty minutes, we'd seen two doilies, and there were at least forty more around the room under glass cases. Some were framed on the wall like art.

I was beginning to feel like I fucked up.

"Where do you go to find doilies?" Finn asked, and Dot launched into a long story about this time she visited a doily store in Vancouver.

He was supposed to be bored out of his mind, not *making friends* with the owner.

Thirty minutes later, Dot clapped her hands together. "I'll go find that map for you, Finn, there's an antiques store in

Nanaimo that may have something similar if you're hoping to find one for your own home." Her eyes slid to me while she hid a playful grin. "Or perhaps as a gift for a special someone."

"That would be great," Finn said, his arm returning to my shoulder. His fingers played with the ends of my hair, sending tingles down my neck. "I know a *special someone* who loves doilies."

Dot hustled out of the room and the second she disappeared, I lodged my elbow in his ribs.

"Ow," Finn said, laughing and jerking back. "What's wrong, baby?"

"Stop dragging this out," I hissed.

He looked shocked. "*Dragging this out*?" he repeated in a low voice so Dot wouldn't overhear. "I thought you brought me here because you knew I'd love it."

I caught myself. Before I could say anything, he leaned in, caging me in against the glass display case behind me.

His mouth brushed my ear. "You look so fucking cute in that ugly shirt."

Heat flared between my legs at the way his breath tickled me, and the intensity in his voice.

"You're a pervert."

He snorted, chest shaking with laughter. Dot hustled back into the room. She spread the map out on the display case and began explaining the store location in detail.

Two hours later, the tour of the doily museum came to an end. Finn's arm returned to my shoulders and my stomach flip-flopped at the contact.

I had to get home. I had to get away from Finn.

"Thanks, Dot," I said in a rush, glancing at the door. "It's been so fun, but we've got to get going."

Dot's expression fell like I told her I was taking her dog away. "I was hoping you'd stay for some tea and cookies."

Finn's arm squeezed my shoulders closer to him and I

tilted my chin up to look at him. My eyes begged for mercy. *Please*, my eyes said. *Please don't make me stay here.*

Finn's mouth curled into a wicked grin and his eyebrows lifted once.

Fuck.

"We would *love* to stay," he told Dot. "We're starving."

She clapped, elated. "I'll go set out the doily!"

———

"LIV, I GOTTA SAY," Finn said as we wandered down Main Street, a tin of cookies tucked under his arm. "You sure know how to plan a date."

My gaze met his. My stomach fluttered and I fought the urge to laugh. Despite my best efforts, it seemed like he had fun today.

I'd have to try harder next time.

"If you enjoyed today," I told him, "you're going to *love* our next date."

His mouth quirked. "Not so fast. It's my turn to plan a date."

"I like doing it," I volleyed back, keeping my voice light.

"Liv, a strong relationship is built off equality." He gave me a teasing, chiding look and I fought a laugh.

"Been in a lot of relationships, have you?"

He stopped walking and caught my hand, pulling me to stand in front of him. His smile dimmed but his eyes were soft. "Nope. You ruined me, but I'm not mad about it."

My heart dipped, swooping and dropping in my chest, and I blinked at him. I wished he wouldn't say things like that. Things that sounded so sincere.

"What about you?" he asked in a low voice, eyes on me. "Anyone serious?"

I had dated in university. It usually fizzled out with one of us getting busy with exams and then going home for the summer, or sometimes we just stopped texting each other. During the first year of my PhD program, I dated a guy in my program, Noah. We broke up at the end of the school year when he told me I wasn't invested enough in our relationship. That it seemed like I didn't care enough.

I guess I didn't.

I shook my head at Finn. "I was busy with school."

His gaze roamed my face before searching my eyes. The full weight of his attention drugged me, slowing my brain down but making my pulse race. He rubbed light strokes up and down my palm, and it was hard to concentrate. "You ever fall in love with anyone else?"

Like I was hypnotized, I shook my head.

The corner of his mouth turned up into a slight grin. "Just me then, huh?"

He tilted his head, eyes dropping to my mouth. Did he step closer? It seemed like he moved closer.

"What are you doing right now?" I whispered, eyes wide.

His lopsided grin hitched higher, but his eyes stayed locked on mine, pulling me in. "Trying to make a point."

Clarity cut through my thoughts like a knife. Finn wouldn't give up until he got what he wanted. He'd lure me in, pull me underwater with his thumb strokes, smirks, and tattoos, and when I resurfaced, he'd be gone. He'd get sick of me and move on to something new.

"I have to get going." I crossed my arms over my chest and glanced down the street.

He nodded, eyes narrowed while he studied me with a little smile on his face like he had won something. "One more kiss."

My head whipped up. "What?"

He lifted one shoulder, mouth twitching. "Yesterday was a little chaste, don't you think? We should try again."

"I haven't brushed my teeth today," I lied.

He looked like he was trying to hold back a laugh. "It's four in the afternoon."

"Sometimes I forget." I never forgot.

His eyes shone with amusement. "I'll risk it. You know, for *love*."

I held back a groan. Seriously, this guy.

Finn's eyes gleamed. "What's the matter, Liv? You seem like you're trying to run me off or something."

We held each other's gazes and deep in my lizard brain, I wondered what it would be like if I just kissed him.

I'd like it. I knew I would. I could still remember how he tugged my hair to tilt my head back and deepen the kiss. The slow, consuming glide of his tongue, the soft press of his lips against mine. A muscle low in my belly twinged and I sucked in a sobering breath.

"I think I'm getting sick." I lifted my elbow and coughed once, turning away from him. "Bye."

"Oh, and Liv?"

I paused and turned.

"I'll see you at Miri's class career day tomorrow afternoon."

I frowned. Miri Yang taught at the local elementary school and had asked me to talk to the class about forestry sciences.

His eyes glittered. "She asked the fire hall for a volunteer." His shoulders lifted in a shrug. "I love setting a good example for the kids."

A laugh of disbelief scraped out of my throat. "You, a good example."

Something flickered through his eyes but he kept the cocky grin. "Yep. You wait."

"You've broken every limb at least once."

His Adam's apple bobbed as he held my gaze with a look of determination. "I'm turning over a new leaf."

From the way his smile fell, it was obvious I didn't believe him. "I bet. See you later."

As I walked down Main Street, I felt his gaze on me.

You ruined me, but I'm not mad about it.

I shook it from my mind. Finn wasn't going to woo me. By the time I was done with him, he was going to be so sick of me he was going to wish he'd never come back to town.

Today hadn't worked like I wanted, so I had to up my game.

13

Finn

I PULLED into the school parking lot, turned the engine off, and studied my reflection in the rearview mirror.

There was a bright red mark beside my left eye, and the surrounding skin was turning a darker purple by the hour. When I pressed on the bruise, I winced, showing the new gap between my teeth.

A black eye and a missing tooth—not a great look after I'd announced my plan to change to Liv yesterday. Wyatt and I had gone surfing this morning, and I'd lost my balance on a rough wave. The board had bonked me in the face and chipped my front tooth.

I glanced over at the front doors of the school. I couldn't cancel, that'd be even worse. Besides, it wasn't like I could hide out without people knowing. Liv would find out.

When I opened the front door, the receptionist greeted me with a cheeky smile.

"Here comes trouble," she called, standing and shaking her head.

I gave her a close-lipped smile. "Hi, Mrs. Flores."

She gasped, eyes on my mouth and black eye. "Did you get in a fight?"

"What? No." I'd never even been in a fist fight. "Surfing."

"What a relief," she said, hand over her heart. "Goodness, Finn, you look so handsome in your uniform."

I looked down at myself with a little laugh. I'd gone all out today. For the kids, but also for Liv. Her seeing this side of me, seeing how seriously I took firefighting, would help change her mind.

Mrs. Flores shook her head with that same knowing, cheeky smile. She wagged a finger at me. "I know you're still that little devil, though." She pointed at the framed photo outside the principal's office, and I held back a sigh.

That photo was *still* here? It was my grade twelve school photo, and below it, there was a small plaque. I already knew what it said. The principal had showed this to me at graduation.

Finn Rhodes—record holder for number of visits to the principal's office

"A few kids have come close," she laughed, "but no one's beat your record yet."

It used to be inside the principal's office, and now it hung outside for everyone who passed in and out of the school to see.

My shoulders tensed. No wonder I had a reputation. Jesus Christ.

"Ms. Yang is ready if you want to head straight to her class," she said with a bright smile, pointing down the hall. "Right at the end. The door should be open."

I thanked her and headed down the hall, my boots thumping on the linoleum floor as I approached.

A woman stepped through the classroom door in front of me and I stopped short.

"Jen." I straightened up. "Hi."

My stomach tensed. Living in Queen's Cove over the years, I'd run into Olivia's mom once in a while, and it was always awkward. Every time I saw her, I heard what she said to me outside the principal's office. Her words had weighed on me for years.

Jen Morgan was a nurse at the Queen's Cove hospital. I didn't realize she'd be here for career day. I hadn't asked Miri who else had agreed to come.

"Hi, Finn," she said, gaze flicking over my eye.

Fuck. I had such stupidly high hopes for today and it was sliding downhill, fast.

"Jen." I pushed my shoulders back. I felt like I should be wearing a tie or something. I pointed at my eye. "This is from surfing."

She nodded once. "I heard you moved in above the bar."

My ears burned hot. "Yep."

Yes, I moved in above the bar knowing Olivia would hate it, but I was desperate to spend more time with her.

"Joe really helped me out." I cleared my throat again. "Not a lot of options coming into the busy season."

She raised an eyebrow. "Mhm."

We stared at each other.

"Finn." Olivia appeared in the doorway, pink haircut pulled back into a bun, choppy bangs held back with a black headband. She wore a black tank top with a green plaid shirt open over it. She stared at me in surprise.

I knew she had worn that stupid Guy Fieri shirt the other day to get to me. No way would she wear it normally. A smile curved up on my mouth at the sight of her. She looked fucking cute in that tank top.

She made a face at my black eye. "Did you get into a fight?"

"No," I sighed. "Surfing with Wyatt."

Frustration hitched in my shoulders. I was going to be correcting a lot of people over the next few days.

She glanced up and down at my firefighter's gear. "Nice uniform." The corner of her mouth kicked up like she was trying not to smile, and energy crackled in my chest.

I *knew* it was a good idea, wearing my gear. I gave her a beaming smile. I could practically see her walls crumbling. True love, here we come. Any minute now.

I wiggled my eyebrows at her. "Hell, one of these kids might grow up to be a firefighter like me."

Jen smiled but it didn't reach her eyes. "You can't say hell in front of seventh graders, Finn."

"Shit. Sorry. I mean—" I caught myself again. "Heck. Shoot."

Liv snorted.

Thank *fuck* Miri Yang appeared beside us with a big smile. "Hello, volunteers."

"I'm going to use the ladies' room before we start," Jen said, stepping away.

Miri gasped at my eye and missing tooth.

"Surfing," I cut in before she could ask. "My surfboard hit me in the face."

Miri shook her head. "My goodness, Finn, trouble finds you everywhere, doesn't it?" She glanced between Liv and me, and her expression turned smug.

At slightly over five feet tall, Miri was physically tiny but socially powerful. Emmett had admitted that convincing Miri Yang of his and Avery's fake engagement had been key to winning over the entire town. The woman was feral for gossip.

She sighed, looking wistful. "I always knew you two would get back together." She nudged me with her elbow. "Didn't I say it at Sadie and Holden's wedding? You remember?"

How could I forget?

Four brothers, four weddings, she had said with a gleam in her eye.

No, I was quick to tell her. *No way*.

At that time, I believed what everyone else did—I was bad news for Liv.

Now, I wanted her to have the job of her dreams, and I wanted to be the right guy for her.

"What?" Liv's eyebrows shot up and she shifted. "What are you talking about?"

"Four brothers, four weddings," Miri sang, bouncing with excitement.

Olivia's eyes widened with terror and I stiffened.

"Oops!" Miri grinned and made a mouth-zipping motion. "I've said too much. I'm going to get the class's attention and we can get started."

She hustled into the classroom and Liv turned to me with a look of disgust.

"Please tell me you're not going to propose."

I huffed a laugh. I knew how that would go. She'd toss the ring off a cliff.

"I'm not going to propose." My mouth hitched. "Not yet."

"*Finn.*"

I snorted, grinning wider. "What? I'm not going to push you to do something you're not ready for. I didn't make you kiss me yesterday, did I?"

She rolled her eyes. "Like you're ready to get married."

"To you? I'd get married this afternoon," I said without thinking. "Would have done it twelve years ago if I was smart enough."

Panic streaked through me. I didn't mean to say that. I didn't want to freak her out. I shot her a wary glance, and she blinked up at me, expression blank.

"You don't mean that. You're messing with me." A little frown grew between her eyebrows and I itched to trace it with my fingers. Before I could respond, she stepped into the classroom.

I watched her make her way to the seats at the back, where the other volunteers gathered.

"I surely fucking do mean it," I muttered under my breath before I followed her.

———

"PUTTING out fires is only one small part of my job," I told the class when it was my turn to present. "On a typical day, we might do routine checks of smoke detectors and fire alarms," —I pointed to the smoke detector on the ceiling—"or we could be running safety drills at our training facility. If the paramedics are too busy, we answer emergency calls. And because Queen's Cove is a small town, many of the firefighters double as Search and Rescue."

The kids were enthralled and I was freaking *nailing* this. Emmett was a genius for telling me to clean up my image. From the back of the room, Miri beamed and gave me an enthusiastic thumbs up. Even Jen seemed to be warming up to me. Her expression had softened as she watched me present.

"Do you get to ride in a helicopter?" one of the kids asked.

"I sure do," I told her. "Does anyone know why someone would call Search and Rescue?"

Several kids put their hands up and I pointed to one.

"Do you work with girls?" the kid asked.

I nodded. "Yes, there are three women on the crew. My boss, Chief Bell, is a woman, too. People call Search and Rescue when they get lost or injured—"

Another kid cut me off. "What happens when the girls aren't as strong as you?"

I should have thanked this kid for lobbing me that softball. I fought the urge to crack my knuckles because I was about to nail this.

"First, we refer to them as women, not girls, because they're grown-ups. Understand?"

The kids stared back at me. When I glanced at Liv, she wore a little smile on her face, which filled me with confidence. One gold star for Finn Rhodes.

"All firefighters are required to pass a series of tests before being hired on to the crew, which means all the female firefighters are strong enough. They're an important part of our crew and I'm lucky to work with them."

Miri clutched her heart and pretended to swoon. *Whoosh* —that was the sound of me *slam dunking* this. My chest puffed out with pride. Miri slipped out into the hall to speak with a volunteer who had just arrived, and I opened my mouth to continue talking about safety in the back country.

"Have you ever been drunk?" another kid asked.

"Uh." I hesitated. Of course I had, but I didn't think I should say that. "Alcohol is bad."

"My parents drink wine," she volleyed back.

Uh. "A little is fine but getting drunk is bad. So, one of the main reasons people need to call for help is—"

"You didn't answer us," a girl in the front row said, raising her eyebrows. She turned to the class. "He's drunk right now. That's why he has no tooth."

"I'm not drunk," I rushed out. My ears were going hot again. What the fuck? "And I knocked my tooth out surfing this morning. Sure, I've been drunk before, but as you get older, the hangovers will hit you harder..." I caught Jen's bemused expression and Olivia rolling her lips, trying not to laugh, and cut myself off. "Let's stick to talking about hiking safety."

"Have you ever smoked weed?" the girl prodded.

"Uh." I glanced at Jen, who raised an unimpressed eyebrow.

I glanced at the doorway. Miri was still fucking *chatting* in the hallway. I exhaled heavily. I couldn't *lie* to them, they'd see right through me. Besides, it was more responsible to tell them the truth and give them the tools to make good decisions, right?

A kid in the front row held up his phone. "Is this you?"

I leaned forward and nearly choked at a photo of me in my early twenties, doing a bong rip with some friends.

I reared back. "Where'd you find that?"

She tapped something on her phone and the phones around the classroom started pinging and buzzing.

"I put it in the group chat," she said to the class, and everyone pulled out their phones to look.

Fuck. Okay. I was losing control of this.

"Yes, I have smoked weed," I admitted, glancing nervously at Jen. "Drugs are bad. I mean, not all drugs—"

She frowned.

"—most drugs are bad," I continued, starting to sweat.

"How do we know which ones are bad?" the nosy girl asked.

"Anything in pill form. Pills, crystals, powders, that stuff can kill you. We see people overdose sometimes." Good, okay, this was good. Back on track. "Don't take anything people offer you."

"Are mushrooms bad?"

"How do you make weed brownies?" another one asked.

The nosy girl started filming me. "How many beers can you drink before you're drunk?"

"What's a Jäger-bomb?"

"My mom went to school with you and she said you're a hot mess express."

Fucking hell. This wasn't a class presentation, it was a firing squad. Under my jacket, I was sweating through my t-shirt.

"Have you ever been arrested? My dad said you've been to jail."

"The drunk tank isn't *jail*," I said, for some stupid fucking reason. *Finn, shut your goddamned mouth.*

Jen turned and gave Liv a look.

Fuuuuuuck.

"And our next presenter is…" I gestured at the back. "Jen Morgan! Everyone give her a big round of applause."

The kids ignored me while I strode to the back of the room, heart beating in my ears. Jen started talking about nursing and I dropped into the seat beside Liv.

A wry smile stretched over her face. "That went *really* well."

I raked a hand back through my hair.

This date I was going to take Liv on? I needed to plan something *good*.

———

ON THE WAY back to the fire hall from the school, I passed a car on the side of the road. One of the tires was sagging. I slowed and pulled over to the shoulder and got out.

The driver straightened up from where he was fumbling with a tire iron. He scanned me in my gear, and he was breathing hard. I'd seen people experiencing a stress response like this during Search and Rescue.

I put my hands up. "Need help?" I asked in a reassuring tone. "I know how to change a flat."

His gaze flicked between me and the highway behind me. "Yeah." He nodded quickly before swallowing. "That would be great."

I was swapping out the flat for his spare when a familiar white 4x4 drove past. Liv's car. I gave her a wave and a big smile and returned to tightening the bolts.

Today had started out shit, but this guy's flat was a small gift from the universe.

14

Olivia

"HI," I called as I stepped inside my parents' house that evening.

"In the kitchen," my mom called back. Classic rock played in the living room so I knew my dad was still home.

I kicked my shoes off and followed the sound of my parents' voices.

"...I'm telling you, Joe, blood *everywhere*, all over the floor," my mom was saying, seated at the kitchen island as my dad unloaded the dishwasher. Her gaze shot to my hair and she slumped in relief. "Oh, thank god you got your hair fixed. Those bangs are cute on you."

This afternoon, Sadie had dragged me to the salon to have it fixed. The stylist had given me wispy curtain bangs and a shoulder-length cut with a seventies vibe to it.

"Thanks." I raised an eyebrow. "What are you talking about?"

My mom shrugged. "I said I had the day from hell and Joe asked what happened."

"Jen, no." He shook his head, wincing. "I can't hear this stuff."

She started laughing. "You asked."

"Mom, you can't talk to us the way you talk to other nurses."

She rolled her eyes, smiling. "You two. The kids loved hearing my gross stories today."

"Oh, right." My dad leaned on the counter. "How'd that go?"

My mom and I exchanged a look. The air snapped with a strange tension. She adopted a polite, pleasant expression, which meant she was thinking about Finn and how badly his presentation had gone today.

Have you ever been in jail? The drunk tank isn't jail. I turned and winced out the window.

"Fine," my mom told him.

"Yeah, fine," I added. "The kids were more interested in how to make drinks than my thesis."

My dad folded his arms over his chest and exchanged a look with my mom. I arched a brow.

"What?" I asked them.

My mom glanced between my dad and me, shifting on her stool. My stomach dipped, suddenly nervous.

My dad blew out a long breath. "I'm going to sell the bar."

My eyebrows shot up. "*What?*"

He nodded, rubbing his jaw. "Yeah. I think it's time." He smiled at my mom. "We're ready to retire. We realized last year that we didn't want to wait until our seventies to do all the fun retirement stuff."

"And I'm not fully retiring," my mom added. "I'm going down to part time."

Thoughts toppled over each other in my mind like balls in one of those lottery tumblers. Last year, when I was struggling to find the flower, I admitted to Sadie that if I didn't finish my dissertation, I wanted to buy the bar when the time came and take it over. My dad had done so much for us, and he loved that place. I wanted to do it for him.

Was it my dream? No, being out in the forest was my dream, but it was a good second choice. It was good enough.

But now my fallback plan was being yanked out from beneath me.

"I want to buy it," I burst out. "I want to buy the bar."

They exchanged another look, like they expected this.

"No," he said, studying my face with concern. "I know it isn't what you want, honey."

"But—" I started.

"*No*, Olivia." He watched me, eyebrows creasing. "I appreciate all the hard work you've put in. We never could have gone traveling if not for you holding down the fort last year." He shook his head, sighing. "But I can't help thinking you want to buy the place out of obligation, and in the end, we want you to be happy."

I dragged in a shaky breath. "Can't it be both?"

He shot me a sad smile before walking over and wrapping me in a bear hug.

"My mind is made up," he said before dropping a quick kiss on the top of my head. "Okay?"

I nodded against his shoulder, feeling anxious and agitated even though I knew he was right.

———

"I CAN'T WATCH *WILD* AGAIN," she protested.

"It's been at least six months." My thumb hovered over the button on the remote, ready to press play.

My mom huffed a laugh. My dad had headed to the bar and we were sitting in the living room eating takeout sushi, ready to put a movie on.

"Fine." She sighed but I could see she didn't mind that much. "We talk through it anyway."

I started the movie and settled back into the couch.

She looked at me out of the corner of her eye. "Are you upset about the bar?"

My head tipped back against the back of the couch and I hummed. "I can see where you guys are coming from." I knew in my gut it was the right choice, but that didn't make it any more comfortable that my career safety net was falling out from beneath me. "I just—" I folded my arms over my plaid shirt. "Dad has done so much for us."

"What do you mean?"

"Without him, who knows where we'd be? We wouldn't have been able to buy this house from Grandma and Grandpa." When I was born, my mom and Cole lived with her parents to save money. Cole moved out when they broke up shortly after I was born. My dad made them an offer on the house the day he proposed to my mom, when I was five. "We may not have been able to afford university for me."

My mom frowned and searched my face. "Honey. You don't owe Joe this. Those are the kind of things that dads do."

Not all dads. The thought scraped, painful and raw. Some dads left. Some dads lost interest in their kids' lives. Some dads lost touch.

Sometimes, I wondered if Cole even thought about me. Did he remember my birthday or my first word?

Joe did. He remembered every detail. He was there on every birthday, showed up to every parent-teacher conference, even picked me up from school when I got in trouble with Finn.

I let out a long sigh and flattened my mouth as I glanced at my mom.

"Baby," she said softly, looping her arm around my shoulder. "We worry that you're stuck." She exhaled through her nose, looking pained. "You're so focused on that flower, but what if you don't find it?"

Her doubt seared me, and my stomach twisted. Another person who thought I was wasting my time.

"It feels like you're treading water." Her shoulders lifted. "And we've noticed that you don't date."

I choked. "I've dated."

"No one serious, though." Her expression changed and she rolled her eyes. "And we're going to talk about this whole Finn thing."

"It's not what you think—"

"Hold on." She put a hand up. "I just want to say, I think Joe selling the bar is a good thing. It'll force you into the next phase of your life." She gave me a soft look, full of love. "All we want is for you to live a full, happy life." She searched my eyes. "Okay?"

I nodded, throat tight. "Yep. Okay."

She squeezed my shoulder before pulling her arm back and I hesitated. Her eyebrow arched.

"So you've heard about me and Finn."

"Uh-huh." Her tone was dry.

My mom wasn't Finn's biggest fan. Any time I had a kid over from school who wasn't Finn, she'd be thrilled and overly encouraging, especially as I got further into my teen years and Finn's antics started getting worse.

She was relieved when he left. She'd never say that because I was obviously upset, but I think she saw Finn leaving as a bullet dodged.

On the couch, I told her about my plan to get him to lose interest in me.

"Ohhhhkay." She pointed at my hair. "I get the bad haircut now." She studied me for a moment before letting out a laugh and burying her head in her hands. "Oh my god. Baby. You're playing with fire here."

"It's fine. I have it all under control."

"I don't know about this." She shook her head, worrying her bottom lip. "He's just…"

I waited. "He's just what?"

"He's something else." She didn't say it like it was a good thing. "And he's always been your weakness."

I huffed. "Wow. Not mincing words tonight, are you?"

"I'm sorry, baby, I didn't mean it in a bad way. Guys like Finn? I know guys like him. Or, I knew one." She laughed but it didn't reach her eyes. My stomach twisted again at the comparison between Finn and Cole.

"I told you, it's fake."

"You can't rely on them." Her expression was pained. "They don't stick around for long. Finn has been in and out of this town for years."

"I *know*." My shoulders tensed with irritation.

"You can't change them."

I shook my head, squeezing my eyes closed. "I don't want to talk about this anymore. I have everything under control. Everything you're saying, I already know. Finn's the only one who doesn't realize he's going to leave again, okay? I'm ready for it."

She chewed her lip, her blue eyes holding mine. "Yeah. Okay." She winced through a small smile. "Just trying to protect my baby."

"I'm not a baby anymore."

"You're not *a* baby, but you're still *my* baby." She looped her arm around my shoulders and made squeaky kissy noises against my face.

I laughed and tried to push her away. "Stop it."

We turned back to the movie, and while we watched, my mind wandered to Finn.

My mom was right. This was the reminder I needed. I had replayed the quick brush of his lips over mine in the bar a hundred times, and when he looked at me yesterday after our date at the doily museum with heat in his gaze, I *wanted* him to kiss me.

You ruined me, and I'm not mad about it.

I had to be careful around him. My brain knew he was

bad news, but my body? She wanted action with the hot, bright-eyed firefighter covered in tattoos.

Later, after I ran upstairs to use the washroom, I lingered in the open doorway of my old bedroom.

Except for removing my posters and pictures on the walls, my parents had kept the room the same. It was a guest room now for visitors. I wandered in, approaching the window that faced Finn's old room.

I peered out but Finn's old room was dark, so I couldn't see inside. I'd stolen peeks over the years and from this distance, it also looked mostly the same. My gaze passed over the Rhodes' front yard, where I'd seen Finn sneak out and back in on grad night.

My shoulder bumped the window frame as I looked out.

Everywhere I turned, I was flooded with memories of Finn. I thought about what my mom said.

You can't rely on them. You can't change them.

If I let Finn break my heart again, I was going to spend the rest of my life haunted by memories of us.

15

Olivia

FINN RHODES HELPS *local car thief escape*.

In my pajamas, I stood in the kitchen of my apartment, brushing my teeth and reading the article Sadie had sent me.

My mind wandered to a few days ago when Finn showed up looking like he'd come from a bar fight, and then got slaughtered by those kids. On my way home, I'd seen him on the side of the highway, changing someone's tire.

There was a knock at the door.

"It's open," I called.

Finn opened the door and leaned on the frame, roguish grin rising on his mouth. His black eye was starting to heal, going green at the edges as it faded, and a temporary crown filled the gap in his front teeth seamlessly.

His eyes snagged on my hair.

"You changed your hair again." His grin hitched higher. "It looked so nice before."

I rolled my eyes. Liar.

His hair was damp like he just got out of the shower, tousled and messy, and I pictured him rubbing a towel over it to dry it. Water dripping down his hard chest.

Low in my stomach, there was a funny tug, and I blinked. *Stop that*, I told myself.

I held my phone up. "Heard you helped a criminal out the other day."

His face fell. "That was an accident." He rubbed a hand over the back of his neck, looking sheepish. "I didn't know the car was stolen. Honest, Liv. I didn't. I was trying to help someone out."

I believed him, but on top of the the kids rooting up his past the other day, the black eye, and the chipped tooth? Warning rose in my stomach.

Did Finn think he was proving anything to me?

He glanced around my apartment, hands braced on the doorframe and hanging forward a little. His gaze came up to mine expectantly.

I gestured for him to enter. "Don't touch anything."

"You're cute when you're grumpy." He took a seat at the kitchen table and leaned back, arms behind his head, muscles rippling.

I headed back to the bathroom to rinse my mouth out. When I emerged from my room, dressed and ready to go, Finn stood in my living room, studying my bookshelf with his head tilted to the side.

"Thanks for waiting," I said, tone brisk and all business while I pulled on my hiking boots.

Finn did a double take at my pants. I busied myself with adjusting the straps of my bag, turning to hide my grin.

"Those are…" he trailed off, gaze snagging on the zippers on the pant hems.

I bit my lip. These pants were *hideous*.

Normally, I wore yoga leggings in the forest because even though summer was approaching and the weather was warming up, it got cold in the mountains. Someone in town gifted me these pants a few years ago. They were hand-me-downs from someone's brother's daughter and I couldn't donate them because then they'd find out, so I had stashed them in my closet.

They made my ass look flat and super long, like it stretched from my lower back to the bottom of my knees. They made an annoying swishing noise when I walked and had a hundred pockets. Also, they zipped off at both the thighs and the calves.

When I had my face under control, I straightened up to look at him. "Do you like them?"

His eyebrows lifted before his gaze rose to mine. A smile curled up on his mouth. "I do. You have the ankles of a porn star."

Do. Not. Laugh.

I stared at him and he stared right back, daring me. "You like these pants," I repeated.

"Yep." His chin dipped in a nod and his eyes danced with amusement.

My stomach swooped and the side of my mouth twitched but I didn't dare laugh. No fucking way.

"Great," I chirped in a voice completely unlike my own. "I'm ready to go."

I picked my bag up and frowned at how light it was before I opened it. "My water is gone."

"It's in mine," he said. "I'll carry it."

I frowned at him. "No."

He huffed a laugh, and his hair fell across his forehead. "Yes, Liv."

"I can carry my own."

"I *know* you can carry your own. You can do everything on your own. No question about that." He looked up at me, standing with my hands on my hips. "But maybe I want to carry your water. Ever think of that?" His eyebrow arched and that amused look passed through his eyes again.

There was something about him looking at me like that,

like I was cute and funny and like he *liked me* that made me feel shaky, silly, and excited.

I hadn't felt like this in a long time.

Ugh. *Get a fucking grip, Liv*.

"You okay, Morgan?" His eyes danced, bright and amused.

I threw my hands up, mind whirring and totally scrambled. "Fine, you can carry my water." I hauled my backpack on. "Let's go."

———

HALF AN HOUR LATER, we parked my car off the side of the logging road and began the hike. We made our way through the forest in silence as the sun rose higher. Sunbeams cut through the tree canopy and steam rose from where they hit the ground. Birds chirped, our boots sank into the soft earth, and somewhere above us, a woodpecker clacked against a tree.

God, I loved being out here in the woods. It was like all my problems faded away into nothing.

"Happy?" Finn asked with a chuckle, and I blinked.

"Hmm?"

"You sighed." His eyes crinkled as he glanced between me and the fallen tree he was stepping over. "Your shoulders fell a couple inches and you looked relaxed. I almost forgot you wanted to kill me."

I snorted and made a strange face. "I don't want you dead."

"Uh-huh. Sure."

"I don't," I insisted, laughing a little.

He shot me a grin that told me he didn't believe me.

"For a long time, I wished I'd never met you, though," I admitted.

The grin on his face faded, and his eyebrows pulled together.

I looked to the ground, watching where I stepped. I'd already searched this area a couple months ago but I scanned back and forth, desperate for a task to keep me anchored and focused.

Maybe that was too harsh to say, about wishing I'd never met him.

"And that," he said quietly, stopping and turning abruptly, "is why I'm not giving up. Because with the wrong guy, you would have been relieved. You would have been over me by now, but you're not, are you? You can barely look at me. You're terrified to let yourself relax around me."

"That's not true," I whispered, my eyes flicking up to meet his before I glanced back down to the ground.

His hand came up and his fingers brushed below my chin, tilting my face up to look at him. He stared down into my eyes and my heart skipped a beat.

"I know what you're doing," he murmured in a low voice that made my heart beat harder, "with these ugly pants and the haircut and the doily museum."

"So you admit they're ugly," I whispered.

His mouth twitched into a grin but heat flashed through his eyes. "I'm going to do everything I can to show you I'm different." His voice dropped to a whisper. "I'll never make the same mistake again."

My heart twisted and I wanted to believe him so, so badly. A part of me did believe him. He was here, wasn't he? Hoofing it around the mountains when he could be doing anything else. He'd endured a three-hour mind-numbingly boring doily museum tour.

Maybe he wasn't the same Finn who'd stepped all over my heart.

But what if he was, and he was just fooling everyone, himself included? What if I let go of all this anger and heartbreak that I had grown around and let him fill in the gaps and make me whole again? When he left, I'd have nothing holding me together. I'd fall apart for real this time, and harder. Smaller pieces were harder to put back together.

Fast as lightning, Finn's hands framed my jaw and he stole a kiss from my mouth. His lips were warm and his stubble brushed me, sending sparks across my skin. I gasped and he pulled away, flashing me a grin and a wink.

"Come on, Morgan," he called over his shoulder, continuing on through the forest while I gawked at him. "I've got all your water and you're still struggling to keep up."

A shocked laugh scraped out of my throat while I stared after him.

Warmth bloomed in my chest and I bit my lip to hide my grin. What a fucking asshole.

16

Olivia

WITHIN TWO HOURS, we reached the area I wanted to search today. I dropped my pack and pulled out my notebook to study the map and glance over the printouts of the flower.

"Do you want to look?" I held the images up for Finn, but he shook his head and pulled out his own notebook.

"Got my own." He flipped the book open and showed me images of the plant taped to the pages.

I frowned. "Where'd you get those?"

"The *internet*." He said it like it was a novelty while studying his page. "I've been doing a little reading."

I stared at him. "On the flower?"

"Mhm." He reached down for a bottle of water and nudged my elbow with it. "Drink."

"I'm fine."

He undid the cap and nudged me again. "If you get dehydrated, I'll have to carry you." His mouth curled and he narrowed his eyes at me. "Bet you'd like that, huh, Liv? Been fantasizing about me carrying you, firefighter style?"

My expression turned to a glare and I took the bottle from him, holding eye contact as I drank. A smug grin pulled onto his face as he turned back to his notebook.

"That's what I thought. You're such a fucking brat," he murmured, eyes on the page.

"You wish." I rolled my eyes and adjusted my swishy pants. The stupid zippers were scratching up my inner thighs. I should have worn shorts underneath. No wonder that person gave these pants away.

I eyed my backpack. I had a pair of leggings in there as a backup but putting them on would be a defeat in this battle against Finn.

Besides, my leggings were like a second skin, hugging my curves and making my ass look incredible. I was *not* going to play with that kind of fire today. I was trying to turn Finn off, not wave a red flag in front of a bull.

When I took a step, the zipper scraped my skin again and I winced.

"What's wrong?" Finn asked, brow creasing with concern. It was unnerving when he turned serious like that.

"Nothing." I tilted the book so he could see the map. "This is the area I want to search today."

He peered over my shoulder, studying the map before he nodded. "Let's get to it."

We spaced out so we could search in corridors while keeping each other in eyesight, and I breathed a sigh of relief. Being in Finn's vicinity was doing weird things to my brain. My concentration was shot. Every time he got close, I replayed his quick brush against my lips earlier today.

This guy was driving me insane.

We searched the area before I checked it off on the map and we moved to the next section. We worked in silence, keeping each other in sight.

My mind wandered to the printouts he had shown me, and I held down a smile. A flush of happiness hit me in the chest. He didn't take anything else seriously, but he cared about me finding the flower and finishing my PhD.

We might be friends after all, once this was all over.

I took another step and winced as the zipper scratched my skin. Pain seared my inner thigh and I clamped my mouth into a thin line to hold in the groan. Fucking hell, that hurt.

"Liv, you want to break for lunch?" Finn called over.

"Sure."

He gestured to a big log with a clear area around it. "Over here."

I made my way over, trying to walk in a way that didn't agitate the zipper against my skin. He shot me a funny look.

"Did you hurt your ankle?" He cocked an eyebrow and glanced down at my legs and feet. "You're walking weird."

I took a seat on the log and he dropped to kneel at my feet, reaching for my ankle.

"I'm fine," I said, swatting him away.

He frowned. "Liv."

I stared at him before relenting. "These ugly pants are scratching my legs up."

His head fell back and he let out a bark of laughter. "I knew you were wearing these to fuck with me." He opened his bag and dug through it, pulling out a first aid kit. "I have some bandages in here. Unzip them."

Alarm shot through me. This was dangerous territory. "No."

He tilted his head, watching me with a patient look. "Liv, it's going to get worse and we have a long way to go."

My teeth gritted. I knew that. I *knew* wearing these stupid pants was a mistake. "Fine." I held my hand out for the first aid kit but he ignored me.

"Unzip." He sat and opened the small kit, shuffling through the different sizes of bandages.

You know what? This was nothing. It was no big deal, and if I was in the field with a colleague, I wouldn't think twice about this. People got scrapes and blisters and cuts, and then they dealt with it.

It wasn't a big deal. It didn't matter than Finn was here.

I yanked the zipper on the pants, turning them into shorts. God, I hated these pants.

Finn shook his head at my newly bare legs. The fabric ballooned out around my ass. "They're even worse as shorts."

A snort escaped me and my chest shook with laughter. Finn's gaze snapped to mine, surprised and delighted, before I covered it with a cough.

"Sit," Finn said, tilting his chin at the log.

I ignored him, holding my hand out. "I'll do it."

He stared back at me with that annoying, smug little smile. "*Sit down*. Jesus Christ, Liv, I'm trained at this."

Okay, fine. He wanted to be *professional* about applying a bandage to my inner thigh?

Deep down, I wanted to see another flash of that heated look he gave me once in a while, like he was thinking about us on grad night. I took a seat on the log and he knelt at my feet.

His fingers tapped the inside of my knee, and sparks shot up my skin. "Can I get in there, please?"

I tapped my tongue against my top lip, watching him. This would be an exercise in getting stronger, I told myself. Like exposure therapy to Finn's hotness.

I could totally handle this.

17

Olivia

I SHIFTED my leg open a little more, studying his face for any sign of teasing. My stomach was molten, twisting in weird anticipation.

"Thank you." He pulled out a bottle of antiseptic and shook it, expression neutral.

I frowned.

His hand came to my thigh, warm and solid, and his gaze met mine. "I need to disinfect it."

I nodded, swallowing. Did I remember to shave my legs? I didn't want to glance down and draw attention to them. Fuck, his hand on my thigh felt nice. He gave me a light squeeze, holding my gaze. His gray eyes were so clear and bright, rimmed in dark lashes. My heart thumped harder in my chest.

"Deep breath in," he said, eyes on me.

I sucked in a breath.

"Let it out in eight counts."

There was something very calming about this version of Finn. It was probably part of Search and Rescue training, learning how to keep people relaxed.

One, two, three—Finn sprayed the antiseptic on me and pain seared across my skin. I gasped and flinched.

"Ow." My mouth fell open. "That hurt."

He made a comforting noise in his throat, and something weird flipped in my stomach. He ripped the bandage package open and pulled the wrapper off.

"Poor Livvy," he said in a low, teasing voice, eyes on where his fingers applied the bandage with care. My pulse tripped at the nickname. "Trying to look ugly and even that doesn't work." His eyes flicked up to mine with a little smirk on his face before he brushed the bandage lightly to make sure it stuck.

That brush zinged all the way up to the apex of my legs. A sharp clench around nothing, a flash of quick heat. I sucked a breath in and swallowed.

"I wish you'd stop calling me that," I whispered.

"Why?"

Because it made me feel things. Because it was sweet and nostalgic. Because it made me forget why I hated him so much.

He arched an eyebrow. "You want me to call you something else? Like *girlfriend*?"

Oh my god. I ignored the pulse in my chest and stood. "Thanks for the help."

He rocked back onto his heels and watched me move around, picking up my bag and digging around inside for nothing to keep my hands busy.

"You should put those other pants on."

My gaze cut to his. "You'd like that, wouldn't you?"

He burst out laughing. "I would, but that's not why I said it. The zipper on those shorts is going to bug you all day."

I was torn. The yoga leggings would make my ass look amazing, which seemed dangerous, but even I wasn't stupid enough to keep wearing these pants.

"Fine," I told him, pulling them out of my bag before I pointed at him and twirled my finger in a circular motion. "Don't look, though."

"I won't." He stood and turned.

I paused with the pants in my hands, nerves running through me. "I'm serious, Finn."

He sighed. "Liv, when I see you without pants on, it won't be against your will, okay? You'll be begging me to take them off."

I blinked, heat flashing through me. "Whatever."

He snorted, and even with his back turned, I could see his smugness turned up tenfold. "Yeah, whatever. Right." He crossed his arms over his chest. "Do your thing, I won't peek."

Once I had removed my boots, I yanked the shorts from hell off and threw them onto my bag before pulling on the yoga pants as fast as possible.

"Okay. Thanks. Let's eat lunch."

Finn nodded once before we pulled our food out and ate. After our sandwiches were done and we had polished off another bottle of water, Finn reached into his bag and tossed me—

I gasped at the crinkly orange bag. "Cheezies?!" My face lit up with a big smile. "Oh my *god*. I could so fucking go for some Cheezies right now."

His smile hitched, and embarrassment at my excitement over the snack had my skin feeling warm. He leaned his chin on his palm, watching me. "So go for them. I brought them for you."

My eyebrows shot up. "You did?"

"Are they still your favorite?"

I tore the bag open. "They sure are."

"Then I brought them for you."

I bit into one and closed my eyes. "Oh my god. So good."

Cheezies were absolute trash junk food. They were made of space dust, chemicals, and salt. They glowed bright radioactive orange and were in bizarre little cat poop shapes.

They were delicious.

I crunched one, dancing in my seat as the salt hit my tongue. "Mm. So good. I love these."

Finn watched me with bright eyes. "Good."

I smiled at him. "Thank you. I almost forgot that you touched my inner thigh today."

He snorted. "I was a gentleman and a professional."

"You were." My eyebrows bobbed as I chewed. "I'm kind of impressed. Being a gentleman is so unlike you."

Something moved through his eyes. Determination and regret. Worry pinched in my gut. Should I not have said that? Was I being a dick?

"I'll have to keep showing you what a gentleman I can be, huh?" His gaze held mine and my stomach did a lazy roll.

After we finished eating, we packed up our garbage and sat around for a few minutes, staring at the forest and listening to the birds chirp around us.

My mind wandered to the flower. It was already June, which meant it was definitely in bloom by now. If I couldn't find it, the last five years of my life would have been a huge waste of time. No one was going to hire a researcher who hadn't finished school.

A researcher who most people were laughing at behind her back.

"Hey," Finn said, eyes soft. "We're going to find it. I know it's out there."

My eyebrows pinched together. The way he said it, the confident, assured expression on his face, it filled me with a weird rush of gratitude for him.

"Are my thoughts that obvious?" I joked.

"Yes," he said. "We saw it. I believe you."

My heart squeezed. When he said things like that, he gave me hope, and I didn't know if that was a good thing anymore.

"I think you're the only person who does."

"You'll show them, Liv." He slid down to sit beside me,

back against the log. His warm arm brushed mine. "I know you will."

————

WE SPENT the rest of the afternoon working in silence, aware of each other walking through the trees in the forest but focused with our eyes on the ground, stopping for snack breaks before getting back to work. When we were three hours from sunset, Finn called out that we should head back to the car, and we began the hike back to the logging road.

"Don't worry," Finn said as we got to the car. "We'll find it."

I nodded, avoiding his eyes.

"How're your inner thighs?" He tossed his bag in the back and shot me a smirk. "You need me to take another look?"

I couldn't hide the grin. Even if I didn't want to, Finn always knew how to make me laugh.

"They're fine, pervert."

He chuckled and closed the trunk. "I'll drive back if you like." He tilted his chin to the keys in my hand.

I massaged the spot on my shoulder where my pack strap had rubbed all day. After a full day out in the woods, my batteries were drained in the best way—that bone-deep tired from being outside, breathing in the fresh air. My gaze flicked up at him.

He cocked a grin at me. "Come on, let me drive. I'll go the speed limit and I won't help any criminals get away, promise."

I rolled my eyes and tossed him the keys.

"You working tonight?" Finn asked a few minutes later as he drove the car down the bumpy logging road that led back to the highway.

I shook my head. "Nope."

"Good." Instead of turning left toward Queen's Cove, he turned right.

"Finn." My eyebrows shot together and I straightened up. "Where are we going?"

He slid me a sly smile before turning back to the road, drumming his fingers on the steering wheel. "Let's get some food."

My mouth opened, ready to protest, but the words didn't come. Aside from finding out Finn had unwittingly helped someone steal a car, today had been fine. More than fine. Nice, even.

My mind wandered to the bag of Cheezies he had brought for me, and his focus in the forest as he searched for the flower, like it was important to him.

Like my goals were important to him.

I sat back and watched the forest as we passed, and Finn turned up the music.

18

Finn

THE BELL on the door rang as we stepped inside the diner off the highway between Queen's Cove and the next town.

"Sit anywhere you like," the server called.

I grabbed Liv's hand and led her to a booth in the corner, slipping in after her and propping an arm over her side. She glanced back at my arm with alarm, and I rolled my lips to hide a grin.

I'd been thinking about how to hold her hand all day. It was like we were teenagers again.

"Go sit on the other side," she said, tilting her chin at the other side of the booth.

"I'm good here."

"There's not enough room."

"Sure there is."

The server appeared with her pen poised. "What can I get you two?"

"We're going to split an order of curly fries," I told her.

Liv loved curly fries. Or she used to.

She straightened up with a start. "I forgot my wallet in the car. It's in my pack."

I didn't budge. "It's fine, I've got it. What else do you want?"

She shook her head. "Nothing."

Bullshit. She'd burned thousands of calories today. She was just being stubborn.

"Two club sandwiches," I told the server. Liv could change the order if she wanted but I wasn't going to let her skip dinner. "A slice of apple pie with vanilla ice cream, and two glasses of water, please. Thank you."

The server jotted this down and hustled off.

I turned to Liv, my gaze sliding over her cheekbones, where more freckles had popped up since a few days ago. On the top of the booth, my hand twitched, itching to touch her. The smell of her shampoo had me considering burying my face in her neck.

She glanced at me with a snort. "Stop drooling."

I leaned in closer, my mouth an inch from her ear. "What, I can't buy my *girlfriend* dinner?"

The corner of her mouth lifted before she rolled her lips to hide it.

"This doesn't count as a date, you know," I told her.

She leaned forward, resting her elbows on the table. "Yes, it does."

"I'm not wasting my date on a crappy diner off the highway."

She reached out to fiddle with her napkin, and her arm brushed my fingers. She sat there tearing tiny pieces off it.

"What are you thinking about?" I asked, my gaze on the curve of her dark eyelashes.

She was quiet a moment. "My dad's going to sell the bar."

"Wow." My eyebrows shot up. "Are you okay?"

She pulled her bottom lip between her teeth. "I don't know. I think so."

I waited, desperate for more of this version of Liv—

honest and real. Walls down. Unguarded. Being herself. It was intoxicating and addictive.

Her lashes fluttered as she blinked, frowning to herself. "I have to find a new place to live if he sells it." She glanced at me. "You do, too."

I nodded, running my fingers over her arm. Her skin was like silk. "We'll figure it out."

"Buying the bar was supposed to be my backup plan."

I made a noise of acknowledgement, remembering what Sadie told me at her wedding to Holden. "If you don't find the flower."

"Yeah."

"But you will."

"Maybe." She ripped another piece of napkin off.

"You will."

Her hair had been up in a ponytail all day but pieces in the front had come loose, waving around her face. Feeling bold and brave, I tucked a lock behind her ear before my arm dropped to her shoulder, fingers brushing the hem of her t-shirt sleeve, running across her skin. Her eyes shot to mine with a flicker of surprise, and under my arm, she shivered. Warm brown eyes locked on mine, lingering. Something new flared in my chest.

"You will," I whispered, and her eyes dropped to my mouth.

"They're worried about me." Her eyes flickered with something vulnerable. "My mom thinks I'm stuck."

My eyebrows pinched together. "Do I have anything to do with them being worried?"

She paused, frowning to herself. "My mom doesn't think it'll last."

I narrowed my eyes, tapping my top lip with my tongue. Stubbornness formed like a rock in the middle of my chest. Once Jen saw how happy Liv was with me, she'd come around.

"You'd love that, wouldn't you?" I quirked her a teasing a smile.

Her eyes widened for a split second before a smile curled on her pretty mouth. A mouth I wanted to kiss. "What makes you say that? I'm *crazy* about you."

My chest shook with laughter. "You've always been a bad liar." My finger brushed down her arm, stroking the soft skin. It was barely a graze, downright *pure*, and yet her eyelids fell halfway and her breath hitched.

My cock woke up.

I stared at her mouth. I remembered how it felt to kiss Liv, to consume her mouth and for her to come right back at me with just as much desire and need.

When I dragged my gaze up to hers, she was looking at *my* mouth. Her eyes met mine with a start.

"Busted," I whispered.

Her lips parted before she blinked. "Can you stop that with your hand? It's distracting."

I pulled my arm back up onto the top of the booth. Did she look a little disappointed?

"I think you like being distracted like that," I said as the server dropped our plates off. I thanked her and slid the curly fries over to Liv.

Off her questioning look, I rolled my eyes. "Don't even pretend you don't like them. You used to devour them."

She let out a laugh and I memorized the sweet sound. I slid her sandwich over in front of her, beside the fries.

"Eat," I said.

She gave me a funny look before shoving a fry in her mouth. "You're so bossy."

I nodded. "I am. You're going to need your strength this summer. I'm not going to wait around while you catch your breath." My knee bounced under the table as energy buzzed inside me, waiting for her reaction.

Another laugh burst out of her. "While you've been doing

bong rips with your bros, I've been hauling my ass all over these mountains looking for that stupid flower."

I ate another fry. "My body is a temple."

She rolled her eyes. "I'm sure. Tell yourself that when you're jerking off to pictures of yourself."

I snorted. "Liv, the only photos I've ever jerked off to were yours."

Her hand paused, curly fry dangling halfway to her mouth, and a pink flush spread over her cheeks. Her gaze cut to mine, and the heat behind her eyes sent blood rushing through my veins.

A slow, wicked grin curled up on my mouth. "You love that idea, don't you?"

"No." Her nose twitched and her jaw tensed.

Jesus, she was so fucking sexy, all pissed off and grouchy like this. I wanted to tickle her until she laughed. She'd try to scratch my eyes out, no doubt.

My brain flashed with a memory of her scratching me in a different context. Skin on skin, hands fisting sheets and each other's hair and her teeth nipping my shoulder as she tensed under me.

My body hummed. For so long, I'd been remembering short bursts of us together on grad night, fumbling around, excited to finally explore each other, and while those memories met my needs with my hand wrapped around my cock in the shower, a low buzz ran through my veins at the idea of more.

I leaned in, letting my lips brush her ear. "Do you remember how it was, Liv? Because I do. I remember every inch of your body." Could she feel my heart slamming against my chest, pressed against her shoulder? "And soon I'm going to show my *girlfriend* all the things I've been thinking about doing to her."

Her lips parted and when I nipped her earlobe, she let out a breathy squeak. My cock hardened.

"Eat your fries, sweetheart," I told her, straightening up. "You can daydream about me later."

When we were done and I had paid up, we headed to the car. I held her door open and she glanced at it with a small frown before getting into the passenger seat.

I pulled onto the highway, Liv turned the music up, and we drove back to Queen's Cove without talking, just listening to music, me tapping my hands on the steering wheel and Liv staring out the window, lost in thought. By the time I parked behind the bar, her eyes were closed, her head leaned on the window, and her chest rose and fell in a steady rhythm.

I took the quiet moment to study her and wondered whether it would feel like this every day if we were together for real. We'd spent the rest of the time at the diner talking about our upcoming hike, planning a route and pitching ideas to each other about future trips around the mountains. Liv's eyes had lit up and warmth gathered in my chest at the knowledge that I helped put that look on her face. When she dropped her knives, being with Liv was so fucking easy. It always had been. We had been best friends for a reason. We just clicked.

I sucked in a deep breath and let it out slow, tracing the slope of her nose with my gaze. I'd cover that nose with kisses if I didn't think she'd punch me in the dick.

I reached out and gently shook her shoulder. "Liv," I murmured.

"Mmm." Her eyes stayed closed.

"Liv, we're home."

My heart twisted at the familiarity of the words. Home. One day, we'd live in the same place. My mouth turned up at the thought and I gently shook her again.

"Wake up, baby, or I'm going to toss you over my shoulder and carry you up the stairs myself, and that'll really get people talking."

Her eyes shot open and she inhaled a sharp breath. "Awake. I'm awake."

I grinned. "Mhm. Come on."

I got out of the car and went around to help her, but she was already stumbling out with a jaw-breaking yawn that made her eyes water. I closed the car door behind her and led her to the bar.

"I'll bring your pack up later," I told her. "My girl needs to sleep." I held the back door open and a chorus of noise hit us from inside.

"I'm not your girl," she grumbled, walking past me inside.

A smile twisted up on my mouth. "We're back to that, huh? No more sweet Liv stuffing her face with curly fries and talking to me about hiking? That's fine, I can deal. I'm persistent."

"I know you are." She started up the stairs. "Stop staring at my ass."

"I'm not," I said, eyes on her ass.

Fuck, she had a great ass. I *dreamed* about that ass, round and soft and smooth.

She rolled her eyes and turned the key in the lock. "Goodnight, Finn. Thanks for dinner." She opened her door.

My heart flipped. I didn't want to say goodbye. Not yet. "Wait."

She paused.

I swallowed, suddenly nervous. "Stay right where you are."

"Why?" She stood there frozen, eyes wide.

I leaned closer, so fucking slowly so as not to scare her off. I gave her time to lean back and get the fuck away from me if she wanted.

"I'm going to kiss you goodnight."

Alarm rose in her eyes. "What?"

"You heard me." An inch closer.

Her gaze dropped to my lips. "Um." She blinked, lashes

fluttering. Her gaze was going hazy, eyes on my mouth. "Okay," she said, surprising me.

I drew closer, closer, until at the last second I paused a hair's width from her lips. My chest brushed hers. Her breath moved over my skin, and wide brown eyes stared back at me. I quickly turned and pressed a soft, lingering kiss to her cheek. She shivered under my touch.

"Goodnight," I murmured in her ear.

"Goodnight," she whispered back before she whirled around and closed the door.

I stared at it, smiling to myself.

Liv still had feelings for me, whether she realized it or not. Now, I had to take her on a date that reminded her why.

19

Olivia

THREE DAYS LATER, I was still thinking about the pastel purple sticky note that had been sitting on my bookshelf when I got home from the diner with Finn.

It was a cartoon drawing of a bird with a choppy haircut. He must have put it there while I was changing out of my pajamas. I'd set it on my bedside table, and when I woke up, it was the first thing I saw.

"*Olivia.*"

I snapped to attention with a sharp inhale. My head whipped toward Sadie, leaning on the bar with crossed arms and a funny smile on her face. "What?"

"You've been drying that glass for five minutes." She grinned wider, her green eyes shining.

I dropped the cloth and set the glass on the rack above my head. "Just thinking about my research."

"Right." She nodded, still smiling. "Your research. And how's that going?"

I shrugged. "Fine."

"Mhm." She leaned in, narrowing her eyes.

Nerves squirmed in my stomach.

"Your shirt is weird." She glanced at the t-shirt I bought

online last week.

It was a murky, unflattering brown, almost like it had been tie-dyed, and smack-dab in the center of my chest was a giant poo emoji.

She gave me a funny look. "What's up with you?"

I swallowed and shrugged again. "Nothing," I lied.

"You're lying."

She pinned me with her gaze and I glanced between her and the counter. "I'm going on a date with Finn tonight."

"Oh my god. I knew it." She gasped in delight. "Do you like him now?"

I opened my mouth to deny it but nothing came out. At the diner the other night, he had been so sweet, and talking with him was so easy. I shook my head while my mouth opened and closed.

"No. I don't know. I don't think so."

My forehead wrinkled and I put my face in my hands.

I was a fucking mess, and I'd been a fucking mess for days. Finn living across the hall was driving me insane. The walls were so thin I could hear when he got home or left for the fire hall. If he wasn't working, he'd hang out in the bar in the evenings, watching sports with his brothers or chatting with the other regulars or my dad. I had lost count of the times I'd turned around with a tray full of drinks and met his gaze while he was mid-conversation. I felt the prickle of his eyes on me at all times. It shot a skitter of nerves down my spine.

Yesterday, there was a bird cartoon sticky note on my car window of the bird driving a car. It said *bird needs an oil change —leave the keys with the asshole across the hall and he'll get it done.* This morning, I opened my front door to a coffee with a sticky note of the bird half asleep and drinking coffee, with little z's floating out of its head.

My head was full of thoughts of Finn. I thought about the way he smelled, sharp and clean and fresh. The way his eyes crinkled when he smiled at me. His fingers on my inner thigh.

The way his hands felt framing my jaw as he kissed me quick. Him nipping my ear in the diner.

The worst part? I'd been having sex dreams about Finn. Even my subconscious couldn't stop thinking about him.

I was so, so fucking horny, and all I could think about was going further with Finn. Kissing Finn. Getting naked with Finn. Licking a line up his throat. His mouth on me. His hands everywhere.

I shuddered. That's why I was wearing the ugly poo emoji t-shirt. Finn tried to kiss me the other night and I let him. If Finn wanted to pull me into his apartment and touch me until I couldn't think, I'd let him do that, too.

And then everything would be totally fucked.

"Your eyes are doing that weird thing again," Sadie said. "Where are you going tonight?"

"I don't know. I haven't asked." I sucked in a breath. "It's getting harder to…" I trailed off and met Sadie's eyes. She was one of the few people I could be myself around. "I'm forgetting why I hate him. He's…"

"Really hot?" she supplied.

I snorted. "Yeah. He's really hot."

I remembered how sweet he was, doing first aid on me. *And nice, thoughtful, and funny.*

"Is it possible he's not the guy you remember?" Her voice was quiet and she studied her nails, acting casual.

I knew what she was doing. She was trying not to freak me out.

"Stop planting the seed of doubt."

Her gaze shot up and she grinned. "Sorry. Busted. I just remember at my wedding when he asked me about you. He seemed so sad, like he wished he still had you in his life." Her mouth twisted in a rueful smile. "He still cares about you."

"I know he does." My heart squeezed up into my throat and I crossed my arms, hugging myself.

He cared about me before and he still left.

Sadie's gaze caught over my shoulder. "Hello," she said with a bright smile.

I turned to see Dot, the doily museum owner, standing on the other side of the counter.

"Hi, Dot." I blinked in surprise. With her tweed skirt suit, white silk shirt with a lace collar, and neatly pinned up gray hair, she stuck out in the dingy dive bar.

"Hello, Olivia." She reached down into her handbag before placing a doily on the counter.

Or, it was supposed to be a doily. It was a mangled mess of yarn and white fabric, like a kid had made it. Sadie and I stared at it on the counter.

"Finn forgot to take it with him after the workshop," she told us.

"The workshop?" Sadie repeated.

Dot nodded. "He attended my doily workshop last week. Attendance was low this year but we had a lovely time. After the workshop, he insisted on taking me out for lunch. He's a very nice boy." She smiled, the wrinkles around her eyes multiplying.

Sadie placed a hand on my arm, a silent way of saying *see?* I swatted her hand away.

Dot smiled at the doily before wincing and leaning in, lowering her voice. "I'll admit he isn't very good at making doilies, but it was nice to have the company. He loved hearing about the hiking trip my Roger and I did in the eighties."

I stared at her. Finn went to a doily workshop? I had a sneaking feeling in my gut that he wanted to make this lovely little old lady happy. My heart tugged.

My mind flicked back to the empty doily museum and how happy Dot had been when we arrived.

"Stay for a drink," I told her. "On the house. I'll make you whatever you like."

"Yes, stay!" Sadie beamed at her.

"Well, alright then." She made her way up onto the stool.

"I can't remember the last time I had a cocktail in such an interesting establishment." Her gaze lingered on the alien dildo hanging off the wall.

I smiled at the excitement in her eyes. "What do you like?"

Dot listed drinks she liked and I made her a New York sour—bourbon, lemon juice, simple syrup, egg white, and red wine. Her eyes lit up when I slid it across the counter to her.

"Red wine reminds me of my nun days," she said, taking the first sip, eyebrows bobbing at the flavor.

I blinked at her. "I'm sorry?"

She nodded. "I used to be a nun, but that was before I met my Roger. He was the mailman at the convent." She let out a laugh. "They were so surprised when I ran off with him. I'll never forget their faces."

I stared at her.

Movement caught my eye. I turned to see Finn stepping out of the hallway that led upstairs and my stomach did a slow roll forward.

He wore a navy-blue button-up shirt, done all the way up to the collar. He should have looked like a dork with that shirt but knowing he was covered in tattoos underneath woke my brain up. The shirt stretched across his broad shoulders. His hair was damp and curling. Every time I saw him with damp hair, I thought about him in the shower, water running down his muscles and tattoos. His hand on his cock, thinking about me with his eyes closed and lips parted.

Alarm rose in me. Tonight was a bad idea. I should have made an excuse.

His gaze met mine and he shot me a wicked smile as he strode over. He stopped right in front of me and I caught a whoosh of his clean scent. He must have seen something flickering in my eyes because his eyes flashed with endearment.

I was so fucked.

"Hi," he said, voice low and eyes on me.

"Hi." I rolled my mouth into a line, unable to tear my

gaze away.

"Nice poo shirt."

Behind him, Sadie snorted. I shot her a *shut up* glare.

"Ready to go?" he asked, eyes still glittering with amusement.

"Yep." My voice sounded small and my entire stomach was full of butterflies.

He turned and spotted Dot. "Hi, Dot, how are you?"

"Hello, Finn." She smiled back at him and gestured to her drink. "Olivia here made me a wonderful drink. It's called a New York sour."

Finn glanced at me with appreciation. "She's good at mixing drinks. I'll have to get her to make me one of those later."

I tilted my chin at the doily on the counter. "You've been busy," I told him.

He shot me a sheepish smile and swiped it off the counter, tucking it in his back pocket. "I have." He slipped his big, warm hand around mine and tugged me to follow him. "See you later, Dot. Come in again and we'll have a drink together," he called over his shoulder as he led me down the hallway and through the door to the alley.

The second we got outside, he spun me around and walked me backward so I was pressed against the wall. My eyes widened as he stepped into my space, one arm leaning on the wall beside my head, the other still holding my hand. My pulse skyrocketed at his nearness and I couldn't tear my gaze from his. He smelled incredible, masculine and clean, and the sharp, delicious scent made my thoughts blur.

That wicked grin curled up on his mouth again.

"Back to your old antics," he said, gaze flicking down to my t-shirt.

"It's laundry day," I lied. My voice sounded breathless and I *hated* that Finn Rhodes did this to me. That he made me into this swooning, light-headed woman who couldn't focus on anything except the infuriating, cruel tilt of the corner of his mouth and how fucking badly I wanted to suck on it.

"Mhm. I'm sure it is." His gaze roamed my face. "You think a t-shirt like that is going to distract me from how nice your tits are?"

Heat pooled low in my belly and I blinked. "Um. I don't know."

"It isn't." He held my gaze and my stomach rolled back and forth with nerves and excitement. His hand gave mine a little squeeze and my lips parted. His eyes darkened. "You heard what I said in the diner."

Did I fucking *ever*. I'd been hearing those low words in my sleep. *I remember every inch of your body*. A muscle low in my stomach tightened.

We stared at each other for a long moment in the quiet alley while cars drove past on the street and people chatted on the sidewalk twenty feet away. My breasts felt heavy and my pulse thrummed between my legs.

He glanced down at my mouth and my heart sped up even more.

I should have kissed him. Why not? I wanted to, and I couldn't remember why I shouldn't—

Finn pulled away, tugging my hand toward his car. "Come on, Livvy, let's go."

He opened the passenger door and guided me in. What just happened? I studied his face as he made his way around the car and got into the driver's side. He turned the engine on with a little smirk.

Oh my god. He was dangling sex in front of me like a carrot. That was it. He was going to wait for me to make the first move. It was like all the games we used to play, all the competitive little jokes we played on each other. Always in competition.

Well, I'd been freezing him out for a decade. I could control myself for *one night*.

20

Finn

THE SHIRT WORKED.

I couldn't fucking believe it. Emmett's stupid dorky shirt idea *worked*. The second I stepped into the bar, her eyes did that sexy, hazy thing like she wanted to drag me back upstairs.

That was the look she gave me on grad night, right before I slid the strap of her dress off. Pure fucking *yearning*.

Poor Liv, all horny and worked up. I smiled, sending her a quick glance before turning back to the road. I knew she was getting the sticky notes. I'd left one on a coffee this morning outside her door and a couple hours later, it was gone. The one of her car window had disappeared, too.

I thought back to the diner, how she admitted those things to me. My heart had twisted in half, seeing her vulnerable like that around me. It was almost like we used to be, like she knew I wouldn't hurt her. My chest twinged but I shook it off.

I was so close.

Until she trusted me, no messing around. No sex stuff. Getting into bed with Liv was significant—I'd been thinking about it for *years*. A third of my life, I'd been dreaming about us back together. It meant something. If we slept together and things didn't work out, it would destroy me. The idea loomed in the back of my mind, big, dark, and unwelcome, and tension bled into my shoulders.

In her seat, she shifted, crossing and uncrossing her legs, and I bit back a smile.

We weren't having sex, but I could still tease her.

"Where are we going?" Liv asked, pulling my attention back to the present.

I smiled. "It's a surprise." I winked at her. "We'll be there in ten minutes. You want to pick some music?"

She nodded and pulled out her phone to cue a playlist up before cracking her window as I drove. Her hair fluttered in the wind and my stomach dipped.

Fucking hell, she was pretty.

"You went to Dot's doily workshop," she said, her gaze on the passing trees.

I huffed a laugh. "Yeah, I did."

Her eyebrows pinched. "Why?"

"Because she seems kind of bored." I shrugged. "And she's interesting to chat with once she moves on from doilies. She tell you that she used to be a nun?"

She laughed. "Yeah. She did."

"She and her husband hiked all over the Rockies after they got married. And they did the same hikes when they were in their eighties. She said he was her best friend."

Liv's gaze was on the passing trees. Was she wondering the same thing I was—would we ever be best friends again? Would we have adventures in our eighties, hiking around the mountains and teasing each other?

I fucking hoped so. I'd fight like hell to get that. I couldn't picture my life with anyone but her. Even when I was twenty-two and stupid, when I told myself I wasn't destined for anything long-term, my mind would wander back to Liv.

When I pulled up to the park, half the town was there. Anticipation curled in my chest, and my heart rate picked up speed.

Our date tonight was about showing Liv that we were meant to be, but that didn't mean I couldn't have a *little* fun with her. I knew she was lying through her teeth about wanting us to be a couple again, and seeing her keep the charade up was becoming an addiction. The flare of her nostrils, her twitching nose, the amused glare she shot me—it felt like we were *us* again.

"What's this?" Liv asked, stepping out of the car, gaze sweeping over everyone sitting on picnic blankets.

"Movie in the park. They're playing *Superbad*." I opened the trunk and handed her a blanket. "We have a couple hours until sunset, though. Can you carry that?"

She took it from me and a little smile curled up on her mouth. "I love that movie."

"I know." I smiled at her and hauled out the cooler.

We wandered through the people on the grass, saying hello to Emmett and Avery seated on their own blanket, waving to Miri Yang and her husband Scott, who shared a blanket with Miri's best friend, Don, who ran the town news blog, and his wife. I recognized some people from our high school, some with their own families, some on dates or with friends. Liv waved at Hannah's dad, Frank Nielsen, sitting with his partner, Veena, who owned the bakery. I spotted the elementary school principal, and even some of the brats who had skewered me in front of Jen and Liv the day of my class presentation.

Everyone was here. Exactly what I wanted.

When we found a spot on the grass, we laid out the blanket and I unpacked our dinner. I had received a confirmation text earlier this afternoon, and now all I had to do was wait. I tapped my thumb against my leg, scanning the sky.

"What's up with you?" Liv asked as we ate dinner. I'd brought pulled pork sandwiches with coleslaw. Emmett had shown me the recipe the other day.

I froze, trying not to grin. "What do you mean? Nothing."

Her eyes narrowed. "You're twitchy."

"No, I'm not." Yes, I was. I was listening hard for the low sound of the motor.

"You keep looking up at the sky." She glanced around. "What are you looking for?"

I shrugged and made a face like I had no clue what she was talking about. "It's such a nice evening, don't you think?"

"I guess." She studied me, skeptical, and I bit back a smile.

Then, I heard it. The low, buzzing sound of a plane. I sucked in a breath, tongue tapping my upper lip as I watched the horizon from the south, where Mark said he'd be flying in from. The drone of the plane got louder but Liv didn't notice it.

There. My stomach flipped as the plane appeared.

Mark flew for us as part of Search and Rescue, and ran a small airline company on the side with flights to and from Victoria and Vancouver. He'd been on board immediately with my idea.

"Oh my god," Miri hollered, jumping to her feet, pointing at the plane. The banner behind it was visible but not yet legible. "It's a message in the sky! I've always wanted to see one of these!"

Everyone started murmuring and watched as the plane approached. Delight unfurled in my chest, light and sparking, and out of the corner of my eye, I glanced at Liv.

She gave me a strange look. "What have you done?"

"What does it say?" Don called, standing and peering at the sign.

"It's getting closer!" Miri yelled uselessly. "It's approaching."

Everyone watched in rapt attention as the plane flew toward the park, and my gaze flicked between Liv's wary expression and the plane.

My mouth was an inch from her ear. "This is payback for

the haircut, the doily museum, the pants, and the ugly poo shirt," I murmured.

Her jaw dropped when she read what the banner said. "Are you fucking serious?"

One by one, people turned to us, smiling as they read the banner. A few *aww*s rose up. Emmett slow-clapped.

OLIVIA MORGAN LOVES FINN RHODES FOREVER

Liv glared at me and my chest squeezed with excitement.

"I'm going to kill you in your sleep," she hissed, and I thought my chest might burst. "What the actual *fuck*." Her voice was a low growl, for my ears only, but she wore a strained smile.

"Olivia," I said loudly so everyone could hear. "That's so sweet. I love you, too, baby, and I can't wait to be with you *forever*."

She gave a tight smile to the people around us, and I held back a laugh.

I lowered my voice. "I wanted to make it clear to everyone that you've only got eyes for me." I put my arm around her shoulder and pulled her closer. There was the nostril flare I liked so much. "I didn't want any of the single guys in town to get the wrong idea."

Her gaze shot to mine before going back to the banner. "I can't believe you." The corner of her mouth twitched but she closed her eyes and shook her head. "A banner in the sky. How much did you spend on it?"

"Doesn't matter. I thought about hiring a skywriter but I thought he'd get too nauseous."

She snorted, burying her face in her hands. "Oh my god. You are so relentless."

I leaned in so my mouth brushed her ear. "You haven't seen anything yet."

Miri approached with tears streaming down her face. "You

two are meant to be." She started clapping and everyone followed.

Across the park, Avery and Emmett watched with big grins. I gave Emmett a thumbs-up and he laughed and shook his head.

"Kiss, kiss, kiss," I started chanting, head whipping around like someone else had said it. "Oh my god? What's that?"

Liv snorted. "Finn—"

It was too late.

"Kiss, kiss, kiss," fifty people chanted, clapping.

I beamed at her. "Well? I think it's time for our first real kiss, don't you?"

Her eyes narrowed and the corner of her mouth kicked up. She cocked her head. "Yes, I do."

I hesitated. This felt like a trap. "Okay, great." People were still chanting *kiss!* around us. "Let's do it."

"Great." She watched me, eyes dancing. "Ready when you are."

"I'm ready now." My hands came to her jaw and I tilted her face up to me, leaning forward. "Want to count us in?"

Her eyes were bright, like she was entertained. "Three."

My gaze dropped to her lips and need rushed in my blood. Her lips were the prettiest shade of pink and all I wanted to do was suck on her bottom lip until she moaned.

"Two," she murmured, biting it.

The crowd of people around us fell away from my consciousness, leaving only her. My skin was tingling.

"One," she whispered before she tipped her mouth up to mine.

The world stilled, narrowing down to the connection between us, and it was like no time had passed. My body remembered Liv, her soft lips, the flutter of her dark lashes against her cheekbones, the brush of her skin against mine. In my chest, my heart thumped hard, and with my hands on her face, I stroked the side of her jaw.

She shuddered under my touch. I was vaguely aware of applause around us.

A sharp pinch on my lower lip made me jerk back. A cat-like smile spread over her mouth as I rubbed the sting on my lower lip, blinking in surprise.

I snorted. "You bit me."

"Mhm." She wiggled her eyebrows.

My gaze lingered on her mouth. Was it wrong that I still found that insanely hot? Our eyes met again and heat and amusement rose in her eyes. I grinned at her.

She shook her head and rolled her eyes, but her smile lingered. "You're unbelievable."

I held her gaze. "You like me."

"Whatever."

"Say it." I poked her side and she batted me away. "Say you like me, or I'll tickle you." My fingers dug into her ribs and she let out a sharp laugh, wiggling to get away. I tucked one arm around her so she couldn't escape, and I caught a whiff of her scent—sweet and spicy. My laugh died out as she met my gaze.

Her eyes were warm as she studied my face.

"Fine," she said, and I watched the way her lips moved. "I like you."

My heart tripped like a clumsy teenager.

21

Finn

"WHAT'S your favorite hiking spot around here?" I asked her later, when the sun had almost set.

Her eyes narrowed as she thought about it. "Sitka Mountain, I think. The hike is tough but not too tough, just a short overnighter, and when you wake up in the morning and stick your head out your tent with a view of those turquoise lakes, it's—" Her expression melted into something relaxed and nostalgic, and I couldn't look away. "—gorgeous. Serene. It feels like I'm the only person on the planet."

"Sounds nice."

Her eyebrows bobbed. "It is. You should go."

"You should take me." My brows lifted and she smiled. "Where will you work once you finish your PhD?"

"There's a forestry research center in Port Alberni." That was a town near Queen's Cove, about an hour's drive. "They don't have much funding, so I'm not sure if I could get a job there even with a PhD." She chewed her lip and her eyes met mine. "I might have to move to Victoria." That was the biggest city on Vancouver Island, a three-hour drive from Queen's Cove. "Or the mainland, Vancouver or something in the interior of BC."

I nodded, taking this in. People had to move for work, that wasn't a big deal or out of the ordinary. Still, my stomach tipped over as I pictured Liv moving away.

I'd go with her, if she let me.

"Are you ready to leave?"

She pressed her mouth into a line, frowning. "No. I love this place. I hated leaving to go to school. Vancouver's nice but it's so busy and chaotic, there's a lot of traffic, and—" She cut herself off, shrugging and shaking her head. "It's not here."

"Yeah. I know what you mean."

"Do you miss firefighting?" She played with a tassel on the blanket. Her eyes flicked up to me, curious. "Forest fires, that is."

"Sometimes," I admitted. "It's an organized chaos out there when the fires are raging." I shot her a lopsided grin. "I feel in my element there."

"And here?" Her gaze stayed on her fingers.

I swallowed. "Sometimes I'm in my element here, too. Like when we go hiking."

She glanced up and gave me a smile. My chest squeezed, warm and tight. I'd be replaying this moment for the next few days.

I knew she felt it too.

She nodded. "You're good at it. I feel safe hiking with you."

"Yeah?" My brows lifted and my mouth curled into a smug smile. "You feel safe with me?"

She rolled her eyes, trying not to smile. "You know what I mean. You talk enough to scare the bears away."

Her cheeks flushed pink. So fucking adorable.

"Mhm." I gave her another grin. Her ankle was inches from my thumb so I drew a line over it. Her breath caught. "You feel safe with me."

"Whatever," she muttered, grinning at the thread on the blanket, pulling her ankle away.

She wore a playful smile on her lips and something tugged under my heart, but her smile faded.

"You're going to get bored in this town," she whispered, and my gut tensed. We were as close to Liv finally telling me the truth as we'd ever been, and I felt like I was walking around fucking landmines. "You're going to miss the chaos."

I shook my head. "I won't. There's a lot of stuff I don't miss about it, Liv. Living in camps, falling into bed exhausted every night, missing my friends and family. This is my home." Our gazes held, and something big and bright pulsed between us. "You're here."

Her eyebrows pulled together in worry. "You can't stay somewhere for one person."

"I can, and if you got a job in Victoria, I'd happily move there for you."

"What about your family?"

"We'd visit."

She glanced over at where they were setting up the screen, worry clouding her gaze. "You can't last more than seven or eight months in one town."

"That was before."

"Before what?"

I rubbed my jaw, frowning down at the blanket. The time to tell her was now. "Before I ran into your dad. Your biological dad."

Her gaze whipped to mine. "Cole?"

I nodded. "In Whistler. He lives there now. Runs a handyman business."

She chewed her bottom lip, listening and watching with a wary expression. "I looked him up a few years ago."

"You didn't reach out?"

She shook her head.

"He has your eyes."

She nodded, playing with a loose thread on the blanket. "I know. I remember."

"Your laugh, too. Kind of quiet and sarcastic."

Pain flashed across her expression and I had the urge to haul her into my chest. "Why are you telling me this?"

"Because…" I huffed another deep breath. Shit. I was losing her. I was upsetting her, but she had to know. "He's why I changed my mind. I was ready to come back and convince you to get your degree before I left again, but—" There was a rock in my throat.

Her gaze snapped up.

"The guy was sad, Liv." I leaned forward, gaze locked on hers. Discomfort washed over her face and she hugged herself tighter but she had to hear this. "Sad and lonely. He was in there a lot, and always alone. He drinks a lot." Fear twisted in my gut. "I don't want to be like him. He hurt you by leaving and everyone paid the price. He never fixed it, never apologized and never made it better."

When someone on a neighboring blanket glanced over, I realized how sharply I'd spoken. I didn't care, though. Liv needed the truth.

"Liv, I never want to be Cole. I know I hurt you. I know I fucked up. I told Sadie that I was coming back, and that was because I thought you weren't going to finish school. I was going to…" I shook my head. "I don't know what I was going to do. I'd been thinking about you for years. I didn't want to spend the rest of my life regretting that I wasn't good enough for you, and that I didn't even try."

She frowned at the picnic blanket. The sky was dim now, and more people filtered into the park, taking their seats, but the woman across from me held my full attention.

"I'm going to do everything I can to fix us, understand?"

She gave me a tiny nod, eyes still on the blanket.

"Please look at me, baby," I whispered.

Her chest rose as she inhaled before she let it out slowly, raising her gaze to mine. She nodded again. "Okay."

In my chest, my heart thudded. Something lifted in my chest, and it felt a lot like hope.

Her hands brushed her arms and she shivered.

"Is the poo shirt not warm enough?" I asked, cocking my head.

She grinned. "Shut up."

I moved to standing. "I have a jacket in the car. Be right back."

When I returned to the blanket, I took the seat directly beside her, holding out my jean jacket with the shearling collar for her to slip into.

"Thanks," she said, pulling it around her.

"You look cute wearing my jacket." My mouth hitched and I pictured her wearing other items of my clothing. My t-shirt. My hoodie. I imagined her waking up in my t-shirt, and me pushing the hem up with my head between her legs.

Fuck, I liked the idea of that.

Across the grass, the screen flickered to life and the movie started. Liv shifted, tucking her legs beneath her.

"You remember when we saw this movie in the theater?" I whispered to her.

She nodded at me, smiling. We had just been teenagers.

I leaned in a bit closer. "During the movie, your knee brushed mine and I got a boner."

She choked, snort-laughing. "What?" she whispered back, grinning. "Ew. Why are you telling me this?"

I shrugged. "I had a crush on you."

"Keep your boner story to yourself." She shook her head but amusement lit up her eyes.

I winced. "Liv, there are lots of boner stories. Basically, anytime I was in your bedroom."

She groaned and I laughed again.

"No," I continued, ducking lower so my mouth was a few inches from her ear, "but during the whole movie, all I could think about was how to get you to hold my hand."

She turned her head, giving me a side-long look. "Really?"

"Mhm." I nodded, holding her gaze.

She turned back to the screen, the corner of her mouth turning up a little. "I guess that's a little cute."

Fireworks burst in my chest. Liv said I was *cute*.

She shifted again, and a second later, her hand settled on the blanket in between us. I glanced between her hand and her face with a question in my eyes.

She rolled hers. "It's not a big deal. Don't get a boner over it."

My grin broadened and I settled my hand over hers. "No promises."

She snorted and turned back to the movie, a smile playing at her lips as my thumb stroked over hers. At one point, she shifted, stretching her back, and I patted my chest.

"Lean back," I said.

She arched an eyebrow at me.

"I should have brought chairs. Lean back on me so I don't feel guilty."

To my total fucking surprise, she didn't put up a fight. She just turned around, scooched between my legs, and settled back into my chest. My arms wrapped across her front and my head rested on top of hers as we watched the rest of the movie.

Like this, Liv and I didn't feel like best friends… we felt like more. Like partners. We belonged together. My heart expanded in my chest, squeezing out any doubt or worry that she wouldn't come around.

She already *was* coming around. Maybe it was this stupid shirt or all the time we were spending together. I didn't know, and I didn't care. I wanted more of *this*. More cuddling in the park, more hand holding, more talking about hikes.

My chest swelled with affection for her, wrapped in my arms, her back warm against my chest, looking fucking delectable in my jacket. It was huge on her.

Liv was it for me, and I was going to be as patient as she needed. I'd play this dumb game with her pretending to be my girlfriend and trying to get me to dump her, because moments like this were worth it.

22

Olivia

A FEW DAYS after Finn organized that horrifying banner in the sky, we set out to search for the flower again. Our search area was further into the mountains now that we had covered so much ground together, and we had agreed on a multi-day trip while Finn had time off from the fire hall.

After dinner, we sat against a log from a fallen tree, watching the fire we had built in a small campsite. In my head, I replayed moments from the day, working in silence with Finn a hundred feet away, listening to the birds chirping in the forest while the sun shone down on us. Hauling my heavy pack had made my legs and back burn with fatigue, but after a day in the forest, calm satisfaction eased through me.

Finn stood and took my empty bowl from dinner. A little smile quirked on his mouth. "I brought you a treat."

"You did?"

"Mhm." He reached into his pack and pulled out a bag of Cheezies. My face lit up and he laughed.

He tossed it to me and I caught the bag and tore it open. "You're a god."

His eyes flashed with heat. "You haven't seen anything yet."

Warmth tugged between my legs and my brain stumbled. My mind flashed with images of Finn and me on grad night, him on top of me, being careful not to hurt me. Eyes clouded with lust.

That night had been the first time for both of us. We had no clue what we were doing, although I suspected Finn had bugged his brothers for some pointers because some of the stuff he did… a virgin shouldn't know how to use his tongue like that.

I shivered.

Finn's eyes crinkled. "You okay, there?"

"Um. Yep." I stood. "I brought you something, too."

His grin hitched, surprised. "You did?"

I smiled and nodded. "Be right back."

"Where are you going?"

"To the creek," I called over my shoulder. Five minutes later, I returned with two cans and set them down between us.

Finn's face burst into a big grin. "You brought beer."

I couldn't help the smile creeping up on my mouth. A warm, pleased flush moved through my chest. "Yep."

He picked one up. "And it's cold."

"I put it in the creek while we ate dinner."

He tilted his head, staring at me with an expression of pure affection. My mouth twitched and I struggled to meet his eye.

A tiny dose of panic hit my bloodstream. I wasn't supposed to be bringing him cold drinks and making him smile. I was supposed to be repulsing him.

"Come here." He set the beer down and held his arms out.

I stiffened. "Huh?"

"I want to give you a hug."

"Why?" I took a step back.

Softness and amusement melted in his eyes and he flashed that wicked grin again. "Because I like you, Liv, and I want to say thank you for bringing me a cold beer. It's just what I wanted right now. And that's what couples do. They hug," he said in a condescending, teasing tone that made me want to roll my eyes and laugh. His gaze sharpened. "Among other things."

My heart hammered at his words and I blinked.

"I'm coming in," he said quietly as he stepped forward and slowly wrapped his arms around me, pulling me into his chest. "That's it. You're doing great."

I snorted. "Shut up." God, he was warm.

He squeezed me tighter. "You're supposed to put your arms around me, too."

"Do you find yourself funny?" His chest felt nice, broad and firm, and I had the urge to rest my head against him.

"I can show you if you need help."

I rolled my eyes at him but my lips pulled into a grin as I wrapped my arms around his lower back.

"There we go," he murmured, dipping his head down so his mouth hovered inches from my ear.

I dragged in a breath, inhaling his scent. His deodorant, his body wash, and then something uniquely Finn. Probably sweat. His scent made a muscle pull low in my stomach. His hands smoothed across my back in calming strokes and I let myself lean into him. A low hum escaped him as he exhaled, and he brought his lips to my temple.

"Thank you for bringing me beer, Liv," he murmured against my skin, and my eyes closed.

"Mhm." I didn't trust myself to say anything more. I might accidentally moan.

He inhaled once more, his chest expanding against mine, and I didn't even care that my boobs pressed into him. He was warm and comfy and I didn't want to let go, but I unhooked my arms and stepped back.

He smiled down at me with hooded eyes. "That was nice."

I shrugged. "Yep." *Coward.*

"Say it."

My gaze snapped up and I saw the dare in his eyes. "What?" My eyebrow shot up.

"Say it. Say that you enjoyed hugging me. I know you did."

I stared at him and he stared back in challenge. "Fine." I lifted my shoulder, so casual. "You give good hugs."

His mouth curled up. "That wasn't so hard, was it?"

I rolled my eyes. "Whatever."

He laughed and shook his head before he sat down and opened his beer. He took a long pull before his head fell back. "Jesus Christ, that is so good."

I smiled. "It's shitty beer."

"I don't care. It's cold and I'm a happy guy sitting here with *my girl* in the forest." Finn's gaze slid to mine, smug and knowing. Challenging me.

Something sparked in my chest at his words. The last time he called me that, when I fell asleep in the car after the diner, I'd blurted out *I'm not your girl* by mistake. This time, I knew enough to hold my tongue. We were supposed to be together, after all.

I'd never admit it, but I liked the way the words sounded.

We sat there in content silence, drinking our beers and listening to the noises in the forest and from the fire, watching as it burned down to the ashes.

"I'm going to wash off in the creek before bed," he said as the sun began to set. A question quirked on his face, playful and coy. "You want to join?"

My eyes rolled but I grinned at him. "You'd love that."

"I sure would." His eyes flashed again. "Be right back. Don't talk to bears."

I laughed. Whenever Finn and I would go exploring as kids, our parents would say *don't talk to strangers!* As we got older and spent more time traipsing around the forest, we'd respond, *there's nothing but bears out there,* so Elizabeth started saying, *okay, don't talk to bears!* and we'd laugh.

When Finn returned, I was staring into the fire. I'd added a small log to get it burning again as the sun set, but my mind was lost in thought, reliving those days where we used to play together. He stepped closer to the fire and my gaze swung up to him—

Shirtless. Ink spanning his skin, shifting over the ridges, valleys, and hard lines of his muscles. Abs. Pecs. Chest hair smattered across his sternum, tricking down his stomach into his waistband.

It was the first time I'd seen him shirtless in over a decade. His tattoos were on full display, and my eyes searched, memorizing every detail. The birds flew up and around his muscular arm, all the way to the shoulder. I'd seen the moon and stars on the other arm before, but now I could see the stars creeping up across his shoulder and sternum, blending into the sky above the forest spanning his collarbone. I'd seen the tops of the trees poking out of his shirts, but now I could see the lake beneath them. I caught a peek of the mountain range over his ribcage and was struck with the familiarity. That was the mountain range around Queen's Cove. The area over his heart was blank.

This wasn't the skinny teenager I'd fumbled around with in the dark. Finn was a man now. He had put on more muscle, collected a torso full of tattoos, and I could imagine the brush of his chest hair against my skin.

While I window-shopped his body, Finn watched me with a cocky, heated smile, like he was enjoying it. A rush of lust hit me between my legs, swirling heat and pressure, and I shuddered, clenching. I couldn't tear my gaze off him. He smirked before pulling a shirt over his head. His biceps and triceps danced as his arms moved.

"You have a lot of tattoos," I said uselessly.

As he took a seat beside me, he smirked like he had a secret. "A few."

My gaze skimmed down his left arm, covered in a half-sleeve of the solar system. I reached out and my finger brushed the edge of a moon, barely bigger than my fingernail. While I traced the constellation of stars, he studied my face. Goosebumps rose up on his arm and I pulled my hand away, face flushing at the intimacy.

"How many birds are on your arm?"

"Twelve. I get one on our birthday every year," he said quietly, and my pulse tripped.

My gaze shot to his, searching for insincerity or humor or *something* that would take away from the heaviness of this information.

If Finn turned out to be a romantic, I swear to god, I couldn't handle it.

He held my eyes, steady and certain. I was supposed to be avoiding situations like this, but all I could think about were excuses to get his shirt off again.

Did it mean anything? Would he get another bird tattoo this year?

A sensation loomed in my chest, too big and intense to even think about.

"Do you have any?" His voice was low.

"A couple trees on my side," I answered as I gazed into the crackling fire.

He dragged a breath in, like he was trying to calm himself. "I can't wait to see them," he whispered, eyes darkening, and I shuddered.

Finn and I sat there for a long time, watching the fire and listening to the sounds of the forest as the sun sank lower and the sky turned dark.

A canopy of twinkling lights stretched overhead and I sighed. Somewhere in the trees, an owl hooted.

I hugged my knees, feeling funny. How many times had Finn and I sat on his roof, staring up at the sky? We'd climb out his window, usually when his parents were asleep. Their bedroom was on the other side of the house so they wouldn't hear us if we were quiet. We'd lie on the roof, stare at the sky, and point out shooting stars, whispering back and forth. Sometimes our hands or arms would brush. Once, Finn reached his foot out and rested it against mine, and we stayed like that for an hour, neither of us moving, connected by that square inch. The side of his socked foot against mine. His socks had Bigfoot on them. I had thought about that for days after.

For every star in the sky, I had a memory with Finn. My head was full of them, and the more time we spent together, the more resurfaced. It was like I was waking up, I realized, and shaking the last twelve years off.

I glanced at his mouth, the perfect line turned up at the corners in a cruel, smug smirk. Vulnerability wavered in his expression though, and my heart tugged. God, I hated that mouth, and yet I wanted to kiss him again so fucking badly. In my head, I replayed the kiss at the movie in the park, the moments before I nipped him.

It was *good*. It was the kind of kiss I'd wanted without realizing it—deep and consuming and desperate. That kiss was like one bite of the best chocolate cake, and it wasn't enough. I wanted the whole slice. I wanted *more*.

It would be so fucking good. I didn't even care that Finn had hurt me, that he left and he'd leave again because guys like him didn't stick around even if he truly believed he would. I didn't care.

He got those tattoos for me. I knew he did. Why was that so hot? Why did Finn have to get so much hotter over the years?

It wasn't fair.

What if I gave in?

He'd stick it out in town for the summer, at least. I could

admit that I'd never been attracted to someone the way I was to Finn, not when we were teenagers and definitely not now, as adults.

Grown up, Finn was impossible to resist.

What if I enjoyed him while he was here? I could keep my heart out of it. It would just be sex. Messing around. Nothing serious.

"We should make out," I said, staring at his mouth.

The fire reflected in his dark gaze, eyes hooded and full of heat. His smirk turned up even more. "Yeah?"

I nodded, meeting his eyes. *Confidence, Olivia.* He couldn't see how fast my heart was beating.

"That's what couples do, isn't it?" My tone was light, cocky, and playful, like I'd taken notes from him. I mentally high-fived myself. "Among other things."

His Adam's apple bobbed and his mouth curled into a wicked grin. "Come here, then."

23

Olivia

MY PULSE TOOK off as I settled in Finn's lap, straddling him. His eyes were on me, heavy and clouded. He gripped my waist, head tilted up to me, watching with wonder. Under my hands, his shoulders were warm and firm. My finger traced the skin above his collar, and his breath caught. Between us, the air crackled with tension.

No smirk in sight, I noticed.

My heart slammed in my chest as I studied his face. He was so fucking handsome. I'd never seen someone as good-looking as Finn, not even celebrities whose *job* was to look hot.

Something about Finn, his face and his body, the knowledge of those tattoos lingering under his clothes, it lit my blood on fire.

I lowered my mouth to his, and he groaned into it. On my waist, his fingers dug in as I brushed my lips over his. My hands slipped into his hair, and it woke something up in him. He sat up straighter, his arms slid up my back, and he coaxed my mouth open, sliding inside.

This. I shuddered as his tongue swept over mine, steady and firm and unrelenting. This was *so* like Finn to kiss like this, like he knew exactly what I needed. Like he'd been thinking about it forever. Like he was ready to take what he wanted.

Heat spread through me, over my skin, through my chest, building and swelling at my center. My fingers twisted in his hair and when he sucked my tongue, I think I pulled his hair a little because he groaned again, low and desperate.

"I should teach you a lesson for biting me the other day," he said in between kisses, and my thighs clenched around him. A low laugh rumbled against my mouth as he leaned into me.

Every sensation blended together—the scrape of his stubble against my chin, the slick, hot glide of his tongue against mine, his hands, one on my ass and one threaded in the hair at the back of my neck, pulling lightly, and the thick, firm press of his cock beneath me. I was pulled under, drugged, intoxicated, totally fucking *addicted* to the hot bliss that was making out with Finn Rhodes.

"Fuck, you're hot," he said, kissing down my neck. "I can't stop thinking about you, Liv. Every night, I fuck my fist thinking about how good your pussy feels." His eyes were so dark as he said this, and he pulled me back to him for another hungry kiss. "I remember it like it was yesterday."

A shiver ran through me. "Want a reminder?" I gasped as he squeezed my ass. Between my legs, I was aching, wet, needy. I should have been embarrassed at how fast that happened, but I was too drunk on Finn to care.

I sucked on the side of Finn's neck and he moaned—the sweetest sound I'd ever heard — and I rocked against him. The sharp, delicious sensation of my clit against him made me gasp.

Finn stiffened.

"We should stop," he rasped, breathing hard. By the dim light of the fire, I could see his pupils were blown.

What? I sat back, frowning, breathing hard. "No."

He blinked a few times like he was clearing his head. He

pulled his hand out of my hair and sucked in a deep breath. "*Yes*. Liv. Come on."

Disappointment, shame, rejection—they squeezed the lust of out me and I hurried off his lap, blinking like I'd been slapped.

I thought he wanted me.

Ugh. This was exactly what wasn't supposed to happen. I was supposed to be cold, calculating, and careful, and here I was, melting for him, practically offering myself on a platter.

Want a reminder? I was going to die of embarrassment. My face burned.

"I don't want to rush this." His words were quiet but determined, and his eyes were full of heat.

Anger and frustration bubbled up in me. "Then what the fuck is with all the cheek kisses and hugs and stuff? Are you trying to drive me crazy?"

There was that wicked grin again, quick as a flash before it faded into something more serious. "I don't want this to be a fling. No friends with benefits bullshit."

I didn't say a word. When Sadie and Holden tried being friends with benefits, it ended just how Holden had wanted—with them married.

Finn traced a line down my arm and when I glanced up at him, his eyes were soft. "I'm playing the long game," he said before gesturing at the front of his pants. His erection stretched out the fabric, and another twinge pulsed between my legs. "Don't think that I don't want you." He snorted. "I'm going to have blue balls all weekend, if that makes you feel better."

"It does," I said, and Finn laughed. A smile cracked on my face. "It really does."

A warm, heavy weight expanded in my chest, pushing the shame out. Finn wanted more from me, more from *us*. The Finn I grew up with shot first, thought later. Usually it was shoot first, apologize later. That's how we got into this whole mess in the first place.

It was for the best that we stopped. We were playing two different games, and I was dangerously close to fucking it all up. I rubbed my arms as the chill in the air gave me goosebumps.

"Cold?"

I nodded. "I haven't camped out here in a while. I forgot how cold it gets."

He stood and walked to his pack.

"It's fine," I started, but he turned and held his hoodie up for me.

"Come on." He gestured for me to stand up. "Don't be stubborn, Liv."

I snorted and tried to take the hoodie from him but he held tight, eyes dancing with amusement.

"Arms up." His mouth curved as I rolled my eyes.

"I can dress myself."

"Maybe I want to do it."

I wanted him to, if I was being honest. So stupid, so meaningless, and yet when I held my arms up, the way he slid the hoodie over my head so slowly and carefully made me feel warm and loved.

He was messing with my head. Camping was a terrible fucking idea.

"I'm going to go to bed," I said quickly. "I'm tired and I won't be able to sleep once the sun's up."

He nodded with a small smile, like he thought I was cute. My stomach flipped over as he stepped forward.

"Alright. Goodnight, Liv." He wrapped his arms around me and pulled me in tight to his chest. "Thank you for bringing me beer."

I let myself close my eyes for five seconds, counting in my head, inhaling him and leaning my face against his chest.

"Goodnight," I whispered.

He let me go and I felt the absence of his warmth but unzipped my tent and got inside. I lay in my sleeping bag, listening to the sizzle of the fire as he put it out, the soft thumps of his boots on the ground as he headed to his tent. The zip of his tent's fly, the rustle of him getting into his sleeping bag, and finally silence, punctuated with noises from the forest—a coyote yipping, an owl hooting.

I was starting to like Finn, not just lust after him. We were becoming friends again, pulled together like magnets. I burrowed further into my sleeping bag, trying to warm up. With my nose against the neck of his hoodie, I inhaled a lungful of Finn.

He wouldn't do any sexy stuff with me because he didn't want it to be a fling. It prickled in my head, the shame of rejection coupled with the spike of pleasure at knowing he was willing to wait for something good. Me. I was that something good.

I pictured what my mom's expression would be if she ever ran into Finn and me together. She'd see right through me. She knew me better than anyone. She would *know* I was—

I was what? Falling for him?

No. I wasn't.

I squeezed my eyes tight, breathing in his scent again. I was totally stealing this hoodie. All of this shit? I'd deal with it another day. So Finn and I were becoming friends again. So what. So I wanted to sleep with him. *So what.*

In a few months, I'd be searching for a new job, with or without a PhD, and that might mean leaving town if there was nothing in the immediate area.

But right now? I wanted my friend back. No one understood me like Finn, no one made me simultaneously flustered and at ease.

I was happy to know him again, even if it was temporary.

I WOKE to my tent's fly being zipped open. My chest shook from the cold, hands and feet almost numb. A phone flashlight lit up the tent.

I lifted my head, squinting. "Finn?"

The tent rustled as he crawled in, crouching while he did the fly back up. He was shirtless.

"What's going on?" My voice was gravelly with sleep.

"Your teeth are chattering so loud they can hear you back in town." He unzipped my sleeping bag and cold air rushed in.

I squeaked and burrowed further into the sleeping bag. "Why do you hate me?" I demanded through my sleep-fogged haze.

Finn slipped in beside me, sitting to zip the bag back up before looping his big arm under my neck and pulling me backwards into his chest.

I moaned. Oh my god. *Warm.* He wrapped his other arm over me, tucking me under his chin. His hand found mine, hidden within the long sleeve of his hoodie, but I could still feel his heat.

"Better?" he murmured. He caught my feet with his.

"Mhmm." The tension in my muscles eased and my shivers slowed. "Thank you."

His hand squeezed mine. The sleeping bag was meant to fit one person, not two, but instead of feeling claustrophobic, it was cozy and snuggly. Finn's body melded against mine and I felt the beat of his heart against my back.

"Go to sleep, baby," he whispered into my hair.

I closed my eyes and was out within a minute.

24

Finn

I WOKE up with my arms around her, my steel cock pressing into her. She made a sweet murmuring sound, half asleep, and pushed her ass back into me. A groan slipped out of me.

"Jesus fucking Christ, this feels too good," I rasped into her hair.

She rolled over in my arms to face me. Her eyes were puffy with sleep, hair all messy. I wanted to keep her like this forever. We could spend the rest of our days out here in the woods, wandering through the trees and staring at the stars together.

She blinked the sleep from her eyes, gaze on my face, and my mouth hitched.

"Good morning," I whispered.

"Morning."

My arm tightened around her and she sighed, eyelids drooping with comfort. She didn't need me warming her up anymore now that the sun was out but hell if I was going anywhere.

"Thanks for, um—" She cut herself off, flattening her mouth. "Thanks."

I gave her a small nod. The second I heard her shivering,

protectiveness had surged in my chest and I was out of my tent in a shot. My girl was cold. As if I wouldn't do anything about that.

I watched her lashes flutter. She had a healthy flush of pink across her cheekbones that I wanted to press my lips against.

She shifted and the movement pressed her against my cock. My eyes fell closed and I groaned.

"You're so hard," she whispered, eyes wide.

My expression turned rueful and I winced. "Sorry."

She shook her head. "It's okay." She swallowed, her gaze dropping to my lips. My cock pulsed and her lips parted, eyes meeting mine. "Felt that."

I huffed a laugh. My control balanced on a knife's edge, teetering. Her warm, soft body pressed up against me, curves against my hard lines. That sweet, sleepy expression on her beautiful face.

I never got to wake up with her, not like this. Our parents never would have let us have a sleepover, even if we had insisted nothing was going on.

And now? We weren't kids anymore. My pulse picked up as my heart pounded against the front wall of my chest, where Liv's hands were tucked.

Her gaze turned molten. "Why are you teasing me like this?"

I closed my eyes, dragging in a deep breath while reminding myself of the end game. Hooking up with Liv now and scaring the shit out of her, versus keeping my hands off her and waiting until she felt the same way.

"You know why," I told her, my voice low and teasing.

She squirmed against me and the thread of my control strained.

Maybe we could fool around a little—

No. Not yet. Not until she wanted me back, and not for a quick fuck. Forever.

I rolled onto my back and unzipped the sleeping bag, willing my erection to go away.

"Come on, Livvy. The day is young and the flower is out there."

I unzipped the tent, stepped outside and stretched, tilting my head up at the blue sky. The forest was drenched in that perfect morning light, clear and bright, with sunbeams cutting through the canopy around us. I leaned down to peek into the tent, where Liv hadn't moved.

She lay back in the sleeping bag with a grouchy expression, eyes cataloguing every muscle on my bare torso before her gaze snagged on my erection.

Her eyes shot back up to meet mine.

I let out a loud laugh. "I'll get coffee started."

―――――

WE SPENT another day scouring the mountain for the plant with no luck. I sent a glance over at Liv on the way back to the campsite. As she walked, her pink ponytail bounced. Wisps of bangs cascaded off her tanned cheekbones, and a smile lingered on her mouth, like she was happy and content. My blood hummed with satisfaction.

"Are you free next weekend?" Liv asked after a few minutes.

I nodded. "You want to do another camping trip?"

"It's my turn to take you on a date."

Mischief glittered in her eyes. I could see it right under the surface, my favorite side of Liv. Silly, mischievous, egging me on and challenging me.

"You going to take me somewhere nice?" I asked, grinning back at her. "Should I wear a suit?"

She held her smile down, trying not to laugh. "No suit necessary." Her eyes sparkled. "You'll see."

I held her gaze, biting my lower lip. Oh, this was going to

be fucking good. The doily museum didn't work so now she was going to ramp it up. Anticipation rolled through my chest, filling every crack with light.

Fucking hell, being with Liv was fun. There was no one like her, no one who knew how to push my buttons like she did. No one I enjoyed bugging like her.

I shook my head, staring at her, taking in her pretty face, her big brown eyes glittering in the golden hour light. "I missed you so fucking much."

She blinked, stunned, and for a second, I thought she'd shut down.

She didn't, though. Her cheeks turned pink and she smiled. She pulled her delicate bottom lip into her mouth with her teeth and I watched, fascinated.

I should have kissed her this morning.

AS THE SUN set and the temperature dropped, she retrieved my hoodie from her tent. She hadn't given it back this morning and I hadn't asked, and when she pulled it over her head, I couldn't wipe the grin from my face.

She yawned for the fourth time and I nudged her. "Bedtime."

She nodded and started to get up.

I thought about our kiss yesterday, and I couldn't help myself anymore. "I'm coming in," I said, leaving no room for argument.

She nodded again, hand slipping into mine and tugging. She didn't have to pull hard. I followed her to the tent, yanking my shirt over my head as she got into her sleeping bag and I took the spot beside her. The cold didn't affect me like it affected her.

Same as last night, she moved to her side and I wrapped my arms around her, pulling her to my chest, tucking her under my chin. My mouth brushed her temple in a quick kiss.

"Goodnight, baby."

"Goodnight," she whispered.

I lay there listening to her breathing even out until she fell asleep while I memorized the feel of her against me. Her warmth, her softness, the curve of her ass in her leggings. Her chest expanded and contracted under me with her breathing.

If this didn't work, it would crush me.

25

Finn

NEXT FRIDAY NIGHT, Liv's front door swung open and I stared at her... dress. Or whatever it was. "Wow."

"I said I'd pick *you* up." She crossed her arms.

"I'm ready now." And I liked watching her putter around her apartment, at ease and comfortable. Like we lived together or something.

I wrinkled my nose at her dress. It was a lot of fabric, and tough to tell if it had a skirt or it was one of those romper things. "Where'd you find that thing?"

She raised an eyebrow, eyes sparkling. "You don't like it?"

It had short sleeves and came to mid-thigh, but with the amount of ruffles and tenting on the fabric, I could barely tell Liv's shape. I couldn't see her tits, that was for sure. The thing buttoned up to her neck before the fabric plumed out, like one of those Shakespearean collars.

A laugh threatened to bubble out of me but I held it back. She'd outdone herself tonight.

I shook my head, grinning. "Liv, Liv, Liv. You're gorgeous in everything. This dress, though?" I tilted my chin at the frilly white fabric. "You look like a baby about to get baptized."

"How dare you." Her gaze held mine, and the corner of

her mouth twitched. "My grandmother was buried in this dress." Her eyes glittered as she reached for her bag and I shook with laughter. "Let's go. I'll drive."

"You sure?"

Her mouth turned up. "Absolutely."

Outside, I crowed with laughter when I saw why she had insisted.

In her usual parking spot in the alley, a rusty, beat-up minivan sat waiting, flames painted up the sides. The bumper was held on with duct tape. Two of the doors were dented. I circled the van, whistling long and low, running my fingers over the orange and red flames while Liv stood with her hip cocked. Or at least, I think her hip was cocked. Hard to tell under that giant loofah.

"Nice ride," I told her, nodding with appreciation. "You sell your car?" I asked, knowing she didn't. She'd never trust this piece of crap up those logging roads.

"It's getting an oil change."

I frowned. "I said I'd do it for you."

"I can do it myself."

"An oil change takes a couple hours. Why'd they give you a loaner?" My eyes narrowed as I watched her fumble through her lie.

She scratched the side of her nose, adopting an innocent expression. "The shop was busy." She shrugged.

Liar. Delight lifted in my chest, and I shot her a wicked grin. "They gave you this gnarly ride so I guess you showed me, huh?"

She pushed a giant ruffle out of the way so she could fold her arms over her chest. "We're going to be late," she said, acting casual.

I rolled my lips to hold back my laugh. She wasn't going to win this. My chest strained with excited energy and I made my way to the passenger seat.

Liv turned the car on and it roared to life; apparently the

muffler had fallen off. As she drove down the street, I rolled my window down and stuck my head out, waving at the residents of Queen's Cove walking along the sidewalk, and even the tourists. Miri Yang's eyes widened and she whipped her phone out to take a photo for the social media account she ran for the town.

"Can you not?" Liv hissed when I leaned over at a red light and honked the horn. She swatted my hand away, face going bright red. "Stop that."

Her embarrassment was like blood in the water for me. My head buzzed with excitement.

"What's the matter, Liv? I want everyone to see us in this sick ride. Look, it's Emmett." I leaned out the window and put my hands up to my mouth. "*EMMETT!*" I waved and he turned, jaw slack. I jerked my thumb over my shoulder at the ride. "Got that minivan you suggested!"

"Oh my god," Liv muttered, hitting the button on her door to roll up the window.

The window whirred beneath my hands but I held it down. The motor died and I leaned my chin on my palm, smiling as we passed people, waving like I was on a parade float.

"This is going to be a fun night." I nodded at Liv, smiling at her flared nostrils. "I can tell."

26

Olivia

I PULLED the junky minivan into a parking spot in front of Avery's restaurant, The Arbutus. The car backfired and people on the street ducked like a gun had gone off.

My stomach tightened and warning bells rang in my head.

One spot over, the Thompsons' car was rocking as they ferociously made out in the front seat. I winced.

"I changed my mind," I told Finn. "Let's have dinner at my place."

Finn's smile turned smug. "Hell no," he drawled.

My eyes darted to the restaurant. Through the windows, I could see Avery hustling around, greeting diners and coordinating with the staff, totally in her element. She used to manage the restaurant and when the previous owner was ready to sell, she couldn't get a bank loan to buy it, so Emmett offered to cosign on her loan if she pretended to be his fiancée for his mayoral campaign. She bought the restaurant, Emmett won the election, and they got married. Last year, she hired a new chef and the restaurant had been featured in some major foodie publications. The place was packed every weekend during tourist season.

"We can order in." I kept my gaze on the restaurant, heart

rate speeding up. "We can cuddle on the couch. I'll do anything you want." My voice had a desperate, unhinged edge.

Finn laughed. "Nope. I want to see whatever you had planned."

Fuck.

I chewed my lip. "I'll wear lingerie."

One eyebrow lifted. "You don't own lingerie."

"I do, I just never wear it."

His gaze sharpened, pinning me. He was considering it.

He shook his head. "No way. You're getting desperate so I know this is going to be a good time." He opened the car door and walked around to open mine. "Let's go, Morgan. Out of the car."

I sighed.

I left the Thompsons in their vehicle and led Finn up the walkway to the restaurant. Maybe they'd get so busy in there, they'd forget what I had planned.

Avery greeted us with a big grin. "Hey, you two—oh." Her gaze dropped to my outfit before she rolled her mouth into a thin line, eyes bright with laughter. She wrapped me in a hug. "You look terrible," she whispered in my ear. "Nice work."

She pulled back and gave Finn a quick hug before leading us to our table. People glanced at my outfit on the way and my stomach dipped.

I'd already taken the joke too far. This evening was supposed to get a rise out of Finn but it was a mistake planning it at The Arbutus. I didn't care if people were laughing at me wearing something weird but I didn't want to bring drama to Avery's business. My heart thumped beneath the ruffles and I sucked in a breath as I took my seat.

Finn glanced at the other two place settings. "Are we expecting guests?"

"Mhm." My voice sounded strangled.

The front door flew open and Shannon Thompson strode in. She saw us and lit up.

Finn spotted her and choked with laughter, hiding it with a cough.

"Oliviaaaaaaaa," Shannon sang as she approached the table. Diners glanced over at her volume but she didn't notice. Her bracelets jangled as she walked. She leaned down and gave me a kiss on each cheek. "Mwah, mwah. Finn!" He stood and she wrapped him in a tight hug, squeezing for too long. The corner of his mouth twitched.

"Hi, Shannon," he said, patting her gingerly while raising his eyebrows at me.

"Love your outfit." Shannon's hands rustled through my ruffles while she admired it. "You're like a big sexy baby."

Finn snorted but I refused to look at him.

"Okay." I took my seat. "Where's Jackson?"

"He needed a moment in the car." Shannon slipped into the chair across from me, brushing her silk scarf over her shoulder. The restaurant door opened again and Shannon glanced over her shoulder. "Here he is."

Jackson appeared at our table with a sleazy smile. A thick cloud of cologne consumed the table, forcing all the air out of the room. I coughed.

"Olivia, stunning as always." He leaned down to give me an awkward side hug before shaking Finn's hand. "Finn."

"And who's this beautiful young woman?" Jackson leered at Shannon while she preened, flipping her hair back.

"I'm not interested," she said in a haughty tone.

"Like hell, you're not interested." Jackson grabbed the back of Shannon's hair and kissed her. She moaned into him as her hands fisted his shirt.

Beside me, Finn leaned back, looping an arm over the back of my chair, studying his menu with a grin. Other diners peeked over Shannon and Jackson wrestled with each other's tongues. Avery brought out another table's food and stopped dead in the middle of the restaurant, eyes wide as she spotted them making out.

My face heated even more. Why did I do this? Stupid, stupid, stupid. I should have taken Finn to see some boring movie instead. I should have known he'd be more entertained by this than anything.

Finally, they broke apart and Jackson took his seat, readjusting his pants. Ugh. Gross.

"So, Finn," Shannon started, smiling at him. "How do you like being back in town?"

"It's great." His hand snuck into my lap, resting on my bare thigh, and he gave me a squeeze. "I've missed everyone."

Shannon inhaled deeply and let it out with a sigh. "Ah, Queen's Cove. So much to miss. Are you here to stay for good?"

Finn's mouth turned up and he glanced at me, giving me another thigh squeeze. His hand was so warm on my leg, and I resisted the urge to place my hand over top of his.

"I'll be wherever Liv is, let's put it that way."

I rolled my eyes but smiled at my menu.

"Oh my gosh." Shannon put her hand over her heart. "That's so sweet." She turned to Jackson. "How come you never say things like that?"

He made a face. "What do you mean? I said you had magic hands back in the car."

I held back a disgusted grimace and tried not to picture the context.

Shannon scoffed. "I jerk you off and you can't even be romantic about it?"

My hand settled over Finn's, and I dug my nails into his skin.

He smiled, waving a server down. "We're ready for a few drinks," he told her.

After the server left with our orders, Jackson turned to Finn.

"Finn, my guy. I'm telling you, the first few years of marriage, you got sunshine and rainbows coming out of your dickhole, but ten years in? You gotta do more to keep the magic popping, you know what I mean?"

Finn glanced at me with amusement sparking in his eyes. His hand was still on my thigh. "Please go on," he managed, like he was trying not to laugh.

Shannon sighed, head falling back with drama. "Enjoy this phase of your new relationship because soon enough, all you'll be talking about is toenail fungus." She shook her head and jerked her thumb at Jackson. "This one has struggled with it for years. We *cannot* get rid of his toenail fungus."

She waited like she expected me to say something but I blinked. "Okay," I replied, nodding. "Wow."

"What kind of fungus?" Finn asked, and I stared at him in shock.

His expression said *politely interested* but when his eyes flicked to mine, they said *oh, you wanna play? Let's play.*

Butterflies filled my chest and stomach. He shifted his hand, wrapping his fingers around mine.

"What kind of fungus has Jackson *not* had, more like," Shannon answered before going on a long, rambling rant about how tough it was to eradicate toenail fungus because Jackson kept going barefoot in the gym showers.

"I've got your drinks here," the server said sometime later.

"Thank fuck," I whispered under my breath and Finn gave my fingers a squeeze.

Shannon pointed a spiky nail at me. "Olivia, be sure to check Finn's feet for fungus every night after he gets home."

Jackson shook his head. "It would have been so easy to treat if we caught it early. I wouldn't have lost the nail."

I buried my face in my hands. If I went to the washroom, I could slip out the back.

"Yeah, Liv." Finn's eyes glittered. "I'll do you if you do me."

I gave him a dry look. "I doubt that you'll *do* me. I've offered."

A broad smile stretched over his face. "Maybe tonight's your night."

My stomach flip-flopped at the idea of something sexy happening tonight. A flash of nerves hit me in the gut.

Finn leaned in and I shivered as his mouth brushed my ear. "You're going to have to work a lot harder than this to get me in the sack, Morgan. I'm not putting out that easy."

I relaxed. It wasn't happening tonight.

"Finn," Shannon added as he took a sip of beer, "you need to be checking her for skin cancer on her labia as well."

Finn's beer sprayed out his nose in a storm of coughing. Over at the bar, Avery shot me a *what's going on* expression and I returned it with a wide-eyed thumbs up.

These people were batshit crazy, and I needed to get them out of here as soon as possible. I'd ask Avery to rush our meals, I'd eat as fast as possible, and as soon as the meal was over, we'd get the bill and get the absolute fuck out of here.

I flagged the server down. "Can we order? We're in a rush."

Shannon leaned forward on her hands. "No leaving early on us." She let out a loud laugh and Jackson chuckled.

"We're not in a rush," Finn told the server, shaking his head before shooting me a wicked grin. "We've got all night."

27

Olivia

ONCE WE PLACED our dinner orders, Finn turned to the Thompsons. "Tell us more about how to keep your relationship alive after ten years of marriage."

Oh my god, *Finn*. What the fuck was he doing? He was *trying* to get them to say more weird shit.

Shannon opened her mouth. "Butt pl—"

"Hiking." I cleared my throat. "Finn and I love hiking and camping. We used to do it as kids and then teenagers so it's nice to spend time out in nature together again." I glanced at him. "I missed doing that."

His gaze softened as he studied my face and his mouth tipped up in a sincere smile.

"I missed it too, baby." He gave me a lingering, sweet look before his eyes turned wicked. "Shannon, Jackson, you should join us sometime."

I sucked in a breath. *No!*

Shannon gasped. "We would *love* that." She leaned in and lowered her voice. "Have you guys ever seen a Sasquatch?"

Finn's hand twitched on my thigh. "Not yet."

Jackson glanced up from scrolling on his phone. "If you do

see one, you should capture it so you can sell it to the government."

I blew a long breath out and glanced at the door. I should leave and walk straight into the ocean.

Shannon clapped her hands together. "We know so many camping songs." She elbowed Jackson and he flinched.

"What?" he asked.

"I was saying that we know so many camping songs." She waved her hand. "What was that one about the raccoon?"

"Oh, uh." Jackson rubbed the bridge of his nose, thinking. "Little Timmy something."

"Yes!" Shannon lit up. "Little Timmy Trashrat."

"I don't know that one." Finn cocked his head. "Sing it for us?"

I closed my eyes and fought the urge to sink under the table.

"*Little Timmy Trashraaaat*," Shannon sang and Jackson joined in, slapping the table to create a beat. Half the restaurant was staring at us. "*Timmy loves to forage through trash*," she sang in falsetto. She closed her eyes, swaying. "*He visits at night and the bins go—*" She pointed at me, waiting.

I shook my head. "I don't know this one." It wasn't even about camping.

"*Crash!*" she finished before they sang the rest of the song about a racoon who ate garbage, three more verses. She drew out the last few notes then bowed in her seat to Finn's applause. My face was burning red.

Jackson looped an arm around Shannon's waist and dragged her closer. "God, Shan, you're so fucking hot when you sing," he growled.

She shot him a sexy smirk, narrowing her eyes. "Behave and you'll get to hear more."

He bit the air in front of her face. "I'm going to spank you for being a bad girl."

Uh.

"Do it. Do it now," she snarled.

My eyebrows shot up to my hairline. Were they this weird with everyone?

"I will," Jackson said, chomping at the air. "God, you're so sexy." He leaned in to sniff her neck and she moaned loudly. He whispered something in her ear and her eyelids drooped.

Jackson sat back in his chair and slugged back half his wine while Shannon fanned herself. Her chair scraped as she stood quickly. "I'll be right back. I have to use the ladies' room." She widened her eyes meaningfully at Jackson, who wiggled his eyebrows at her.

I sucked in a breath. Noooooooooooo. Not here.

Shannon disappeared to use the washroom and Jackson's eyes followed her. I could see him mouthing *eight, nine, ten* before he stood.

"I need to use the washroom as well," he informed us before he followed his wife.

"You think he's checking her labia?" Finn asked, and I guzzled half my glass of wine.

"You say that like you even know what the labia are."

He snorted. "You say that like I didn't make you come twice that night."

A shimmer of lust hit me between my legs and I sucked in a deep breath, ignoring the heat. "Whatever."

"Mhm. Whatever." His voice teased me but I refused to look at him.

"When our food arrives, let's eat as fast as possible so we can go home."

He pulled my chair closer to his and looped his arm around my shoulder. "Go home, huh? You got something planned after this?" His breath tickled my ear.

"You know what I meant. The bar. Where we both live."

"Come over for dinner tomorrow."

I turned to meet his gaze and his sincerity struck me right in the chest.

"Come on," he whispered, winking. "No weird poo emoji t-shirt, no ugly bag dress, just you and me eating dinner. I'll put a movie on and we can hang out. You don't even have to check my feet for fungus."

My mouth curved up against my will. "Promise?"

"I promise I'll never ask you to check my feet for fungus. Ever, Liv."

I snorted. "Okay. Tomorrow, then."

He pulled me a little closer to his chest and I smiled. This was nice, sitting like this. In an alternate universe, we would have been sitting here on a Friday night, eating dinner together. Maybe we'd already be married. We'd go home to the apartment we lived in together.

My heart twisted thinking about all these sweet thoughts, and a stab of worry pierced through. Those things weren't real.

Something caught my attention and I turned toward the hallway with the washrooms. Beside the bar, Avery's eyes narrowed as she listened with a frown.

Oh my god.

Moaning. There were moaning sounds coming from the bathroom. And was that…*slapping*? Oh my god.

Finn lowered his voice to a whisper. "Do you think that's him spanking her or his balls slapping against her?"

Avery's eyes went wide as she realized what was happening in there. The moaning was increasing in volume and she gestured frantically at Max, the manager, pointing at the music.

"Turn it up," she mouthed at him, pointing at the ceiling.

The music got louder, barely drowning out Shannon's wailing from the bathroom as she climaxed.

"When they come back," Finn murmured, "let's ask them to be the godparents of our children."

I sighed, closing my eyes and ignoring the little pulse of pleasure at *our children*. "Finn, I want to leave."

"What about our food?"

My eyes pleaded. "I'll fake sickness. I'll say I got my period."

"Alright." He shook his head at me, eyes bright. "You've had enough torture for tonight." He gestured to our server for the bill.

A crashing noise came from the hallway and Shannon stumbled out, pulling her dress down over her thighs, tears streaming down her face.

"Baby, I'm sorry!" Jackson hurried after her, buckling his belt. "I was kidding."

"You always call me a bad girl," Shannon sobbed, stopping in front of our table. "How come you never call me a good girl?"

Finn and I, along with the entire restaurant, watched in stunned silence.

"I can't spank you *and* call you a good girl," Jackson protested. "Those things don't go together."

"It's never about what I want," she wailed before lurching for her wine glass.

I clutched Finn. "Oh god."

Shannon threw the glass of red wine in Jackson's face and people around us gasped. The wine splattered all over my baptism dress.

Jackson wiped his face off. "See, you are a bad girl."

"Ugh!" Shannon grabbed *his* glass of wine and tossed *that* in his face before storming out.

Jackson followed, hot on her heels. "You do this on purpose to make me horny, Shannon. Get back here."

The front door slammed and the restaurant sat in silence, watching through the big windows as they argued outside.

"Oh no," Finn droned in a flat voice, glancing at all the wine that had stained my dress. "Your dress." He reached for his glass and tipped the rest onto my lap.

My eyes widened even more and I held back a laugh.

"Wowwwww." Avery appeared at our table. "You brought the Thompsons here, huh?"

I winced. "I'm so sorry, Av. You can drink for free at the bar for the rest of the summer."

She snorted. "Deal."

After Finn and I argued over the bill—he won—we left, climbing into the beater minivan I had begged to borrow from the mechanic.

Finn laughed all the way home.

28

Finn

"YOUR FACE," I said, shaking my head as we got back to the bar. My face hurt from laughing. "When Shannon brought up your labia, your face turned so red."

She turned from the step in front of me and her eyes bugged out. "Oh my god. We need to stop saying that word. And you nearly choked when she said that."

I couldn't help my grin as I followed her into the hall between our apartments. Her weird dress was stained with red wine, and it made a swishing noise as she walked.

"You look like an egg in this thing," I said, pointing at her outfit.

She tried to glare at me but her mouth twitched, giving her away.

I leaned on her doorframe. "You had fun tonight."

She snorted. "Right, I brought two insane people to Avery's restaurant and we didn't even get dinner. So much fun."

"I think you *did* have fun. I think you like poking at me, trying to get a rise out of me."

The line of her throat moved as she swallowed. Her gaze flicked up to mine with a little frown. She pulled that plush lower lip into her mouth to bite it and I thought about her straddling my lap while we were camping last week, rocking against me as I tasted her.

In an instant, my cock was half hard.

I studied her pretty face, freckles scattered across her nose and cheeks, a pink flush from being in the sun and a little left over from her dinner plans gone awry, dark brows quirking up. The delicate line of her lips sloping up to her cupid's bow.

"You didn't eat," she said suddenly.

Opportunity lifted its devious head in the back of my mind. Any chance to spend more time with Liv and I was in. I'd sit through a dozen more dinners with the Thompsons with a smile on my face if Liv was within arm's reach.

"Neither did you."

"I'm going to order pizza." She unlocked her door. "Come on."

I followed her in, watching as she flicked lights on and opened windows. I kicked my shoes off and took a seat on the couch, hands behind my head and gaze on her. She sent me quick glances before turning away, like she was nervous or something.

My eyes narrowed. The air in her apartment felt different from the last time I was here, waiting for her to put her boots on before we went hiking. Tonight, it felt charged, electrified. Sparking.

She tugged at her lacy collar like it was too tight. "I'm going to change."

I nodded, eyes on her legs. They were lean, strong, and tanned from hiking. When I rested my hand there tonight, her skin was soft as silk. I wondered if she'd like it if I scraped her inner thighs with my five o'clock shadow. If she'd gasp.

She walked into her bedroom, but she left the door cracked. My gaze locked on that crack of light as I listened hard. A drawer sliding open and closed. A rustle of clothing. Another rustle. A grunt.

In her room, she sighed. "Finn?"

I sat up straight. "Yeah?"

The door opened. An adorable pink flush spanned her cheeks as she stared at me with a resigned expression. "I can't get it off."

I barked a laugh.

"Don't." Her nostrils flared. "Don't you dare fucking laugh."

I let out a loud *ha!* "You need help?"

"Only if you're not going to be a dickhead about it."

"I'm always a dickhead, Liv." I stood and strode over to her.

That wicked part of me? It was fucking *singing*. My blood rushed through my veins. Her eyes widened as I advanced and I arched an eyebrow at her before whirling my finger in the air.

"Turn."

She spun around, giving me her back.

"What the fuck?" I grimaced, lifting a ruffle. "There are a thousand buttons on this thing."

"I know." She turned and winced at me. "Sadie helped me put it on."

"Didn't think this through, did you?"

She shook her head.

I leaned in, mouth by her ear. "Or maybe you did."

Her breath caught. "Are you going to help me or not?"

My mouth curled up. "Liv, I'll always help you, even if I'm a dick about it." I stood back and frowned at her outfit. It started out hideous, and now that it was stained in wine, it was going in the garbage.

I grabbed the top of the collar with both hands, fingers brushing Liv's shoulders, and a shudder rolled down her back before I yanked the fabric.

She gasped as buttons flew, baring her back to me. I saw a

flash of ink and black lace before she turned, clutching the remaining fabric to her chest. I was fully hard.

"Thanks," she whispered, eyes wide.

My blood thickened watching her clutch the fabric like that. I could see the pulse going in her neck, a little *tap-tap-tap*, and her chest rose and fell faster than normal. Her brown eyes darkened as her pupils dilated and she did that fucking intoxicating lip-chewing thing that drove me up the wall.

"Aren't you going to get dressed?" I murmured, daring her.

She dropped the fabric and it fell to the floor, pooling at her feet.

"Oh, fuck," I muttered, raking my hands through my hair.

Liv stood there in a thin black lace bra and panties, and my cock ached, straining against my zipper. I put a fist to my mouth as I memorized her body. The flare of her hips from her waist. The swell of her cleavage around her bra. I wanted to run my tongue over her. My heart thumped against the front wall of my chest. I pictured her long legs wrapped around my neck while I made her moan. A tattoo of a Douglas fir tree ran up the side of her torso, up her rib cage.

"Fuck, Liv." My voice was raw.

Her gaze flicked down to my erection and her eyes hooded before she turned to grab the shorts and t-shirt lying on her bed. My control hung by a thread. I pictured us doing a thousand things in that bed. She pulled her t-shirt on and I stared at the curve of her ass in that thong, wanting to tear it off her. She bent over and pulled the shorts up before turning to me.

"What's the matter, Finn?" she teased and I blinked.

I was so hard, it hurt. I got a flash of skin and I wanted to sink into her, fuck her into the mattress, make her come again and again until her voice was hoarse from shouting my name.

She breezed past me and the scent of her shampoo whooshed up my nose. My hands flexed and I dragged in a deep breath.

Tonight was going to test my control.

———

FORTY MINUTES LATER, we sat on the couch watching *Bridesmaids* and eating pizza.

I shifted to face her. "Did you know dinner was going to be *that* bad?"

She snorted and shook her head. "No. I'm so sorry."

I shrugged. "Don't be. I loved watching your face get more and more red."

"I can't believe she threw *two* glasses of wine."

"You've been working in a bar for years, you've never seen someone throw a drink?"

She shifted, tucking her feet under her legs. "No. I've always wanted to see it, though."

"So you're saying you crossed something off your bucket list tonight."

She grinned. "I guess so. I'll bring Avery apology donuts tomorrow."

"What else is on your list?" I asked her before taking a bite of pizza.

"Well, finding the flower." Her mouth twisted and she wiggled her eyebrows at me. "You know that."

"Mhm. What else?"

"Finishing my PhD, although I don't care about having the letters after my name. I just want to work in forest research." She glanced out the sliding glass door at the setting sun splashing orange and pink across the sky. "I think I want kids." In her lap, her fingers hooked around each other as she fidgeted. She met my gaze and pressed her mouth into a thin line before shrugging.

This slice of Liv's heart made my chest ache. It felt like she had peeled back one layer of the armor around herself to show me her skin, even if I hurt her before.

"Multiple kids?"

The corner of her mouth ticked up. "Yeah. Being an only child can be kind of lonely. I got lucky."

"How?"

Her gaze warmed. "Well, there was a whole house of kids next door."

"Mhm." I kept my eyes on her, even if she could barely look at me. "Having me made you less lonely?"

She nodded. "There's no guarantee of having a kid next door to be best friends with like I had. I know kids are expensive and have tantrums and ruin your sleep but I want two."

I reached out and set my hand on the couch between us, palm up like I had a handful of birdseed, waiting for a wary bird to land and say hello.

"You want two because you want your kids to have what we had? Best friends like that?" I asked.

She stared at my hand, nodded, and dropped her palm into mine. My heart thumped a steady, excited rhythm in my chest at the contact of her warm, soft skin. I stroked my thumb back and forth, back and forth.

"Liv?" My voice was low.

Her gaze lifted to mine.

"Do you want to…" I trailed off, huffing a laugh.

"What?" Curiosity and heat rose in her eyes.

"Do you want to throw a glass of wine in my face?"

29

Finn

I STOOD in Liv's shower while she held the bottle, wine glugging into the glass on the counter. When she raised her eyebrows at me, her eyes shone bright.

"You should take your shirt off," she said. "It'll stain."

I shot her a wry look. "Uh-huh. I see why we're in here now."

Her mouth curled into a pretty smile. "You offered."

I reached over my shoulder and yanked the shirt over my head. Liv kept pouring the wine but her gaze strayed to my chest and stomach.

"Pants, too."

In the back of my mind, the level-headed part of me told me to step carefully. That Liv and I were still on shaky ground and this was a slippery slope. The other part of my mind, the one that reached my hand out on the couch and melted when she put her hand in mine, that part wanted to push Liv a little further, see how she'd react.

And that part of me liked the way her gaze lingered on my body. My blood beat a little harder in my ears at the idea that Liv thought I was hot.

That part of my brain made me unbuckle my belt slower

than normal before sliding my jeans down my legs. She finished pouring the wine and stood there staring at me with heat in her eyes.

Blood rushed to my cock. I was already erect, standing on display for her like this in my boxer briefs.

Her eyes flicked up to mine and a smile twisted onto her mouth. "Ready?"

I grinned at her.

"How dare you!" she gasped before tossing the wine at me.

I burst out laughing as it splashed over me, running down my neck and chest. Liv grinned ear to ear, wiggling her eyebrows as she studied me covered in wine.

"That was fun." She set the empty glass down on the sink and pulled a towel out from the closet. "Here you go."

"Hold up." I arched an eyebrow at her. "What about me?"

She froze, hands on the towel, crooked half-smile on her face. "What do you mean, what about you?"

The wicked part of me that I was trying to hide so badly rattled his cage. "My turn."

She blinked and a flush spread over her cheeks. "Fine."

She lifted the bottle and poured another glass of wine before handing it to me. I gestured at the spot beside me in the tub but before she stepped forward, her hands came to the hem of her shirt and she pulled it over her head.

Oh, *fuck*. There was that bra again, the tattoo running up her side. All that smooth skin begging for attention. She pushed her shorts down.

"Wow," I said, staring at her. My balls ached. Liv was half-naked in the bathroom with me, and as she stepped into the tub, into my space, it was almost too fucking much to handle.

"Wow," I repeated, staring at the soft swells of her tits.

"You already said that."

I swallowed, nodding, memorizing her curves. The flare at

her waist where I had held her when she straddled me. The hollow at her collarbone where I'd run my tongue.

"Finn?" Liv's voice was soft and her eyes flashed with amusement.

"Hmm?" God, those fucking thighs. They'd feel so good around my neck, warm and soft, squeezing me as I worked my tongue between her legs.

"Throw the wine."

"Right." My heart was beating so hard. My dick strained against my boxers. "Close your eyes."

Her mouth turned up, her eyes closed, and I tossed the contents of the wine glass in her face. She chuckled and sputtered, eyes still closed, dripping in red wine. Droplets rolled down her nose, her chest, into her bra, down her stomach.

She wiped her face and opened her eyes, studying me with a coy smile. I reached to set the glass on the counter before turning back to her. That asshole who rattled the cage inside me earlier, telling Liv to strip down, he was back. My hands framed her jaw, tilting her face to mine.

"That list earlier, your bucket list?" I whispered.

She nodded.

"I want it all. I want to be all your firsts. Everything. I want those things with you."

Her throat worked under my hands but she didn't move.

"Do you understand, Liv?"

She nodded, eyes big and full of something brave. "Yes."

We held each other's gaze for a moment, understanding passing between us.

I want to find the flower with you.

I want to have kids with you.

Let's live a long, happy life together.

My lips pressed against hers and a groan ripped through my chest. Soft. Sweet. Her breath tickled my face and her hands came to my chest. I slanted my mouth over hers, coaxing her open before slipping in to taste her.

She moaned and my hands threaded into her hair. Her delicate mouth tasted so fucking sweet, so Liv. My tongue stroked hers and she nipped my bottom lip. I felt the little bite all the way to my cock, pressing into her stomach.

"Fuck, Liv," I whispered, looping an arm around her waist to pull her to me. "Fuck."

Kissing Liv was fucking heaven. We should have been doing this since the day I got back to town. We should have been doing this for years. I tilted her head back, opening her up more, taking her deeper, and one of her hands came to the back of my neck, tugging my hair. The other palmed my length.

"God, you taste so fucking good." My voice was rough in between kisses. I reached behind her and turned on the shower. Water poured down on us, rinsing the wine off, and I backed her into the spray, getting her hair wet. Our kisses were getting faster, more needy, more hungry, and behind her back, I undid her bra before tossing it aside.

Her tits. Jesus Christ, Liv's tits. My palms covered each breast, stroking and rolling and gently tugging the pinched nipples while Liv made these delicious fucking moans into my mouth. Her hands were everywhere—in my hair, grazing my chest, scratching up and down my abs, digging into the back of my neck. Seeing this side of Liv was intoxicating.

"I knew you wanted me like this," I rasped in her ear. "Knew you wanted me like I want you."

"Shut up." She pulled my mouth back down to hers and I laughed against it. My fingers found the waistband of her panties and tugged down, baring her. She kicked them off before yanking my boxers down. My cock sprang free, beading with pre-cum, and her arms looped back around my neck, soft lips returning to mine as she practically hung off me. I dragged a breath in, slowing our kiss down and looping an arm around her back to pull her tight to me.

Something crazy was happening in my chest. My heart squeezed, expanding into every corner of my chest.

This was right. This was real. It was big and intense and special and meant to be. I pulled back to search her eyes, heavy with desire, such a warm, gorgeous brown. Her wet hair dripped down her forehead, down her chest, and the moment felt so goddamn intimate. Like we were the only people that existed.

"You're so fucking beautiful, baby," I whispered.

The corner of her mouth curled up and I wished I could hear her thoughts but she wrapped her warm hand around my cock and my mind blanked. She gave me a long, firm stroke and I groaned into her neck as pressure built in my balls.

Wait. My head snapped up, head pounding with lust.

"Hands on the tile," I told her. "You can touch me when I say you can."

Her lips parted and she pulled in her bottom lip, eyes daring and ready to challenge me.

"You want to fool around? We're doing it my way."

Her eyes blazed as she leaned back against the wall. "Make it good, then."

30

Finn

"YOU'RE A BRAT," I told Liv, pressing a soft kiss to her mouth before running my mouth down her neck. "I know there's a good girl in there, though."

My lips found a nipple and I sucked. Her head fell back with a moan that I felt all the way to my balls. "Uh-huh. I remember how sweet you can be."

With my fingers on her other breast, I gave her gorgeous tits all the attention they deserved, licking and sucking and tugging as she arched on the tiles. She was trying to keep quiet, clamping her mouth closed tight, but once in a while, a breathy moan or groan would escape and I'd smile against her skin.

I straightened up, towering over her, caging her in.

"Do you like when I'm in control like this?" I murmured down at her.

Her eyes danced with fire and heat. "You're stalling. Do you need me to walk you through it?"

I shot her a wicked grin, shaking my head. "Morgan, when I'm done with you, you won't remember your own name. I don't need a reminder. I know what works on you."

She swallowed and her hands flexed against the tiles. My

fingers trailed a slow line from her breasts down her stomach, watching her eyes until I slipped between her legs.

She closed her eyes and moaned as I stroked her wet heat.

"Jesus Christ," I muttered, watching where my fingers glided over her. "You're so fucking wet and soft."

"You've been teasing me for weeks," she gasped as I circled her clit.

"Yeah? You've been thinking about this for weeks?" I flattened my fingers and dragged them in slow strokes over her clit, watching her eyes roll back as I added pressure. "There we go. I'm going to make you come, I know it."

Steam rose around us in the shower and she closed her eyes, breathing through her nose as she flattened her mouth, trying not to make a noise. Her abs tightened and her hips bucked against my hand and I felt like a fucking god, doling out pleasure to her one ounce at a time.

"You won't," she gasped, but her strained expression, her parted lips said I would.

I dipped a finger inside and she moaned. I pressed my mouth to where her shoulder met her neck, teeth scraping her skin while her pussy squeezed my finger.

"Oh, yeah?" I stroked in and out slowly until I found the ridged spot on her front wall.

She made a choking noise, hips bucking again.

"Oh, yeah," I said, giving her a cocky smile. One of my arms was propped above her while I fingered her, watching her gorgeous face. Watching her melt as I wound her tighter. I added a second finger and she whimpered. Her eyebrows pulled together and she bit that pretty bottom lip as I pushed into her tightness.

"Finn," she whined in desperation.

The devil inside me liked the way she said my name. "Say it, Liv. Say you're my girl."

She huffed. "Shut up."

My grin turned wicked as my fingers worked her. She was

getting wetter, slipping all over my fingers, and I added a third finger. "Uh-huh. Keep fighting it. You're getting tighter. Is my girl going to come?"

She shook her head, eyes closed, head tilted back against the shower. I kissed up the long line of her throat. Her pussy tightened when I licked the sensitive spot beneath her ear.

"You sure?" I murmured in her ear, massaging her G-spot. "You sure you're not going to come?"

"Doubt it." She squirmed, tits out and begging for attention. My lips met one nipple and I sucked hard.

"Fuck, fuck, fuck," she whispered. Her walls squeezed and rippled around my hand. I slipped my thumb over her clit and her eyes flew open. "Oh, shit."

"There we go. There's my girl." My voice was low and jagged, and my gaze flipped from her face to between her legs. "This pussy is so fucking sweet, baby, and soon, I'm going to bury my face between your legs and make you moan my name."

"Not your girl," she bit out.

"Yes, you are." I rubbed the pad of my thumb over her clit, circling with pressure.

"You fucking *wish*." Her eyes clenched closed, her back arched, and it was like watching an angel come undone beneath me. My heart slammed in my chest.

I did wish, and my wish was coming true.

"Can I touch you?" she gasped. "Please?"

My cock was dripping pre-cum but the second she touched me, I'd be in trouble. "Not yet. Wrap your arms around my neck, baby."

She looped her arms around me fast, like she was desperate for skin-on-skin contact, and she clung to me as I worked her inner walls. My pulse beat in my ears as her muscles began fluttering around my hand.

"Finn," she moaned, lips against my throat. "Finn."

"I knew it. I knew you'd fucking come," I growled into her

hair as she clung harder to my neck. "Deep down, Liv, there's a good girl in there who wants me to fuck her, isn't that right?"

She moaned again, wrapping her leg around my hip to let me get deeper. She squeezed tighter and tighter and her hips moved in time with my hands.

"Just like that, baby. Fuck yourself on my hand and let me make you feel good."

She started nodding and I knew that sign.

"Fuck," she gasped, head tilting back, and when her eyes opened and met mine, I saw disbelief, wonder, and pure pleasure. Her muscles rippled and clenched my fingers and she let out a long, low moan. "Finn, I'm coming."

"Yes, yes, yes, there we go," I murmured into her hair, holding her against me as she clutched my chest. "Touching you is so fucking sweet, Liv. I'm going to come thinking about this for months."

She bucked and her moans echoed in the bathroom as she rode out her orgasm. Her spasms slowed and she sighed into me, boneless. Under my arm, she caught her breath and tipped her face up, eyes hazy. I pressed my mouth against hers.

"You look so fucking good when you come," I whispered.

Her hand slipped down between us and wrapped around the base of my cock.

"Oh, shit," I gasped. She squeezed and my hips bucked in her hand. "*Oh, shit.* Olivia."

The corner of her mouth turned up and she watched my face while she stroked. Her other hand came to my balls, lightly rubbing and tugging. Heat coursed through my blood and I watched her face, so studious, careful, and curious as she jerked me off. My arms came up around her head, propped on the tiles while I leaned my forehead against hers and kissed her.

"Oh my fucking god," I gasped against her mouth.

Liv stroking my cock while we made out in the warm shower was the best thing I'd ever experienced. My thoughts scattered in the air like stars in the sky and my skin felt too hot, too tight, like I couldn't contain this desire for her.

"We're going to do this again." My voice was low and rough. "So many fucking times."

There was that smug grin on her face again, eyelids at half-mast before her gaze dropped to my cock. That little smile played at her lips while she worked my length, like she was admiring me.

She licked her lips and the idea of her mouth on my cock made me pulse in her hand. A pathetic whimper slipped out of my mouth and I huffed.

"Now who's going to come?" Liv whispered.

"What did you expect, looking at me like that?" Pressure boiled up my spine as I tried to hold on and my eyes clenched closed. "Been dreaming about your hand on my cock for years."

"Finn, kiss me."

My mouth fell to hers and I stroked into her, tasting her, getting my fill of Liv Morgan, the woman of my fucking dreams. Need whipped through me, pressure built in my balls, and with a gasp, I came all over her hand and stomach, moaning her name into her mouth.

"Oh, fuck." My head dropped to her shoulder as I caught my breath.

She kept a hand on my chest but moved out from under my arms. My brain was hazy as she opened a bottle of shampoo and gestured for me to lean down so she could reach my hair. Liv washed my hair before I washed hers, and as the water ran down our bodies, I felt a warm, intimate thrum in my chest.

After the shower, we toweled each other off, got dressed, and returned to the living room to watch the movie.

"Come here," I said, gesturing for Liv to curl up against me.

Her tongue darted out to wet her bottom lip as her eyes

narrowed in hesitation, but a second later, she slumped against me, head on my chest, my arm around her shoulders. I pressed a kiss to the top of her damp hair and she sighed. When the movie was over and Liv didn't move, breathing a steady rhythm on my chest, I reached for a nearby blanket, turned off the lamp, and settled back on the couch with her sprawled on top of me.

Everything I wanted was happening for Liv and me. We were spending more time together, she was trusting me, and we were getting closer. Soon enough, we wouldn't be where we were before, we'd be more *us*, deeper in this friendship, woven tighter together. Inseparable. Like we were meant to be.

A nervous, ugly chill slithered through my consciousness.

What if she changed her mind? I lay there in the dark, staring at the ceiling as Liv slept on my chest. What if she woke up and realized I was exactly who I was trying not to be?

I let a long breath out, pushing the thoughts out of my head and replacing them with memories of tonight, of Liv and me in the shower, of her embarrassed face at dinner, of the way her eyes glazed over with trust and pleasure as I made her come.

It was working, this plan of mine. Now I had to stop myself from fucking it up.

31

Olivia

ONE MORNING THE FOLLOWING WEEK, I zipped my pack up and stood in my kitchen, staring off into space.

We were just hiking. No big deal. We went hiking before and nothing happened.

That was before the shower. Before Finn made my brain disintegrate while he touched me. He had made me come so hard I couldn't think. Every night this week, I'd crawled into bed and slipped my hand between my legs thinking about Finn in the shower, towering over me with that smug expression, like he *knew* I was going to come.

Years ago, I thought my first time with Finn was a fluke. Losing your virginity was supposed to be awkward, fumbly and uncomfortable. With Finn, though? It had been hot and fun, and the second he touched me, it felt like he knew me. He knew exactly *how* and *what* and *where*. None of my later hookups had compared, and even when I dated that guy for a few months in school, the sex never got to that level. It always felt unsatisfying, like eating a bowl of popcorn and still feeling hungry.

But in the shower with Finn… holy shit. Maybe it was the

buildup, his height over me, or him being in control. Maybe it was him telling me I was his girl.

In my kitchen, I shivered and shook it off.

I'd been avoiding him all week and he knew it. The morning after, he had been so *warm* against my cheek when my head was on his chest, and his fingers played with my hair, light and gentle. I'd made an awkward excuse about needing to use the washroom before kicking him out. When he sat at the bar in the evenings, I had the other staff wait on him while his eyes followed me, heated and intense.

He was giving me space on purpose, and that irritated me even more, like he was being careful with me or something. Like I'd snap on him.

I already felt like I'd snapped. His gaze lit my skin on fire, his smirks and smug, knowing looks made me squirm, and the slow, cocky way he said *hi, Liv* in passing made me shiver. He was still leaving me cartoon doodles of the bird. The bird reading a textbook, with an $A+$ in the corner and a graduation hat on its head. The bird eating Cheezies by a campfire. The bird throwing wine in another bird's face, which made me chuckle.

I really wanted to fuck Finn Rhodes.

Today, though, we were just hiking.

I hauled my pack on and stepped into the hallway. Usually, Finn was at my door a few minutes early. He liked watching me move around my apartment, getting ready, tugging my boots on and checking my pack to make sure I had everything. I knocked on his door and listened to the slow footsteps on the other side. I frowned. Something was off.

The door opened and Death himself stared back at me.

"Oh my god." I grimaced. "You look like garbage."

Finn gave me a half-hearted, wry smile. His skin was pale but shiny, like he was sweating. A dull, tired glaze replaced the usual spark in his eyes.

"Sorry, running behind today." He turned and gestured for me to come inside before he sat down at the table.

"Are you hungover?" I asked.

He scrubbed a hand over his face. "Just tired. Long night at the fire hall." He took a deep breath like he was steeling himself and began to lace up his boots.

I frowned. A warning twinge, like something was wrong, lodged between my ribs. "I forgot you were on shift last night." He would have gotten home early this morning. "We should go tomorrow instead so you can get some sleep."

He shook his head and gave me a weak smile. "It's okay. I'll be fine once we're outside." I chewed my lip, hesitating, but he stood and hauled his pack on. "Let's hit the road."

I followed him downstairs and out of the bar to my car in the alley.

"You want me to drive this time?" he asked.

Drive? The guy was about to keel over. "I'll drive."

In the passenger seat, Finn sat back and closed his eyes while I drove through town and merged onto the highway. A few minutes in, he reached out and gripped the door handle.

"Liv?" He rubbed a hand over his face.

"Yeah?" My gaze whipped between him and the road. "What's going on?"

"Pull over."

The second I pulled onto the shoulder, Finn threw the door open and threw up on the pavement. I winced as he heaved, digging out a water bottle and some napkins.

"You're sick," I told him when he sat up again, breathing hard. His forehead was damp with sweat and his skin had a gray tinge.

"I'm fine. I think there's something going around at the fire hall. Let's keep going."

"No."

It zapped his energy just to turn his head. "We have to keep searching for the flower. I promised you."

"You're *sick*. We're not going today," I snapped, putting the car in drive and doing a U-turn on the empty highway.

"Liv."

"Shut up." I frowned at the road. My chest felt weird and unhappy every time I glanced at him looking all shitty like that. "We're going home and you're going straight to bed."

He closed his eyes but the corner of his mouth kicked up. "Worried about me?"

"No. I just don't want to haul you down the mountain when you keel over."

"We both know you'd leave me there."

I snorted. "Shut up."

We arrived back at the bar and even though I forced him to leave his pack in the car, he was still winded at the top of the stairs. Inside his apartment, I waited for him to kick his boots off before I guided him to his bedroom and pulled back the covers.

"Get in." My voice sounded more authoritative than I felt. "You're going to sleep this off."

"Worried about nothing," he mumbled, settling against the pillows.

I walked over to the window and pulled the blinds closed. His room had a wooden bed frame in a dark stain, a bedside table, and a lamp, and that was it. His clothes were neatly hung in the closet. My lip curled.

"Dude, your room bums me out."

"What do you mean?" His eyes were still closed.

"You need some art or something on the walls."

He sighed. "I won't be staying long," he mumbled.

I blinked like I'd been slapped. "Oh. Right." My stomach knotted.

Of course. I studied his face. Did he realize he had said that? My stomach sank. He was leaving, and that stuff in the shower the other night had just been us messing around.

It hadn't meant anything.

Ugh. I felt so stupid and embarrassed. I knew this about Finn, and yet I couldn't help myself around him.

I set a glass of water on his bedside table before I returned to my apartment and pulled out my laptop to work on my thesis. Except for finding the flower, my research was done, and now I just had to finish writing the thesis itself, organizing the data to explain my work. I opened the document and stared at it, mind wandering to Finn's apartment.

A minute later, I went back across the hall and sat down at *his* kitchen table, an old table from my parents' house when I was a kid that my dad stored here. From my spot in the kitchen, I had a view into Finn's room so I could see if he needed anything.

I was editing a graph when I heard the rustle of sheets. My head whipped up to see Finn throw the bathroom door open and heave into the toilet.

Oh god. I ran to the bathroom.

"Liv, go home," Finn gasped in between rounds.

"No." Fuck. I didn't know what to do. "You're sick."

"I'm fine. It's just a stomach bug." He leaned over and threw up again.

I put my hand on the back of his neck. His skin was so hot. "You're burning up." Nerves twisted in my stomach. "I'm calling Beck."

Finn sighed. "Liv, I'm fine."

In the kitchen, I scrolled through my contacts until I found Beck's name. He answered on the third ring. There was noise in the background, people talking. He must have been at the hospital.

"Hey. What's wrong?"

Guilt nudged my stomach. Beck was the guy people called when something was wrong.

"Finn has a fever and he's throwing up." I glanced at Finn sitting on the edge of the tub. "I don't know what to do."

"Sounds like the flu. What's his temperature?"

"I don't know." I should have taken his temperature before calling.

"It's okay, just take his temperature after we hang up." Beck's voice was calm and steady and a couple knots loosened in my stomach. "If it's above 102 Fahrenheit, call me back. He needs sleep and fluids. If he's throwing up for more than six hours, call me. If he has a hard time breathing, call me. Does that make sense?"

"Yep." I sounded breathless. "Got it."

"Olivia, don't worry. He's healthy. I did his routine checkup for the fire department last month. He'll be fine. If you get freaked out, call me."

"Yep. Okay." I nodded to myself. "Thanks, Beck."

We said goodbye and I followed Finn back into his bedroom. I helped him into bed before I just sat there, watching him fall asleep, broad chest rising and falling softly. The guy felt like absolute garbage but he had been ready to endure a two-day hike to help me out.

I couldn't leave him to fend for himself. I had to take care of him.

He'd do it for me.

32

Olivia

HALF AN HOUR LATER, I sat on the bed beside Finn, taking his temperature. The thermometer beeped. A hundred and one Fahrenheit.

"Am I going to die?" Finn mumbled.

"Hilarious." I frowned and reached for the orange juice I had bought at the pharmacy. "Are you still nauseous?"

He shook his head and sat up, drinking the orange juice. Even after I brought all my blankets from my apartment and loaded them on top of him, he was shivering.

He scanned my face with weak amusement. "Don't look so worried, frowny face." The corner of his mouth lifted but the smile didn't reach his eyes. "I'm not going to die."

My brow furrowed. "I know."

He finished the orange juice and lay back into the pillows. "You don't need to stay here. I don't want to get you sick."

"I'm not leaving." I stood and retrieved my laptop from the kitchen before taking the spot beside Finn on the bed. "Let me know if you want lunch. I bought soup."

"You bought soup?" His smile lifted again.

I rolled my eyes. Seeing Finn like this was making me grumpy. "Go back to sleep."

Finn slept the entire day. I sat on the bed beside him working on my thesis until I couldn't stare at it anymore. When he opened his eyes in the late afternoon, I was watching an old season of a reality show on Netflix.

"You're still here." He squinted, adjusting to the light from the lamp beside him.

"You want some food? You should have something to drink."

"Sure." His eyes only opened halfway.

That nagging sense of wrongness stayed lodged in my ribs. Finn was supposed to be bulletproof, so healthy and strong and full of life, and he was a tired, weak mess. In the kitchen, I microwaved the soup with some toast the way my dad had made for me when I was sick as a kid.

Finn sat up against the pillows and ate his dinner. "Thank you, baby."

I nodded, ignoring the pulse of warmth in my chest when he called me that. He finished his food and I took the bowl away before returning to the bed beside him. His eyes were closed again but he was still sitting.

"Hey. Lie down," I whispered, and he moved back to his back. "What do you need?"

"Blowjob," he mumbled.

I snorted. "Unbelievable."

With his eyes closed, his grin hitched and I sat there watching his perfect smile, studying the way his hair fell into his eyes. I grabbed the thermometer from the bedside table. He groaned when I stuck it in his mouth again.

I waited for the beep. Still one hundred and one. Shit. Without thinking, I reached out and pushed his hair off his forehead, chewing my lip. He made a rumbly noise of appreciation, eyes still closed, as I stroked down the back of his head all the way to his shoulder. His shirt was damp with sweat.

"Finn, I'm going to change your shirt."

"I'm cold."

"I know, I'll put a long-sleeve t-shirt on you. Where are they?"

"Closet."

I dug around in the closet for the t-shirts, lifting one out of the built-in drawer. Papers fluttered to the floor, and I bent down to pick them up.

My heart stopped. *Relocation of the Pacific Trail fern—a study in plant movement due to environmental changes*. It was the first paper I had published in my program, when I was trying to prove that plants could thrive in new environments as the forest changed. There was my name on the byline, *Morgan, O.*, as well as my advisor and the other students involved. I glanced through the papers. All four of my published papers were here.

Why were my research papers sitting in his closet? There were handwritten notes in the margins, phrases underlined with the definitions scribbled near them, and stars next to the findings. My lungs felt tight like I couldn't catch my breath, and I shot a glance over my shoulder at Finn, already fast asleep again.

He had read my papers. My stomach did a slow roll forward and I felt a weird pressure behind my eyes, like I was going to cry or something, which was stupid, because this was nothing.

Right?

This was nothing.

In his flu haze, he admitted earlier that he was leaving. Maybe he didn't even realize he was leaving, but he said it. What the fuck was I doing, getting attached to someone who couldn't bear to stick around this boring town for longer than a summer?

His words from the shower popped into my head, about how he wanted to be all my firsts. How many times had I pictured those things with him over the past few days? As soon as he said that, I couldn't get it out of my head. Us buying our first place. Us having kids together.

The papers rustled as I shoved them back where I found them.

After eating my own dinner, watching more TV on the bed beside Finn, and stepping over into my own apartment to brush my teeth and wash my face, I settled onto the bed next to him.

This wasn't weird. We weren't sleeping together, it was because he was sick. What if he got sick again in the middle of the night? What if he had trouble breathing, like Beck said?

Beck had texted me while I was brushing my teeth. *Everything okay?*

I stuck the thermometer back in Finn's mouth. I'd taken ten temperature readings today. One hundred degrees. My eyebrows lifted. This was good. His fever was going down.

He's been sleeping all day. Temperature down to 100F.

Good. I'll check in tomorrow morning, he replied.

I rubbed my sternum, swelling with gratitude for him. Next time he came into the bar, his drink was on me.

Finn was leaving. I swallowed past a thick throat. I didn't know what to think anymore. A pressure built in my chest but I shoved it away. I didn't dare let myself be disappointed. Disappointed over what? This thing with Finn was temporary. I crawled under one of the blankets and settled into bed, letting the steady rhythm of his breathing lull me to sleep.

———

I WOKE in the middle of the night to Finn sitting up beside me.

"Liv?" He frowned in the dim light.

My hand came to his shoulder. "I'm here."

He made a soft noise of acknowledgement before relaxing back into the pillows, and a muscle in my chest tugged. He needed me. He was comforted that I was here. We'd never done this before. When we were teenagers, our parents took care of us when we were sick.

I'd never taken care of anyone when they were sick before.

I blew a long breath out. Oh, shit. This was a relationship thing. This was what partners did.

"So glad you're here." His eyes were closed again.

I put my hand on his forehead. He felt cooler than before. I breathed a sigh of relief. He wasn't back to normal but better. So much better than before. Good.

"I love you so fucking much," he mumbled, reaching for my hand and tucking it to his chest, and I froze.

My mind whirled, repeating what I had heard. Where he trapped my hand against him, I could feel his heartbeat.

Finn was leaving, he said it himself, but he also read all my research papers, something even my parents hadn't done. He told me he wanted to have kids with me. He told me we were meant to be. He was trying to woo me.

My forehead creased and I winced. I was so, so confused.

"You said you weren't staying earlier," I said softly. "Where are you going?"

He clutched my hand, half asleep. "Going to buy us a house."

I stared at him. "What?"

He cleared his throat, turning onto his back, eyes still closed. "That old house at the edge of town. Holden said he'd help me fix it up. Four bedrooms for Cora's cousins."

The one we passed every time we drove into the mountains. The one we used to ride our bikes to as kids. He knew I loved that house. My nose was practically against the windshield whenever we drove past it.

My pulse picked up and I stared at Finn's face, pressing my mouth into a thin line so I wouldn't smile. Bubbles fizzed in my chest.

He wasn't leaving. He just meant he wasn't staying *here* in this apartment.

Don't you dare get your hopes up.

I wanted to, though. I really fucking wanted to get my hopes up. Would I regret not giving us a shot? Fifty years from now, would I think about Finn Rhodes and wish I'd said yes?

I thought about Cole. He and my mom were high school sweethearts. They loved each other, and they had a *kid* together and he still didn't stay.

I bit my lip, watching Finn sleep. I had no freaking clue what to do.

33

Olivia

"WE CAN'T HAVE your baby shower at a strip club," I told Sadie as the four of us gathered in the living room of the home she shared with Holden. Around us, paintings hung on the walls, some Sadie's and some other local artists'. The home in the woods had huge windows, dark wood floors, and a mix of antique and modern furniture, giving it an old library vibe.

Sadie pushed her phone at me. "It isn't a strip club, it's a special *event*. Miri's planning it."

Avery snorted. "Of course she is."

"She hired a bunch of male strippers from Victoria," Sadie continued with a big smile. "Everyone's going to be there. We can't miss it."

I scanned Miri's Instagram post. She was renting out the town community center and bringing in an *array of talented male exotic dancers*.

Hannah leaned over. "Can I see that?"

"Really?" My eyebrows shot up in disbelief, handing her the phone. "You, too?"

She blushed, laughing. "I've never been."

On the couch, Sadie rested a hand on her bump. Every

time I saw her, it got bigger. Now that she was out of the first trimester, the morning sickness had gone away and she said she was feeling more like herself. Her skin glowed, her hair shone like a shampoo commercial, and even though she still fell asleep at nine every night, she seemed like she had more energy.

"It'll either be a blast or terrible," she said.

"Or both," Avery pointed out.

"Won't your man be jealous?" I asked Sadie. Holden wasn't home. Sadie had said he was having dinner with Wyatt and Cora.

She gave me a knowing look. "Won't *yours*?"

Going to buy you a house. Four bedrooms for Cora's cousins.

We stared at each other, and a smile curled up on my mouth.

She pointed at whatever my expression was. "That's what I thought." She frowned and tilted her head. "Where've you been this week? He's been at the bar but you haven't been working."

I squirmed, fiddling with the edge of the blanket on the couch. I was back to avoiding him because I was a coward. Thankfully, the bar was fully staffed this week and they didn't need me most nights. The tipping point wasn't him telling me he was going to buy us a house, and it wasn't finding my research papers in his closet, or even him telling me he loved me.

It was the way he'd looked at me the next morning when he woke up, like he was relieved I was still there. The soft, affectionate way he had smiled at me made me want to be there when he woke up every day.

Fuck. I was so fucked. The feelings tightened around my throat.

"Busy with school stuff," I lied, giving her the same excuse I'd given my dad.

The truth was, I couldn't face Finn. I needed a breather

from him. He was too intense, too hot, and around him, my walls of ice were melting.

"He's different this time," Hannah said quietly, mouth twisting to the side as she watched me.

Avery frowned and nodded. "Yeah. I've noticed that but I can't put my finger on what it is about him."

Hannah smiled. "He keeps offering to babysit."

I made a face. "Really?"

She nodded. "Yep. He spends a lot more time with family than he used to."

"Oh, yeah," Sadie said, narrowing her eyes. "He's been hanging out with Holden a ton."

Avery hummed, biting her lip, glancing at me with uncertainty.

"What?" I prodded. "Go ahead. I know you want to say something."

"I have a theory."

My brow arched. "Okay."

She tapped her finger with her lip. "In the past, when Finn would be in town, either living here during the year when you were away or visiting, he'd keep his distance."

I frowned.

Hannah nodded at Avery. "Yeah. That's it."

"He spent a lot of time on his own or working. At family dinners, he'd usually leave early. It felt like…" She shook her head. "I don't know, like he didn't want to get too attached. And he'd be kind of mopey in the weeks before he shipped off to the interior of BC."

Sadie pointed at her. "That's totally it. He's not like that this time around. It feels like he's trying more."

The three of them turned to me and I frowned down at my hands.

I couldn't hear this kind of stuff. My defenses were already weak with him, and now this?

I had caved and let myself fool around with him, but I

wasn't going to fall in love with him. If he was trying to put roots down here, he was fooling himself.

I'd been fooled once—it wouldn't happen again.

"Let's talk about the baby shower invite list," I said, changing the subject.

———

WE STAYED at Sadie's until she started yawning and Hannah had to get home to help with Cora's bedtime. Avery and I, the night owls, headed to her place to finish planning Sadie's baby shower, and by the time I got home, the bar was closed.

Perfect.

I unlocked the door from the alley, expecting darkness inside, but the lights were still on. I frowned and walked down the hallway to the bar to turn them off.

In the empty bar, Finn sat in his usual spot, watching the TV above the bar. His easy gaze rested on me while I stood there, confused and frozen.

"What—" I started, shaking my head.

"I told your dad I'd turn the lights off."

"Were you waiting for me?"

He nodded. "Wanted to make sure you got home okay."

Liquid warmth wove through my chest. "Are you worried about me or something?"

"Always." The corner of his mouth hitched. "When I'm not here, I'm thinking about you." His eyes glittered and I shivered under the full weight of his attention. "You've been avoiding me."

I cleared my throat and broke our eye contact. Sometimes, the way he looked at me, it made my pulse act like I was on a rollercoaster. "How are you feeling?"

"Great. Full health, thanks to you."

I shrugged. "I didn't do anything. Beck said it himself,

you're young and healthy so you would have recovered anyway."

His eyebrows shot up. "You called Beck?"

I blinked. Busted. "No."

Keeping his unnerving, knowing gaze on me, he walked around the bar counter until he was in front of me, towering over me. His cruel mouth turned up and his eyes were so bright. "You called Beck. You were worried about me."

My face was going red. "Whatever."

Wow, amazing comeback. God, I was so fucking transparent. I probably had fucking hearts popping out of my eyes like a cartoon.

Finn leaned down so his mouth was beside my ear. "You held my hand and got me blankets. You bought a thermometer. You were worried about me."

His fingers stroked the back of my neck, sending shivers down my spine. His other hand came to beneath my chin, tipping my face up.

"I missed you this week," he murmured.

I stared back at him, worry creasing my brow. My gaze flicked toward the hallway behind him, my escape route.

"Don't you dare." He backed me against the counter. "Say it, Liv. Admit why you've been dodging me this week."

My throat worked and his eyes flared with heat, something dark and pleased.

I shivered. "Things are weird." I met his gaze, biting my lip. My stomach was tumbling like I was rolling down a hill.

"You have feelings for me."

I closed my eyes. Defeat.

"Olivia." He tilted my face up. "Time to come clean."

"I know," I whispered, keeping my eyes closed. A weight sank in my stomach and I nodded to myself.

It was time to stop pretending I was unaffected by him. That I was anything less than falling for him like he had planned. That *my* plan wasn't working in the slightest.

"I have feelings for you," I whispered. My voice was so small and quiet. I opened my eyes to meet his gaze and the affection I saw there nearly made my heart stop.

"Baby. You say it like it's a bad thing."

I groaned in frustration.

"Was that so hard?" he asked, voice soft.

I turned away. The last time I told Finn how I felt, he left the next day.

"Hey." He dipped his head to meet my eyes. "I know you're scared."

Alarm rose in me. Could he hear my thoughts?

"I'm scared too," he admitted, a hint of worry in his eyes. "I'm scared you'll wake up and realize I'm not even close to being good enough for you, and I'll never see you again."

I frowned. Why would he think that? "You are good enough for me. Don't say that."

Saying it out loud clicked something into place in my chest, and for the first time, I wondered if I was making a mistake, trying to get him to dump me.

When he smiled, I didn't like how it didn't reach his eyes. "I'm not, but I'm going to do everything I can to be that guy for you, Liv. We're going to find the flower. I meant what I said about buying that house for us. Do you understand?"

I nodded. Showing Finn this tiny corner of my heart and him catching me like this filled me with confidence.

My heart beat like a drum in my ears and my gaze snagged on his mouth, the line of his lips. His eyes, so sharp and piercing and rimmed in thick lashes. My arms looped around his neck and my hand worked into his hair. His eyelids drooped when my fingers ran over his scalp.

"I understand," I whispered, before I leaned up on my toes and kissed him.

34

Olivia

IT HAD ONLY BEEN a week since I'd seen him, but Finn kissed me with a hungry urgency that made my skin hot. My pulse whooshed in my ears and the hesitation I felt earlier evaporated.

This week, I had missed him, too, and being with him like this, it was too good to stop.

He walked me back against the bar, tilting me open for him so he could taste me. His stubble scraped me and I moaned into his mouth at the sensation.

He broke our kiss, resting his forehead against mine with heat in his eyes.

"When you look at me like that," I whispered, "I feel…"

A smug smile pulled at his mouth. "You feel what, Liv?"

"Flustered." I sounded breathless. "Like I don't know where my thoughts went."

His eyes darkened. "Good. You don't need to think all the time. Let me take over for the next while."

A muscle pulled low in my stomach and my brain turned hazy.

He must have seen something he liked in my eyes because he smiled and his lips returned to mine. He coaxed my mouth open so he could slip inside, and I shivered at the drugging glide of his tongue against mine. Lust swirled low in my stomach, between my legs, warming my blood and making me squirm for him.

"I can't stop thinking about my fingers in your gorgeous pussy," he whispered.

I nodded, temporarily stupid. "Uh-huh."

He smiled. "You're so cute when you're horny for me."

His cocky, knowing tone made irritation prickle at the back of my neck. Ever since he made me come the other week, it was like he had flipped a switch in me. I found myself daydreaming about us in the shower a hundred times a day.

He didn't need to know that, though. His ego was big enough.

He ran his hands down the back of my neck with firm, dominant pressure, and I fought the urge to let my eyes roll back. His palms came to my breasts while he pressed kisses down my neck and collarbone, then he pulled the neckline of my shirt and bra cups down to toy with my nipples.

I gasped at the sharp pleasure.

"You going to come for me tonight?" he murmured into my ear as his fingers pinched and rolled the tight peaks.

I clenched my teeth so I wouldn't moan. "Doubt it."

He laughed silently against my temple. "God, you're such a fucking liar. You're practically coming with my hands on your tits, and you won't admit it."

"You clearly have no idea what it looks like when I come." My voice was ragged. I was wet, and an urgent pulse thrummed between my legs. I gripped the bar counter behind me.

His low chuckle made me clench with anticipation. "I remember. I remember back then and I remember last week." He leaned down to pull a nipple into his mouth and the hot slick of his tongue made my jaw go slack.

Holy fuck. I sucked a deep breath in through my nose and

closed my eyes. Too good. Too fucking good. What Finn Rhodes lacked in responsibility and trustworthiness, he made up for in tongue skills.

"You can moan," he whispered against my chest.

I shook my head. "No, thanks."

He laughed, sucking hard, and I squeaked, eyes squeezed tightly closed.

"Oh, fuck," I whispered.

"Good?"

"It's fine." My voice was high and breathy. "You're still learning."

He straightened up and did that towering-over-me thing again. His eyes flared with amusement and challenge and he set a hand beside each of mine. He was all around me, blocking me in, and I loved the twist of nerves low in my belly. My nipples pricked with a chill from the air after the wet heat of his mouth.

He shook his head, watching my eyes, mouth turned up in a wicked smile. "We always loved playing games, didn't we, Livvy? Always loved racing each other to the finish line. Well, we're adults now, and we're going to play a different kind of game."

Excitement arced through me but I kept my face neutral. I lifted one shoulder in a shrug. "Fine."

He nodded slowly, holding my gaze. "Fine." He stepped back and made a twirling motion with his finger in the air. "Turn around."

Anticipation thrilled through my chest. I blinked at him. "Excuse me?"

He didn't move, just held my gaze with that cocky, demanding expression. "Turn. Around."

"No."

His brow arched and the heat in his eyes lit me on fire. "Do it."

"Make me."

He huffed and his head fell back. "Jesus Christ, Liv. You're going to drive me insane, you know that?" He stepped forward until he was less than a foot from me and placed his hands on my shoulders. He turned me slowly with unrelenting pressure until I faced the rest of the bar. He wrapped his arms around me, palming my breasts. His fingers toyed with me and my breath caught.

"Mhm." His mouth was on my neck. His chest rose and fell against my back and something about his height, how he surrounded me like this, made the apex of my legs warm.

His hand slipped down, brushing the skin above the waist-band of my jeans. "Undo the button."

On the bar counter, my hands twitched, desperate to do as he said, but I held them still. "Why am I not surprised that you have a hard time undressing women? Maybe that's why I still have my bra on."

He reached around my back, pulled the band of my bra and let it go, snapping me. A laugh of surprise burst out of me at the sharp sting.

"Undo the fucking button, Liv." His voice rumbled in my ear.

I did as I was told. A tiny part of me huffed in irritation but the rest of me? She liked this game. She liked this game *a lot.*

His teeth scored my neck and I shivered. "Good," he murmured.

A shiver of pleasure rolled down my back and I bit my lip. God, I hated how much I liked this side of him.

With one of his hands gripping my hip, holding me steady, he slipped the other into my jeans, straight past my panties. His fingers brushed my clit and I whimpered.

He made a noise of appreciation. "I knew you'd be wet for me."

My face heated as he slid his fingers through me with unhurried strokes. Sparks danced through my limbs, tension coiled, and I pressed into the hard length of him against my backside. Arousal rushed to where he touched me and I sighed.

"Oh my god," I whispered, eyes closed, chasing friction and pressure.

"Need more?" His other hand dug into my waist, anchoring me.

"Uh-huh." I bit my lip. The way he was touching me, it was winding me higher but not enough to get me to the edge.

Finn must have noticed the desperate squirm of my hips or the way my breath caught every time he ran the pads of his fingers over my clit, because his hand stilled.

"Bend over."

My eyebrows lifted. "What?"

Over my shoulder, he grinned at me, lazy, roguish, and full of heat. It made my insides twist with anticipation. His hips pinned mine, locking me against the bar, and his hand came to my shoulder before he gently pushed me down.

I let him.

With my head tilted to the side, my cheek was flat against the counter, but his hand moved between my shoulders with more pressure.

"All the way."

My bare breasts pressed against the cool surface and I let out a quiet gasp at the sensation.

"Good girl."

Oh, *fuck*. My blood surged with heat. From where they gripped the edge of the counter, he moved my hands to lie flat over my head. This position felt... submissive. Totally at his mercy. Like I was serving him or something. My center ached to be touched again. My breath caught as he slid my pants down my hips.

I was exposed and open to him. Shame threatened at the edges of my consciousness but something bigger took over.

"Just like that," he whispered, his hand rubbing up and down my back in languid strokes. "Perfect."

Pleasure melted into my blood and I smiled with my face against the counter. How many times had I stood at this counter and taken someone's drink order, or chatted with one of the regulars? My throat worked as I swallowed the grin.

Finn was a bad influence, but right now? I didn't mind one bit. I'd follow the devil right into the depths of hell if he made me feel like this.

In the back of my mind, that old version of myself from a couple months ago was outraged and incredulous. *What are we doing? This is Finn Rhodes, we hate him! He's a backstabbing dickhead who we don't trust!*

But the thing was, I did trust him. I didn't hate him. And the rest of me? She wanted this. Badly. My pulse was racing, my face was flushed, and the pressure and heat between my legs were nearly unbearable.

He made a noise of admiration. "Fucking gorgeous." He palmed my ass, running his hand over my skin, and I shivered.

"If you move off the counter, I'm stopping. Clear?"

I scoffed like I didn't care. "Fine."

"Good."

He delivered a sharp smack on my ass and I yelped in surprise. A wave of heat hit me between my legs, exposed and open to him.

Ugh. *Olivia.* Who *was* I right now? Finn turned my brain to mush.

"What the fuck?" I hissed.

He huffed a laugh. "That's for the double date from hell."

When the next slap landed, I clenched and a low moan slipped out of my mouth.

"That's for thinking a bad haircut or an ugly dress would scare me off."

Another smack and I bit my lip to keep quiet.

"That's for distracting me all fucking week, thinking about

you in the shower, tightening up around my fingers, moaning my name."

He smoothed his hand over my skin, soothing me. I was soaked, dripping, and my face burned with heat.

I was melting. That was the only explanation for why I was enjoying this so much. I hadn't had a drop to drink but I felt drunk, like my mind was spinning with pleasure and adrenaline.

"And this—" His hand slid from my backside to between my legs, massaging over my clit. I moaned with relief. "—is for taking care of me when I was sick."

His pressure was *just* right. Enough to make my hips tilt up for more.

One finger pushed inside me and my eyes rolled back as he stroked in and out.

"Jesus *fuck*, you are tight. I love that this is mine," he ground out.

I huffed. "You wish."

Behind me, he laughed and added another finger, stroking me and making my mind go blank. He found the spot he'd found in the shower and pressed.

"*Finn*," I gasped.

"There we go."

My back arched.

His other hand palmed my ass while he fingered me. "Your ass is so perfect. You look so pretty like this, bent over for me. You're soaking my hand, Liv, do you know that?"

I was so wet, I could hear his fingers moving in and out of me. Heat twisted between my legs and I moaned. On the bar top, my hands tensed.

Something warm brushed my clit—Finn's tongue.

"Finn," I gasped again, eyes wide and unseeing as my hips tilted for more.

"Yeah? Didn't mind that, huh?"

"God, I hate your stupid, cocky voice." I groaned. "Do that again."

I heard his low chuckle before his tongue returned to my clit, swiping lazily, and I winced at how good it was. Warm, liquid and pleasurable. He groaned and drew circles against the tight bud of nerves.

"You taste like heaven, just like I remember. So fucking sweet."

He pressed harder on my G-spot while the warmth and softness of his tongue made my head spin. My hands pressed harder into the countertop and I squeezed his finger, eager for more. I was going to burst out of my skin.

I moaned. "Please."

"Please, what?" His words were muffled against my pussy and his breath tickled me.

God, I could picture his stupid grin right now. A fading part of my brain snarled at his smug, satisfied tone. The rest of me needed release. "Please, let me come," I moaned, forehead on the bar. "Please, Finn."

He straightened up and I missed the heat of his mouth on me immediately. I groaned with frustration.

"Call me baby."

"Baby," I gasped. Anything. Anything to come.

"Say this means something."

"What?" I lifted my head.

His hands were off me immediately. "You want me to stop?"

"No. Fuck, no." My cheek returned to the bar, and a moment later, his hand came to the back of my neck, gentle but firm.

"Say. It. Means. Something." His voice was sandpaper, gritty and rough. "Say this is special. I'm yours, Liv, and I want to hear it." His thumb stroked the side of my neck and I shuddered. His gaze weighed me down while I was bent over the counter for him. "Make it convincing this time."

My mind swirled, fixated on the pleasure between my legs, just out of grasp.

"It means something." His finger swiped my clit and I bucked. "It's special." Another slick swipe, making my hips shake. "Oh, fuck, I'm so close, Finn."

"Keep talking."

"I'm yours. I'm yours, Finn. Please make me come. Please."

His fingers moved back and forth too slow, holding me *right* at the edge. Was this how I died? I couldn't stay here forever, I was tearing apart at the seams as his fingers glided over my sensitive nerves.

"Are you my good girl?"

"*Yes.*"

"Are you going to come on my fingers?"

"Uh-huh." God, I wasn't even fighting it anymore. That girl I used to be, the one who put up barriers, she was miles away.

"Are you going to stop fighting this between us?"

I moaned an acknowledgement. "Please."

"You know what I want to hear."

"We're together for real." My voice was thin and full of need. He had me right where he wanted me. "No more fighting it."

He groaned. "Fuck, you look so good when you let go for me. Every time you're back here, I want you to think about this. Think about my fingers in your pussy, think about my hand on your neck, think about my tongue on your pretty little clit."

With that perfect pressure on the back of my neck, holding me down, he swirled his fingers fast over my clit. The pressure built quickly and a moan tore out of me. My release barreled through me and I pulsed around nothing as my thoughts scattered in the air in a burst of sparks. My focus was on his fingers, his low voice in my ear, urging me on, saying *yes* and *good girl* and *there you go, look at you, so fucking pretty when you come*.

When the pleasure had drained out of me, I shuddered against the countertop, heaving for air. "Oh my god."

I was boneless and stupid. Not a thought left in my head. Finn leaned over me and I felt his heat against my back as he kissed the top of my spine. My brain swam with warm, happy sluggishness and I grinned against the counter.

"Thanks," I mumbled, wishing we were in a bed right now so I could curl into him.

"We're not done."

"Hmm?"

"You're going to do it again."

35

Olivia

I LIFTED my head and made a noise like *whahuhh?* but his hand pressed me back down against the counter and his mouth returned to my slick center.

"I can't," I gasped, eyes clenched closed, writhing as his tongue stroked me. Fuck, I was so sensitive.

"You can, and you will. I know you can." He sounded so certain. "I want you to come on my mouth and that's what I'm going to get. We'll stay right here until sunrise if we have to."

The delicious threat melted into my blood and my inner muscles tightened. He laughed, low and dark.

I should have been humiliated. This shouldn't have been so hot.

"You love that idea. You like thinking about me worshipping this pussy until the sun comes up and people start knocking on the door."

He made a noise of appreciation as he licked my clit in steady strokes. "God, you're so wet and sweet. Love how you get so wet when you come." His fingers pushed back into me while his tongue worked and my eyes went wide.

I felt that familiar pressure low in my stomach. Oh, shit.

This was working. My thighs were damp as more heat thrummed between my legs. I squirmed, bent over, pushing further onto Finn's mouth as he fucked me with his fingers at a demanding pace.

His other hand palmed my ass and I moaned, clenching.

"Oooh, there we go. Squeeze me like that, Liv. I can't wait to fuck you hard." He sucked my clit and I bucked. "I'm going to fuck you in front of a mirror so you get used to seeing us like this."

The image of it sent more heat, more pressure, more wetness to my core and I arched, forehead on the bar.

Holy shit. He sucked hard and my second orgasm closed in on me.

"Is my good girl going to come again for me?" He sucked more pressure on my clit and I broke, crying out and writhing against his mouth and fingers, pulsing around his hand, soaking his face while he groaned and let me ride it out on his face. My vision turned white and a cool chill ran down the back of my legs, like my nerves were fraying.

I tumbled back to Earth with four brain cells left.

"Holy fuck," I panted, slumped over the bar.

"Come here." His voice was low and soft. His hand snaked beneath my chest and pulled me up, turned me, and wrapped me against his chest.

I moaned, sinking into his warmth, face against his shirt, huffing in his scent. He lifted his hand and sucked the wetness off his fingers with a low groan.

"Fuck, that's good."

I'd be thinking about that later, his expression as he tasted my orgasm on his hand. I tilted my face up and gave him a lazy smile. He stared down at me like I was everything to him. The fierce, possessive look in his eyes burned me, and my hand came to the front of his pants.

His lips parted as I stroked his thick length through his jeans.

Finn had big dick energy because he had a big dick. I remembered how it felt that night, filling me, stretching me, pushing into me and eventually *driving* into me. My mouth watered and my hands came to his belt, holding eye contact with him.

His eyes darkened. One of his brows arched, and I shot him my own wicked smile. He leaned against the counter, hands braced at either side while I fumbled with his belt. The bastard wouldn't even help me, wanted to watch me struggle, and even though that was kind of fucked, I liked it.

I liked that he was in charge.

Fuck. I'd deal with that later. I got his belt undone, slipped my hand in and wrapped it around his straining length.

He made a noise in his throat, watching me with that dark, hot, hungry expression. I squeezed the base and he groaned, long and low.

"Take your shirt off," I whispered. "I want to see you while I suck your cock."

His eyes darkened further, and the corner of his mouth turned up. "Say please."

Asshole. I stroked his length. His skin was like fire, so warm. "Please."

He reached over his head and pulled the shirt off, messing up his hair, making me smile. I lowered to my knees and he swore. His cock was long, thick, and beading with pre-cum.

"You look so good on your knees, Liv." His eyelids drooped. "Dreamed about this."

I held his gaze, watching the flare of heat in his eyes as I licked the drop off the tip.

He bit his lip and shook his head slowly. "Don't you dare torture me, baby. I've been so patient."

I shot him a little smile and nodded. "You have." I licked a long line up his cock and he shuddered.

His hand came to the back of my head and without a word, I opened my mouth and let him push between my lips.

He groaned, head falling back as I took him to the back of my throat.

"My fucking *god*, Liv. Your mouth."

I let my tongue run up the bottom of his shaft as my mouth bobbed back and forth, slow at first while I kept my gaze on him. The ink on his abs rippled, tightening as he watched me. His hand rested on the back of my head, letting me lead, light enough pressure to make me wet all over again. To remind me that he was in charge.

I slipped my tongue over the sensitive tip and he groaned again. His other hand came to the back of my head.

"Yes, baby. Like that." His head fell back before he snapped it up, eyes trained down at me on my knees for him. "You're so pretty with my cock between your lips."

Pleasure weaved through my veins and I sucked, hollowing out my cheeks, taking his length in my mouth while his chest heaved.

He let out a sharp laugh. "Not going to last when you look and feel like that."

I hummed an acknowledgement, grinning around him, and stroked his base harder while I took him deeper.

"Liv." His voice was strained. His fingers dug into my scalp and his hips began to shuttle back and forth, and we found a rhythm as he fucked my mouth with his thick length.

I loved every second of it. I loved having him at my mercy, even for those few moments.

"Gonna come," he gritted out, watching me with furrowed brows and a tight jaw.

No wicked grin in sight, I noticed.

His expression turned to agony and disbelief as his abs tensed and he came in my mouth. His low, drawn-out groan was the best thing I'd ever heard.

"Swallow," he said through a clenched jaw. "Every drop, Liv. That's yours."

He held my head, kept his thick cock in my mouth while I

did as I was told. Embarrassment and pleasure twisted through me. My face warmed and I knew I was blushing but I couldn't tear my gaze from Finn's. His eyes blazed with heat as they pinned me.

"Jesus Christ, you're a sight." He hauled me up to standing and kissed me hard, tongue slipping into my mouth. I could taste our orgasms and from his low, pleased groan and the way he deepened our kiss, sucking on my tongue, he could too.

Our kiss broke and he began to put my clothes to rights, straightening my top and doing my fly up, and I did the same for him, ignoring the panic sitting at the edge of my consciousness at how intimate this was. His hands landed on my shoulders, slipping up to frame my face.

When he put his hands on my face and gazed down at me like I was the only person in the world, I forgot all the reasons Finn and I shouldn't be together.

"Never letting you go." He searched my eyes, stroking the sides of my face. "How do you feel about that?"

I quirked my eyebrows at him, smiling. "Fine."

He snorted, shaking his head, but he smiled and it reached his eyes. "We'll work on that answer." He pressed a soft kiss to my mouth and my heart squeezed.

Finn led me upstairs to my apartment. He sat on the edge of the tub while I brushed my teeth, watching with a little smile, then he climbed into my bed, eyes all over my body while I changed into a sleep shirt.

"Getting comfortable?" I asked with raised eyebrows. Sarcastic on the outside, but on the inside, my heart leaped at the idea of him spending the night.

Olivia, you stupid, stupid woman.

"I'm sleeping here," he said, holding the covers back for me.

I climbed in and he pulled me into his chest, tucking the covers around me. He watched my face with pure affection while I settled against him, heavy, floaty, and drowsy. His hand came to my hair, brushing it back, and I gave him a small smile.

"Goodnight," I whispered.

"Goodnight, Livvy."

While Finn fell asleep, my mind whirred with thoughts.

What if Finn was going to stay? What if a judgement from years ago wasn't fair, and he had grown up?

What if we were meant to be together, and if I didn't take this chance with him, I'd never get another one? Anxiety twisted in my stomach at the thought.

It was so easy with Finn. When I let go, he caught me. He was right there, waiting and thrilled, and all I had to do was jump.

A thought pierced through and my breath caught. It was too late. If Finn left, he'd take half of me with him. The stupid plan to get him to dump me wasn't working.

I was falling back in love with Finn Rhodes, whether I wanted to or not. The guy was sleeping beneath me in my bed, and I couldn't be more content.

This was a disaster. I should be running, packing up my belongings and moving to the next town to get away from him.

Never letting you go, he had said, and I wanted it to be true more than anything.

I didn't want to run anymore. I wanted to jump, and I wanted Finn to catch me. I'd held on to *Finn is evil* for so long that letting go of it made my throat knot, but what if it didn't serve me anymore? What if it was in the way of something better?

In my head, I saw my mom's narrowed eyes of disapproval when she found out Finn and I were back together for real, and my stomach churned.

I didn't want to think about this anymore. I shifted on his chest, shoving the thoughts from my head, and took a deep breath. For the first time in my life, I didn't need to have a plan. I didn't need everything mapped out. It fit, didn't it? I had no fucking clue where the flower was, had no idea where I was going to work or live come October, and I couldn't force Finn to stay in town. I would never want someone to stick around out of obligation. I'd rather be alone.

So what if I went along with it, floated with the current and enjoyed being with Finn? Perhaps I wouldn't try so hard to control everything.

Maybe it was my turn to be reckless.

36

Finn

"WHERE'S YOUR TENT?" Liv asked as we loaded our gear into her car a week later. The sun was rising, washing shades of pink across the sky.

I straightened up and closed the trunk, holding her gaze. "I didn't bring one."

Silence stretched as we stared at each other. She pulled her bottom lip between her teeth, and the corner of my mouth hitched.

This past week had been different. She was different. Lighter. Less guarded. At the bar, she had actually smiled at me a few times.

In public.

She still rolled her eyes at me, gave me that long stare when I irritated her, but now, she did it with a playful smile on her lips, like she was enjoying it.

"That okay with you?" I asked, keeping my voice low and my eyes on her.

She lifted one shoulder in a shrug, eyes glittering. "Fine."

I took a step toward her, smiling down at her. "I take my role of keeping you warm *very* seriously."

She suppressed a grin. "Good." Her tone was soft but bossy.

I dropped a quick kiss onto her lips, stepping away before she could pull me closer. "Let's go. If we start fooling around, we'll never leave."

She huffed a laugh, and I knew I was right.

———

"WE CAN SPREAD out more if you want," I said to her that afternoon as we made our way down a hillside to a creek Liv had flagged on her map. I arched a brow at her as she leaned a hand on a nearby tree for balance and stepped over a log. "Cover more ground."

She shook her head. "It's okay."

I glanced over at her, pink hair swept up in a ponytail, bangs fluttering around her face. "Worried you'll get lost?"

She snorted. "Fuck you."

I smiled down at the ground as I stepped over a gnarled tree root. It was happening, things with Liv and me. Behind the warm pulse in my chest, panic dripped into my blood, one drop at a time, barely detectable, and I heard the same voice I'd heard years ago.

The last thing Olivia needs is a guy like you dragging her down.

My gut boiled. Where it mattered, I wasn't that guy anymore. So I had a few speeding tickets. So I ran my bike over Miri Yang's roses when I was sixteen. Even the stuff the kids in that class dug up, the picture of me smoking weed and the night in the drunk tank—none of that mattered. That was the old version of me.

I cocked a smug grin at her, the one that she both hated and loved. "It's okay, baby. Stick close to me, I'll protect you."

She tried to give me a cold glare but her mouth turned up. "This cocky thing isn't working for you."

I winced. "I think it is."

Being there for Liv, supporting her in her career, making her dreams come true, cooking her dinner at night. Those were the important things. Everything else was in the past.

"Whatever." Twin flushes appeared on her cheeks and she rolled her eyes. "Have fun sleeping on the ground tonight."

I crowed with laughter and she grinned, eyes glittering in the clear forest light.

———

THAT EVENING AFTER DINNER, we sat by the fire, roasting marshmallows. The sky was an inky blanket above us, punctured by an infinite number of stars, and beside me, Liv wore my hoodie. I smiled down at her.

Her wearing my hoodie sent a ripple of possessive pride through me.

"What?" She gave me a strange look. There was a little piece of marshmallow at the corner of her mouth so I lowered my head and licked it off. Her breath shuddered out of her.

I quirked a smile down at her before turning back to the stars.

She stuck another marshmallow on the stick. "The Thompsons keep asking me for another date."

My chest shook with laughter. "I know. Shannon found me at the bar and I said to talk to you about it."

"Thanks." She gave me a flat look.

My head fell back as I laughed. "Baby, this one's all on you."

"I know," she groaned.

A thought flicked into my head. "We should take your parents out for dinner."

She stiffened. In her lap, her hands came together, twisting. "Why?"

A knot formed in my throat but I ignored it. "Because I

want your mom to get to know me. Or, the grown-up version of me." Jen's face at the class presentation appeared in my head, amused but not impressed. "When she knew me, I was just a stupid kid." My gaze lingered on Liv. "I want her to be on board with us."

"Maybe." She shrugged, studying the stick she was using to roast marshmallows. "It's still new to us, you know?"

Unease threaded through my gut and I frowned. "What's new about it? We've been friends since before we could walk. Your mom should have known we'd find our way back to each other."

An unwelcome thought rose in my head. Liv still had reservations about us.

I folded my arms over my chest and my brow furrowed.

Her hands twisted. "I want to give it a bit more time. I'm not saying no, I'm saying… not right now. I want things to be easy."

Her eyes pleaded and I nodded. "Okay. I get it."

I had hurt her, and now I had to be patient.

"Thanks." Her teeth worried that pretty bottom lip but her shoulders inched down in relief. Her eyes searched my face a moment. "Can I ask you a question?"

I nodded.

"Why did you go cliff jumping that night?" she asked, voice soft.

In an instant, I was transported back to that night. The terror I felt, the shame, the worry that she'd see who I was and toss me aside. I raked a hand back through my hair as I put an answer together.

"I was terrified," I told her. "I, uh." My chest tightened. "I liked you for so long and then it was real. A part of me knew I wasn't good enough for you." Our eyes met. "I'm still not."

She frowned. "Don't say that."

"I wasn't drunk."

She stared at me in confusion. "What?"

I blew a breath out, wincing at the dark forest. "I wasn't drunk when I got home. I'd had two beers over two hours."

Her eyes narrowed. "But you tripped when you got out of the car. I saw you."

"I *did* trip, but that was because I'd left my bike across the path to the front door, and I didn't see it."

"You were slurring your words," she whispered. "You slumped against the door."

Shame snaked through my gut, and I swallowed with difficulty. My heart was banging in my chest. "I did that on purpose."

"Why?" Her eyes were wide.

"When we told each other—" I cut myself off, not ready to say it again. "I wanted you to hate me. It was easier that way, Liv. It was just a matter of time before you saw me the way your mom did, the way everyone else did. So I left before you could leave me."

"And now?" Her voice was quiet.

"And now I'm willing to take that risk." I thought about her biological father in the bar. "I'm not Cole." Anger weaved through my chest and I shook my head to myself. "I'd never leave you, never leave our kid." The image of Liv with our baby was almost too sweet to picture, and the idea of leaving her again, leaving *them*, made my stomach churn. "Jesus, Liv. I can't even think about doing that. Even if you wanted out, I wouldn't leave town again. I'd buy the house next door and watch you raise our kid with some other guy if I had to." I scrubbed my hands down my face, dragging air into my lungs. "Fuck. I hate that idea."

Her hand was on my thigh. "Stop picturing it. That's not going to happen."

The tension in my chest eased a notch. "I fucked up, Liv. I fucked up in so many ways, but I'm trying to fix it." I turned to meet her gaze. "Do you understand?"

She nodded.

"Good." My voice was low while I stared into the fire, arms crossed, and a second later, Liv pulled my arm out and took my hand. I studied our joined palms, fingers laced, the nails on her delicate hand. My thumb stroked back and forth across her skin as my pulse slowed.

"What did you mean by the way my mom saw you?" she asked, frowning.

The knot was back in my throat. With my free hand, I rubbed the side of my jaw. "Remember that time we got in trouble in grade twelve for skipping?"

Her eyes narrowed as she remembered. "Yeah. We got ice cream."

I nodded. "It was the first nice day of the year."

She huffed a light laugh. "Right. We were so stir crazy after a month of rain."

"Mhm." I squeezed her hand, remembering how we ate our ice creams in the marina in town, letting the sun warm our faces. When we returned for the last class of the day, we both got called to the principal's office, and our parents had to pick us up. "Before you left with your mom, she pulled me aside."

I repeated the words to Liv, words I had repeated so many times to myself. In the past, during a weak moment when I thought about calling her, they'd ring in my head. I knew that sentence by heart, better than my own name.

"*Dragging me down*?" she repeated, face falling. "Why would she say that?"

I tilted my head, giving her a dry look. "Come on, Liv. I got you in trouble so many times."

She blanched. "And I willingly went along with your bad ideas. I could have left. I could have said no. I could have ditched you a thousand times." She shook her head at me. "Finn, what the fuck?" Her eyes flashed with frustration and anger, and she pulled her hand out of mine before she slapped my chest.

"Wha—?" She smacked my arm and I let out a yelp of surprise, jerking back. "Are you mad at *me*?"

She stared hard at me. "*Yes*." She grabbed her marshmallow-roasting stick and whipped it at my boot.

I squawked a laugh and threw my hands up. My mind whirled. I had just confessed one of my darkest, deepest secrets and she was slapping me?

"Why?"

"Oh my god." She tossed the stick aside before closing her eyes and rubbing the bridge of her nose. "Because you *believed her*." She shook her hands out, inhaling a deep breath. "I'm so fucking mad at you right now. All of this because you believed something someone said about you."

"It's not just Jen. Everyone says it. Even my mom calls me the devil, Liv."

Her throat worked and she nodded to herself. "Yeah. I guess so."

She exhaled before scooting closer to me. Her hand slipped back into mine and her head settled onto my shoulder, and the worry and tension that had me by the throat as I told her the truth began to fall away.

"I missed you," she whispered. "I hated you but I also missed you, and I'm happy you're back."

A pulse hit me square in the chest and I smiled. "Me, too."

"I like the cartoons. I save them all."

"Yeah?"

She nodded, hiding her smile. "Yeah."

I switched hands so I could loop my arm around her shoulder to keep her warm. We were quiet for a few minutes, staring at the fire, watching sparks crack and arc in the air before fading out.

In moments like this, with Liv's head on my chest, our fingers intertwined, everything felt right. It was like the universe was finally putting the puzzle pieces of our lives into place.

My mind wandered back to Liv's bad haircut, the date with the Thompsons, and the ugly clothes. She'd stopped avoiding me after that night in the bar, and after tonight, when she admitted she missed me?

It felt like she was all in.

Wariness surged in my blood, and I really fucking hoped Liv didn't have something up her sleeve. She'd crush me.

I turned my head and pressed a kiss into her hair, inhaling her scent. After what I did, I deserved it.

When the fire burned down to the ashes and Liv could barely keep her eyes open, we climbed into the tent. She reached for me, but I held her wrists.

"You're tired," I told her. "You're half asleep already."

She made an unhappy noise. "What's the point of us staying in the same tent then?" She sounded pissed, and it made me grin. Maybe she was thinking about the other night in the bar as often as I was.

Fuck, that had been hot, her bent over and submitting to me. The number of times I'd jerked off thinking about that in the last week was obscene.

"Come here," I said, pulling her to me so we were spooning. My hand slipped into the front of her leggings and she moaned as I found her clit. "You're wet already. How'd that happen?"

"Shut up," she murmured, grumpy, and I grinned and massaged her. Her ass ground into my cock and my balls ached. "Did you bring condoms?"

"No, because we're not doing that tonight." I pressed kisses up the side of her neck and felt her shudder. "When we finally fuck again, I'm going to take my time."

She shuddered under my touch. "Rude."

I slipped two fingers inside her and she whimpered. My other hand was under her top, pinching her nipples, making her gasp, and within minutes, she was an arching, moaning mess, calling my name and pulsing around my fingers, soaking my hand.

When she was done, I sucked her release off my fingers. She tried to turn around but I held her to my chest. "No. Go to sleep."

She wiggled under my arms and I laughed as she fought me before she relented, sinking back into me.

"I'll get you back," she mumbled, half asleep.

"Yeah? How?"

"I'm going to take you on another date."

"Pass. Your dates are terrible. It's my turn."

"I like torturing you." Her words slurred with sleep.

I grinned and pulled her closer, keeping her warm. She wasn't trying to get me to dump her anymore, she was toying with me. I liked her torturing me, too, and even if she dragged me on another terrible date, I'd gladly go just to spend more time with her.

37

Olivia

"DOT'S GOT A SET OF LUNGS," my dad commented from behind the counter as we watched her sing Bon Jovi's 'Living on a Prayer' at the bar's karaoke night.

I smiled as the bar patrons cheered her on. She didn't even need the lyrics on the screen, she knew all the words.

"When I sell this place," my dad continued, "I'm going to stipulate that the new owner needs to do at least four karaoke nights per year. They're so fun."

I grinned. When my parents were traveling last year, we didn't do karaoke night. I had enough going on with training Sadie, ordering, inventory, and payroll. I hadn't heard the end of it though. My dad *loved* karaoke night.

My dad gave me a side-long look. "You feeling okay about all of that?"

"About you selling the bar?" I arched a brow.

He nodded.

I thought about what my mom had said, and what Finn had said about how he only wanted to see me happy.

"Yeah," I said, giving him a small smile. "I know you'll pick the right person."

"Good. You know I love you, right?"

I nodded, smiling wider. "Yep." My throat was tight with emotion. "I love you, too."

He pressed a quick kiss to my temple before walking away to introduce the next karaoke singer. A server dropped off a table's order and I got to work mixing drinks.

My conversation with Finn resurfaced in my mind. I'd been replaying it over the past week, thinking about how different life might have been if we hadn't kept secrets over the past decade. If he'd told me what my mom had said, if I told him that I missed him earlier… round and round I went, picturing different scenarios.

It broke my heart, hearing what my mom had said to Finn. I hadn't talked to her since we got back from the hike. I didn't know what I would say. She didn't realize what she had done, but she had hurt Finn, helped him believe he wasn't enough, and in the process, she had hurt me too.

In my mind, I saw Finn sitting by the fire, hair falling across his forehead, eyes shining in the firelight. He was so beautiful, it made my heart hurt.

My mouth hitched as I turned and glanced at the cartoon he had left on the bar for me tonight. I'd tucked it onto a shelf above the bar to keep it safe. Two birds holding hands with hearts swirling around their heads. This thing between us was becoming bigger than I had expected. Once I let go, once I let it grow out of my grasp, it was so easy between us. It felt meant to be.

I smiled to myself as I shook the cocktail shaker.

Finn was making me feel whole again.

Another person had been sneaking into my head lately— Cole. With Finn, I had been so certain things were the way I perceived them, but there had been another side to that story. A whole other person to factor in with their own experience, feelings, and baggage.

When I was a kid, Cole was younger than I was at present. When I was five, he was twenty-five. He was a kid with a kid.

What if I lived my entire life without knowing him because of some stupid misunderstanding?

I kept hearing Finn's voice saying how miserable Cole had seemed in Whistler. Maybe he regretted things with me and my mom.

Anxiety tightened in my chest but I breathed through it. I had to see for myself, or I might always regret it.

A woman about my age slipped onto the bar stool in front of me. Her long red hair was loose around her shoulders, and her tall, willowy frame made her navy blazer and dress shirt look like a magazine ad. She met my gaze with a tired expression.

"Hi," I said, raising my eyebrows at her.

"I need booze," she responded, leaning on her elbows, rubbing her temples. "All of that," she added, referring to the liquor bottles stocked behind me.

I snorted. "Bad day?"

Her eyelashes fluttered as she frowned. "I have no idea. Long day, I guess." She ordered an old-fashioned and I got to work. "I had an interview," she added as I gathered ingredients. "For my dream job." She winced and shook her head. "Sorry, I don't talk to bartenders. I'm not that person."

I laughed again and shrugged. "I don't care. You can talk to me."

This happened sometimes, people coming in alone to chat. Again, my mind flicked to Cole sitting alone in a bar, unloading his problems to the bartender. That joke that bartenders were a drunk's therapist? It wasn't a joke. I'd heard everyone in Queen's Cove's problems at some point.

"How'd the interview go?"

She leaned her chin on her palm. "No idea. I couldn't read the interviewer at all." She waved a hand over her face, making a blank expression. "He gave me nothing."

I wrinkled my nose. "Bummer." I slid her the drink.

"Yeah." She held it up to me. "Thanks. Cheers."

My eyes narrowed, studying her. I didn't recognize her. "You're not from here, right?"

She shook her head. "Vancouver. Well, a small town in Northern BC before that, but Vancouver for the last ten years." She bit her lip. "I don't know if I'm ready to go back to small-town life."

I laughed to myself, thinking about all the stupid antics that went on in this town. "That's fair. Queen's Cove can be a lot."

I glanced around the bar at Dot sitting at a table full of regulars, making them laugh with stories from her life. At my dad talking about sports with his friends at another table. I thought about Miri shrieking at the sky as the plane with the banner flew overhead.

"If you get the job, you should take it," I told her with a shrug and a smile. "The people in this town are special. They're weird," I added and she laughed, "but they're special. You might like it here."

She watched me for a moment with a small smile. "Thanks. I'll think about it."

———

THE NEXT HOUR PASSED QUICKLY, and I stayed busy mixing drinks, keeping the bar clear, and chatting with regulars.

"Hi, sweetheart."

My head whipped up from where I was restocking limes. Elizabeth leaned on the counter. The apples of her cheeks popped with her smile.

"Hi." I swallowed, and my stomach clenched.

For years, I'd been dodging Elizabeth Rhodes. She'd ask if I wanted to get coffee to catch up and I'd shut her down. She'd compliment my hair or my outfit and I'd freeze her out. I had wanted nothing to do with Finn's mom, who was so sweet and nice and warm. I'd admitted to Sadie once that it always felt like she held a candle for Finn and me, like she was waiting for us to get back together, and I couldn't take the pressure.

"I won't bother you." Her hands came to her necklace as she took me in. Elizabeth had this funny way of looking at people like she was admiring them. It had always made me feel like shrinking into the background, but tonight I stood my ground. "I wanted to see if Finn was here."

"He's at the fire hall."

"Oh." She shrugged. "Okay, I'll try to catch him tomorrow. Bye, honey." She waved.

"Wait."

She stopped and turned, eyebrows raised.

I chewed my lip. A strange, nervous energy flowed in my blood. "We have a new red," I told her.

She blinked at me. "Oh."

"Lambrusco. It's sparkling, which is weird, but it's good. My dad calls it trash wine, but it's not. It's good," I repeated. "The bubbles are tiny. It's fizzy and fun."

She tilted her head, watching me with a funny smile like she thought I was cute but strange. She reminded me of Finn right now, amused and entertained by me.

For years when I ran into her, I always saw Finn's impish, wicked smile, and I never wanted her to get her hopes up about me and Finn.

"You might like it." I cleared my throat. "I'll have a glass with you."

She watched me for a long moment and I felt like I might crawl out of my skin under the intensity of her gaze, but she dropped her bag on a stool and hopped onto the one beside it.

"I'd *love* a glass, honey. You know I love a weird wine."

I snorted. "Yeah. I do."

"So," Elizabeth said as I poured her a glass. "I can't wait for Sadie's baby shower."

I burst out laughing and we smiled at each other. "It'll be memorable, I'm sure."

While karaoke continued, I hung out behind the bar, chatting with Elizabeth while we drank wine and I mixed drinks for other customers. It was nice, being able to chat openly with her, and for once, I didn't mind that she was holding out for Finn and me.

Elizabeth checked the time. "I should get home. I have book club in two days and I haven't even started the book."

She told me the title of the book and some of the plot, and my jaw was on the floor.

"Hannah and I had a romance book club," Elizabeth explained, "and then we merged with Miri and Don's book club. It's easier that way."

An idea hit me and I narrowed my eyes at her. "Can anyone join?"

She brightened. "Absolutely. We're meeting Sunday afternoon in Hannah's bookstore."

"Great." My smile stretched wide as delight and mischief spread through my chest. "See you there."

38

Olivia

ON SUNDAY AFTERNOON, I led Finn down the street to our next date.

"What are you grinning about?" Finn murmured in my ear, wrapping his arm around my shoulder.

"Just excited to take you on a romantic date." I flattened my mouth so I wouldn't laugh.

God, I couldn't wait to see his face when he figured it out. I'd given up trying to get him to dump me, but I still loved trying to rattle him.

A little part of me wanted to see how he'd react, too. Would he get me back? In my mind, I heard the smack of his hand on my ass.

"Cold?"

"Hmm?" I looked up at him. "What?"

"You shivered." His eyes glittered. Even though there was a light breeze coming off the nearby marina, the sun was warm and pleasant.

"Oh." My face heated and I hid my smile. "Nope. Not cold."

His gaze flicked down the t-shirt dress I had on. I didn't wear skirts or dresses often but something about Finn holding off on us having sex made me want to tease him a bit. His eyes lingered on the neckline, pinning me with something focused and hungry.

We stopped in front of Pemberley Books, Hannah's bookstore.

"We're here," I told Finn, stomach bubbling and fizzing with excitement.

God, I couldn't wait to fuck with him.

He narrowed his eyes at the store but I pulled him inside.

Hannah's bookstore was gorgeous. Her mom had started it when Hannah was a baby, and after she passed, Hannah and her dad ran it. A few years ago, with the help of Wyatt and his family, Hannah had fixed it up into something whimsical. The wallpaper burst with big flowers, fluffy lighting hung from the ceilings, and the bookshelves were new, sturdy, and gleaming. Outside, a bright, spectacular mural decorated the side of the building. She sold only romance books, because that was her favorite genre and the books made people happy.

Hannah had changed when she and Wyatt got closer. She had always been painfully shy, but remembering her belting out the Spice Girls at the bar karaoke night always brought a smile to my face. Wyatt helped her come out of her shell and shine brighter.

Hannah processed a customer's sale at the desk while Wyatt wandered the store with Cora in his arms. She was pointing at all the different book covers and babbling while Wyatt watched her with a sweet, adoring expression. Cora waved at her mom and Hannah beamed and waved back.

Is that what happened when you fell in love? You turned into a better, brighter version of yourself? My stomach flipped as I glanced at Finn and he sent a wink back at me.

Being with Finn made me better. He made me less grumpy and more playful, and everything was more fun. Around him, I couldn't think of things to be grumpy about.

I couldn't even imagine how good it would be to feel like

this forever. It couldn't possibly last. The thought sent a chill through my blood.

Hannah glanced up.

"Hey, you two." She gave us an odd smile. "Are you here for the book club?"

I nodded. "We sure are."

Her eyes went wide and she bit back a grin, glancing at Finn. "Okay, then."

Finn nudged me. "Book club, huh? I know the kinds of books Hannah sells." His gaze flared and he lowered his voice to a whisper. "If you want me to read smut to you, Morgan, all you have to do is ask."

I coughed to hide my laugh. This was going to be so good.

At the back of the bookstore, a few people from town gathered. Miri and Don were there. Naya, the artist who painted the mural outside, was chatting with Thérèse, one of Hannah's friends.

"Oh, look," I said in a casual tone, tapping Finn's arm. "Dot's here." Dot chatted enthusiastically with a woman who worked at the grocery store.

Finn frowned. "Okay."

The door opened and Elizabeth walked in.

Beside me, Finn stiffened. "Mom."

She paused inside the door, regarding us with an amused smile. "Hello, Finn. Olivia."

I gave her a nod, glancing between her and Finn.

Finn's eyes narrowed and he glanced down at me. "Are you kidding?"

"Nope."

He winced. "Is this going to be weird?"

"Yep."

He chuckled and shook his head. "Alright, you're on. I'm going to go chat with Wyatt for a bit."

I took a seat and watched him wander over to his brother and niece. Elizabeth took the seat beside me.

She studied me with that little smile. "Is this going to be a regular thing?"

"Probably not."

She smiled wider. "I figured as much. I'm beginning to think Finn isn't the only devil around here."

"I'm trying to expand his mind, Elizabeth." I adopted an innocent expression.

"I'm sure." Her eyes glittered and she opened her mouth to say something but hesitated, studying me.

I raised my eyebrows at her, waiting.

"I'm sure you'll be working but we're having a family dinner the last Friday of the month." Her smile lifted as she watched me. "We'd love for you to join."

She said it like she expected me to say no, the way I always said no.

"Sure," I told her. I had a shift but could easily find another bartender to fill in for me. "That would be great."

The apples of her cheeks popped as she smiled wider. "Excellent."

I nodded, and my gaze strayed to where Finn was holding Cora, bouncing her up and down while she laughed.

My heart squeezed. Holy hell, that was cute. Finn with a baby, being silly with her, smiling at her like that? My ovaries did backflips, begging for attention. I couldn't tear my eyes off them. Wyatt leaned against the bookshelf, glancing between his daughter and Hannah on the other side of the store, and a funny tension wrapped around my heart.

Longing.

For the first time, I wanted what they had.

Maybe I had always wanted it, I just never let myself consider it.

Finn blew a raspberry on Cora's belly and her giggling filled the entire store. I remembered what Finn had said about wanting to be all my firsts. Wanting to fill a house up with a bunch of kids.

I turned back around and clasped my hands together in my lap. Hesitation rattled my chest, like I was getting too close to a good thing and the bubble would pop, or I'd wake up from the dream.

Elizabeth pulled a paperback from her tote bag. The pages were littered with colored tabs, and she flipped to one of them.

Beside me, Finn took his seat as Wyatt and Cora waved goodbye to Hannah. Elizabeth's gaze flicked to Finn and mischief sparked in her eyes, reminding me of him.

She leaned in, close to my ear. "Shall we make this fun?"

Anticipation fluttered in my chest. "Yes, please."

Miri strode into the seating area and encouraged everyone to take their seats. "First, I'd like to welcome our two guests, Olivia and Finn." She smiled at us. "Welcome to this month's book club, where we will be discussing the third book in Rinalda Davenport's My Big Sexy Alien series, *The Warlord's Thunderous Desire*."

Oh my god. This was better than I could have *imagined*. It wasn't uncommon for Hannah to shove books at me; she had a knack for recommending the perfect book for each individual. When things at school were stressful, I'd read a few chapters before bed and it helped me forget about the endless list of things I had to do.

Some of those alien romances? They were *dirty* in the best way. I snuck a peek at Finn. His face was blank.

He had no freaking clue what was about to happen.

He slid an amused glance at me. "*Thunderous Desire*?" he mouthed, and I wiggled my eyebrows.

Miri flipped her book open. "We all know what we need to discuss first."

"The penises," Elizabeth said, and Finn snorted.

"Do we ever." Don threw his hands up. "They're getting out of hand. Literally. They're so big the main female character couldn't get both hands around it."

Finn's eyes were wide. "Wow."

Dot cut into the conversation. "One of my favorite tropes of alien romance is that they can go bareback." She nodded with enthusiasm. "It really is better."

Finn bowed his head and I smiled at Dot. Out of the corner of my eye, I saw Hannah put a hand over her mouth.

Elizabeth put her hand up. "I loved the plethora of *penises*," she announced. "And I agree, Dot, that bareback is the way to go as long as it's safe. For our guests, I'll read a quick description." She glanced to Finn. "Of the alien *penises*."

He winced.

Miri nodded as if Elizabeth was offering her a cup of tea. "We'd love that."

Elizabeth cleared her throat before reading from the page. "*His member was thick and long like a Subway sandwich.*"

Hannah snorted before she hid her face in her book. I couldn't help the huge grin on my face. This was going even better than I had hoped. Beside me, Finn stared at his mom in horror.

"*The sac hung heavy between his legs, swinging like two hefty water balloons,*" Elizabeth continued, ignoring Finn.

What a champ. She wasn't even laughing.

"*Thick liquid dripped from the tip of his gargantuan hog, indicating his desire for his mate. When Lily's wide eyes met with the intimidating member, it began to buzz.*"

Don and Miri broke into applause.

"A vibrating *penis* with a clit massager at the base," Elizabeth said, shaking her head in wonder. "The multitude of *penis* features in alien romance is perhaps my favorite part of the niche."

I held a giant laugh in. Finn's eyes burned my skin. It was like Elizabeth was trying to say *penis* as many times as possible.

"Shall we talk about the plot?" Thérèse asked.

"We'll get there," Miri assured her. "If there's time. I loved the author's use of peppermint-flavored semen."

Elizabeth nodded. "It seemed like it was a toothpaste consistency, didn't it?"

Don pointed at her, eyes wide. "Like toothpaste squirting out of the tube."

Beside me, Finn closed his eyes, probably trying to evaporate into the air or block this afternoon from his memory.

"*Toothpaste*," I whispered, and he met my gaze, shaking his head.

"*You are so dead*," he whispered back, and a thrill ran through me.

Elizabeth flipped through the pages to about three-quarters of the way through the book. "Let's discuss the inclusion of *butt stuff* in this novel."

Finn shook his head. "No," he begged his mom.

"Finn." She gave him a long look and I nearly burst out laughing. "Please be mature about this. In my experience, anal sex can be *quite* romantic."

A delirious laugh rose up my throat but I held it down. Across the circle, Hannah stared at me, shaking her head slightly with bright eyes.

I owe you, I mouthed at her, but she grinned, looking equal parts horrified and amused.

I'm used to it, she mouthed back, sliding her gaze to Don and Miri.

To Finn, I raised my eyebrows. *Giving in?*

He dragged in a deep breath like he was steeling himself for war before shaking his head.

Miri lit up. "What an exciting surprise that was. Who knew anal sex could be so romantic?"

"In *my* experience—" Elizabeth started.

"Welp, this is fucking horrifying." Finn grabbed my hand and stood. "We've got somewhere to be."

"So soon?" Elizabeth gave him a bright smile, and I saw that Finn had inherited every ounce of his troublemaking from this woman.

He hauled me to the door. "Thanks for having us," he called over his shoulder.

"Come back next month, we're discussing a polar bear shifter romance!" Miri's voice rang out as Finn pulled me through the door.

In the alley beside the bookstore, he backed me against the bright yellow mural with fire and amusement in his eyes.

"Did you find that funny?" he asked in a low voice.

"Yes." My voice was a whisper. A laugh sat right below my vocal cords. "I did."

He blinked slowly, holding my gaze. "So on the next date, we get to do whatever I want, right?"

My nerves spiked. "What do you mean?"

The cruel line of his mouth hooked up and something dangerous and playful flared in his eyes. Between my legs, heat coiled. I didn't think I'd ever had so much fun.

"I mean," he said, low and dark, "that you've had your fun, and next time we go out, I get to have my fun."

A thousand images projected in my mind of Finn and me naked, tangled in the sheets. Skin on skin. Chests heaving for air, his hand between my legs. His *tongue* between my legs, firm and unrelenting. Gripping his hair, shuddering around him as he thrust inside me.

"Okay." My voice was so quiet. "Fine."

"Good." His expression turned wicked and smug before he brightened up. "Hungry?"

I beamed at him and nodded.

———

WE SPENT the rest of the afternoon at The Arbutus, eating a late lunch and then sharing drinks with Emmett and Avery, talking and laughing on the patio.

We walked home down Main Street, and Finn took my

hand. My mind wandered back to my realization the other day about my biological father.

I peered up at him. "I'm going to reach out to Cole."

His eyebrows shot sky-high. "Really?"

I nodded, and when he squeezed my hand, I felt a boost of support, like the ground beneath my feet was more solid.

"What changed your mind?"

"You." I pulled my bottom lip between my teeth. "When we laid the cards all out on the table, there were two sides to the story." My shoulders lifted. "It wasn't right and wrong."

He was quiet a moment as we walked. "And you think that might be the case with Cole," he said quietly, and I nodded.

"I don't even know what I would say to him." My stomach twinged with worry. *Hi, remember me?*

Oh, god. What if he didn't remember me?

"Hey." Finn stopped and turned me to him, worry written on his face. "Whatever it is, we'll figure it out. I'll help you. We can call him together if you like."

It was so unfair how he could be such a devilish asshole one moment, and the next, he was the sweetest person I could ever imagine.

"Thanks," I whispered.

He winked at me, hands on my shoulders.

"Your mom invited me for dinner," I said with a little smile.

"Yeah?" His eyebrows lifted as he gauged my reaction. "And?"

I shrugged. "And I said yes."

His gaze bored into me. "Like, with everyone, or just us four?"

"She said family dinner, so I think that means everyone."

"Baby." His smile stretched ear to ear and my stomach did backflips.

I rolled my eyes. "Relax."

He walked me backwards until my back was against the

nearest wall and he was staring down at me with bright eyes. "This is big."

I shrugged. "Whatever." My hands were on his chest, smoothing over the fabric of his t-shirt, the ridges and muscles beneath.

"Mhm." His eyes danced as he dipped his head down. His hands threaded into the hair at the back of my neck and against my will I sighed, making his smug grin hitch higher. "This is big."

He kissed me against the wall. I melted under his touch, opening for him as we made out like teenagers for everyone to see. People passed us by and I didn't care.

I just liked being with him. I was falling for Finn Rhodes, slipping down the slope into a life with him, and I didn't want it to end.

39

Finn

WHEN WE PULLED up to our usual parking spot at the end of the old logging road a few days later, there were already seven cars there. People stood around in the early morning light, chatting and drinking coffee. Avery, Sadie, and Hannah gathered around the bed of Holden's truck, eating muffins, while Holden, Wyatt, Emmett, and Beck peered over a map. Aiden, a friendly, annoyingly good-looking guy who worked for Rhodes Construction, chatted with Joe and Jen.

"What's going on?" Liv asked, twisting around in her seat as I parked. "Why is half the town here?"

"I invited them." I killed the engine.

Her expression turned baffled. "Why?"

I chuckled. "So we can find the flower."

She stared at me, frowning, before opening the car door and stepping out. She stood watching everyone in confusion.

"Sadie and Holden aren't coming, they're just here to see everyone off, and I think Hannah and Wyatt can only stay out until the early afternoon. Beck, Aiden, Randeep, and a few others are going to camp with us."

Emotion rose in her eyes. "They are?"

I smiled at her and nodded. "Yep."

Another car of people pulled up behind us and a family poured out—Emmett's best friend Will and his wife, Nat. Will was our other neighbor growing up.

"Hey, Olivia!" Randeep passed Liv, decked out in his hiking gear. He lifted both hands up, giving her a double high-five. "Flower power!"

"Yeah," she said, watching him walk away with confusion all over her face. She turned back to me. "You did this?"

I shrugged. "I suggested it and people were interested."

A slow smile pulled up on her mouth, and her eyes softened. "Finn."

I opened the trunk and pulled our packs out. "It was nothing."

She came up behind me, wrapping her arms around me and leaning her head against my shoulder. "Thank you."

My heart thudded against the front wall of my chest, steady and strong, and my hands settled over hers.

———

THAT EVENING, a small group of us sat around the campfire, chatting and making s'mores. Across from me, Liv talked with Randeep but our gazes kept meeting over the fire. Her skin glowed in the firelight, and I was counting down the seconds until I could pull her against me in the tent and bury my face in her hair.

"Glad you could get away from the hospital," I said to Beck beside me.

He made a noise of acknowledgement and tipped back the last of his beer. "It wasn't easy. We can't catch up these days." He glanced at me. "Olivia was worried about you a few weeks ago when you were sick."

Again, my eyes met hers across the fire and her mouth curved up. She'd been so light and happy today, hiking with everyone. The old Liv was back again. I didn't know why I didn't think to invite people before.

When I turned back to Beck, he was glancing between Liv and me with a funny smile. "Must be nice."

"The prom king's having issues with the ladies?" My smile quirked up.

Beck was tall, like me and my brothers. The guy hit the gym regularly. People in town joked that he was Queen's Cove most eligible bachelor.

I arched a brow at him. "You save babies for a living and you have a boat. What's the issue?"

He shrugged. "Finding someone is one thing. Finding the *right* someone is another. Do you ever feel like…" He sighed and settled back against the log. "Like you're never going to meet someone interesting enough to spend your entire life with?"

I thought back to my years in the field, fighting forest fires. How I'd compare every girl in every bar to Liv but no one came close. Across the fire, she stuck her tongue out at me, fast as lightning, and I grinned.

"I can't say I do, buddy," I told him.

Beck snorted. "Of course not. Forget I said anything."

A pang of empathy threaded through my chest for him. Beck was a good guy. He deserved what I had with Liv.

"Is this the part where I'm supposed to tell you that love will find you when you least expect it?" I asked with a wry grin.

Beck's chest shook with laughter. "Wow. Thank you for the sage advice." He rolled his eyes. "Especially from the guy who's with his childhood sweetheart. So unexpected."

I smiled at the fire, gaze finding Liv once again.

"Hey," he said, "do you think this strippers thing is going to get out of hand?"

"Strippers?" I repeated, laughing. "What?"

He chuckled. "Miri organized a ladies' night at the

community center and hired male strippers to drive in from Victoria. Sadie's doing her baby shower there. I want to know if I need to be on-call that night." He winced. "Miri can get out of hand."

Ever since Liv dragged me to the book club and made me listen to my *mom* talk about alien dicks, I'd been waiting for an opportunity to get her back. A slow, wicked grin curled up on my mouth, and across the fire, Liv narrowed her eyes at me, smiling.

I had just found it.

40

Olivia

"YOU LOOK HOT," Sadie said, nodding with appreciation, wiggling her shoulders in the crowded community center.

She had insisted we sit in the front row. Music pumped through the sound system while people filed in the door and took their seats, and her eyes glittered in the dim lighting. Across her torso, a sash read *Hot Mama*.

She sipped her drink as her eyes came to my chest. "Your boobs look good in that dress."

My boobs *did* look good in this dress. It was a simple black t-shirt dress but the cotton was soft and clingy and the neckline dipped low. I had slipped a black velvet choker on, drawn a subtle but sharp winged liner, and added two coats of mascara.

A little flicker pulsed in my chest, wishing Finn could see me like this. Imagining how his eyes would flare, heat tugged on something low in my stomach.

I grinned. "So do you. What's Holden doing tonight?"

"Probably prowling outside."

We laughed.

"No, he's at home." She smiled and her hand rested on

her bump. "I told him not to wait up but I'm sure he will. He's very protective these days."

"More than normal?"

She rolled her eyes with a smile.

Avery and Hannah returned to the table with another round of drinks. Max, who worked with Avery, and Div, who worked with Emmett, sat at the table beside us. Elizabeth and a group of her friends, including Avery's mom, were at the next.

My gaze floated over the crowd. Half the town was here.

The music volume dropped and everyone rushed to take their seats. As the lights dimmed, the conversation faded out.

"Citizens of Queen's Cove," Emmett's voice came over the sound system, "are you ready?"

The crowd started screaming and we all turned to Avery with confused expressions.

She shrugged. "Miri asked him if he wanted to MC and he said he'd love to."

"They're handsome, they're ripped, and they work very, very hard to please," Emmett continued. A low beat started playing in the background. "All the way from Victoria, please welcome your entertainment for tonight!"

The crowd cheered and applauded, the music turned up, and five shirtless men strode on stage, wearing fitted gray sweatpants and sneakers, and carrying chairs. The second they appeared, the crowd went wild, and Sadie and I burst out laughing. The music turned up even louder and the men started dancing, thrusting and rolling their hips in time with the music. Dot immediately threw a handful of bills on stage, clapping with enthusiasm as a man in his twenties dropped to his knees in front of her, smiling at her.

In front of us, another dancer crawled toward me and Sadie. He eyed her sash and shot her a wink.

"Hey, Mama," he said with a grin, and she laughed.

The dancers spun their chairs on one leg before tilting

them back and thrusting against them in an insinuating way. Miri was almost jumping out of her seat with excitement.

"Why are they wearing sweatpants?" Sadie sipped her drink and peered at them with curiosity. "I thought they'd wear something like cowboy outfits."

One of the dancers stepped closer to us. The outline of his package was clearly visible beneath the fabric of his pants.

"Oh," I said, eyebrows going up. "I guess that's why."

He danced closer to Elizabeth, and she stood and tucked a twenty into his waistband, wearing a cheeky smile that looked like Finn's. She wiggled her eyebrows at me and I shook my head, laughing.

The guys performed a series of dances, eventually stripping down to glittery gold thongs, until Emmett announced an intermission, and everyone stood up to get more drinks and use the washroom.

Sadie leaned into our table. "This is so fun. I'm glad we got all dressed up. Getting checked out is good for the soul, even if we are all going home to our loves."

"Are we?" Hannah asked, watching me over the rim of her glass.

I shot her a weird expression. "Are we what?"

Her teal eyes glittered. "Are we all going home to our *loves*?"

My heart stuttered and I blinked. "Um." A funny, weird, pleased warmth melted into my blood.

Avery waved a hand. "Don't bug her about it." She cleared her throat, all business. "So, Olivia, tell us about Finn's dick."

I choked on my drink and we all started laughing.

"Yeah." Sadie toyed with a long lock of hair. "Does the family curse run down the whole line?"

Hannah's face flushed bright red but her eyes shined with laughter. I tried to hide it but my grin stretched ear to ear.

"He's your brother-in-law," I said, shaking my head. "You perverts."

Avery put her hands together and slowly moved them apart, glancing between me and her hands. "Say when."

We dissolved into another round of giggles.

"We haven't had sex yet," I admitted. I didn't tell them that Finn's cock had barely fit in my mouth.

Sadie's eyes bugged out. "What?"

"I mean, we slept together once when we were teenagers, but not in this decade. He's trying to…" I rubbed my forehead, frowning. "… go slow."

"Oh." Avery tilted her head, watching me with confusion.

Hannah's eyes sparkled. "Finn is trying to go slow," she repeated.

"Yep." My stomach fluttered at their surprise.

Finn, going slow for me. Finn, trying not to freak me out. Finn, who wanted me and would fight his instincts and desire for me so we could have something special long-term.

"Damn." Avery smiled down at her drink. "I thought he'd be banging down your door every night."

Sadie snorted and I rolled my eyes.

"Okay, folks." Emmett was back on the mic from backstage. "We have a *very* special surprise for you tonight. While our guests oil their muscles backstage, we have some additional entertainers for your viewing pleasure."

Miri glanced over at me with a smile, and alarm plucked in my stomach.

"Please welcome the Queen's Cove fire department!"

41

Olivia

I STARED with a mix of horror, shock, and amusement as six men from the fire department entered the stage in their full gear. The crowd went crazy, screaming and hollering and stamping their feet. Miri choked, having inhaled a feather from her boa.

Finn locked eyes with me from the stage and shot me that wicked grin.

I couldn't breathe.

Sadie howled with laughter. "What?" she shrieked, laughing into her hands. "Did you know about this?"

"No," I squawked, unable to tear my gaze from Finn's.

Unlike the professional dancers before, the fire department didn't have choreography, but as the song played, they slowly peeled clothing off until they were stripped down to their boxer briefs.

The crowd ate it up. I'd never heard so much screaming. Bills fluttered through the air, landing on the stage as the pile of clothing behind each firefighter got bigger and more skin was visible.

My eyes were on Finn the entire time, and his eyes were on me.

I already knew Finn was hot. I already knew his muscles looked airbrushed, every ridge and line cut into his body like stone. I had seen the ink spanning his skin and how it moved with him.

But like this? In the dim lighting, with music playing, with his eyes lighting me on fire like that? He was like a god, and I had the urge to run my tongue over each tattoo.

I tore my gaze up from his body to his eyes and he smiled wider, more arrogantly. Rakishly, even. His gaze traced my skin, lingered on the choker around my neck, on the swell of my breasts. He stared at me like he wanted me. Between my legs, I twinged.

It made me fucking horny.

A slow, sexy smile appeared on his face and he lifted an eyebrow. I shivered.

"Show our gentlemen how much you appreciate them," Emmett said over the mic, and another roar of cheers rose up.

The music volume decreased, and Emmett continued.

"These fine firefighters have asked the audience for a volunteer."

Gasps rose up, and everyone turned to Sadie.

She shook her head, smiling. "Hell, no."

"It's your baby shower," I persisted, laughing. "This is what you wanted."

"Who's the lucky winner?" Emmett's voice rang out, and Sadie grabbed my arm and yanked it up.

"What?" I croaked, shaking my head, trying to pull my arm back. "No way!"

Pregnant women were *strong*. She waved my arm in the air, but Finn's gaze had never even left me. He advanced on us and my gut dipped.

Sadie leaned into my ear. "It's my baby shower, I get to choose." She started clapping. "Olivia, Olivia, Olivia."

Of course, the crowd around us joined in, chanting my name.

Finn drew closer and my face flamed hot. He dropped off the stage, standing right in front of me as more raucous cheering rose up around us.

"Hi, Liv," he said, grinning.

The opening bars of Ginuwine's 'Pony' played, and the crowd lost their minds.

He stepped forward and leaned down so his mouth was beside my ear. He brushed the shell with his lips, and I sucked in a lungful of his scent. It made the spot between my legs pulse.

"This is for your last stunt," he murmured.

My mouth fell open and I huffed, half amused, half turned on. Firecrackers went off in my chest as I gazed up at him, hovering over me with that smirk.

Fuck. That smirk was so hot. I hated that I was so easily lured in by it.

I shook my head at him, holding his gaze. I couldn't wipe the grin off my face. Round and round we went, getting back at each other, and I didn't mind one bit.

Finn stepped forward, hands on the back of my chair as he stood with my legs in between his. His hips started rolling, making his abs ripple.

His eyes didn't leave mine once.

"Shameless," I whispered and his pupils blew, reading my lips.

His hands came to the backs of my knees and he yanked me forward, sliding me down the chair so I was directly beneath him. My eyes widened, and another round of screams and hoots rose from the crowd as he worked his hips against mine.

His abs danced as he moved, his obliques popped and jumped, and the ridges of his chest and stomach begged to be traced by my finger. His tattoos mesmerized me. I reached out but he grabbed my hand in his.

"Ah, ah," he warned, eyes dancing. "No touching."

I huffed a laugh. We were in a room full of screaming people but I barely noticed.

He dropped to his knee and my breath caught. My smile dropped. He quirked a funny, delirious look at me, an expression that said *now what?*

The way he was posed on one knee like that—

My heart shot into my throat. I was vaguely aware of people screaming *oh my god! Oh my god!*

"Finn," I hissed, sending him murder eyes.

If he proposed like this, I was going to kill him.

"Do *not*." I sounded like a demon, voice tense and raspy. "Do not."

A slow, wicked smile hitched on his mouth. His smile said, *but what if I did?*

I blinked. My chest was a shaken-up pop can, ready to explode and fizz everywhere. What if he did?

His eyes narrowed, so cocky and sexy. "It would be an incredible story."

This was crazy. I choked out a laugh and his grin widened. I wasn't actually considering this, was I? My stomach tumbled like I was on a roller coaster, and my pulse went haywire.

He stood and lowered himself over me, and I breathed a sigh of relief.

One of his corded arms reached out to support himself on the back of my chair while the other hand threaded into my hair, anchoring me. My pulse thrummed between my legs as my eyes settled on his.

His eyes flashed dark and wild and I felt drunk, strung along by my intense attraction to Finn Rhodes. Up, down, left, right, he yanked me with him, along for the ride, and I didn't even mind anymore.

My lungs felt tight like I couldn't get a full breath as we watched each other.

His irises were dark like dusk. "Look at you, Olivia," he said, and it sounded like an accusation. Like how dare I look so hot tonight? Awareness shot through me, and I shivered at the way he said my full name.

He leaned in. "Are your panties wet?" he asked, for my ears only.

I pulled back, giving him my own smug smile, and slowly shook my head. "Not wearing any."

His eyes blazed wild before he closed them, sucking a breath in.

Was this doing anything to convince me of the new, improved Finn? The responsible, reliable guy? Nope.

Did I care? Not even a little.

He tucked a lock of hair behind my ear and my mind slurred, drunk on lust. "Thought you said no touching," I called over the music.

"That was just a suggestion."

His mouth dropped to mine and the noise from the crowd turned deafening. Every person in that place must have been screaming. The windows were probably shaking. Noise roared to the rafters, but I was consumed by the taste of Finn, his tongue in my mouth, stroking me, firm and unrelenting, hungry and needy. His hands in my hair. His warm skin brushing mine.

His kiss felt like sex and I needed more.

My hands were in his hair, on his chest, raking down his back. He groaned as my nails scratched him, and I hoped I left marks.

Good. Show everyone. Let everyone see that I desperately wanted to fuck him and be fucked by him.

———

I DIDN'T SEE Finn after he left the stage, but I thought about him all night. I thought about him as we went for drinks at the cocktail bar of a hotel in Queen's Cove. I thought about him as I got a ride home. And I thought about him as I stepped inside my apartment.

Was he inside his apartment, thinking about me?

A pressure tugged between my legs and my eyebrows pinched together in frustration. I threw the flimsy lock closed and raced to my room, not even bothering to close my bedroom door before flopping on my duvet. My hand slipped under my dress.

The first brush of my fingers sent a warm squeeze of pleasure through me, and my back arched. I let out a long, slow breath, closing my eyes and thinking about Finn between my legs. Thinking about him bending me over the bar, stroking me, spanking me, and licking my pussy. The groan he let out when he tasted me, how his mouth vibrated against my clit. The way he took control and made me take my pleasure. I thought about him kissing me tonight, how hot his tattoos had looked on display. I shuddered, moving my fingers in fast, light circles, dragging wetness over my clit. My skin was fire and ice, and I squirmed.

God, being fucked by Finn was going to be so good. So *fucking* good. His cock was thick and I remembered how it had felt for him to push inside me. Seeing the expression on his face as he stroked into me would send me over the edge. Even now, even imagining it, I was soaked.

An idea formed in my head and I stopped. My own wicked smile stretched across my face as I reached for my phone.

I opened up a new text to Finn and hit the button to record a voice note.

Danger thrilled through my blood as I touched myself, heightening every sensation. The phone caught every gasp, every moan, every whimper as I edged toward my climax. I bit hard into my lip, grinning at the picture of Finn's expression in my mind as he listened to it.

"Finn," I moaned as my fingers worked faster.

Finn might be the devil, but I could be, too.

With Finn on my mind and my hand between my legs, I found my release. White heat arced through me, blinding me, and my hips bucked as the waves of warmth and tension and pleasure crashed through me.

I sighed back into the pillows and hit send before typing *Listen to that alone*. A chuckle slipped out of me as I stared at the text conversation.

He was going to lose his mind. My smile stretched and I sighed again, relaxed but not fully sated. Nothing was quite as good as sex with Finn.

I lay there for a few moments, catching my breath and willing myself to get up and get ready for bed with no success.

A noise in the hallway caught my attention. Footsteps.

Three loud, booming knocks on my front door. My eyes went wide and my pulse turned erratic.

"*Olivia*." His voice was thick. "Let me in right now."

Hand over my mouth, I laughed silently, butterflies tumbling around my stomach at his dangerous tone. He could wait. This game was too fun.

With a crack, the door burst open. I sat straight up, eyes wide as I took in the splintered doorframe, and Finn stepped inside my apartment, eyes blazing.

"I'll fix that tomorrow," he said in a low voice, eyes raking over me where I lay in the middle of the bed like a present to him.

42

Finn

MY BLOOD PUMPED in my ears as I prowled toward her, slamming her bedroom door behind me. She jumped and her pretty lips parted. They were swollen like she'd been biting them.

That *voice note*. Holy fuck. I had almost disintegrated, listening to it in my apartment.

"You little tease." I crawled over her on the bed and she fell back against the pillows, hair wild. On her neck, her pulse fluttered. I dropped my head down to lick it, and her breath caught under my tongue. "You look so fucking hot in this dress. The second I saw you in it, I thought about bending you over, flipping it up, and fucking you hard."

A moan slipped out of her and I dragged my mouth across her skin, down her neck until I hit the spot between her neck and shoulder. My teeth grazed her. Between my legs, her thighs pressed together.

"Finn," she breathed.

"What's the matter?" I crooned, sliding a palm up her smooth, soft thigh. "I thought you already took care of yourself."

The needy heat in her eyes stirred everything up in me,

made me want to tear her dress off and sink right into her tight, wet pussy.

I lowered my hips to notch myself between her and her mouth fell open as my thick length pressed against her. "Yeah." I nodded. "That's from your dirty little voice note."

Her eyes glazed and she bit back a smile.

"Fuck, you're bad." My fingers threaded into her hair and I kissed her, coaxing her mouth open before running my tongue over hers. She moaned into my mouth and my cock twitched.

"I can't stop thinking about you."

I groaned as her sweet words shredded what was left of my control. The soft brush of her lips, her tongue against me, it undid me. She lifted her hips, rubbing against me, desperate and needy, and that last thread inside me snapped.

I dragged a breath in. "You're mine. You said it yourself."

She nodded, eyelids heavy. My hand moved up her inner thigh until I felt the wetness slicked over her thighs. She wasn't lying earlier about no panties. Jesus Christ, when she had said that, I felt the pre-cum dripping from my cock. My fingers found her clit and I stroked as lightly as I could. She was swollen, hot, and still soaked. Her eyes fell closed as I massaged her with increasing pressure.

"Finn," she moaned.

"I love when you say my name, baby. I went so long without hearing it."

Under her dress, I slipped a finger inside her, locating the ridged spot that made her go insane with need. Like last time, it was easier to find after she'd come once. I pressed it and she gasped.

"Take your tits out," I demanded, watching as she slipped the shoulders of her dress down and pulled her bra cups down, revealing her gorgeous breasts. "Fuck, I love these," I groaned out, watching them as she arched. I leaned down to suck a stiff nipple into my mouth, rolling the peak between my lips and teeth, and a low, guttural noise scraped out of her throat.

She was perfect with her walls down like this.

I added a second finger, making the slow *come hither* motion on her G-spot, thumb skating over her clit. With my other hand, I pulled myself out of my jeans and stroked my length while I stared down at her.

"You look so good like this, ready to come on my fingers," I told her. I wore a wicked smile as I urged her toward her orgasm. "Come on."

She clung to my gaze, eyes heavy and chest heaving for air as I stroked her, stroked myself. She watched my cock and the lazy, languid way I touched myself. Pre-cum appeared at the tip and I wiped it off with my thumb.

"Open." It wasn't a question.

Her lips parted and I slipped my thumb between them. Her tongue swirled and heat twisted around my spine, making my cock jump. She made a pleased humming noise.

"Good girl." Her pussy tightened around my fingers. "You love being called that, don't you? You love pleasing me." I worked my fingers harder, massaging her inside and out, and she moaned.

"Finn."

"Say you love it." My voice teased as I pulled back on the pressure, dangling what she wanted just out of reach.

"*Finn*." Frustration dripped off her voice and I laughed, low and dark.

Jesus, she was so warm and wet, I could have done this forever. "Say you love pleasing me."

"I love pleasing you," she admitted in a rush, slicking my hand again.

I chuckled. "Good. That wasn't so hard." My free hand skimmed her breasts, rolling and pinching the nipples until she whined. I worked her pussy harder, stroking and massaging and fucking her with my hand until I felt the first flutters.

"There you go. Look at you." She arched, pressing her breast into my hand, eyes clenched tightly closed as she squeezed me between her thighs. One of her hands came to my cock, jerking me, and the other gripped my forearm as I pinched her nipple tighter.

Her eyes opened and locked on me, hazy and fucking beautiful. "Gonna come," she managed.

"Yes, you are." Smug pride burst in my chest.

"You're so good at this."

"I know."

She bit her lip. "Asshole."

I grinned, swirling pressure on her clit, and she fell over the cliff, twisting and squirming, bucking on my hand. She squeezed my cock at the base and I scrambled to hold on to control. Her muscles spasmed around me as she gasped my name, and I felt like a king, doling out pleasure to her like this. Her thighs were slippery with her arousal.

I could come from watching her shatter like this.

My hands came to her hips and in a swift movement, I flipped her onto her stomach.

"You sent me that voice note of you coming on your fingers, gasping my name, because you wanted me to fuck you hard." I slid her dress up, baring her ass. My hands squeezed her soft skin. "Didn't you?"

She squirmed, pushing into my hands.

"*Didn't you.*"

"Yes," she gasped, and I gave her a sharp smack on the ass. She moaned.

"Brat." I slapped her ass again, watching her writhe. "Such a fucking brat." I dragged the head of my cock up and down her pussy, coating myself with her arousal.

"Finn, please." Her fingers clutched the duvet and I felt her shudder.

"Please what?"

"Again."

"Beg. Me."

"Asshole," she gasped with frustration.

A low laugh slipped out of me as I rubbed up and down the smooth skin of her ass, pushing her dress higher. She looked so good like this, dress hitched up and ready for me to fuck her.

Years of her hating me, wanting nothing to do with me, while I missed her and hated myself, and now this.

"Beg me." My tone was cruel but I'd give her what she wanted. As soon as she gave me an ounce of what I'd needed for years. "Ask me like you mean it."

She growled and glared at me over her shoulder, and my mouth twitched with amusement. "Fuck me right now."

My blood crackled with electricity. "No." She made a noise like a pissed off cat and I chuckled. "You were always so much fun to play with."

"Finn—"

I lay down on the bed beside her and gestured for her to climb on top of me. "Come here."

Slowly, she raised herself up and crawled over me, limp and boneless. My fingers threaded into her hair and I kissed her, sucking her tongue gently and running my hands through her silky hair. Her hand drifted to the back of my neck, toying with my hair, lighting up my nerves.

We were so fucking good together. Sex had never been like this with anyone but Liv.

"You're so fucking pretty, Liv," I murmured. "So perfect. So good at coming for me."

She let a soft moan out into my mouth, settling her weight on me. My cock ached to fuck her.

We couldn't though. The realization cut through my racing heart, my clouded thoughts. If we had sex, she'd freak out. It would mean something. It would be intense, and big, and heavy, and there was no going back.

She couldn't handle it yet.

I glanced at the mirror in the corner of her bedroom, and an idea formed in my head. "Lift up for me, baby."

She blinked, frowning, and I helped her move her weight to her knees and elbows before I slid down the bed so my face was between her legs.

"Finn," she gasped as my tongue swiped her. "I can't."

"What's the matter?" I smoothed my palms over her ass, squeezing and pulling her against my mouth. "You can come again." I lavished her clit with attention and she bucked against my mouth. "There you go."

She let out a low moan and I grinned, slipping two fingers inside her. I gave her ass one last squeeze before fisting my cock, stroking myself as she rode my face.

"One more time, baby. You can do it. And this time," I paused before pointing at the mirror. "You're going to watch yourself in the mirror while you do it."

"Oh, god," she whimpered, leaning on her forearms.

"Are you watching?"

Her pussy squeezed my fingers. "Yes." Her voice was thin and needy, and satisfaction rose in me.

"Good. I want you to get used to the sight of yourself riding my face. It's different now." She was already clamping up on my fingers. Not long now. "Understand?"

"Uh-huh." Another rush of arousal around my fingers, another tremor.

I stroked my length, dragging my tongue up and down her swollen sex, letting her work herself on my mouth to find the rhythm she liked.

"That's it, baby. Find what you need. Fuck, you taste so sweet." My voice was a low, demanding growl.

"Gonna come," she gasped, one hand sliding down to grip the back of my head as she rode my face. Her thighs tightened around my head and my dick pulsed in my hand. "Gonna come again."

My brain sizzled with lust and pleasure as one of my

fantasies came true. As her tight channel gripped my fingers and her pussy soaked my face, my balls tightened close to my body.

"Finn," she wailed, muffled by the duvet. Her walls pulsed around me and heat seared up my spine, erasing my thoughts as my release closed in. Pride sparked in my chest from her being able to come again, and from helping her do that. At the base of my spine, the pressure burst and I moaned into the apex of her legs as I came, shooting ropes of cum up my stomach and all over her ass, moaning her name.

This. This was where I belonged, pleasuring Liv and feeling connected with her. I drew in a deep breath and pressed a sweet kiss to her inner thigh, wet with her arousal.

"Baby," I whispered. The word was a pathetic replacement for the three that I wanted to say, but I held them back.

She watched me as she caught her breath. Vulnerability flashed in her eyes and I wondered if she wanted to say it, too.

When she was ready, I'd be here.

43

Olivia

"EVELYN! COME ON," my mom called down the beach and Evelyn barreled toward us on the sand, drool flying and slinging over her snout, jowls flapping. She galloped past us and did a loop on the beach before splashing through the sparkling water. The sun was out, warming my skin, and the sand was soft under my bare feet. A light breeze drifted in off the water and I inhaled the clean air. Surfers lay on their boards in the water, catching waves.

God, it was beautiful here.

I smiled at my parents' chocolate Lab. "She loves it here."

My mom laughed as Evelyn ran over for scratches. "She sure does. If I'm ever feeling lazy about taking her out, I remember this is the best part of her day, getting to run around outside. You're such a good baby," she cooed, and Evelyn's tongue hung out the side of her mouth while my mom rubbed the sweet spot behind Evelyn's ears.

"I want to get a dog." Finn would love to get one.

My mom glanced up with interest. "Someone to join you on hikes?"

I smiled, imagining a big dog wedged between Finn and me in our tent. "Yeah, that would be nice."

A weird tension hovered in the air when we didn't address the other *someone* who'd been joining me on hikes.

"I heard you had a fun time at Sadie's baby shower." Her mouth twisted to the side in a smile.

I huffed a laugh, and heat spread up my neck and cheeks. My god. Everyone in town had been talking about the show, about Finn dancing for me and about us making out in front of everyone. Half the town was there, and the other half had been able to hear the noise from the community center. Miri had posted a picture of us kissing, Finn hovering over me, my hands in his hair, us surrounded by screaming people.

I couldn't stop thinking about what we did in my apartment after.

"Um, yeah," I told my mom, turning away to hide my smile. "I did."

"And the whole getting-him-to-dump-you thing…?"

I chewed my lip, searching for the words.

She sighed. "I knew this would happen."

Frustration spiked in my blood and my shoulders hitched with tension. I blinked, at a loss for words. Evelyn brought me a stick and I hauled it as far as I could before she raced to retrieve it.

"It's new," I said. "We're figuring it out."

She made a humming noise, gaze on the beach ahead of us with a wrinkle in her brow. I studied her. My mom had me at twenty, which put her at forty-nine now. Freckles splashed over her nose and cheeks. We had the same nose and face shape.

I didn't remember much from before Joe came into our lives, but I remember her being stressed. My grandparents were still working when I was born, so they couldn't take care of me during the day. I remember my mom scrambling for childcare, and occasionally bringing me to work with her, having me sit with crayons at the nurses' station.

After Joe came into the picture, it was easier. He worked

evenings, so he did the school pick-ups and drop-offs when she was at the hospital. Even when she wasn't working, he was happy to take on just as much parenting. With Joe around, she finally had time for herself.

A memory appeared in my head of a birthday party. I was turning nine or ten, and Finn and I were having a joint party like always. My mom kept glancing at the side of the yard, watching.

I found out later she had been waiting for Cole, but he never showed.

On the beach, she turned to me with a sad, tense expression. "I don't want you to go through what I did."

"I won't." My throat felt tight, talking about this.

She was quiet as we walked along the beach. It was high tourist season so even on a Monday afternoon, there were people having picnics and kids making sandcastles. Seagulls hopped along, picking at things in the seaweed, and the waves crashed on the shore.

I thought about what Finn told me last month when we were camping, what my mom had said to him about dragging me down.

"He's not Cole," I told her quietly.

Our gazes met briefly, hers loaded with worry. She raised her eyebrows.

"Did you ever consider that it's unfair to compare them?" I continued. "Finn and I aren't teenagers anymore." I swallowed, hesitating. I thought about how vehemently he had reassured me that he would never leave me, never leave our kid. "If we had a family, he wouldn't ditch us the way Cole did."

My mom swore under her breath. "Are we really talking about you having a baby with this guy?"

Anger rushed through my blood. *This guy?* "Don't do that. Say his name," I spat out.

"Fine. Finn. For real?"

"Yes," I burst out, surprising myself. "Not today and not even this year but maybe one day. I don't know." I tucked my arms around myself as my stomach flopped around, uneasy and uncertain. The words locked up in my throat. "I don't know anymore. Finn is different now and I might have been wrong. It isn't fair to judge someone for the dumb shit they did when they were seventeen."

My mom sighed out at the water, chewing her lip. "This is hard for me."

"I know."

Evelyn dropped the stick at my mom's feet before sitting, waiting, and my mom dipped down and chucked it down the beach. Evelyn took off after it.

"Every cell in my body is screaming at me to protect you," my mom said, eyes on Evelyn.

"That's because all you know is the guy who fucked up."

"Yeah."

"I'm a grown-up now," I told her. "I can protect myself."

She shot me a sad smile, wincing. "I know you can. I'm sorry. It's my mama bear instincts."

"I want you to try to like Finn."

She pressed her mouth into a thin line, and it was like staring into a mirror.

"And I want you to try to forget who he used to be."

Evelyn dropped the stick at my feet and I threw it for her. She took off, sand spraying behind her.

A few of the knots in my stomach loosened but my pulse picked up at what I was about to say. "I'm going to reach out to Cole."

"*What?*" My mom's jaw dropped. "Are you kidding?"

I shook my head.

"Olivia." Her expression was a mix of worry, shock, and warning.

I knew what she was thinking. Why on Earth would I try to find the guy who fucked our lives up? The guy who couldn't be bothered with us? He had let us down. He was supposed to love us and didn't.

"He's in the past," she said, shrugging and shaking her head. "I worry that you're setting yourself up for disappointment with him."

I explained what Finn had told me, how he had seen Cole in Whistler, how he'd seemed sad and full of regret.

"I hate this," my mom said, shaking her head. "I can see how this will go. He'll be who he's always been and you'll be devastated."

"So maybe I'll be devastated." My voice was soft. "I can handle it. I just need to know. What if he needs me to reach out first? He might have no one."

My heart twisted. I just had to know.

My mom dragged a breath in and let it out on a sigh. "This scares me."

"I know."

Her face was etched with worry as her gaze lingered on me. "I'll give Finn a shot." Her eyes widened in emphasis. "You're right." She nodded to herself. "He was just a kid."

Warmth squeezed my chest and I smiled at her. "Thank you."

My heart beat like a drum, slowing only when my mom changed the subject to dispel the tension.

LATE THAT AFTERNOON, I sat at my kitchen table, arms crossed, staring at the Google Maps listing for Wright Handyman Services in Whistler, BC. Anxiety wrenched in my stomach as I read through the reviews. They were positive, citing that Cole was trustworthy, showed up on time, and charged a fair price for quality work. He didn't have a website, but there was a phone number listed.

I had been hoping I could email him. I hated talking on

the phone. Besides, if he never responded, I could have told myself that it went to his junk mail.

What was I even going to say?

Finn had offered to be here with me while I did this, but I said no. This was something I had to do myself.

Before I could lose my nerve, I dialed, heart beating in my ears. My mouth went dry as it rang.

"Hi," a low, gravelly voice answered, and my blood spiked with adrenaline. "This is Cole Wright. Leave a message and I'll get back to you."

Voicemail. My gut eased a fraction before it beeped and I sat there, frozen.

What was I going to say?

Fuck.

"Hi," I said, blinking. "Um. This is Olivia."

My heart beat out of my chest, and I was struck by an ugly thought.

What if he didn't remember me?

No, I countered. Obviously, he'd remember me.

The side of me that wasn't frozen and blinking was baffled at how hard I was fucking this up.

"Your daughter," I added. It felt like my mouth was full of sand. "And I'd like to meet you."

Oh god, what if he thought I wanted something from him? Alarm shot through me.

"I don't want money or anything," I hurried to add.

Wow. Olivia. My ears felt warm.

"I want to talk." I paused a moment. "Okay, bye."

I hung up and stared at my phone with wide eyes. That couldn't have gone any worse.

A pulse of pride flicked through me. I did it, though, and I couldn't wait to tell Finn.

44

Olivia

THE NIGHT OF OUR DATE, I stood in front of my bathroom mirror, squirming with nerves.

This was so stupid. So unlike me to be nervous. For what, even? We were probably getting food and a drink and maybe we'd make out for a bit. Maybe we'd go see another movie in the park. I had no reason to be nervous, I told myself while I applied winged liner and mascara.

It was just a date, I thought while I pulled on a pair of high-waisted shorts that made my ass look good. The top I had selected showed off a bit of cleavage, and I could already picture Finn's gaze snagging on the neckline.

A shudder of anticipation rolled through me.

It was just a date. It wasn't a big deal.

My gaze strayed to the new door Finn had installed the other morning. He had tossed me two sets of keys and pocketed a third with a rakish grin.

"So I don't have to break it down next time," he said with a wink.

Another shiver rolled down my spine as I pictured him storming into my room. The dark, hot look in his eyes.

On my bedside table, my phone lit up with a text.

Sadie Waters: *Are you working tonight?*

Olivia Morgan: *Not tonight. Date with Finn.*

Sadie Waters: *Ooooooooooooooh.*

Olivia Morgan: *Stop it.*

Sadie Waters: *:)*

I grinned and rolled my eyes at the phone before pulling a necklace off my dresser. Behind me, the phone lit up again.

Sadie Waters: *Should I be on the lookout for a vintage Porsche?*

My stomach wobbled, dipping and swaying, as I stared at her text.

The car meant something. What did it mean, though, that my heart lifted at the idea of Finn showing up in that car?

Olivia Morgan: *I hope not.*

When Finn knocked on the door, I opened it to him holding a bouquet—a mix of plum, pink, and orange flowers. He wore a white t-shirt. So simple and yet so, so fucking hot. His eyes burned bright as his gaze raked down my form and the corner of his mouth turned up in a pleased, smug smile.

My stomach dipped again. I rolled my eyes, failing to hide my own grin. "Hi."

"Hi, baby." His voice was soft as he leaned in and brushed a kiss onto my cheek. My eyes fluttered closed and his smell whooshed at me.

He stepped inside while I placed the flowers in a jar with water. If the green car was outside, would I get in? My blood thrilled at the idea of getting in the car. When his back was turned, I inhaled the bouquet, filling my lungs with the sweet, sharp scent.

"Like them?"

I whipped around. He was leaning on the kitchen counter, watching me with a funny expression. Not smug this time. More like… proud.

I nodded. "Thank you. Where are we going tonight?"

"We're going on a little adventure."

My eyebrows lifted, half amused, half concerned, and he laughed.

"Ready to go?"

I nodded again, speechless. My gaze strayed to him in his t-shirt, fabric pulling gently across his broad shoulders, ink crawling down his corded arms. His forearms were tanned and I had the urge to lick them.

Like he could read my thoughts, his eyebrow arched and he grinned, holding the door open for me.

"Lots of time for that later, Morgan," he murmured as we headed downstairs, and another shiver shot through me.

I turned to head to the back door leading to the alley, but Finn cocked his head toward the bar.

"This way."

My heart pounded. If the green car was out there waiting for me, everyone would see me get inside. Everyone would know what it meant. They'd tell my mom. She'd have to hear about it from Miri Yang or someone instead of me. And once I got in the car, there was no going back. If falling for Finn was like being on a rollercoaster, getting in the green car was like boarding the ride.

Would that be so bad? I thought about the flowers upstairs, the sweet way he kissed me on the cheek, the softness I caught in his eyes sometimes. How he was helping me find the flower, hiking tough terrain with bugs and thorns and shitty camping food so I could find something that might not exist.

He had organized a town hiking event. My heart squeezed. He did it for me.

Maybe it wouldn't be so bad, getting in that car.

As we approached the front door, he winked at me over his shoulder and my stomach lodged in my throat. I followed him outside, scanning the street in front of the bar.

No green car.

I let the air out of my lungs. My stomach sank a fraction. It was just a dumb car. I wasn't disappointed.

I wasn't.

"Are we walking?" I asked.

"Nope." He stepped over to where two bikes leaned against the wall of the bar.

A surprised laugh ripped out of me. It was my old bike from when we were teenagers. I used to store it in Finn's parents' shed in their backyard beside Finn's bike, and when Finn left, I didn't bother taking it out. I hadn't ridden it since. After over a decade in a dirty old shed, it should have been rusty and grimy, but it looked preserved in a time capsule. My gaze roamed the midnight-blue frame, speckled with stars, and I reached out to trace one of the brake lines, smooth and untouched by age. The seat was different. There was a new basket on the front.

"How...?" I frowned.

Finn crossed his arms, watching with a tentative grin. "I replaced the brakes and got you a new seat. And I fixed a few other things."

His bike stood beside mine, cleaned up just as nicely.

"And you added a basket."

His head dipped, pleased and a little embarrassed. His bashful, boyish expression made my heart stammer.

"I couldn't resist. Almost added a few sparkly streamers on the side to piss you off."

I chuckled, reaching out to run the pad of my finger over the wicker basket. Butterflies whipped around in my stomach and chest as I scraped my teeth over my bottom lip.

"Do you like it?" he asked in a low voice.

I shot him a silent nod, smiling.

His eyes turned soft like velvet, and my stomach flopped. "Good."

Before I could overthink it, Finn was on his bike, slowly meandering down the sidewalk while I scrambled to catch up.

The first push of the peddle woke something up in me, a sparking energy in my stomach that made me smile as we rode through the streets of Queen's Cove to the marina. We leaned our bikes at the top of the marina and headed down to the tiny fish and chips shack, busy with summer tourists.

After we ordered and received our food, we carried it up to the bikes.

"Let's eat at the beach," Finn suggested.

"Which one?"

His gaze lifted and behind his eyes, I saw something hesitant and hoping. "Castle."

A beat passed between us. Castle Beach wasn't known to tourists. It wasn't on a map, it wasn't on Google, and locals didn't post it on Instagram. Even Miri knew better than to spill the beans about it. Boaters couldn't access the beach due to signage about underwater rocks. The highway access was nearly impossible to find unless you knew what to search for, but Finn and I knew another way via a back road.

As kids and teenagers, we used to go there all the time. We used to watch the sunset and build bonfires. I remembered sitting there wondering if he liked me *like that*.

"Race you." I held his gaze while the challenge lingered in the air. The corner of his mouth turned up and he lifted one eyebrow.

"Oh, yeah?"

"Mhm." I rolled my lips to hide my smile. My stomach danced with excitement. That thing that woke up in me earlier? It sat up, yawned, and stretched. Blinked the sleep out of its eyes. I smiled wider, wiggling my eyebrows. "Unless you're worried I'll kick your ass, like when we hike."

He let out a bark of laughter. "Morgan, you're trying to rile me up."

"What if I am?" I tried to take the food from him to place in the basket but he tucked it in the backpack he had brought, waving me off.

"I'll carry it." He did the zip up before straightening and regarding me. "Alright, you're on. Get ready to dry your tears."

I smiled so hard my face hurt. "Never."

We agreed to ride at a casual pace until Main Street and the traffic were behind us. We picked up speed, passing houses, the elementary school, the mechanic, our parents' houses.

We reached the back road to Castle Beach, slipping through a short path, bumping over the gravel until we reached the pavement.

I sent a delighted, daring grin at Finn before I was off.

45

Olivia

HE WAS right on my tail.

The wind whipped my hair and that version of myself who'd woken up got out of bed, wandered to the window, and smiled at the sky. I glanced over my shoulder and locked eyes with Finn. Whatever was on my face lit him up like a sparkler, and he beamed back at me. No smirk, no roguish grin, no smug smile. Just pure happiness.

A laugh burst out of me as he gained on me. My thighs burned, my eyes watered from the wind, and my cheeks *ached* from smiling. I was so fucking happy and light, riding bikes and racing Finn Rhodes down the street.

This felt like where I belonged. I whooshed past the entrance to the beach a hair in front of Finn and let my bike slow. My chest shook with laughter as I circled back.

"Beat you." I was breathing hard, legs, back, and lungs burning.

He smiled openly at me. His cheeks flushed pink and my heart flipped over. "You did. Do me a favor and don't gloat about it, okay?"

I scoffed. "Whatever."

He laughed and I followed him through the path to the beach. We left our bikes at the edge of the sand.

Finn tilted his chin at the basket on my bike. "There's a treat for you in there."

I flipped it open. A beach blanket covered a bag of Cheezies, and I wiggled my eyebrows at him. "Thank you."

His eyes gleamed. "Those are disgusting."

"I know. I still love them."

"I know." He smiled and tilted his head to the beach. "Come on."

We set out the blanket on the empty beach, unpacking the food and opening the drinks Finn had brought. The salt from the fries burst in my mouth and I hummed, surveying the ocean as the evening sun dipped low in the sky. I watched the sand soak up the tide from the waves crashing in and out. A light breeze pushed my hair back and I caught Finn studying me, like he was trying to remember this. My heart twisted.

"Happy?" he asked, leaning back on his elbow as he ate.

I nodded, inhaling the fresh air and letting it out slow. I took another bite of fish, sighing with pleasure at the crunchy deep-fried batter. "They gave us extra tartar sauce. How could I not be happy?"

He chuckled, and his pleased expression made my heart beat faster.

"Thank you," I told him.

His gaze lifted to mine. "For what?"

"I'm having a good time with you."

His eyes softened. "Me too, baby."

I chewed my lip, glancing at him. "I reached out to Cole."

"Oh, shit," he said softly, eyebrows going up like he was impressed. "How'd that go?"

I shrugged. "I don't know. Weird. I left him a voicemail. I haven't heard back from him."

His gaze roamed my face and the corner of his mouth quirked up. "That took guts, Morgan. I'm proud of you."

My face heated and I hid my smile.

He opened his mouth to say something before closing it.

"What?" I prompted.

"Just thinking about how I'm going to challenge you again."

"You could find the flower before me." I ate another fry.

He shook his head, eyes dancing. "I'd never do that to you."

We watched each other. "I know."

Something popped into my head, and my stomach twisted with worry. His expression turned serious, like he could see my emotions painted all over my face. I used to be good at hiding my emotions. I used to have the best resting bitch face in town, but over the summer, I seemed to have misplaced it. Or maybe Finn stole it. He could always read me like a book.

"I started job hunting," I admitted. "For October."

"Oh." He picked up a fry but didn't eat it. "Find anything?"

"The research center in Port Alberni has nothing, which is no surprise. They're underfunded and because they're underfunded, they're becoming obsolete, which means they're getting fewer grants."

"Which means they're becoming more underfunded," Finn supplied, and I nodded.

The next words caught in my throat. "There are a few jobs in Port Hardy."

Finn blinked before nodding. "Hmm."

Port Hardy was on the northwest end of the island, a six-hour drive from Queen's Cove. I wouldn't be commuting back to town every night with that drive.

"And they have a few jobs that don't require PhDs," I continued, staring at the ocean. "Although they seem boring. Just lab work. Stuff I did in undergrad."

He hummed again, understanding the underlying

message. I didn't want those jobs, and I didn't want to move to Port Hardy.

"I'd move with you." His careful gaze met mine.

"Your job."

He watched me, still smiling. "I'm sure they have fires there."

I chewed my lip to keep from smiling back at him before I let it go, let the smile lift on my face. "We'll see."

"Yep." He nodded.

A twist of frustration hit me and I blinked. Queen's Cove was my home, and I didn't want to leave. Everyone *else* got their happy ending. Even if Finn came with me, I didn't want to leave.

I thought about Finn's brothers and my friends. Except for Emmett, they all owned their own businesses and made their own destiny. My forehead creased. It didn't work like that for me. I couldn't start my own research lab here in Queen's Cove; half the field thought I was a quack on the hunt for something that went extinct. No one in their right mind would give me hundreds of thousands of dollars to lead studies. Not if I didn't find the flower.

A slow, sinking feeling hit my stomach.

"Hey." Finn's hand brushed my arm. "We're going to figure it out, okay?"

I nodded, not believing him. My gaze swung out to the water, reflecting the sun dipping lower in the sky. I didn't want to feel like this, not here. Not on the date Finn had planned for us.

"We should move to the forest," I said with a snort. "We could build our own cabin, drill a well for water, and pedal our bikes to keep the lights on."

He cocked a grin at me. "Boil water for baths?"

"Too much work. We'd swim in the creek."

"What about in the winter?"

"You'll keep me warm."

His smile lifted higher and he chuckled. The sound fizzed over my skin. The frustration from moments before popped like a bubble as I grinned back at him.

Glancing at Finn propped on his elbow, hair falling into his eyes, a muscle in my chest twinged and I realized something.

I didn't want this summer to end.

We stayed on the beach, chatting and watching the water until the sky began to dim. We rode back to the bar at a comfortable pace, meandering down the streets.

"I don't know why I didn't get another bike years ago," I admitted to Finn as we leaned them against the wall in the hallway inside the door of the bar.

"Now you don't need to."

He dropped a kiss on my cheek, too quick and fast for my liking, before tugging me upstairs.

I bit my lip in anticipation. When we reached the hallway between our apartments, he kept walking to the end and my expression turned confused. A ladder sat against the wall, and he dropped my hand to set it up below the roof hatch. After opening the hatch, he stepped down, helping me up as I climbed onto the roof.

When I saw the blanket spread out on the roof with a pile of throw pillows, I laughed.

"What's this?" Across the sky, the sun was setting.

"Thought we'd watch the sunset." He dusted his hands off and led me over to the blankets. "If you want."

"I want." I smiled at the sky, dusty purples and indigo blues.

We sat on the blanket, staring at the sky. Up here, we could hear the chatter from outside the bar, the light din of traffic, the laughter of people walking down Main Street. Our town was so full of life, full of people enjoying their lives.

A funny thought struck me and my heart clenched. How long had it been since I enjoyed my life like this? Without

Finn, what would I be doing right now? Working at the bar or obsessing about my studies. Maybe camping by myself, eating packaged pasta and staring into the fire.

Finn had blown back into town and knocked all that aside. He showed me the moments that were worth living for.

"Come here," Finn whispered, lying back against the pillows, corded, tattooed arm out and open for me. I tucked myself into his side, sighing as I relaxed into his warm, hard chest, eyes on the sky.

"You smell amazing." My voice was quiet. His hand came to my hair, toying lightly, and he chuckled.

We watched the sky as the sun sank below the horizon. The sky darkened and tiny pinpricks of light appeared while I listened to Finn's heartbeat against my ear. His chest rose and fell as my world narrowed to our little bubble—the soft brush of his t-shirt against my cheek, his warmth, the sounds from the street below, the tickle of his fingers in my hair. My hand on his flat stomach.

At one point, I lifted my head to look at him and he watched me back. We stared openly at each other, connected in a way I'd never felt before.

I lifted up on my elbow and kissed him.

He exhaled against me as my lips grazed his. The light scrape of his stubble against my chin sent sparks across my skin and as I deepened the kiss, he lifted me on top of him. His tongue slid against the seam of my mouth and I let him in.

He groaned against my mouth, stroking my tongue with his. The sound of pure pleasure hit me between my thighs, and beneath me, he hardened. I was breathless but I couldn't stop kissing him. My hips tilted against his, and even through our clothes, his cock against my center flooded me with heat. The rhythm of his tongue against mine wound me higher, tighter. The way he moved in my mouth was like how his fingers moved between my legs, firm and unyielding, doling out pure pleasure at his pace, not mine.

"Tonight?" I whispered against his mouth in between kisses.

His eyes devoured me. He knew what I meant. "Not tonight."

Frustration ached between my legs.

"Why not?" I breathed.

He pulled back to study me. The corner of his mouth twitched but his eyes burned hot and possessive. "I'm waiting until I think you love me."

I searched his eyes, frozen. The words I wanted to say were like glitter in water. I could see them but when I reached for them, they slipped through my fingers.

I blinked, annoyed with myself. It shouldn't be this hard. Some people said it all the time—to their parents, to their friends, to their kids and their pets—but lying on a blanket entangled with someone I'd known my whole life, someone who might know me better than any other person on the planet, I couldn't say it.

A question appeared in my head, and my muscles tensed. If I said the words, would the chase be over for Finn?

My throat locked up and I swallowed.

"It's okay." Finn's gaze was careful. His hand squeezed my thigh, draped across him. "I'm not going anywhere."

The knots in my chest and throat eased and I nodded, shooting him a small smile. He winked at me and I relaxed more.

"Liv, I can't be without you. Can't you see that?" His eyes were so clear under the stars, and his voice was so confident.

I blinked, searching for what to say, coming up with nothing except a bright warmth in my chest. I slipped my hand into his and the warm brush of his skin against mine, the light scrape of his callouses against my fingers made my blood hum. His thumb moved against the back of my hand, back and forth in comforting strokes.

I could lie here forever with him on the roof, staring at the stars.

"Look," Finn whispered, pointing.

A shooting star spilled light across the inky sky, there for a moment and gone in a flash. My mind scrambled to make a wish. To pick something good.

Maybe I couldn't be without Finn either, and I wished I'd never have to.

46

Finn

"THANK you *so* much for helping today," Miri said as Liv and I loaded the boxes into the trunk and backseat of my Mustang.

Tomorrow, we were heading out on another hiking trip, but today, we were helping Miri with some errands around town. With her packed schedule of volunteering and social events, she was busy, so when I offered to help her out, she jumped at the chance. She had been thrilled when I dragged Liv with me.

"Don't forget the box with the holes in it," Miri added. "They need to go to the turtle sanctuary. They've got air and food so they should be fine for a couple hours. They're still half-frozen so they're a little loopy, anyway." She whirled her finger around her temple in the sign for *crazy*.

Liv and I exchanged an alarmed look.

Miri shoved the list into my hand with all the deliveries for today. "Thanks, you two, you're lifesavers!"

"Bye, Miri," Liv called as I studied the list. The boxes of books in my car were going to the school. After that, we'd pick up meals from local restaurants and drop them off with people who were homebound. It was a town program for people who were unable to leave the house. There was a box that needed to go to town hall, and then there was the box with air holes. A rustling sound came from inside and I winced.

"I'm going to put this one in the backseat," I told Liv, and she wrinkled her nose and nodded.

We climbed into the car, I pulled out of Miri's driveway, and Liv examined me from across the front seat.

"Are you Mr. Volunteer now?"

I shot her my most winning smile. "Sure. Something like that."

Her eyes narrowed, but the corner of her mouth twitched up. "What do you have planned?"

"Nothing." I shook my head. "We're just running errands for Miri."

This was one more way to show Liv and the town that I wasn't the irresponsible, reckless brat from a decade ago. That guy never would have volunteered a whole day of his time to do deliveries.

"You're trying to cause mayhem?" Liv prodded.

I choked with laughter. "No."

She arched a brow in amused disbelief, and I shook my head.

"I promise," I told her, grinning. "I'm an upstanding, responsible, community-oriented guy, like Emmett."

She snorted. "Okay."

"Miri trusts me."

"Mhm." She smiled out the open window.

"No mayhem, no chaos, no getting in trouble today. Just good old-fashioned volunteering."

She grinned. "You're so weird."

I reached across the seat and placed my hand on her thigh, giving her a light squeeze. "Thanks for coming with me today. This'll be way more fun with you around."

Her eyes met mine, and the warmth in them made my heart flip. She shrugged. "Happy to."

———

THREE HOURS LATER, we had two deliveries left—the box to town hall and the box that was going to the turtle sanctuary. It felt like we'd run into every person in town today, and I felt a funny pride in my chest, helping out like this. Catching up with people I hadn't seen in a while, making conversation with some of the older folks we delivered meals to who didn't get out much, and even seeing how excited the teachers were when the books arrived—it felt nice. Rewarding, even. It felt like I was a part of something.

I'd keep this up, volunteering with Miri. It felt good to be a part of the town again, and not just be counting down until I left.

We pulled up to town hall, and Liv turned around to study the box with the holes in it. A rustling noise came from inside.

"We can't leave them in the car," she said. "It's getting too hot."

We climbed out and I pulled the box for town hall out of the trunk.

"Here," I said, handing it to her. "This one's light. I'll take the turtles inside with us."

Inside, the receptionist glanced up from her phone. "Hi, you two."

"Hey, Anna. We've got a delivery for Div."

She pointed down the hall before swiping left on a dating app. "He should be in his office. Go right in."

"Thanks." I gestured to the box in my arms. "Can we leave this with you for a moment? We'll be right back."

"Sure thing." She turned back to her phone and gestured over her shoulder. "Just leave it on the floor."

I slid the box down below the desk, and when I straightened up, Emmett was passing through the lobby, carrying a takeout bag from Avery's restaurant.

"Hey," he called, waving. "What are you two up to?"

My gaze met Liv's and she rolled her lips to hide a smile. I widened my eyes, a silent way of saying *don't tell Emmett what's in the box.*

Emmett didn't like turtles. As a kid, he accidentally rode his bike over one and killed it, and ever since, he'd had a *thing* against them. When they were dating, Avery dragged him to the turtle sanctuary. Behind Miri's back, he called it Miri's House of Turtle Horrors.

I shrugged. "Just dropping a box off for Div."

He brightened up. "Nice." He glanced at his watch. "Gotta go, there's a class from the school doing a tour here soon." He nodded at us. "See ya."

"Bye, Emmett," Liv said lightly as he walked away. "We need to get that box out of here *now*."

I laughed. "Okay, let's go then."

When we arrived at his office, Div sat at his desk, typing an email. As always, he wore a full suit. He turned to see us in the doorway and gave us a discerning expression.

"Olivia. Finn." He nodded once, looking me up and down with an arched brow. "Nice to see you with clothes on."

I burst out laughing and my ears heated. I'd been getting a few comments around town after my stunt the other night at the community center.

For the thousandth time, I pictured the hot, glazed look on Liv's face as I pulled her beneath me amidst the screaming crowd.

It had been so worth it.

I rubbed my jaw, thinking. "Div, were you the one who threw a hundred-dollar bill at me?"

He cleared his throat and Liv laughed. "I don't know what you're talking about," he said lightly.

I grinned at him. "Well, the Queen's Cove fire department

thanks whoever made that donation. We gave all the proceeds to the food bank."

Div shrugged, all innocence, before tilting his chin at the box we brought.

"What's that?"

Liv set it on his desk. "We have a box for you from Miri."

When he flipped it open, his eyes lit up and he gasped.

"Thank you, Miri," he murmured, pulling out a platform orange shoe and inspecting it. "These are practically new." He wiggled his eyebrows at us. "And my size."

"Nice." Liv perched on the edge of his desk as he kicked his dress shoes off and tried on the orange heels. "When's your next show?"

Outside of being Emmett's assistant at town hall, Div performed in drag shows at a bar in the next town. I'd gone to see a show with my brothers and my sisters-in-law. It was fun, and Div was an incredible singer. In drag, he let a totally different side of himself out.

"Two Saturdays from now," he told us. "It's tropical themed."

Liv nudged me. "We should go."

"Sure. I'd love to."

Div pulled out his phone to send us the details, and we chatted for a few minutes about the drag show, town events, and the next reality TV show night he sometimes hosted with Liv, Hannah, Avery, and Sadie.

His email pinged, snagging his attention.

"We should head out," Liv said, pulling me by the hand. "Bye, Div."

He waved goodbye over his shoulder, already distracted by his screen, and we headed back to the lobby.

When we returned to the front desk, Anna was still consumed by her phone, swiping left at an impressive speed. I stepped behind the reception desk to grab the—

The box was gone.

"Fuck," I whispered.

Liv saw my face and came to my side. Her jaw dropped when she saw the box was gone, and eyes wide, we stared at each other.

"Hey, Anna?" I asked.

Anna's eyes were on her phone. "Mmm?"

"Where'd that box go?"

"I don't know." She shrugged, swiping left on a guy wearing a Santa hat.

Liv and I stared at each other before she snorted with laughter, covering her mouth.

I looked around wildly, scanning the lobby. "We have to find that box."

"I know." Liv shook with laughter.

"Miri is going to kill us." I grabbed Liv's hand and tried to seem casual as we surveyed the lobby. Where was it? Who would have taken it?

Beside me, Liv stiffened. Her gaze was on a group of school kids passing through the lobby and out the doors. They were young, seven or eight years old.

She made eye contact with me and pointed at one of the kids.

"Oh, shit," I snorted, shaking with laughter.

To the complete unawareness of the teacher or chaperones, one of the kids dragged an empty box—*the box*—behind him by the lid.

Liv covered her mouth, doubled over with laughter.

"No, no, no," I said, smothering my own chuckles. "We have to find them."

A loud, blood-curdling shriek rang out, echoing throughout town hall, and we froze.

"Was that Emmett?" she whispered.

"Come on." I pulled her in the direction of the shriek—the same direction as Emmett's office.

We hustled down the hallway, and when we turned the

corner, Emmett cowered at the end of the hall, clutching his sandwich to his chest, dry heaving.

Five small turtles advanced on him, inching forward at a glacial pace.

"Oh my god." Liv's hand came to her mouth.

"Those kids brought them into my office." Emmett tried to climb onto the windowsill, eyes wide with terror as he watched the turtles crawl. He gagged again. "I escaped but they followed me. I'm going to puke."

Liv was laughing so hard she couldn't breathe. Her laughing made *me* laugh, and soon the two of us were doubled over, slapping each other and holding on to each other for support as Emmett dry heaved.

"They're predators. They smell my blood!" Emmett's voice had taken on a delirious edge. His eyes darted to us then back to the turtles. "Stop laughing."

"They smell your food," I called back, wiping my eyes. "Step over them."

Emmett glared at the one in the front. "I recognize her. That one's Sara Beth. She wants revenge!"

Liv let out another peal of laughter. "I'm going to pee," she wheezed.

A small group of people was gathering behind us, watching the spectacle.

"Emmett, come on." I gestured to him. "You're going to make Liv pee herself."

Emmett's gaze flicked to the red fire alarm on the wall. He clutched his stomach. "I'm going to pull the fire alarm."

"No," Liv and I yelled in unison, laughing even harder.

My abs hurt from laughing. "Don't do that. That's not going to help."

"What's going on?" Div asked behind us. He saw Emmett and rolled his eyes. "Oh my god. How did those get in here? We have a policy." He sighed and turned around. "Can we get a box, please?"

"I'm going to do it," Emmett yelled, nostrils flaring as his gaze jumped between the turtles five feet away and the fire alarm. He slid an inch over on the windowsill. "I'm getting closer." His stomach heaved.

One turtle paused, lagging behind, and Emmett stiffened.

"That's one's going to jump," he said, pointing at the small one at the back of the pack.

"Emmett," I called, shaking my head, trying not to laugh. "It's not going to jump. That one's probably tired."

"Alright, take a deep breath," Div said, breezing past us with a cardboard box. He scooped the turtles up with impressive efficiency before snapping the lid closed and handing it over to me. "Can you deal with that, please?"

Liv and I winced at him. "Sorry, Div," I told him.

"It's fine." He gestured at the box. "But please, get them out of here. Now."

With the turtles safely in the box, we hurried through town hall, which was empty since everyone was gathered in the hallway watching their mayor have a meltdown. We passed Anna at reception, still swiping left, and burst out the front doors.

"Mr. Volunteer, everyone," Liv said, applauding me as we set the box in the backseat of my car. Her eyes danced with amusement.

I did a quick bow. "Thank you. I'm available to help where I can."

We climbed into the car and I pulled out onto the street, heading in the direction of the turtle sanctuary.

"No mayhem, no chaos, no getting in trouble," she listed off on her fingers, recalling my earlier words.

"Okay." My chest shook with laughter. "Olivia. You were there. That wasn't my fault."

She shook her head at me. "Wherever you go, trouble finds you, huh?" Her eyes were so bright and warm, they made my throat tight.

She was perfect like this, laughing with me.

"Maybe it's you," I shot back, beaming at her. "You're my little bad luck charm."

Her eyebrows wiggled up and down. "You going to get rid of me?"

"No way." My heart expanded in my chest, glancing at her as I drove. "Not a chance."

Right now, it felt like everything was perfect, like everything was so simple, and even though today hadn't turned out like I wanted, it didn't matter. Where it counted, I was the guy Liv needed. I was there for her, I showed up for her, and I wasn't leaving. Seeing her laugh until she couldn't breathe had lit my soul on fire.

We felt like us again.

Her head fell back and she howled with a big laugh. "*They can smell my blood!*"

"*They're predators!*"

We laughed all the way home, and I begged the universe for this to last forever.

47

Finn

OUR BOOTS CRUNCHED as we hiked up the old path covered in fallen trees, leaves, and other debris from years without use. I slid a glance at Liv, breathing hard as we climbed the steep incline. Her hair was up in a ponytail and she pushed her bangs off her face with the back of her hand.

She turned to face me. "You keep looking at me."

My mouth turned up. "Can't I admire my beautiful girlfriend?"

I tossed the word out, waiting to see her reaction.

She rolled her eyes, turning to hide a smile. "I'm sweating."

"I know."

With her eyes, she shot daggers at me, and I grinned. "Want me to carry some of your pack?"

"Never," she bit out, and I laughed. She grinned and stuck her tongue out at me.

I thought back to this morning, when we left at dawn. She had left her sample collection kit on the table. It was just a resealable plastic bag with more plastic bags, a few plastic tubes, a pen and a notebook.

She never forgot her kit, which meant she didn't think

we'd find the flower on this trip. While her back was turned, I had stuffed it in my bag.

Liv might be giving up hope, but I wasn't.

"How'd you sleep?" I asked her.

She narrowed her eyes at me and I sent her a rakish look. I'd slept in her bed every night this week, not even asking at this point. Each night, she had climbed on top of me, kissing me, tugging on my hair, grinding against me until our breathing was ragged, our cheeks were flushed, and my control was seconds from snapping.

I always flipped her onto her side just in time, tucking her against my chest, ignoring when she ground her ass back against me in protest.

Liv was going out of her mind with horniness and I was right there with her. Every time I stepped into the shower, I was fucking my fist, thinking about her breathy moans in my ear and the glaze in her eyes after I kissed her hard.

"I slept fine," she said lightly.

I grinned at her. "Me too. You're so cute in the mornings."

She narrowed her eyes, probably thinking of something sharp to say. "So are you. I like when your hair's all messy." She picked up the pace and I watched her ass as she climbed the trail with a big smile on my face.

At the top, she turned back to wait for me. "Is there a fireplace in this ski lodge?"

"Dot said there was a wood stove."

We hadn't packed a tent because while having a drink with me at the bar the other night, Dot had told me about the expeditions she and her late husband had done even into their eighties.

"There's a ski lodge on the other side," she had told me, sipping her white wine. "Not a lot of people know about it, especially after the logging road washed out. It's not much, just a simple cabin. No electricity, of course, but it has a loft for sleeping, a table, a wood stove, maybe a few old pots and pans still."

We arrived at the ski lodge around noon, sticky with sweat but relieved that we wouldn't be sleeping outside tonight.

"We can live here if I don't find the flower," Liv said as we slung our packs down.

I straightened up, studying her with a frown. Something in my stomach tightened at her tone.

She raised an eyebrow. "I was joking."

"Were you?"

She blinked at me. The corner of her mouth twitched up as she gestured at the lodge. "I haven't even seen the inside."

I stared harder at her. "Not about that. About the flower. Have you given up?"

Neither of us said anything. In the branches above us, a couple birds chirped at each other.

"No," she said quietly.

"Are you sure?"

She blinked, shaking her head. "What—where is this coming from?"

"I saw your kit on the table this morning."

She blew a long breath out, turning away to open her pack. "I didn't want to carry the extra weight."

My hands came to my hips and I tapped my tongue to my top lip. "It weighs nothing."

My head told me to shut up, that I was picking a fight, but disappointment wrenched in my chest. She couldn't give up, there was too much at stake. This was her PhD, and her dream career.

Her hands stilled on her pack and she straightened before meeting my gaze. Her mouth twisted with hesitation and I saw it in her eyes—defeat.

"If we don't find it on this trip—"

"Liv." I let out a loud sigh. My shoulders tensed.

She stepped toward me and put her hands on my arms,

letting out her own long breath. "If we don't find it on this trip, I don't want to keep hunting."

"What?" I shook my head. "What are you talking about?"

Her eyes dimmed. "What if everyone in my program was right, and it really is extinct? I can't spend the rest of my life searching for it." She rubbed her sternum, frowning. "In October, I'll need to find a new job and a place to live. I don't want to be out here all winter, freezing my ass off. I don't want that for you either." Her gaze met mine, worried and lost. "This summer has taught me that I don't want to be stuck anymore. I want to move forward." Emotion rose in her eyes. "Whatever that looks like. Things are going to be okay either way." Her throat worked. "You make me feel like that."

My chest ached with a twist of emotions. Hearing her want to move forward—with me—made my heart lift, but I hated seeing her like this, losing hope and untethered.

Something struck me, a strange shift in my chest. Since the beginning of the summer, my feelings for Liv had multiplied tenfold. I had thought I was in love with her, but now, it was so much more. I wanted the world for her, and I wanted to keep her heart safe.

In the past, I'd been careless with her heart. I'd never make that mistake again.

My hands framed her jaw. "I'm going to keep searching for that flower, and I won't let you give up."

"You're so dramatic." She let out a soft laugh but the smile didn't reach her eyes. "It's just a stupid flower," she whispered.

I brushed a lock of her hair back, tucking it behind her ear. "It's not just a stupid flower."

Her mouth twisted to the side but her gaze warmed. In the sunlight, her eyes were bottomless pools of caramel that went on forever. Her throat bobbed and she nodded.

"Okay," she said.

"Okay?" I dipped my head down to catch her eyes. "Not giving up?"

She shook her head. "Not giving up. But—" She squeezed my ribs and I jerked back as she tried to tickle me. "I want to enjoy this hike a bit, too. Let's explore this area today. I don't just want to have our eyes on the ground all day."

I nodded. "Alright."

Inside the lodge, sunlight streamed in through skylights. There was a long wooden table with bench seating, a small wooden stove, and a ladder leading to a loft for sleeping, as Dot had described.

Half an hour later, we had unpacked our bags and eaten a quick lunch when Liv glanced up from a map she was studying.

"There's a creek near here." Her finger trailed along the worn paper. "And it flows over a steep elevation drop." She raised an eyebrow at me.

"Waterfall?"

Her expression turned thoughtful. "Maybe. We should be crossing off squares on the grid but…"

Both of our gazes strayed to the map we had been working through this summer, spread out on the table. On each trip, we had drawn an X through the grid squares we searched. There weren't many left.

Something in her eyes told me she needed a break.

"We can search for the flower tomorrow," I told Liv. "Let's go find that waterfall."

———

AN HOUR LATER, we climbed over trees and plants on the way to the creek. Once we spotted it, we'd followed it up the steep incline, exploring.

The black knot behind her neck snagged my attention again. Under her clothes, she had worn her swimsuit, a stringy black bikini. I'd caught a quick flash of her in it while she dressed, and the sight of all that soft skin made me half hard.

She waited with a teasing grin while I chugged water. "Getting tired?"

I gave her a light smack on the ass. "Always uphill with you, huh?"

She laughed. "It'll be worth it."

"It already is." I winked at her and she rolled her eyes, laughing. I let my gaze linger on her, on the slope of her nose, the splash of freckles across her face, the flush and sheen on her skin as she worked hard. The curve of her plush lips, the swoop and dip of her Cupid's bow.

Liv Morgan was fucking gorgeous, and I would happily climb through untouched forests with her for the rest of my life.

Her eyes glittered. "I'm glad we did this. Took an afternoon off, I mean. I like making new memories with you."

I blew a breath out, rubbing the pleasant ache in my chest. Maybe she did love me back.

I cocked a grin at her to hide whatever was threatening to show on my face. "Morgan, when you say things like that, I almost think you have a heart."

She huffed a laugh. "Race you to that giant tree." She pointed at a fallen tree a couple hundred feet away at the top of a ridge. "If I win, you have to eat a Cheezie."

I made a disgusted face. "Gross. Okay, fine, you're on. But if *I* win—" My smile turned wicked and I lifted my eyebrows. "You have to get a tattoo."

Her jaw dropped in outrage but her eyes sparked with fun and challenge.

"And I get to choose it," I cut in before she could protest.

"Unfair," she said, laughing.

I shrugged. "You can choose where you want it." My gaze slid to hers. "You want to change your bet?"

"Yeah, I do." Her hands came to her hips and she cocked her head, fired up. "If I win, *you* have to get a tattoo of my *name*."

My gaze locked on hers and I felt like laughing. "You have a deal, Morgan." I stuck my hand out and she shook it. "No backing out now," I said softly.

The playful, daring, competitive sparkle in her eyes made me grateful for this moment in the forest with her. "You're on."

"Ready?"

She nodded and we planted our feet, ready to run. "Go," she said before taking off like a shot.

Liv hauled *ass* up that mountain, and I watched from a comfortable distance behind her, taking my time. At the top of the ridge, I sauntered to the tree and slapped my hand on it, casual as all hell.

Her expression was equal parts outrage and amusement. "You tricked me!" she yelled, throwing a stick at my foot.

I laughed and hopped out of the way. "I didn't trick you."

"You let me win."

I raised my eyebrows at her. "We both won."

Her nostrils flared and I couldn't tell whether she wanted to tackle me out of anger or horniness. Maybe both. The thought made my dick twitch. Fucking hell, I couldn't wait to fool around with her tonight. I couldn't help myself—the thought of Liv's name on my body made my blood hum.

"I'm not backing down," she said, eyebrows raised. "Even if you threw it, I won."

My mouth curled into a grin. "Good."

"You're getting that tattoo."

I took a step toward her, gaze locked to hers. "Jeez, you must really want your name on me. Feeling territorial? Want to tell others who I belong to?" My voice dipped low and her lips parted.

Her face flushed deep red and she clamped her mouth shut to hide a grin. "Shut up."

My chest shook with laughter, and she whooped as I crouched down and threw her over my shoulder. I was about to make another crack but something in the distance caught my attention and my heart stopped.

"Liv." My smile faded.

Over my shoulder, she kicked and wiggled. "See? You're coming to your senses and have realized you don't want *Olivia* written in Comic Sans across your lower back. Put me down."

I blinked, staring at it, before lowering her to the ground. "Liv."

"What?"

My hands came to her shoulders and I turned her around before pointing.

"Holy shit," she breathed.

48

Olivia

I BLINKED at the delicate pink petals.

At the top of the ridge, the creek cut into the earth, cascading down the jagged rock. Tree roots burst through the cliffs, moss grew on landings, and wherever sunlight hit the cliffs beside the waterfall, a blanket of pink flowers grew.

My heart hammered in my chest.

"Am I hallucinating?" I whispered.

I stepped forward to the edge of the ridge, staring down the waterfall. The flowers ended halfway down as sunlight became more scarce.

"Holy shit," I repeated. "They look so sweet, like they were just sitting here waiting for me."

Finn's hand landed on my shoulder and I turned to him. His eyes searched mine, his Adam's apple bobbed as he gave me a soft smile of disbelief and pride.

"You did it." I'd never heard this tone from him, all wonder and relief. "You found it, Liv."

I glanced between him and the flowers, shaking my head. It was like a dream, the sound of water cascading over the edge, water pooling below. So quiet and serene, and we were the only people who knew about this place. In my chest, something slipped and dislodged, falling loose, fading away.

"I think a small part of me believed them," I told him, dazed. "I believed that it was gone."

He squeezed the back of my neck, warm, firm, and supportive, and I forced myself to breathe. On top of the ridge, the sun was bright and unfiltered. The air was humid from the waterfall and even though it was the peak of summer, the earth beneath our feet was damp. I tested the ground, bouncing my weight on it with a little frown.

Of course.

"It's so simple." I peered at Finn. "They have moisture, they have sunlight, and the rock likely has a similar composition to the sand down on the beaches."

Finn's eyes shone with pride and a laugh burst out of my chest.

"So simple." I shook my head. "So fucking simple."

Holy shit. I had found the flower.

My eyes burned and a hot tear rolled down my face. I wiped it away fast but another one chased it. All this time, all this work, and I had finally found it.

I wasn't crazy. I wasn't a quack. No one had believed me, but I found the flower.

No one but Finn.

I smiled at him through my watery tears. "Thank you."

His eyes welled up and he swallowed. I hadn't seen him cry since we were eight years old. "You did this, baby. This is all you. You found it. You were right."

All the things I had longed to hear. I wrapped my arms around him and he hugged me so tightly I could barely breathe. A sharp, sweet emotion swelled inside me.

We held each other for a long moment, hearts slamming against each other.

I stood there hugging Finn, crying into his shirt, heart

beating out of my chest, and I nearly laughed at how stupid I had been.

I didn't believe in signs, but even I wasn't dumb enough to ignore this one. Finding the flower with Finn meant something. Of course it was him.

It had always been him.

My heart burst wide open in my chest and I knew the truth.

I was fully in love with Finn Rhodes.

All the big moments in life, we had shared. Birthdays, trips, graduation. He was woven into so many of the experiences that had made me who I was.

And now this.

"Sharing this with you," I whispered into his chest, "it's the only way I wanted to do this."

He scooped me up and I wrapped my legs around his waist.

"We're going to have so many firsts together, aren't we?" I asked him, smiling down at him.

His eyes were velvet soft. "Mhm."

I leaned down to kiss him.

———

AT THE BOTTOM of the creek, we left our shoes on the shore while we waded in, letting the cool water run over us. Finn's hand slipped into mine and I leaned against him, quiet and content.

"That's a tough flower," Finn commented, and I smiled.

"Yeah. Everyone underestimated it."

He gave my hand a squeeze.

We returned to the ski lodge with a ton of photos. We'd left my kit here and would return tomorrow to collect samples.

While Finn cooked dinner, I flicked through the photos. He had made me crouch on the ridge, the flowers in the background, while he snapped pictures. In the images, my smile stretched ear to ear.

I glanced at him cooking over the stove, his broad back to me, the muscles dancing as he moved.

I wished I could say it. The emotion simmered under my skin. On the ridge earlier, when we stood together with shining eyes, it had burst and bloomed in my chest.

I really, really wanted to say it.

We ate dinner outside, watching the sun go down as we sat on a log listening to the sounds of the forest.

"Even this dried pasta crap tastes okay tonight," Finn commented, and I laughed.

My nose wrinkled. "Is it bad that I'm relieved we won't have to eat it for a while?"

"Fuck, no. I can never eat this or trail mix ever again." He shrugged, bumping my shoulder with his. "Still worth it, though."

I nodded, meeting his eyes. "Still worth it."

When the light was too dim to see, we headed back inside. I added more wood to the fire in the stove to keep the cabin warm while Finn climbed up to the loft, laying out our sleeping bags. I heard the rustle of him against the slippery fabric, and my pulse picked up as I climbed the ladder.

"It's too early to sleep," I told him.

He was shirtless and my gaze dropped to the pictures across his arms and chest. His eyes followed me, shining in the golden light from the stove and lantern downstairs. "I know."

Sparks shot through me and I crawled into the sleeping bag. He had connected ours together, one on top and one below. Propped up on my elbow, I leaned down to kiss him. His hand came to my jaw, tilting me open to deepen the kiss.

He sighed into me and the next second, I was on my back, watching him hover over me with a devilish smile that was different than usual.

Sweeter. More affectionate. Trusting. Like this was everything to him.

It was everything to me, too.

"You're so beautiful, Olivia." His eyes roamed my face before meeting my gaze. "I look at you and I can't breathe. I can't think. I just want to be with you."

I nodded quickly, feeling like he'd pulled the words from me. My mouth opened and closed but again, the words I wanted to say tangled and snagged. Instead, I nodded again, putting my hands on his shoulders, his warm skin, his muscles.

"Kiss me," I said, and he did.

49

Olivia

FINN'S MOUTH on mine was hungry and unrelenting, stroking deeper and firmer, and every groan and pant from him sent heat to my center. My legs wrapped around his hips, heels digging into him as he broke the kiss, leaning his forehead against mine, chest rising and falling as he gazed at me with fire in his eyes.

"Now?" I whispered, and he nodded. "Thank fuck." My voice was ragged and he chuckled before kissing me again.

While his mouth took mine, he skated his fingers to the hem of my shirt, gliding up my skin until he came to my bra. His fingers brushed over the fabric, circling one nipple before moving to the other, so light he barely touched me, but I felt it all the way to the apex of my thighs.

My hands were on his back, stroking down the bare skin, raking my nails as he shuddered at my touch.

"You going to mark me up tonight, Liv?" he asked in between kisses. "Scratch my back up and show everyone who I belong to, just like that tattoo I'm going to get?"

"You're not getting a tattoo." My voice broke as he dipped into my bra, pinching the aching peak.

"Oh yes, I fucking am," he gritted into my ear before

tapping his forearm, the birds circling it. "I'll get as many tattoos for you as I fucking want. Understand?"

Lust rushed through my blood. So those tattoos did mean something.

His eyes burned me, and my skin heated. "Let's make something clear, Olivia." I shivered at his use of my full name, like when I sent him the voice recording. "I'm not interested in temporary with you."

I'd knocked something loose in Finn, and tonight he wasn't holding back. Electricity ran through me like a bolt of lightning, landing between my legs. I bit my lip.

"Nod so I know you understand."

I jerked a quick nod, and his mouth turned up into something wicked. Paired with the dark glaze in his eyes, the effect was intoxicating. His hand landed on my inner thigh, stroking up and down, closer and closer to where I ached for him.

"Do you want me?" he ground out, still holding my gaze.

"I always have." My words were breathless.

He made a low noise and his hands came to my shirt, lifting it off of me. My bra was next, then my shorts. Beneath him, naked, his gaze lit my skin on fire.

"Jesus," he murmured. He grabbed my wrists and pinned them above my head. "Now you can't rush me. I remember how sweet you are after you come on my cock." His voice was a low purr in my ear and wetness gathered between my legs.

"Finn," I moaned. "Stop teasing me."

"What do you want?" His mouth brushed down my neck, kissing and sucking and nipping, yanking moans and gasps out of my throat.

"I want to come. Make me come."

His eyes darkened and he chuckled again. "Be careful what you wish for."

His hand glided over my slick center. My back arched at the contact, my jaw dropped as I let out a low moan, and Finn drew unrelenting circles on my clit, dragging wetness over me in a merciless motion so pleasurable I thought I'd break right there.

"Let's get the first out of the way. How does that sound?"

I was nodding, I think. He swirled his fingers over me in that delicious way, drawing warmth and pressure and crackling energy out of me.

"Olivia."

My eyes opened and met his. He smiled.

"Good. Eyes on me." Inside me, he crooked his finger to find the spot that made my vision blur. His other hand stayed firm around my wrists, above my head.

"Fuck," I murmured, tilting my hips with the movement of his hand. Heat coursed through my blood.

He hummed, smiling down at me. So confident. I'd always been such a sucker for that arrogant, devilish grin.

"Cocky," I gritted out. "So cocky."

"Your words don't have the same bite when you're on the brink of coming, baby." He added a second finger, letting the heel of his palm bump against my clit with every stroke. My head tipped back as I clenched around him.

"*Fuck, fuck, fuck.*"

He chuckled, watching my face with undivided attention. "I know how to make you come. I've had so much time to think about it, replay every memory. I thought about all the things I'd do once you were mine."

God, his hand. My eyes fell closed and snapped open, meeting his, and his eyes lit up with something pleased and powerful.

"Do you like it like this, Olivia?" he asked in a low voice. "Do you like being underneath me, pinned down and pleasing me like this?"

"Whatever," I gasped, because I felt like playing with fire.

He removed his fingers, stroked lazily up and down my seam, and I growled. His chest shook with laughter.

"Say it, baby."

"Fine. Yes, I like it."

"Good girl." His fingers slipped back inside me, stroking harder, firmer, faster, and I squirmed as pressure grew low in my belly. "You look so pretty when you're under me like this. So pretty when you're about to come on my fingers."

It danced at the edge of my consciousness, closing in, ready to burst open inside of me. Finn's heel pressed my clit harder and my eyes widened.

"That's it." He nodded. "There you go. Almost there. I can feel you getting ready to come, baby. You're tightening up on my fingers and you are so, so wet for me. You're doing so fucking well."

My back arched as the heat and pressure built between my legs, and his gaze raked down my body before he dropped his head to suck on an aching nipple.

White light burst in my vision as I came around his fingers, squeezing and clenching. He murmured encouragement in my ear while wringing pleasure from me, and when I floated back to earth, I was breathing hard.

Finn lifted his fingers to his mouth and let out a low groan as he licked them off. My pussy fluttered again at the sight.

"Great. Nice work." He smiled at me. "That's one."

I moaned and he chuckled.

"What's the magic number, Olivia?"

I was still catching my breath. "Three?" God, I hoped one of those times was with him inside me. His hands and his mouth did delicious things but after today, it wasn't enough.

"Three." He dipped his head and sucked the spot beneath my ear, the one that always made me squirm for him.

His fingers trailed up and down my thighs as he kissed me. The orgasm had taken the edge off my urgency but the desire in Finn's movements, the way he kissed me so deeply, how his hands worked my breasts, slid a heavy ache between my thighs, and soon I was panting and tilting my hips for more.

He let go of my wrists over my head as he shifted down,

pushing my legs further apart, and buried his face between my legs. With his tongue, he dragged a line up my seam, making me buck against his face.

Thank fuck we were in the middle of nowhere, because the volume at which I moaned Finn's name would have woken up the entire town.

"Fuck," I gasped at the soft, dizzying sensation of his tongue on my clit. "Finn."

"Mhm." He did it again, clamping a roped forearm over my hips to hold me down. "You taste so good. So sweet, baby. I fuck my fist daily to the memory of my tongue between your legs."

The image of me bent over the bar, open for him while his tongue worked me, sent a wave of heat to my center. Finn let out a low laugh.

"You just got so wet," he whispered before he slipped his fingers inside me.

I couldn't form words as he stroked my G-spot, licking and sucking and dragging his lips over me. His noises of appreciation drove me higher, and when his free hand slipped beneath my ass to grip me, I felt the first tremors.

"Fuck, you're so close," he rasped, sucking my clit in a pulsing rhythm that made me forget my own name. My pussy pulsed around his fingers, the heat grew low in my stomach, and his groan against me tipped me over the edge. My muscles went taut as I fell, riding his face, listening to his groans of pleasure as electricity crackled through my body.

"Oh my god," I gasped as the spasms slowed and I eased back. "Oh my god."

Finn kissed the inside of my thigh, so gentle and sweet for someone with such a dirty mouth. "That's two."

I laughed with exhaustion or delirium, I wasn't sure.

He crawled over me and kissed me, nipping at my bottom lip as I caught my breath before tilting open for him. I tasted myself on him.

"You're making me crazy," I said against his mouth. "I feel like I'm dying."

He cocked a dark grin at me. "You're not dying, Liv. You're doing great."

His praise made my insides melt and I couldn't hold back my smile. Against my hip, his cock pressed thick and hard through his boxer briefs. I reached for it and he hissed when I stroked his length, rubbing my thumb on the tip over the fabric.

"Now," I breathed, and he nodded, eyes glazing.

He pulled his shorts off before settling between my legs. Instinct had my hips shifting against him, dragging his erection over my soaked center. A flush bloomed on his cheeks and his eyes dropped to my mouth before he kissed me again.

"You okay?" he whispered, and I nodded quickly.

A lock of hair had fallen into his eyes and I brushed it back. My heart squeezed. In the low light of the cabin, with just us for miles around, it felt intimate and special.

It felt like love.

My throat squeezed as I swallowed, and my heart thrashed in my chest, desperate to be seen. Desperate to say its piece.

I wanted to say those words to him. More than anything, I wanted to lift up that corner and show him what was in my heart.

I was so in love with Finn Rhodes.

I didn't think I ever stopped being in love with him. Finn searched my eyes like he could read my thoughts. Did he know? He must have known.

My lips parted and the words were right there—

His expression from years ago flashed into my mind. The disappointment, anger, and regret on his face as he stumbled against his parents' front door, pretending to be drunk. Like it was only a matter of time before he disappointed me. My chest seized as panic loomed in my head.

If Finn left, even if I didn't tell him how I felt, it wouldn't matter. I'd still be devastated.

What did it mean that I couldn't say it?

This was Finn, who was basically an extension of myself. The guy who knew me better than anyone, knew all the worst parts of me and still he was here, looking at me like he—

If I couldn't say it with Finn, what hope did I have? What did that say about me?

My throat locked up, and I still couldn't say it.

"It's okay," he whispered, eyes on me, and the tension in my chest eased. He slipped his hand into mine, lacing our fingers together beside my head. His voice was so soft and reassuring. "It's okay."

I nodded, and the panic dissipated. My fingers squeezed his.

"I'm not going anywhere," he said. Words I'd heard a hundred times, but I needed them now more than ever.

Finn always knew what I needed to hear.

I nodded at him again, wordless, chest pulsing with gratitude for him. He supported his weight on his forearm while his length rested between my legs. His throat worked and I saw the threads of his control snapping.

"I have a condom downstairs." His forehead rested on mine and he shifted his hips, dragging his cock up my center, loosing a low moan from my throat as his hot skin rubbed me.

My head jerked side to side. "I'm on the pill and my last checkup came back clear."

"Me, too." His jaw was tight.

"We don't need one."

"You sure?" he asked in a strained voice.

"Uh-huh." My free hand wrapped around his waist, pulling his hips toward me as the urgency built inside me. My breathing sped up in anticipation. "Now, Finn. Please."

He nudged against my entrance and I gasped at the pressure as he pushed inside.

"God," I managed at the mind-bending burn as he fed his cock into me.

"Fuck, Olivia." He said my name like he was offended at how good I felt. "So tight." His head dropped to my shoulder and I felt myself stretch around him. "Fuck, you feel amazing. Better than anything."

"Oh my god," I was saying over and over again as the sensation overwhelmed me. "Oh my god, Finn."

When he was inside me to the hilt, he paused, breathing hard. "You okay?"

"Uh-huh."

He squeezed his eyes closed. "Jesus Christ," he whispered. "So difficult not to fuck you hard. I need to move, baby."

I nodded, dizzy at the intoxicating pressure inside me. Finn retreated before slowly rocking back in. I felt every inch of his thick length, and I made a moaning noise I'd never heard from myself before.

His gaze made my skin tingle, burning so bright as he stroked. My blood coursed with lust. Deep inside me, the spring wound tighter as he moved. As I adjusted, I wanted more. We could do the slow, gentle sex later, but now, I wanted Finn to lose his mind. I wanted to see him fall apart the way I was shattering around him. We'd break each other and start fresh. We'd wash the last twelve years away as we reformed into new people.

"Go hard, Finn. Please."

Behind his glazed expression, the devilish grin I loved so much flashed, and he jerked a nod. He found a punishing pace and my head tipped back, eyes wide as the pressure swirled around the base of my spine.

"You're mine," he managed. "You've always been mine."

His hand slipped into mine, interlacing our fingers. His head fell forward as he thrust into me, and the scrape of his teeth on my shoulder made my head spin. It was his low moan of pleasure in my ear, though, that made me start shaking again. I listened to the hoarse noises slipping out of him, like being inside me was such a sharp ecstasy that he could barely stand it, and felt my climax closing in on me.

"Again," I gasped before I fell. I gripped his hand as my muscles clenched around him. Heat raced up my spine, my back arched, my feet dug into his ass, and I was vaguely aware that I was saying his name over and over again as every nerve in my body howled with pleasure. Every muscle pulled taut as I shook.

"Gonna come." Finn's voice was rough as he fucked me hard. "Gonna come inside you like I've always wanted."

Through my climax, I nodded and met his gaze, mind clouded like we were in a dream. At the center of the universe, it was just the two of us. Finn's expression turned agonized, wincing with pleasure as he thrust into me hard, shuddering and pulsing inside me.

As we came down together, chests heaving for air, staring at each other with baffled expressions, I knew we were meant to be together.

He collapsed against me and turned to press kisses down my neck. Beside my head, we still clutched each other's hand, interlaced and connected.

"There's no one like you," I whispered to him.

50

Finn

"OH MY GOD," Olivia moaned into my mouth the next morning as she straddled me on the bench downstairs. My hands were on her tits, her ass, dipping below her waistband to massage her clit while she tugged my hair and scraped her nails down my bare back.

"Can't get enough of you." My voice was jagged in her ear as I kissed down her neck. She arched, tilting her head back so I could access the long column of her throat before I pulled her bra down.

The past twelve hours had been a fever dream, a blur of skin, moans, and orgasms. We'd slept a few hours, woken up reaching for each other, and collapsed before repeating it all over again. Now that we had located the flower, the pressure was off and we could enjoy ourselves—and each other—for the rest of the day.

Liv pulled her bra off and tossed it aside before her mouth returned to mine and she began to grind against me. My erection pressed into her and her eyes rolled back.

"Are you sore?" I asked.

Her eyes were glazed. "Yes, but I don't care."

I pulled back. "I don't want to hurt you, I'll just go down on you."

"No." Her nostrils flared and her eyes flashed. Her voice was desperate as she pulled me out of my shorts. "I want you."

She lifted up before sliding down my cock, and we both moaned.

"I knew it would be like this," I managed as she rested her forehead against mine.

Sex with her was all-consuming, intense, and electric. Like nothing else I'd ever experienced. With Liv, it didn't feel like fucking. It felt like more. It felt like love.

She had wanted to say it last night; I saw it in her eyes. It was right there under the surface. It had always been there, waiting, and she had finally figured it out. Liv loved me, she just wasn't ready to say it yet.

I'd wait until she was ready, even if it took forever.

As she rode me, Liv's hand snaked down between us to rub her clit and I watched in fascination and awe as her head tipped back, eyes closed. Liv wore pleasure so well, it made me want to keep her here in this cabin for the rest of our lives. The sound of her orgasm usually triggered my own, and I knew when we returned to regular life, I'd be replaying our time here over and over again.

I had shower material for the next decade.

My balls tightened as she clenched up on me, wincing and moaning.

"Gonna come," she managed, rocking on my length.

I nodded and as her muscles pulsed around my cock, I found my release, spilling into her once again as pressure and heat raced up my spine and made me mindless.

Something about coming inside Liv seared my brain. Made me feel like she was *mine*.

We caught our breaths with our foreheads resting against each other.

"God, we're so good together," she whispered.

"It's never been like this." My hand sank into her hair and I pressed a soft kiss to her lips. "Even our first time."

She nodded, chest still heaving for air. Her eyes had that hot, glazed look I loved to see after she came.

Up and down her back, my hand skimmed lazy strokes. "How about I make you a quick breakfast and then we grab those samples?"

She nodded and smiled. "Okay."

My heart beat with something new. Pride. I took joy in making Olivia food. Providing for her. Supporting her. It was like what I felt yesterday seeing the expression of awe and disbelief when she found the flower.

"I'd do anything for you," I whispered to her before giving her a quick kiss. I searched her eyes for any sign of wariness or worry but she just smiled in that relaxed, sated way.

———

"GOT EVERYTHING YOU NEED?" I asked that afternoon as she sealed the last bag.

"I think so." She crouched beside the bag, flipping through her samples. "I have more photos than I can count, and I have a couple specimens with the roots." She held the bag up to check there was enough moisture before setting it back down. "I have the exact location marked on the map, and I have seeds." She shot me a thumbs up. "We're good."

"Great." I walked to her side. "Stand up for me."

She stood, sending me a confused glance before I leaned down to throw her over my shoulder. She whooped with laughter as I carried her down the hill, and at the bottom, I pulled my shirt off.

Liv's eyes went wide with surprise as my swimsuit came off.

"There's no one around," I told her with a grin, gesturing at the flowers up on the cliffs. "Obviously."

She chewed her lip, returning my smile with hesitance.

"Take your clothes off," I told her, using the tone that I knew made her wet.

Her eyes turned hazy as she did as she was told, and something hot wrapped around the base of my spine. Blood rushed to my cock and her eyebrows shot up as her eyes dropped to it.

"Good girl," I said in a low, pleased tone as she dropped the last item of clothing on the shore. I stepped toward her until I towered over her, dropping my mouth to her neck to skate my lips over her skin. Her breath caught. "You're always such a good girl for me."

She shuddered and I took her hand, leading her into the water. We swam around the shallow pool, racing across the length a few times, splashing each other, and studying the rock formations down the cliffs.

"This is so easy," Liv said at one point, pushing her wet hair back and smiling at me. Her eyes were so soft as she swam to me, letting me pull her into my arms. Her legs wrapped around my waist and my cock stiffened.

I leaned forward to kiss her and that familiar urge that had me by the throat made me lift her out of the water and carry her to the ledge behind the waterfall. Behind the curtain of water, it was dim and misty, and I pushed her back against the wall as my mouth crashed into hers.

"Again?" she murmured against my mouth, already grinding against me.

I nodded, moaning as her hand wrapped around my cock, jerking me.

In the low light, her eyes turned molten. "Your moans are so good, Finn."

This time was different, against the cliff face beneath the waterfall. I forced myself to slow down, not just because she was sore but because being here, in the middle of the forest with the woman I loved, surrounded by the flower she'd been searching for, it was everything. Nothing would ever compare to being with her.

"I love you," I whispered as she began to clench me. "I love you so fucking much, Liv, and I'll wait until you're ready to say it back."

Olivia

"HI," Finn called, pushing the door of his parents' place open. "We're here."

We stepped inside and kicked off our shoes. Conversation filtered through the house, and my pulse beat in my ears.

I swallowed past a rock in my throat, glancing around the familiar foyer. Elizabeth had changed up the side table near the door, and there was a mirror hanging over it. My reflection blinked back at me, face tanned and freckled from being outside all summer.

I hadn't been inside this house since that night, the one before Finn left.

"Hey." Finn's warm arm wrapped around my shoulders and he pulled me into his chest. "You okay?" he murmured against my temple, and I nodded.

"Just nervous," I said with a shrug and a small smile.

He glanced at the door with sparkling eyes, tilting his head. "You want to ditch this?"

I snorted. "No."

"Come on," he teased, voice low in my ear, and a shiver rolled down my back.

Since we got home from hiking, Finn and I had been having a lot of sex.

The best sex. Toe-curling, eye-crossing, crying out each other's names kind of sex. Day and night.

Finn had said he loved me at the waterfall. I'd been replaying the words in my head constantly. He hadn't said it again since, but I knew he felt it.

I wanted to say it too, but every time I tried, my mind reminded me that Finn loved a chase and a thrill. He craved the fun and games part of a relationship. If that was over, he'd get bored.

My stomach tensed. I didn't even want to think about that, after everything that had happened in the past few months.

Cole still hadn't contacted me, so there was my answer. People got bored and people left, so I kept my mouth shut.

For now, though, I was enjoying what I had. I wasn't going to worry about the future. In Elizabeth and Sam's foyer, I shook my head and put on a brave smile for Finn.

Elizabeth appeared around the corner, eyes bright with a big smile on her face. "There they are."

After she gave us warm, lingering hugs, she pulled us into the kitchen, where Wyatt, Holden, and Avery were helping her prep the salad. The guys nodded hellos while Avery hugged us and poured me and Finn glasses of wine.

"Go outside," Elizabeth said, shooing us out the patio door, and I laughed, feeling like we were ten years old again.

In the backyard, Emmett barbecued dinner while Sam, Hannah, and Sadie played with Cora on the grass.

"Hey, you two," Sam called over in between tossing Cora in the air while she squealed and laughed.

Sadie stood and walked over. "Hello, *doctor.*" She wiggled her eyebrows.

I snorted and shook my head. "We're not calling me that."

"We're definitely calling her that," Finn added, taking

Cora from Sam and covering her cheeks in kisses. My heart dipped.

Sadie's arms came around my neck and she squeezed me so hard I couldn't breathe. "Congratulations."

"Thanks." I smiled as she pulled back.

"So proud of you," Hannah said quietly as she gave me a hug, and I flushed.

"When's your defense?" Emmett called from the grill.

In the week since we'd gotten home, when Finn and I weren't tangled up together, I'd been emailing back and forth with my advisor.

"I submitted my dissertation this morning," I told them, taking a seat on one of the patio chairs, "so now they're scheduling the defense with the other researchers. It'll happen sometime in early September."

For the hundredth time this week, relief eased through me. My advisor could move on. *I* could move on.

Sam's eyebrows lifted in curiosity. His eyes were the same color as his son's, that sharp, clear gray. "Feeling okay about it?"

I chuckled. "Yes. My advisor is confident that I have this in the bag." A snort escaped me. "And I've had enough time with the research."

Sam shook his head in awe. "Super proud of you, Olivia."

I smiled at my hands in my lap. "Thanks, Sam."

The others joined us out in the yard, talking and laughing, and by the time we took our seats at the table, my worries had disappeared. Being with these people was easy. How many hours had I spent in this backyard over my childhood and teenager years? It felt like a second home.

"This is a good one," Elizabeth said later, holding her iPad up.

It was a photo from Sadie's baby shower. Finn was mid-hip-roll over me; staring down at me with an expression that would make a porn star blush. In the photo, I was practically drooling over him. In the background, Miri's eyes were feral as she watched.

Everyone laughed.

Holden shook his head at Finn. "Wow."

"What?" Finn asked him. "Liv dragged me to Mom's book club. Do you know how many times Mom said the word *penis* in there?"

Elizabeth shrugged, acting innocent. "As many times as I could." A smile crept up her face as she eyed Finn and me, and her eyes glittered. "And I had a feeling Finn would retaliate. You two are always swiping at each other like that."

Finn's hand drifted to my lap, wrapping around mine, and he gave me a squeeze. I smiled at him.

"Asshole," I said, smiling.

His eyebrows bobbed, eyes gleaming. "You know it."

Wyatt shot Emmett a lazy grin. "Heard you had a bit of a scare at town hall the other day."

Emmett huffed, glaring at me and Finn. "Yeah, and I'm still mad about that."

Finn and I tried to stifle our laughter without success. I covered my mouth with my hand but my shaking shoulders gave us away. Around the table, everyone was grinning. Elizabeth rolled her mouth to hide her smile.

"It's not funny," Emmett told everyone. "At the next town hall, I'm putting forward a proposed ban on turtles in Queen's Cove."

"It was an accident," Finn said through his laughter. "We promise."

Emmett stared at him, shaking his head. "You two always get into trouble together."

Finn's hands flew up. "This one wasn't even my fault." He whirled his finger between me and him. "It was equally both of our faults."

"That's true," I admitted.

Emmett rubbed the bridge of his nose. "No more school trips to town hall."

"Next time, honey," Avery said with her hand on his arm in comfort, "barricade your door from the evil children."

He sighed. "I'll just ask Div to bodyguard for me."

Sadie cleared her throat. "I heard you peed your pants."

Emmett threw his fork down and pointed at me. "Olivia peed, not me!"

My mouth fell open. "I did not!"

Cora waved a chubby hand at Emmett. "Pee."

The table burst out laughing and Cora giggled.

"No one peed," Finn intervened. "But Emmett did almost pull the fire alarm for some reason."

"I was panicking," Emmett said solemnly, and Avery rubbed his arm again.

"Never a dull moment in this town," Elizabeth said, smiling to herself. She glanced at Sam. "Shall we?"

He nodded and they got up from the table, returning moments later with a cake. It read *Congratulations, Olivia!* Pink icing flowers decorated it.

The backs of my eyes burned. Oh god. I was going to cry right here in front of everyone. I blinked fast to clear the tears.

"Veena made it special," Elizabeth added, setting it down on the table. "Chocolate cherry."

My favorite. My gaze met Elizabeth's, and she winked.

"Thank you," I whispered, and she gave my shoulder a squeeze.

As the cake was cut and dished out, and the conversation and wine flowed, a thought struck me. I had so much to lose now. If things with Finn went south, all of this—this second family, these women I had grown to love, these people who knew me so well and had special cakes made to celebrate my achievements—would disappear.

Across the table, Holden frowned. "We're doing the

flooring on Friday," he said in response to whatever Hannah had asked.

Sadie nodded, wincing. "I don't know if it's safe for Cora to be there. There's a lot of dust in the air when they're sanding."

"Sam and I are doing a late afternoon round of golf with the Singhs," Elizabeth said. She thought about it. "We could reschedule."

"Don't reschedule." Wyatt shook his head. "We'll find someone to watch her."

Finn cleared his throat. "I'll do it." He smiled at Cora and stuck his tongue out. She smiled her goofy smile at him.

"You'll watch her?" Wyatt asked.

Finn shrugged. "Sure. I'm not working, and this will give me a chance to take her to the candy store and spoil her rotten."

"Alright." Wyatt shrugged. "Thank you so much."

Hannah leaned forward. "We really appreciate it, Finn."

He waved them off, smiling. "Don't mention it. Seriously." He smiled at me, and again, my heart dipped.

As conversation resumed, my thoughts wandered back to what the girls had said earlier in the summer, how Finn never used to make plans, but now he did. Like he was setting down roots.

I glanced at him sitting beside me, chatting with Wyatt about surfing.

"I want to buy a new board," Finn was saying, arms folded over his chest. "My old one's had it."

He was sticking around, but a part of me held back. I'd spent so long hating him and being angry, and this summer had flown by. I needed a bit more time to adjust, and then I could say the words.

In Hannah's lap, Cora squirmed, pointing at me. I smiled at her.

"She wants to sit with you," Hannah said. "Is that okay?"

I chuckled. "Of course."

Hannah stood and set Cora down in my lap. I leaned forward to smile down at the chubby, adorable kid, and she kicked her feet, giggling. My heart expanded in my chest.

Okay, I could see the appeal of this, having kids and all. The initial stages seemed terrifying, with pregnancy and giving birth, but this? Having a sweet little squishy cutie who resembled me and Finn? Maybe they would have Finn's eyes, or my freckles. Cora reached for Finn and he took her hand, shaking it like he was introducing himself, and I laughed. It would be the cutest thing ever, seeing Finn with our children.

Inside me, my emotions warred, and my jaw locked up. When I was ready, I'd say the words.

52

Olivia

LATER, I headed inside to use the washroom and lingered in the hallway, peering at the family photos hanging on the wall.

My gaze landed on the one of me and Finn on grad night. We were standing under the wooden arch Sam had made in the backyard, laughing and smiling at each other, so happy and young. Elizabeth had snapped the picture at the perfect moment. My breath caught in my throat. In the picture, we looked at each other like we loved each other.

Footsteps made me turn, and Elizabeth stepped up behind me.

"I love that one," she said softly. "I always knew you'd find your way back to each other." She slid a gaze to me, studying my face. "You and Finn see each other."

In my chest, my heart did somersaults.

Her eyes lingered on my face. "Honey, I'm sorry if I ever made you uncomfortable, trying to talk to you over the years. I should have given you more space." A wry smile twisted onto her mouth. "It was hard, not having you around. You were always like a daughter to me." She sighed. "I didn't get a girl, and you were always so special."

Elizabeth's gaze swung to the other pictures—a candid

photo of Avery behind the bar at her restaurant, Hannah smiling with pride in front of her bookstore, and Sadie standing beside a painting during her exhibit at the art gallery in town last year.

Oh. My heart ached, and suddenly, I saw the last twelve years through her eyes. The air whooshed out of my lungs.

"Now you have a whole bunch of girls," I said quietly.

"I do." Her arm came around my shoulders and with her other hand, she tapped the framed photo beside Sadie's.

It was a picture Finn had taken of me in front of the flower, eyes shining in the bright sun. My eyes stung again and I sniffed.

"Even if you didn't find it, honey, I'd be so proud of you and the woman you've grown into." She smiled at the photo of me. "You and Finn getting into trouble never mattered, only that you were there for each other." She pressed a kiss to my temple before letting me go.

"Elizabeth?"

She turned at the end of the hall.

"I'm sorry I brushed you off for so long." I swallowed with difficulty, glancing away. "You reminded me of Finn."

She nodded, eyes bright. "I know. I guess I didn't want you to forget about him. But even if you never got back together, you were still special to me."

She sent me a wink before returning to the backyard, and I took a few more minutes to study the family pictures on the wall.

"Hey," Finn said at the end of the hall.

I straightened up. "Hey."

"Everyone's getting ready to leave."

I nodded. "Okay. You want to go home?"

His eyes glinted as he shook his head. "Not yet." He tilted his head behind him and held his hand out. "Come on."

Finn led me upstairs and into his old bedroom. It was nearly the same, although there was a new duvet cover, and the room was tidier than when he had lived here. Through the window, I could see my old room.

"Finn," I said, laughing. "Everyone's downstairs."

He grinned at me in disbelief. "We're not doing *that*. Jesus, Morgan, you horndog."

My chest shook with laughter. "Why are we up here in your old room, then?"

A moment later, we lay out on the roof, watching the sun set as pastel pinks, golds, and oranges washed across the sky. Birds chirped their last songs of the day from the trees, and Finn's hand snuck into mine. I gave him a quick squeeze.

We heard the front door open.

"Bye," Sadie called.

I lifted my head to watch her and Holden walk down the front path to Holden's truck parked on the street. She turned back and met my gaze before she lifted her hand in a wave. A little smile played at her mouth, and I waved back.

"You know that old house we always pass?" Finn asked, playing with my fingers.

I nodded.

"What kind of changes would you make to it?"

I hummed, letting my mind drift to the old property. "The yard needs a lot of work."

"Yep."

Last time we passed it, the roof was covered in moss. "A new roof."

"Definitely."

"I'd evict all the rats and raccoons that live there now."

Finn chuckled. "Without a doubt."

I thought about the projects Sadie and Holden did and how, when she redesigned a space, she let her imagination run wild. In the inn they owned together, she had convinced Holden to install a secret library with a hidden door in a bookshelf. There was even a treehouse bar in the forest behind the inn. The homes she worked on mixed function and joyfulness.

I pictured living in that house at the edge of town. I imagined it full of our furniture, full of our families as we hosted Thanksgiving or Christmas. The big party we'd host at Halloween, kids in costumes running around the yard.

I pictured being happy there with Finn.

"I'd put a skylight in over the bed," I told him.

His eyes pinned me. "For stargazing?"

I nodded. "Every night before we fall asleep."

The corner of his mouth hitched, but his eyes melted with longing. Again, I thought about the words I wanted to say.

"Thanks for being patient with me," I whispered.

He sighed, smiling back at me. "I'd wait forever for you, Morgan."

In my memory, I heard the word Finn said months ago. He hadn't said it since.

Soulmate.

I peered up at the sky and hoped it was true.

53

Finn

THE NEXT DAY, I sat on a blanket at the park, buried under a small mountain of stuffy toys. Cora babbled to me while she balanced each toy on top of me, and I reached over to adjust her hat. Hannah had been worried about her getting a sunburn when I picked her up an hour ago.

On wobbly legs, Cora picked up another stuffy and placed it on my chest.

"Thanks," I told her.

She garbled something at me, grinning.

Damn, this kid was cute.

"Okay." I watched as she reached down for another toy before putting it on my foot. "You need help?"

"Ellen," she said, stooping to eat a goldfish cracker.

While Cora played, my mind wandered to the last family dinner. We had stayed up on the roof until the stars came out and we were yawning, and I swore, the way she looked at me, she had wanted to say it.

An impatient sliver of me wished she did say it. Why couldn't she? It had felt so right with her there at dinner.

She had always been so stubborn, and now it felt like she was holding out for some reason.

Maybe she was waiting for me to fuck up again. My stomach sank at the thought.

"Ellen," Cora squealed, clapping.

"Yeah, Ellen," I repeated, frowning.

When my parents brought out the cake for Liv, emotion had risen in her eyes like she was going to cry. She felt it, too, I *knew* she did. If only she could summon the courage to tell me how she felt, instead of relying on me to read the signs.

This worry was like a sharp kernel in my chest, poking me. *I'm yours*, she had said when we were together at the ski lodge. I wanted her to be able to say it when she was half asleep. When we were out for dinner. At the grocery store.

After all of this, after most of the summer with me basically on my knees, begging her, she still couldn't give an inch?

My phone buzzed and I glanced over.

My dissertation is booked the first week in September, she had texted.

I tapped out a response. *That's great.*

Typing dots appeared on the screen before her message popped up. *We should stay the weekend in Vancouver.*

My forehead creased. *Absolutely.*

Would we be in the same spot then, with me waiting for her to catch up?

How's it going with Cora?

I smiled and turned to take a selfie with her so we could send it to Liv.

My pulse stopped. Cora was gone.

"Cora," I yelled, shoving the toys off me as I jumped to my feet. "Cora!" My voice boomed around the park, and people glanced over in concern. My heart raced, beating against my chest, blood rushing in my ears. My gaze whipped around the park as I searched for her.

Fuck. Fuck, fuck, fuck. How could I have been so fucking stupid?

Where could she be? I heard a dog barking and turned. A

quiet street bordered the park, and a row of cars were parked along the curb.

The road. My heart lodged in my throat and I took off at a sprint.

"Cora!" I yelled as I passed a parked van, scanning for her.

On the other side of the street, I spotted her as she tripped on the sidewalk. My stomach unwound. She was safe.

"Thank fuck," I muttered, running toward her while she started wailing. "Hey, hey, hey," I said as I picked her up, trying to calm her down. "It's okay."

In my arms, Cora screamed and writhed, flailing her arms.

"Ellen," she sobbed, pointing over my shoulder, and I turned.

Jen Morgan stood there with her chocolate Lab, Evelyn.

Understanding came over me. Ellen. *Evelyn.*

I met Jen's gaze and my stomach lurched again.

"Everything okay?" she asked as she approached. Her tone was dry and wary, like she knew it wasn't.

"Yep," I said tightly as Cora thrashed. I set her down on the sidewalk so she could pet the dog.

Jen watched, and my stomach plummeted even more. "She could have been hurt, Finn."

My ears felt hot, and my pulse was still racing hard. The way Jen stared at me made me hate myself.

"I know." I raked a hand through my hair. "I didn't mean to——" I cut myself off. There was no excuse for what had happened. "I know."

It didn't help that she was what Olivia would look like in twenty years.

Behind her on the sidewalk, a few people gathered, watching. Someone who worked at Veena's bakery, Liya who managed Hannah's bookstore, and a guy I recognized from high school. They shot wary looks over at me, and it was clear they had seen Cora run across the street by herself.

My stomach knotted again and again. Right. Yeah. This was who I was. Finn, the fuck up. The reckless, thrill-seeking devil who couldn't stay in one place for too long.

No matter how hard I tried, I couldn't escape it. I couldn't shake it off. Here I was, trying to change but fighting a losing battle. It hadn't worked. My eyes closed as I thought about what could have happened. Cora could have been hit by a car or a cyclist. She could have been seriously hurt, or worse. I imagined Wyatt and Hannah's expressions, and my stomach turned with nausea.

I had really fucked this one up.

This was a sign. I should have stayed away the first time I learned this lesson. It was only a matter of time before Liv figured out the truth for herself.

"Finn?"

My head snapped up to meet Jen's mistrusting eyes. "What?"

"Why don't I take Cora home?" she asked. Her voice was neutral and strangely calm, like she was trying to keep me calm. "I'm going that way anyway."

My thoughts spun as I raked my hand through my hair, trying to remember the details of everyone's schedules. "Uh. They're not home. It's okay." I shook my head, watching Cora laugh as the dog licked her hands. "I'll take her to Hannah and Wyatt's."

Her gaze flicked to Cora. "You sure?"

"Yeah." Frustration pitched in my chest. Again, I wondered how I could have been so stupid. Hannah was saying the other day how Cora was getting fast at walking. I crouched down to pick her up. "Come on. Time to go."

While I was packing up and putting Cora in her stroller, I felt the gazes of half the park on me. My pulse still drummed in my ears, adrenaline coursing through my blood.

I didn't like this kind of thrill.

I took Cora back to Wyatt and Hannah's. She didn't want to have a nap, so we played on the floor until she fell asleep with her toy in her hand, and I settled her into her crib. I sat there in her room, watching her sleep, thinking about how much I could have lost today because of my own carelessness.

I replayed it over and over, and then I thought about the future with Liv, with our kids.

How could she trust me once she heard about this?

———

WHEN HANNAH GOT HOME EARLY that evening, Cora was still sleeping. I made a quick excuse to leave and got out of there as soon as possible. I didn't tell her what had happened—I didn't know how to. I just said goodbye and hurried out the door.

Pulling up to my parking spot behind the bar, every instinct in my body screamed at me to run, get the hell out of there, away from the whispers and the gossip and the shame. I sprinted up the stairs to the apartments, ignoring the music and chatter from the bar. Ignoring the knowledge that Liv was there tonight, working. In my bedroom, I threw clothes into a bag before hurrying out and down the stairs, back to my car.

Liv was at the bottom of the stairs.

"Hey," she said, brow creasing.

I froze. "Hi." My chest ached. I wanted to tell her what had happened, but if I did, she'd see me the way Jen did, and I couldn't bear it.

I couldn't be around when she realized what a piece of shit I was.

Her gaze dropped to my bag and something dimmed in her eyes. "Where are you going?"

"I don't know." I swallowed with difficulty, unable to tear my gaze from her. I felt stripped bare, like she could see all of me, all the bad parts I had tried to hide from her this summer. "I need to think for a bit."

Her brows snapped together and anger flashed in her gaze. We stood there a moment, staring at each other as noise from the bar traveled down the hall.

She lifted an eyebrow. "Are we done?"

Her eyes were so cold, like this summer had never happened. Like I was a stranger.

"No," I rushed out, shaking my head and wincing. "I—" I rubbed my chest, where anguish and frustration stabbed. "I need to get my head on straight."

She shrugged like she didn't care. "So go."

Without a word, she turned and headed back to the bar, and my heart dropped through my stomach.

54

Olivia

THE NEXT MORNING, I opened my eyes and turned over, searching for him.

My stomach plummeted as I remembered what had happened and I blinked, staring at the empty spot beside me in bed. Yesterday's conversation replayed in my head. After he left, I'd moved around the bar like a robot, unthinking, unfeeling, just going through the motions of mixing drinks and ringing up bills.

He looked so lost last night, with his bag over his shoulder. His eyes had darted between me and the back door like a caged animal.

I frowned and let out a long breath. This didn't make sense. After all this. After this entire summer of him assuring me he was different.

Pain thrashed in my chest, angry and resentful and full of regret.

My phone buzzed and I glanced at it. In the group chat with Hannah, Avery, and Sadie, messages were flying.

Hannah: *does anyone know where Finn is?*

Avery: *no… he was babysitting last night, right?*

Hannah: *Yeah. Liya said something happened at the park with Cora, that she ran across the street to pet Evelyn.*

Understanding dawned on me. My mom would have been there. I could picture her face, so disapproving and totally unsurprised. Fuck. Lying there in bed, I felt sick thinking of how Finn must have felt.

Sadie: *shit. That's scary.*

Hannah: *Yeah. I just want to talk to him. He looked so stressed and upset when he left last night.*

Avery: *Emmett doesn't know*

Sadie: *neither does Holden*

Hannah: *Olivia? Is he with you?*

Hannah: *If you see him, can you just let him know we're not mad? We know it was an accident.*

An unwelcome thought hit me.

If I had told Finn how I felt—how I *really* felt, those three important words—maybe he wouldn't have taken off. A headache formed behind my eyes. This whole time, Finn had said he wasn't going anywhere so I didn't move an inch. I didn't say the words he needed to hear, the words I felt.

I loved Finn. I had always loved Finn, and it was such an integral part of me that I couldn't believe I had tried to ignore it.

A scalding tear rolled down my face. Fuck. My chest ached and I wiped the tear away.

"Stupid, stupid Olivia," I whispered to myself.

———

I WOKE up at noon to my phone buzzing on my night table. My head felt fuzzy from too much sleep, and yet I couldn't will myself to get out of bed. I reached for the phone, saw that it was an unknown number, and ignored it.

A minute later, it started buzzing again.

"What?" I snapped.

There was a pause on the other end before a man said, "Hi... Is this Olivia?"

It was the same raspy, low voice I had heard in his voicemail. My heart caught in my throat.

"Yeah," I said, sitting up in bed, clearing the sleep from my eyes. "That's me. I'm Olivia."

"Uh," he started, and he sounded nervous. "This is probably too short notice, but I'm, uh, here." He cleared his throat. "In Queen's Cove."

I blinked, staring at nothing in front of me. "In town?" I repeated. "Now?"

He made a noise in his throat like regret. "I should have called but I was worried I was going to change my mind and turn around."

In my chest, something pulsed, sad and regretful and weirdly empathetic for the fucking asshole who ditched me.

"You're busy," he said suddenly. "It's okay. I should have known."

"No," I blurted. "I'm not. I have time." I glanced in the mirror across my room. My hair was messy and my eyes were puffy. "Give me half an hour."

55

Olivia

I STARED down the hallway to the bar. It was early afternoon and I could hear a few regulars chatting. The TV was on, playing highlights.

I stepped into the bar. Cole sat at the counter, in Finn's normal seat. My pulse beat in my ears as I studied him. I had seen photos of him when he was younger. He was still handsome, just older, with gray blurring at his temples and lines around his eyes. He wore work boots, jeans, and a t-shirt. His arms and the back of his neck were tanned. There was a white tan line along his hairline at the back of his neck, like he had just gotten a haircut.

He turned and our eyes met. "Olivia."

He had my eyes. His forehead was wrinkled and his skin seemed weathered, not smooth and freckled like my mom's.

His voice was gravelly like a smoker's. There was a glass of soda on the counter in front of him.

"Hi." I didn't move.

He shifted with discomfort before clearing his throat. He gestured to the seat beside him, where Holden usually sat.

"Do you want to take a seat?" he asked. "Or we can, uh."

He cleared his throat again. "We can go somewhere else. I can take you for lunch or coffee. Whatever you want."

Behind him, Joe cleaned a glass, not looking at us, but I could sense his attention. He glanced up and gave me a quick wink, the *I'm here* gesture he had made a thousand times in my life. I nodded back at him.

"Let's walk to the marina," I told Cole.

He nodded once and reached for his wallet. Joe waved him off.

"On the house," he said.

"You sure?" Cole asked.

Joe nodded again with a smile. "You bet."

"Ah. I appreciate it." He got up and gestured for me to lead the way.

We walked down the street to the marina in silence before he finally spoke. "I didn't mean to surprise you like this," he said again, rubbing the back of his neck.

"It's fine."

"You drove from Whistler?" I asked.

He nodded. "It's nice there," he continued. "Lots of trees and mountains."

"Is that your scene?" I asked, keeping my eyes on the road. "Trees and mountains?"

He huffed a laugh. "Yeah, I guess it is. Didn't use to be but it is now."

I nodded like I understood what he meant. Like I knew anything about him. He said it like I knew his life.

We kept walking in silence. The streets were busy because of the Sunday afternoon market, with tables and booths out along Main Street.

Cole let out a low whistle when the marina came into view. "That ice cream place is still here? Shit. You still like ice cream?" His gaze darted to mine, unsure. Like he was nervous.

I nodded. "Yep."

He tilted his head at the busy shop. "What flavor?"

"Anything chocolate, cherry, or coffee. You want me to come with you?"

He shook his head. "You take a seat. I'll be right back."

I sat on the bench while he loped over to the ice cream place. Fuck. This was awkward. Part of me wondered if he was going to make a break for it, take off and leave me sitting on this bench until I figured out he'd left.

Part of me was surprised when he returned with two ice cream cones.

"Don't feed the seagulls," I told him as he sat beside me and handed me a napkin. He'd gotten me the coffee flavor, and for himself, something that looked like strawberry.

He choked on a laugh. "I remember. One near took Jen's eye out when we were kids."

Right. It rushed back at me that they had grown up together, same as Finn and me. The parallel made my heart ache, especially knowing how it had turned out for them.

How was it going to turn out for Finn and me? My chest hurt at the thought.

"You loved birds," he told me before he blinked like he didn't mean to say it.

Silence stretched between us as we ate our ice cream. I barely tasted it. This was the guy I was supposed to be mad at? In front of us, the late-afternoon sun sent a sparkle across the water. Tourists lined up at the fish and chips shack for an early dinner. I caught Beck's eye as he climbed onto his boat. He gave me a wave before he turned the engine on and headed into the harbor alone.

"Joe seems like he'd doing well," Cole said.

"He is."

A weird guilt rose in me. Fuck. This was going horribly. I had wanted to talk with him and now, I could barely say a handful of words.

"I like forests, too," I said, trying not to cringe at the words.

I like forests, too? Wow.

"I looked you up online. I saw the stuff on the university website about your research and finding the flower." He glanced at me and our eyes met. He gave me a quick smile. "I'm proud of you, for what it's worth."

My pulse thudded in my head and anxiety wrapped a tight fist around my throat.

"Why'd you leave us?" I blurted out.

Wow.

He froze, blinking like I'd slapped him.

"I, uh." He winced, rubbing the back of his neck, blinking more. His mouth clamped closed.

Right. I didn't know what I had wanted out of this but I couldn't sit here any longer. I shot to my feet.

"Olivia, wait." He stood and his hand came out like he was going to touch my arm before he jerked back. He made a noise of anguish. "Please don't leave yet."

I folded my arms over my chest and sat back down, staring at the ocean. My lungs felt weighted and heavy.

What had I expected? For him to waltz back into town and throw himself at my feet, begging for forgiveness? For him to say he wished things had gone differently? That he'd fucked up?

He let out a long breath. "It's hard for me to say these things but I'm working on it."

I waited, wanting to disappear into the ground.

"When you were born, my whole world changed," he said, and my heart ached. "You were this blob with eyes and I couldn't stop looking at you. I'd stay up half the night, staring at you. I never knew I could love something the way I loved you." He swallowed, leaning forward and staring at the water. "And everyone thought I was trash. The whole town, Jen's parents, my parents—they were still pissed that I had gotten Jen pregnant. Even Jen was waiting for me to fuck up."

His words rang in my head like a bell and my lip curled.

He let out a heavy breath, his Adam's apple bobbing as he frowned. "Your mom and I split, but we were trying to make it work. Then Joe came into the picture and he was everything I wasn't. Responsible, had a good job, and everyone liked him. Super nice guy. Can't say a bad word about him. That guy is a better father than I could have been." He shook his head. "You loved him, I could see that. You didn't need me," he said quietly. "You were better off with Joe."

Sharp unease twisted in my stomach.

"My therapist says I'm avoidant attachment," he continued, and I turned to him with a bemused expression.

"You have a therapist?"

He nodded, cheeks puffing out as he blew out a long breath. "Yep. Started seeing him this past winter. I was drinking a lot. I've *always* drank a lot, but there was a night this winter I was in the bar getting loaded because then I wouldn't think about what a fuck-up I was, and I just got tired of it."

My gaze shot to his. He winced and turned back to the water.

"I didn't want to be that guy anymore. It flipped my switch. I started going to AA, quit smoking—it wasn't easy, and I fell off the wagon a few times. I'll probably fall off a few more times, too. But my sponsor recommended I start counseling."

"Oh," was all I said, because my mind was reeling.

"He's this old, weathered biker dude in his sixties. I think the guy's been to jail. Tattoos all over his hands and neck. Had a change of heart in his fifties and went back to school for counseling. He says my attachment style is avoidant attachment, and when I'm scared or vulnerable, I find safety in pulling away." He folded his arms over his chest and sat back against the bench. "You were so precious, so tiny and special, and you deserved everything."

His unspoken words rang in the air—*you deserved better than me*. He had never grown bored with me or moved on to a better life without me in it. He had felt unwanted, and neither my mom nor I had helped with that.

My heart sank, like I was watching an accident in slow motion.

Finn had left once because he thought he wasn't good enough, and that it was only a matter of time until I figured it out.

He was supposed to be a drunk deadbeat. He was supposed to be a reckless asshole who didn't give a shit about anyone but himself, but here he was, talking about therapy and me being precious.

"You're not supposed to be like this," I said.

"Yeah, well…" He shrugged. "I'm trying to be better."

My heart squeezed with a weird, stinging emotion, and I felt like crying.

I wished Finn was here. He'd know what to do.

Cole let out a long sigh that I felt in my bones. "I regret leaving, Olivia. I've regretted it every day, every minute of every day. When you called, I knew this was my last shot to make things right." He winced like he was in pain. "I want to know you. I don't want to regret things anymore. I can't change the stupid stuff I did in the past. I fucked up—" His eyes widened. "Sorry. I *screwed* up but I'm taking accountability for my actions." He said the words like he'd said them before, maybe in counseling. "You're well within your right to tell me to leave, tell me you don't want anything to do with me. I'll understand and you don't owe me shit." His eyes widened again. "Sorry. You don't owe me anything." His throat bobbed again and he frowned. "But I can't leave without telling you that. I'd move back if it made things easier."

My heart twisted at his vulnerability, something that had always been so hard for me. I would have liked to know the guy beside me on the bench, and because he hadn't been able to say those things when I was younger, I had never been able to.

Until now.

There was a weird shift in my head, like a door opening, light spilling in, and I finally saw myself for who I was. All these years, I thought this was strength—holding people at a distance. Keeping things locked up inside, keeping my emotions suffocated under a thick layer of eye rolls, snorts, and bitchy glares.

Last night, when Finn needed me, I had pulled away. I'd encouraged him to go. He'd been there for me all summer, and I sent him packing.

Coward, my mind whispered at me. I blinked at Cole, seeing myself in twenty years.

It was suddenly so simple. All of this could have been avoided if he had known how much I needed him. I was just a kid, though, so I didn't know any better.

I wasn't a kid anymore, though, and I was done standing on the sidelines, keeping everything locked up to protect myself.

"You can say *fuck*," I told him.

"What?"

"I'm twenty-nine years old and I spent the last decade working in bars. You can say *fuck*. *Shit*, too."

"What about *moist*?"

"Are you making a joke?" I arched a brow, the corner of my mouth tipping up.

He winced. "Yeah. Sorry. Bad joke."

I snorted. "No, you can't say *moist*. That's gross."

He saw the twitch at the corner of my mouth and some of the sadness left his eyes. "So, what do you think?"

"I think…" The words were hard to say but I shoved them out. "I want to know you, too."

His eyes searched mine as his smile lifted. "Yeah?"

"Yep."

His crinkled. "Great."

Something unraveled in my chest, maybe the knots that had been tying themselves throughout this conversation. I had said the thing, and I didn't die.

Finn's expression of self-hatred from last night flashed in my head. He had given me everything and in return, I gave him the scraps I could spare and nothing more.

And here was Cole, trying to be a better person despite everyone's low opinion of him. Despite fucking up so hard. The deck was stacked against him and he was still trying.

I knew what I had to do. I had to tell Finn how I felt—that I loved him. I had to go get him back.

I looked at Cole. "It's worth something."

He tilted his head. "What's that?"

"That you're proud of me." I nodded. "It's worth something."

His eyes softened, Adam's apple bobbing. "Good."

"I have to go do something." I stood. "But I don't want you to leave. Are you staying in town for a bit?"

He got to his feet. "I have a hotel room. I can stay."

"Maybe we can have dinner tomorrow."

His mouth quirked before flattening, like he was trying not to smile too hard. "That would be great."

I hesitated before I gave him a quick hug. He smelled like pine and citrus, masculine but warm and comforting. It felt weird hugging him because we were both awkward.

"Thanks for this," he said, having a hard time meeting my eyes. "It meant a lot."

I nodded once. "Dinner. Tomorrow."

"You got it."

I waved goodbye as I left the marina, heading up Main

Street, breaking into a jog and then a run. As I ran to Elizabeth and Sam's house, I pulled my phone out, fumbling through a Google search before I found who I was looking for.

"Hello?" the guy answered.

"Hey," I said, breathing hard as my sneakers hit the pavement. "We don't know each other, but my name is Olivia Morgan. I need your help."

56

Olivia

I POUNDED on the front door with urgency until Sam opened it with a baffled expression.

"I need the keys," I wheezed, catching my breath. "To the Porsche. I'm sorry to ask like this but it's an emergency."

He lifted an eyebrow, studying me with curiosity.

"Please, Sam." I straightened up. "I won't crash it, I promise. I need it. I have to go get Finn."

He folded his arms over his chest, watching me for what felt like eternity before he smiled.

"Alright. Meet me by the garage."

Moments later, the garage door opened and Sam pulled a protective sheet off the emerald car. It was spotless and sparkling.

"You know how to drive stick?" he asked, holding the keys out.

I nodded and took them. "My dad taught me."

"Good." He nodded once, folding his arms. "Alright, tiger, go get him."

I got in the driver's side and turned the key. The old engine roared to life, humming under the hood, and I gave Sam a wave as I backed the car out.

Next door, my mom was watering plants in the front yard. She spotted me in the car and her expression changed.

She knew what this car meant. Everyone did.

In the Rhodes' driveway, I killed the engine while Sam lowered the garage door and went back inside. My mom stood there, staring at me.

"What are you doing?" she asked, gesturing at the car.

I dragged in a breath, steadying myself as I got out of the car and walked over to her.

"I'm going to see Finn."

She let out a laugh of disbelief. "You heard what happened?"

"Yeah." My chest felt tight as I folded my arms. "I did."

We stared at each other. Frustration and anguish wove through my gut.

"I love you," I told her, "and also, you need to cut people some slack."

Her jaw dropped at my tone.

"Cole showed up today."

"*What?*"

"Yep." I nodded. "We had ice cream at the marina. He has a counselor and he's in AA. He felt like we didn't need him, that's why he stopped calling and showing up." I shook my head at her. "He saw Joe being Superdad and didn't want to mess up what we had. He felt like he wasn't good enough for us."

She blinked, emotion flashing through her eyes. Shock rose in her expression, along with something else.

Regret, maybe. Pensiveness. Maybe she was wondering how it could have been if we had all just had a conversation.

"Finn told me what you said."

Confusion flickered through her eyes. "What did I say?"

"When we were teenagers, you said something like 'Olivia doesn't need you dragging her down' or something. Everyone called him the devil and joked about what a dirtbag he was, and then you said that and that's why he left when we were teenagers. Because he thought I'd be better off without him." I shifted on my feet. "And maybe you still think that, but I don't." My throat worked. "He's the only one who believed in me about the flower. He hauled ass around those mountains so I could finish my PhD."

My heart twisted.

"I'm not better off without him, and all that other stuff is in the past," I continued, heart slamming in my chest. We didn't talk like this, her and I. "Things with Cole are in the past, and things with Finn are in the past. People fuck up, and I want to move on."

Her forehead creased as she listened. The garden bed she was watering flooded.

I shrugged. "You got pregnant at twenty in a less than ideal situation, but it doesn't make you a bad person, and you aren't defined by your mistakes. Same as them."

The stuff that had happened with Finn in the past? It was only a small part of us. My mind rushed to the good moments —lying on the roof, staring at the stars. Laughing in front of the campfire. Racing on our bikes with the wind in our hair. Him whispering that he loved me.

Those were the moments that had made us. They were so sweet they made my heart ache.

"I lost you in the grocery store once."

My head snapped up. "What?"

She closed her eyes, breathing deeply. "Scariest moment of my life. You were in the candy aisle ten feet away but I'll never forget that terror." She opened her eyes and shook her head to herself. "Finn looked rattled yesterday and I didn't help." Her eyes flickered again with emotion as she met my gaze. "I'm sorry."

In my chest, something eased and I nodded. "Okay." I gestured at the car. "I have to go."

She nodded. "Alright." She swallowed. "Let's have Finn over for dinner next week, okay?"

The corner of my mouth tipped up. "Sure."

I got back in the car, turned the engine on, and backed out of the driveway. I called Miri and asked where Finn was, and she called me back within minutes with a report that Finn's old Mustang was parked in front of a little bungalow a street away from the marina—Beck's house.

Within minutes, I arrived in front of the small, quaint home. Perfectly manicured garden beds sat out front with bright, blooming flowers. There was a white picket fence, and the windows even had shutters. I tried to remember who lived here before Beck.

His black Mustang was parked in the driveway. I parked behind it and turned off the car before heading up to the front door.

I had to tell a guy that I loved him.

57

Finn

ON SUNDAY AFTERNOON, I sat on Beck's back porch. I couldn't stay in my apartment last night; everything reminded me of her, and I needed space to gather my thoughts. I hadn't wanted to go to any of my brothers' places, because either they or my sisters-in-law would want to talk.

I didn't want to talk. I wanted to figure things out.

So I came to Beck's place and slept on his couch. Beck was the guy who everyone went to when they needed help, and I'd make it up to him. Early this morning, he left for the hospital, so I had the place to myself all day.

I hated it. Hated being alone when I could sense her out there, hurting.

I thought about my realization back in the forest, before we found the flower. I needed to keep Liv's heart safe. My eyes closed as my chest ached. I wasn't ready to walk away from Liv. If I did, I was hurting her all over again.

A rock landed in my stomach. There was my answer.

I couldn't make the same mistake I made twelve years ago, I knew that. I thought about Cole in the bar. I wouldn't be that guy.

I had to make it right, something I didn't do years ago. I

wouldn't let her down again. I had to be there for her like I'd promised her all summer, even when it was hard. That was what mattered.

Inside the house, I grabbed my phone, my wallet, and my keys before heading to the front door. I opened it—

Liv stood there, about to knock.

"Oh," she said softly.

"Hi." My pulse picked up, whistling in my ears at the sight of her.

In her plaid flannel, hanging open over a tank top, with her cutoff jean shorts and sneakers, Liv Morgan was the most beautiful thing I'd ever seen. My chest hurt, watching her with her wide eyes, plush mouth, and pretty, sloped nose covered in freckles. Her being in front of me made all our problems seem insignificant.

"Hi," she said back, lowering her hand.

"Liv," I started. "I screwed up—"

She held a hand up. "Shut up for a second."

My eyebrows shot up. Behind her, my dad's vintage Porsche sat parked behind my car.

Oh, shit. My jaw went slack.

Liv nodded. "Yeah. That's the car. This is supposed to be meaningful, and I want everyone to know that I love you."

The words floated through the air, landed on my heart, and sank in. I knew she felt that way, but hearing her say it? It shifted the earth under my feet.

I blinked. "Wow."

Liv Morgan loved me.

She nodded, throat working. "Yeah."

"That's how you greet people at the front door?" The teasing words rushed out of me.

The corner of her mouth twitched, and everything between us settled into place. "Not often," she quipped back, eyes welling up. "Only with you, because I love you."

"You mentioned that."

"It's true." She nodded, lacing her fingers together, and a tear rolled down her cheek. "I do love you. A lot. Like, the most out of anyone who's ever loved anyone. An ugly amount, like I'll kill anyone who hurts you, that kind of love."

"Huh."

"Yeah," she said again, watching me. She licked her lips with a little frown. I could see her chest rising and falling as she gathered her thoughts. "I met Cole. He's here."

"Shit." I whistled, mind reeling.

"Yeah." Her hands made fists, balled up in her shirt sleeves, and she wiped away a tear.

My heart ached with the urge to pull her to my chest, but I wanted to let her say her piece.

"He's in therapy and he's trying to say the things he always meant to say. He stayed away because he thought I was better off without him, like you did."

Her gaze shot to mine, so vulnerable and beautiful.

"And I thought, what's my excuse for being so terrified, if Cole can do it? Don't I get a say in these relationships?" She searched my eyes. "Telling you I loved you meant that you could hurt me, so I kept you at a distance and made you think I didn't care, but I did. I *do* care. I don't want to be that person who forces people to elbow their way into her life. Sadie talked my fucking ear off at the bar—"

I huffed a laugh. Sadie did talk a lot.

"—but she grew on me. But what if she hadn't done that? I never would have gotten to know her." She was picking up speed now, the words tumbling out of her mouth. "Even Avery and Hannah, I only hang out with them if they insist. Your mom wanted to spend time with me for years, but I shot her down every time. I slammed a steel wall up between myself and others so I couldn't get hurt. If I didn't care, it wouldn't matter if they left me."

Her forehead creased with worry. "I don't want to hurt the people I love because I'm scared. I should have gone after you yesterday instead of telling you to leave." She clamped her lips together before she blew out a breath. "I'm sorry. I'm so sorry."

"Me, too." My gaze roamed her face, so worried and repentant when I was the one who should be apologizing. "I shouldn't have freaked out. I screwed up. I'll screw up again, but I'm not leaving. We'll figure it out together."

"I love you," she repeated. "I'm going to keep saying it until you believe it."

"I'm starting to think…" I shook my head. "That you have feelings for me or something?"

A laugh burst out of her, and then it turned into a sob. "Finn."

"Baby." My voice was soft and I held my arms out. "Come here."

She stepped forward and I picked her up. Her arms looped around my neck, her legs wrapped around my waist, and she gazed into my eyes with such intense affection, I swear my heart tripped. Her eyes welled up and I kissed her.

I kissed her like she was mine. I kissed her like I had been hers for a very long time. I kissed her like our hearts were full and connected. I kissed her like she was the best damn thing that ever happened to me, like the universe had put us side by side for a reason.

I kissed Liv Morgan like she was my soulmate.

"You love me?" I asked her in between kisses. "You sure?"

She sniffed and nodded. "I never stopped."

"You still want me?" I knew the answer, but I needed to hear it.

"I always have."

"It's always been you, Liv," I whispered. "Always. I love you so fucking much. All I ever wanted was for you to see me like I see you."

"I want all those firsts with you," she said. "The house, the kids, the new jobs. All of it."

My smile stretched across my face. "Me too, Livvy."

She smiled back at me and I knew we had finally found our way.

In the distance, a low buzzing noise droned from the sky, and Liv jolted with a gasp.

"Oh my god." She turned her head, still in my arms. "I almost forgot. Quick, put me down."

"No." I wasn't letting her go.

"Finn," she laughed, rolling her eyes. "Step into the yard."

I carried her out from the porch, down the steps, and into the front yard. Olivia watched the sky in the east with focus.

I saw it, and my heart squeezed so hard I thought it might explode.

OLIVIA MORGAN LOVES FINN RHODES FOREVER

We watched the plane approach, and as it flew over, my heart was in my throat.

"I know it isn't much," Liv said. "I didn't have much time."

"It's perfect." I watched the banner continue on across the sky. "Perfect."

Layered in with the drone of the plane, the sound of a cowbell caught my attention and I frowned. Liv heard it, too. She tilted her head, meeting my gaze with narrowed eyes as she listened.

"What is that?" she murmured.

Clapping and cheering. The sound got louder, gathering momentum, until it was a low roar.

Our gazes met and we laughed, lit up. The market was today. Everyone on Main Street would have seen the banner, too.

The words were caught in my throat, but Liv wiped another tear from her face. "I told Miri what I was going to do when I was trying to find you. She works fast."

I snorted. Miri must have told everyone in town. The low roar from Main Street persisted. Whistling and hollering filled the air. Metal clanged, like someone was banging pots and pans. "You think that's for us?"

She nodded, warm gaze on me. "I do."

My mouth twisted into a wicked grin. "About time." I tilted my chin at the Porsche. "You going to take me for a ride?"

She beamed at me and I let her slide down to standing before she pulled me to the car.

"Come on," she said, and we headed off to start the next chapter of our lives.

Epilogue 1 - Finn

ONE MONTH *later*

The late September sun warmed my skin as I spread out on the blanket, hands behind my head and eyes closed.

At the sound of her boots approaching, I smiled. I still couldn't believe it was real, our life together.

"Don't you look comfortable."

I opened my eyes to see her standing over me with a wry smile on her pretty face. I winked at her and gestured to the blanket beside me. "Hello, baby."

"Hi." She flopped down and gave me a quick kiss as I unpacked our lunch.

"How'd the media interview go?"

She wrinkled her nose. "They asked the same question three times."

The day after Liv and her advisor published *The Pink Sand Verbena—the Hidden Flower*, her phone and email began blowing up. The media loved Liv's story of persistence and hope when no one else believed in her, although the university didn't appreciate it when she stated that to interviewers in her blunt way. The story of the flower that had remained hidden in the woods for a hundred years gained international exposure, and in the ecology science world, all eyes were suddenly on our tiny town.

Randeep Singh added a tour once we showed him the route.

"*Is there a ledge behind that waterfall?*" he had asked.

Liv and I had exchanged a glance, hiding our grins.

"*Not sure,*" I had told him. "*We didn't go in that area.*"

The best part? Due to the media attention, the research funding was rolling in. Liv's university opened a research hub here in Queen's Cove, where she now worked, continuing her research on how plants adapt to climate change. The researchers who had been laid off from the center in Port Alberni were moving in next week.

"Did Holden say when the flooring would arrive?" Liv asked.

Oh, yeah, and that old house at the edge of town? We bought it.

"Next week. We can install it on the weekend. My dad wants to help." I tipped my chin at her. "You still okay with moving in during renovations?"

Holden and Sadie had offered for us to stay with them, but we wanted our own space.

She nodded. A soft smile spread over her face. "It'll be fine. We made the right call having our birthday party at the bar, though."

We shared a private smile and Liv rolled her lips, eyes glittering. Our birthday party was in two days, and we had invited the entire town. We had something special planned— but it was a secret.

"You ready?" I asked her.

Her smile lifted, and her expression was so soft and sweet, it hurt my chest. "Yes."

My gaze roamed Liv's face, sunlight dancing off her cheekbones and the different tones in her eyes. My heart squeezed.

"Olivia," I said, shaking my head, and her eyes sparked. "You're so beautiful, you make my heart hurt."

She huffed a laugh and peeked down at her hands, still smiling. "I never get sick of hearing you say that."

"Good." I shifted closer to her on the blanket. "I never get sick of saying it." I leaned in and pressed my lips to her temple, inhaling her sweet scent, letting it fill my lungs. Her skin was warm against my mouth and my arm wrapped around her shoulders, brushing the soft sleeve of her plaid shirt. I hummed against her temple and she sighed, leaning into me.

"Do you need to rush back?"

She shook her head. "I have a few minutes." Her eyes turned coy, the smile curling up at the corner of her mouth.

My mouth brushed her ear. "Bet I can make you come in less than five minutes."

Her breath caught but she shot me an amused look of disbelief. "Trust me, you can't."

"Oh, yeah?" I lifted her chin, studying the shades of brown and amber in her eyes. "You think I don't know how to make you feel good?" My voice dropped to a low murmur and her eyelids fell halfway. A ripple of smugness moved through me and my smile lifted higher. "You think I don't know exactly what makes you squirm?"

My knuckles brushed her shirt, lingering on her nipples.

"You're cheating," she breathed.

My hand came up to tuck a lock of soft pink hair behind her ear, and her eyebrows pulled together like she regretted saying that, like she wanted me to keep touching her.

"You know what I've been thinking a lot about lately?" I asked her.

"What?" she breathed.

"Remember two weeks ago, when we took a drive up the coast in my car and you wanted to pull over at that lookout?"

She nodded and my fingers trailed down her neck, slowly skimming over her skin. She shuddered.

"And we sat there in my car, watching the sun go down over the water until the sky turned dark and the stars came out?"

She nodded again, biting her lip. My thumb brushed the base of her throat and she swallowed.

"And my hand trailed higher and higher on your thigh until you couldn't take it anymore, you just *had* to ride my cock in the backseat?"

She made a soft whimper and her pupils expanded. My erection strained against my zipper.

I picked up her phone and showed her the time. "I have until one seventeen."

A light flush grew on her cheeks but she snorted and rolled her eyes. "Good luck."

I grinned at her. "I don't need it. Come here." I shifted to face her and framed her jaw with my hands, pulling her to me so I could kiss her. Her lips were soft and when I licked at the seam of her mouth, she let me in.

I groaned at the hot slide of her tongue against mine.

This never got old. Every kiss from Olivia was a gift.

I tried to go slow, I did, but she kissed me back, tasting me and making these sexy little gaspy moans that lit my blood on fire, and soon enough, she was on her back and I was on top of her, pressing kisses down her neck. Her breath caught again when my teeth scraped the sensitive spot beneath her ear. My hands were on her breasts, pinching and rolling her nipples as she arched into my hand. Smug satisfaction coiled low at the base of my spine as she whispered my name.

"Is this all you've got?" she asked in between moans.

My head tipped back and I laughed. "You're such a little liar. I bet you're soaked." I pulled the neckline of her top down, baring her new tattoo.

A delicate pink flower sat over her heart. I rested my palm

against it for a brief moment before pulling off my own shirt so she could see the matching one over my heart. Her gaze dropped to it and she smiled.

I winked at her.

We got those tattoos the week after she defended her dissertation. The panel of professors had submitted their responses faster than usual—approved. Liv had her PhD.

The flower meant so much more than her getting her PhD, though. It was us, it was the love we shared, persisting over the years, even though it was hidden. Waiting for us to find it.

At the edge of my tattoo, I had the artist incorporate her name, tiny and scripted among the flower's leaves, barely noticeable except to us. Olivia's name right over my heart, where it belonged. I had told her we were fulfilling the bet I lost when we raced to the top of the ridge, moments before we spotted the flower, but Liv knew the truth.

My heart always had and always would belong to Olivia Morgan.

Beneath me, she looked up at me like I was everything to her. I held her gaze as I wrapped my lips around one of the stiff peaks of her breasts. Her eyes glazed and my cock ached, dripping with pre-cum in my boxers.

My hand slipped down the front of Olivia's leggings to find her wet. The breath whooshed out of her lungs as her mouth fell open and she let out a low moan.

"Look at you," I murmured, shaking my head while my fingers dragged slow, lazy circles on her clit. "You're making this too easy for me, baby."

She clenched her jaw. "You're running out of time."

A low laugh rasped out of me as I watched her face. "You taunting me would mean more if you weren't soaking my hand, Morgan."

She huffed a laugh, biting her lip, and when her eyes met mine, my heart squeezed again.

"I love you so fucking much," I whispered.

"I love you, too." Her eyes melted, soft and full of affection. "I've always loved you."

"Alright." I sped up the circles on her clit, and my erection pulsed as she winced with pleasure, arching on the blanket. "Enough of this lovey-dovey bullshit. Time for you to come."

"You wish," she bit out, breathing hard.

I pushed a finger into her tight entrance and we both swore.

"Right there, huh?"

Her eyes were closed when she shook her head. "Barely felt it."

I added a second finger and she whimpered. Around my hand, her muscles rippled, tightening and trembling. Her hips tilted with my movements.

"Really?" I asked. "Barely felt it?"

"Uh-huh." She mouthed *oh my god* and her hand came to my thigh, gripping me like she needed to be anchored.

A wicked smile curled up on my mouth as I watched her fall deeper and deeper into pleasure. "Huh. Guess I'll have to up my game. What about this?" I crooked my fingers to reach her G-spot and massaged the bundle of nerves.

"Fuck," she gasped, eyes squeezed closed. "Fuck, Finn."

"Yeah." I nodded. "That's what I thought. Liv," I drawled into her ear, my voice loaded with smug teasing that made her even wetter, "it kind of feels like you're going to come."

"Nope." She gripped my thigh harder and moaned as I worked her G-spot. "I'm not."

I beamed down at her writhing on my hand, her hair shining in the sun and her tits pressed to the sky. Paradise. This was paradise.

"Oh, you know what I forgot?" I crooned.

"What?" Her voice was thin and from the way she squeezed my hand, I knew she was close.

I shook my head. "I can't believe I forgot your *clit*."

Her eyes flew open. "No," she whined.

I nodded at her with a knowing smile. "Yes."

With my fingers inside her, I pressed down on the tight bud above her entrance with the heel of my hand, giving her more friction and pressure as I stimulated her front walls, and her wet pussy clamped down on me.

"Fuck," she gasped. "Fuck."

"There we go." Her muscles pulsed around my fingers as her hips bucked. She moaned as she came on the blanket in the middle of the forest, looking so gorgeous. "Good girl. Keep riding my hand."

She rippled around my fingers, tits bouncing with her writhing movements as she slowly came down from her climax and opened her eyes.

I made a big show of looking at the time. "One seventeen."

She rolled her eyes, grinning. "Whatever."

I leaned down to kiss her. "Pretty good."

"It's fine," she said against my mouth, her breath tickling my face.

We kissed slowly and unhurriedly this time, and eventually I lifted my head to ask, "Hey, Liv. What's the magic number?"

She laughed. "I'm not answering that."

I tilted my head, and she grinned at my playful expression. "It's three." My hands came to the waistband of her leggings and she lifted her hips without argument as I slipped her pants down, helping her take her boots off until she was bare from the waist down.

"Might as well get rid of this," I said, yanking her shirt over her head, and she laughed.

"You're an animal." She shook her head at me, lying back onto the blanket as I stared at her body.

The smooth curves, the soft skin, her nipples looking so pretty and sweet, her pussy still glistening from my fingers— she took the words right out of my mouth.

"You okay?" she asked softly.

I only nodded, running my hands up her thighs before I pushed them apart. "With you? Always."

She gasped when the pad of my thumb brushed her clit, gentle so I didn't overstimulate her. We held each other's gazes and that overpowering, intense warmth filled my chest. I dragged her wetness over the soft skin between her legs and she bit her lip.

"God, that feels so good," she whispered.

"I know, baby." I leaned down to kiss up her inner thigh, watching her jaw go slack as I slipped my fingers back inside her to find her wet all over again.

When my mouth met her pussy, our groans mixed together. I buried my face between her legs, working her inner walls while my lips and tongue raced over her, lapping up her arousal, winding her higher and higher while my cock ached. I sucked her clit and she rocked against my mouth to get more. Her hands were in my hair, grasping and tugging, urging me on, and she moaned my name again and again as I drew her orgasm out of her.

"Yes," she choked out as she began to shake under my mouth, tightening on my fingers. "Like that."

"Uh-huh." I sucked her clit as she rode her pleasure out against my mouth, soaking my face. Her taste, fucking hell, *her taste*.

"Oh my god." Her chest rose and fell and she looked down at me with a dazed, sated expression. Her throat worked. "Oh my god," she repeated.

"Turn over."

"What?"

"Flip. Over." My hands came to her hips and I turned her over on the blanket before yanking her ass up in the air. "There. Like that."

"Hurry." She arched her back as I raced to undo my belt, pulse thudding in my ears.

My cock was beaded with pre-cum when I pulled it out, and Liv let out a choked breath as I dragged the tip up and down her entrance. Her hips pushed toward me.

"Stop teasing me," she demanded.

"You're not in charge here." I circled her entrance with the head of my cock, loving the way she could barely hold herself up on her forearms.

"Please, Finn." She tilted her hips up to give me access. "Please fuck me."

I grinned. "I love it when you ask nicely. You're always so sweet when you're desperate to come on my cock."

"Shut up," she bit out, and I laughed.

"Say the nice words one more time, baby."

She growled and glared at me over her shoulder. "Please."

My heart danced, happy and smug. "There we go." I fed my cock into her snug entrance and we moaned together.

Oh, *fuck*. After two orgasms, she was soaked, and I pushed through her tightness until I bottomed out.

"Deep," she choked out. "That's so deep."

"I know." My eyes were closed as I let her body adjust to my size. "Fuck, you feel amazing."

She rolled her hips, working herself on my length while I was buried deep inside her, and my brain was already beginning to splinter. So *fucking* good. So warm, wet, tight, and deep. Her pussy gripped me like a fist. My balls ached with the need to come inside her.

"Baby," I gritted out, jaw tight. "Need to move inside you."

Her head bobbed in a jerky nod and I pulled out before pushing back in, moaning. Her pussy clenched.

"Your moans make me so wet," she gasped.

Another wave of her arousal coated my erection. I gave her hip a squeeze. "I can feel it."

I found a rhythm and when her gasps and moans made the pressure around the base of my spine tighten, I reached around to her clit to stroke her into an orgasm. It didn't take long. With Olivia, the third was always the easiest. I brushed her clit with gentle, fast, fluttery strokes the way she had done in front of me the other night, and before long, she was crying my name into the blanket while her muscles flexed and spasmed around me.

"I can't hold out any longer," I told her. "Need to come inside you."

She nodded, still pulsing and squeezing around me, and I began to fuck her harder, thrusting into her as desire sliced through my brain. My balls pulled up close to my body and my head tipped back as heat raced up my spine.

"Olivia," I managed as I palmed her ass, stroking her soft skin before I laid a quick slap across her ass cheek. She moaned and tightened on me again, and I slipped over the edge of control.

My heart banged in my chest as my pleasure boiled over and I spilled inside her. My cock pulsed as I came, filling her and getting her inner thighs even more slick. I emptied into her, pressing my hips into her ass, unable to think, unable to speak, suspended in time and space, buried deep inside the woman I loved.

Where I belonged.

We collapsed onto the blanket together, me still inside her as we caught our breaths. She let out a soft, relaxed noise as I pressed a kiss to the back of her shoulder.

"I love your new job," I whispered into her ear, and she shook with laughter.

Epilogue 2 - Olivia

IN MY OLD apartment above the bar, where I had lived on and off since I was eighteen years old, I stared at my reflection in the mirror. Downstairs, I could hear people gathering for Finn's and my birthday party. My gaze traveled up and down my dress.

I never, *ever* thought I'd wear a dress like this.

I smiled at myself.

Footsteps in the doorway caught my attention and I turned to see Finn leaning on the doorframe, wearing a navy-blue suit that made his eyes stand out.

Even after all this time, all these years of knowing him, I couldn't get over how handsome he was. His hair was unruly and a little curly, the sharp line of his jaw beckoned me to trace a finger down it, and the curve of his lips made me want to grab him by the lapels and make out with him.

"Wow." He blinked at me in my dress. "You look hot."

I snorted. "You're supposed to say I look beautiful."

His expression turned wicked. "You do, but you also look hot." He leaned on the doorframe. "You ready?"

I nodded. "Yep."

I realized what we were about to do and emotion rushed up my throat.

Finn caught the expression on my face and sighed in a dramatic way, making me laugh. "No way. Are you going to cry?"

I winced through my laughter. "I think I might."

"If you cry, I'll cry." He walked toward me, slow footsteps echoing in my old, empty bedroom.

"If you cry," I told him, "your brothers will cry."

"And if my brothers cry, that means everyone else is crying."

I rolled my lips, chest shaking with laughter. "Your mom is going to be sobbing."

He gazed at me, smiling, and let out a sigh, like he could spend forever looking at me. My heart squeezed up into my throat. "This is going to be a shit show, isn't it?"

"Yep."

"Great." He held his hand out to me. "Let's go."

I slipped my hand into his and we left the apartment, pausing at the door. I glanced around the empty space, scattered with a few remaining boxes.

"Are you going to miss this place?" Finn asked.

I hummed, thinking. "A little." I turned to him. "But I can't wait for what's next."

———

THE BAR WENT dead silent as Finn and I stepped out of the hallway, my hand on his arm.

Sadie saw me and started screaming.

"You two are getting *married*?" she screeched.

Finn and I grinned at each other before turning to our stunned friends and family gathered in the bar. Over the counter, a sign hung. *Happy birthday, Olivia and Finn!*

"Surprise," Finn said with his wicked grin, squeezing my arm.

A wall of noise rose up and we were surrounded.

"Oh my god." Sadie's face was inches from mine, eyes wide and shining. "Oh my god." I laughed as she grabbed my face. "I love you so much," she told me.

"I love you, too, Sadie. I'm happy you're in my life."

She stared at me in awe, shaking her head. "Love looks good on you." Her gaze dropped to my dress. "And so does this *dress*."

I glanced down at the short vintage mini-dress, ivory fabric smooth under my fingers. Above the neckline, the pink petals of my tattoo peeked out.

"I *knew* it," Avery told us, shaking her head before wrapping me in an embrace. "I freaking knew it. I knew you were planning something."

Emmett tackled Finn in a big hug, slapping each other on the backs with matching beaming grins.

"Do you have plans in about ten minutes?" Finn asked Emmett.

Emmett's eyes were so bright, and the smile across his face was the proudest I'd ever seen him. He straightened up and adjusted his tie. We had told people to dress up.

"Please tell me I'm officiating," he told Finn.

Finn shrugged. "It's family tradition."

Hannah and Wyatt lingered behind them, smiling. Cora clung to Wyatt's neck, wearing a green dress with ladybugs on it. After the park incident last month, everyone told Finn stories of when they had screwed up. Apparently, when they were kids, Elizabeth had her back turned and Emmett tried to feed Finn rocks. Everyone had acknowledged that mistakes happen, and in the end, the only thing that mattered was that Cora was safe.

"Congratulations," Hannah said softly, wrapping me in a hug.

"Oh my god," Sadie said to Holden, shaking her head, and the corner of his mouth twitched. "I can't believe I didn't realize what was happening."

Wyatt and Hannah switched, and Wyatt pulled me to him in a squeeze.

"Knew you two would figure it out," he said quietly, nodding at me.

"Thanks, Wy."

Holden stepped up and gave Finn a big hug before turning to me. I smiled at him and he nodded, mouth strained like he was holding back a grin.

"Good work," he said. "You two finally stopped being stupid."

We all laughed. For years, Holden had been frustrated that Finn and I were no longer friends. When he and Sadie broke up for a few weeks before they were engaged, he admitted at the bar one night that perhaps things weren't as simple from the outside as they seemed.

"Holden," I told him, shaking my head. "Shut the fuck up."

"Happy for you," he said as we hugged. "You were always family."

My heart expanded in my chest. "Thanks, buddy."

Elizabeth appeared in front of me, already crying, and we all burst out laughing.

"I knew you two would find your way," she said, tears streaming down her face.

"Mom." Finn doubled over laughing. "Come on."

Elizabeth laughed too, wiping her eyes with a tissue that Sam pressed into her hand. "I'm sorry. I've waited so long for all my kids to be happy."

"It's okay." I smiled at her and pulled her into a hug. "Thanks for being patient," I whispered in her ear, and she squeezed me tight.

My parents and Cole were next, hugging and congratulating us. And on my mom's face? Not a lick of hesitation or worry. My chest eased as she and Finn embraced. She had changed in the past month. I didn't know whether it was regret over what she said in the past, or if she saw Finn in a new light now that she was spending more time around him, but her attitude toward him had changed. A weight had lifted in me that I didn't even know was there.

"You're beautiful," Cole told me before pulling me into a tight hug. "I'm so proud of you, honey."

My heart warmed at the words and I smiled, inhaling his woodsy dad scent. He had moved back and started a handyman business here. Every Wednesday night, we had dinner. Sometimes Finn joined, but sometimes he was busy or working, and it was just Cole and me. Cole seemed happy living here. He had found a new AA group, and he and Holden watched hockey together at the bar, even if Cole just drank soda. No one cared. He and Joe were even becoming friends.

"I'm glad you're here," I told him as he pulled back to look at me.

He nodded, mouth pressed tight, and it was like looking in a mirror. "Me, too."

"Alright," Finn said. "Enough crying. Let's do this."

A cheer rose up around us.

Emmett performed the ceremony in the middle of the bar, with our friends and family surrounding us with love and support. Elizabeth sobbed the entire time, and Finn and I kept laughing during the ceremony as more and more people started sniffling until we were all crying.

I smiled at Finn as we said the words in our hearts, the words we didn't say for so long. He held my hand, his thumb stroking over my skin, and I bared my heart for him in front of everyone. He slipped a ring onto my finger—a pale green sapphire we had picked together. On his hand, a white gold band glinted in the low bar lighting, and a possessive, prideful warmth weaved through my chest.

The smartest thing I ever did was let myself love Finn Rhodes.

When the ceremony was over, we opened the champagne. Someone turned the music up. Despite Elizabeth's protests, Finn put the game on the TV behind the bar. The place was filled with laughter, warmth, and love. We took photos, and the alien dildo hanging on the wall beside the TV was in half of them. The painting of Holden sobbing was in the other half.

Our wedding was perfect.

"Hey," Dot called as I stepped behind the bar, swatting at me. "You're not supposed to be back here." She shooed me out and pointed at a bar stool. "Get."

I snorted and took a seat. "How's the new gig?"

Dot had taken a job as the new manager of the bar. My dad had hired her to take over while he searched for the right person to buy it. I could see him glancing around the old building with wistfulness. *I'm excited for new things*, he had told me. *Your mom and I are going to spend the rainy winters in Mexico.*

Dot wiped the spotless counter with a rag. "I love it. I don't know why I didn't think of this years ago."

Beck slipped into the seat beside me, quirking a smile at me. "I think some congratulations are in order."

"Thanks." I smiled at him and Dot slid us each another glass of champagne. "I'm glad you got time off for our birthday party."

He laughed, and the skin around his eyes crinkled. "I saw the note about dressing up and thought it was something I needed to be here for."

I chuckled. "I appreciate it."

Finn slipped into the seat on the other side of me, looping an arm around my shoulder and pressing a kiss to my temple.

"Hello, *wife*."

The word made my skin tingle. He'd been trying it out for days, sometimes in public. I had to shush him to keep the secret. My mind flicked to last night when I gripped the headboard while he took me hard, gritting that word into my ear. In the bar, my face heated and Finn smirked like he knew what I was thinking.

"You're lucky," Beck told us.

Finn and I exchanged a smile. "We know," I said.

Finn leaned toward Beck. "Is the boat done for the season?"

Beck sighed and leaned back in his chair. "It's in my garage until spring."

I studied his regretful expression. Sometimes, it seemed like his boat was the only reprieve Beck had from the demanding hours at the hospital.

"Are things still busy at work?" I asked him.

His eyebrows lifted. "I think things are about to get better. One of my dad's old friends, a specialist from Toronto, is moving here for retirement and he's going to be working part time at the hospital. My dad's hiring another doctor to mentor under the specialist." He frowned. "They brought someone in for a third interview today. I haven't met them, though. They're keeping the interviews private until they make a final decision on the candidate."

"That's good, right? More time for hanging out on your boat."

He laughed quietly. "Yeah, I guess." He stood. "Be right back."

He slipped away and Finn and I sat there, saying hello to the people who came up to congratulate us.

The redheaded woman from earlier in the summer appeared at my side, sending confused glances around the bar. Tourist season was mostly over so we hadn't bothered closing the bar for a private party. Her eyes narrowed as she read the sign above the bar and then took in my dress and Finn's suit.

I beamed at her. "Hi."

"Hi." She winced. "I came in for a drink but…" She trailed off, biting her lip. "I should go."

"Stay." I gestured at the seat Beck had left empty. "Did you have another interview?"

She nodded, a small crease forming between her eyebrows. "I did. I'm Cassidy, by the way."

"Olivia." I gestured to Finn. "This is Finn, my…" Our gazes met and he wiggled his eyebrows at me. "My husband, I guess."

Finn shot me a flat, amused look. "You *guess*?"

I choked out a laugh. "You are. I signed the papers. Everyone saw."

He chuckled and reached out to shake Cassidy's hand. "Hey, Cassidy."

She glanced up at the sign again. "So this is not a birthday party."

I shrugged. "We lied." I gestured around the party. "It's our wedding. Surprise."

She snorted, surveying the room with an amused expression. "This place is weird."

"Yeah." Finn and I grinned at each other. "Queen's Cove is really weird." I turned back to her. "Where are you interviewing?"

"Interviewing," Beck repeated at my side, staring at Cassidy with a weird, tense expression, like he'd seen a ghost. He blinked at her.

Cassidy looked at Beck with a cold glare. "Are you *fucking* kidding me?" she hissed at him.

Finn and I exchanged a charged, curious glance.

Beck's eyes were still on Cassidy. "What are you doing here?" He didn't sound welcoming.

Her back went ramrod straight and she laughed without humor. "Don't tell me you're trying to get the mentorship, too? God, what are you, stalking me or something?"

Beck's jaw ticked. "How'd your interview go?" Sarcasm and something sharp dripped from his tone.

"Great," Cassidy bit out. "I fucking *wowed* them."

Beck's chest rose and fell fast, and his gaze locked on hers. I'd never seen him so pissed. I'd never seen him pissed at all. Beck Kingston was calm, collected, and kind.

He wasn't rattled by anything, but something about Cassidy infuriated him.

Cassidy gave him a wry, smug smile. "Don't get your hopes up, okay? I accepted the job today."

He shook his head, laughing to himself without a trace of humour.

"What?" she demanded.

He rubbed the bridge of his nose. "I already work there." He folded his arms, mirroring her. "We're going to be working together."

She stiffened, blinking like she'd been slapped.

"Jesus fuck," Beck sighed.

"No," Cassidy whispered.

"Yes," Beck shot back.

"Fuck." Her gaze slid to me, eyes darting like she was panicking. "I have to go."

Before I could say a word, she shot to the door and disappeared. I turned to Beck, who stared after her, gritting his teeth.

"Who was that?" I asked him.

"My worst fucking nightmare." He tossed the rest of his drink back with his eyes on the door.

———

IN THE EARLY hours of the morning, as the party continued in the bar, Finn pulled me into the hallway and up the stairs.

"Where are we going?" I asked.

"You'll see." He laced his fingers through mine as he led

me to the end of the hallway, below the skylight. He set the ladder beneath it and climbed up first to open the hatch before descending. "You first."

I gave him a flat look. "Don't look up my dress."

He snorted and gave me a light smack on my ass to make me laugh. When I climbed up onto the roof, my breath caught.

"Finn," I murmured.

He had set out a blanket, covered in pillows and surrounded by tiny tea lights. We curled up together on it and stared at the stars, holding hands, my head leaning against his hard chest, listening to his heartbeat.

"I've never felt this happy," I murmured, and his free hand came to my hair, brushing lightly, lulling me further into a relaxed bliss.

"Me, neither," he whispered. "Sometimes I wondered if I was crazy, and there was no hope for us."

"I'm glad you kept trying."

"So am I." He squeezed my hand and I squeezed back.

A shooting star raced across the sky.

"Make a wish," I told him.

He sighed a happy sound. "I wish that we live a long, happy life together."

"That we get to be as old as Dot."

He made a pleased sound in his throat. "That we spend our eighties hiking through the mountains."

"That our kids are so cute we can barely stand it," I added.

"Oh, yeah. They will be. Have you seen us?" Finn shot me a grin before turning back to the stars. "I wish that for the rest of your life, you never doubt how much I love you, how much I want you, how much I need you."

I squeezed his hand. "You're my best friend."

"I love you, Olivia Morgan."

I lifted up on my elbows, a soft smile curling on my mouth

as I studied his gorgeous face. "Finn Rhodes, it's only ever been you."

———

YES, Beck will get his HEA, but not yet!

In the meantime, read grumpy-sunshine hockey romance *Behind the Net*, the first book in the Vancouver Storm series! Keep reading for an excerpt.

Excerpt from Behind the Net

Pippa

My heart hammers while I stand outside Jamie Streicher's apartment building.

The last time I saw him in person, I had just spilled a blue Slurpee all over my white t-shirt in the high school cafeteria. His cold look of disinterest replays in my head, his green eyes flicking over me before turning back to his conversation with the rest of the hot, popular jocks.

Now I'm going to be his assistant.

He was always an asshole, but god, he was so gorgeous, even then. Thick dark hair, always just a little messy from playing hockey. Sharp jawline, strong nose. Broad, strong shoulders, and tall. *So tall.* Unfairly dark lashes. He never hit that awkward teenager phase that seemed to span my entire teens. His silent, intimidating, grumpy thing both unnerved and fascinated me, along with every other girl and half the guys in school.

Oh god. I drag in a deep breath and enter the number on the keypad outside. He buzzes me up without answering. In the elevator, my stomach wobbles on the way to the penthouse.

I'm not that dorky band girl anymore. I'm a grown woman. It's been eight years. I don't have a teenage crush on the guy anymore.

I need this job. I'm broke and crashing on my sister's couch. I quit my terrible job at Barry's Hot Dog Hut with zero notice after a week, and there's no way they'll take me back, even if I could stand the ugly uniform.

Besides, there's no way he remembers me. Our high school was huge. I was the dorky music girl, always hanging with the band kids, and he was a hot hockey player. I'm two years younger, so we didn't even have classes together or friends in common. He's one of the best goalies in the NHL, with the looks of a freaking god. The fact that he's known for not doing relationships seems to make people even more feral. Last year, someone threw panties on the ice for him—it was all over the sports highlights.

He isn't going to remember me.

I watch the number climb higher as I approach his floor.

He'll be busy with practices and training. I won't see him.

And I really, really need this job. I'm done with the music industry and its famous assholes. I went to school for marketing, and it's time to pursue that path. The only Vancouver job postings in marketing require at least five years' experience, so I wouldn't even be considered. According to my sister Hazel, who works as a physiotherapist for the Vancouver Storm, a marketing job with the team is opening up soon. They prefer internal hires, she said.

This assistant job is my way in. It's temporary. If I prove myself in that job, that's my foot in the door to the marketing job with the team.

The elevator opens on the top floor, and I walk to his door, taking a deep, calming breath. It doesn't work, and my heart pounds against the front wall of my chest.

Need this job, I remind myself.

I knock, the door swings open, and my pulse stumbles like it's drunk on cheap cider.

He's so much hotter grown up. And in person? It's actually unfair.

His frame fills the doorway. He's a foot taller than me, and even under his long-sleeved workout shirt, his body is perfection. The thin fabric stretches over his broad shoulders. I'm vaguely aware of a dog barking and racing around the apartment behind him, but my gaze follows his movement as he props a hand on the doorframe. His sleeves are pushed up, and my gaze lingers on his forearm.

Jamie Streicher's forearms could get a woman pregnant.

I'm staring. I jerk my gaze up to his face.

Ugh. My stomach sinks. That teen crush I had years ago bursts back into my life like a comet, thrilling through me. His eyes are still the deepest, richest green, like all the shades of an old-growth forest. My stomach tumbles.

"Hi," I breathe before clearing my throat. My face burns. "Hi." My voice is stronger this time, and I fake a bright smile. "I'm Pippa, your new assistant." I smooth a hand over my ponytail.

There's a beat where his features are blank before his eyes sharpen and his expression slides to a glower.

My thoughts scatter in the air like confetti. Words? I don't know them. Couldn't even tell you one. His hair is thick, short, and curling a little. Damp, like he just got out of the shower, and I want to run my fingers through it.

His gaze lingers on me, turning more hostile by the second, before he sighs like I'm inconveniencing him. This is how he seemed in high school—surly, irritated, grouchy. Not that we ever interacted.

"Great." He says the word like a curse, like I'm the last person he wants to see. He turns and walks into the apartment.

I knew he wouldn't remember me.

I hold back a humorless laugh of embarrassment and disbelief. I don't know why I'm surprised by his attitude. If I've learned one thing from my ex, Zach, and his crew, it's that gorgeous, famous people are allowed to be complete assholes. The world lets them get away with it.

Jamie Streicher is no different.

I take the open door as a sign to follow him. The dog sprints to my feet and jumps on me. She's wearing a pink collar, and I love her immediately.

"Down," he commands in a stern voice that makes the back of my neck prickle. The dog ignores him, hopping onto my legs and wagging her tail hard.

"Hi, doggy." I crouch down and laugh as she tries to give me kisses.

She's full of goofy, wild energy, doing these little tippy-taps with her paws on the floor as her tail wags so hard it might fall off. Her butt wiggles in the cutest way as I scratch the spot above her tail.

I'm in love.

Jamie clears his throat with disapproval. Embarrassment flickers in my chest but I shove it away. I'm here to help him with his dog; what's his problem? When I straighten up, my face feels warm.

Also, his apartment? It's one of the nicest places I've ever been inside. It's one of the nicest places I've ever *seen*. Floor-to-ceiling windows span two stories and overlook the water and North Shore Mountains, filling the open-concept living room and kitchen with light. The kitchen is sparkling and spacious, and even though the living room is cluttered with moving boxes and dog toys, the enormous sectional sofa looks so comfy and welcoming. There are stairs, which I assume lead to the bedrooms. Through the windows, I can see North Vancouver and the mountains. Even on a stormy day in the worst of the rainy, bleak Vancouver winter, the view will be spectacular.

I bet this place has a huge bathtub.

"What's her name?" I ask Jamie as I pet the dog. She's leaning against me, clearly loving all this attention.

His jaw ticks and the way he stares at me makes my stomach dip. His green eyes are so sharp and piercing, and I wonder if this guy has ever smiled. "I don't know. She's a rescue."

On the floor near the couch, there's a giant fluffy dog bed, and about a hundred colorful toys are scattered throughout the living room. A water bowl and empty food bowl sit on the floor in the kitchen, and on the counter, there's a giant bag of treats, half-empty. The dog runs over to one of the toys before bringing it to Jamie's feet and looking up at him, wagging her tail.

"I have to go to the arena, so let's get this over with," Jamie says, like I'm wasting his time. He stalks past me, and as he passes, his scent whooshes up my nose.

My eyes practically cross. He smells incredible. It's that un-pin-downable scent of men's deodorant—sharp, spicy, bold, fresh, and clean, all at the same time. The scent is probably called Avalanche or Hurricane or something powerful and unstoppable. I want to put my face in his shirt and huff. I'd probably pass out.

As he moves around the kitchen, showing me where the dog's food is, I'm struck by the way he moves with power and grace. His back muscles ripple under his shirt. His shoulders are so broad. He's so, so freaking tall.

I realize he still hasn't even introduced himself. This is something famous people did on Zach's tour when they came backstage, like they expect you to know who they are.

"All our communication will be through email or text," Jamie says. "Walk the dog, feed the dog, keep her out of trouble. I've already taken her to the vet and for grooming." He glances at her again.

I offer him a reassuring smile. "I can handle all of that."

"Good." His tone is sharp.

Wow. Mr. Personality, right here. I swallow with difficulty. He's so bossy.

A shiver rolls over me, and my skin tingles. I bet he's bossy in bed, too.

"Because it's your job," he adds.

A sick feeling moves up my throat but I shove it down. I'm not sixteen anymore. I know better, and I know his type. After Zach, I know not to fall for guys like this—famous guys. Guys with an ego. Guys who think they can do whatever they want without consequences.

Guys who will just get tired of me and cast me aside.

"On game days, I have a nap after lunch," he says over his shoulder as I follow him upstairs. "I need total silence."

It takes all of my willpower not to salute him and say, *sir, yes, sir!* Something tells me he wouldn't laugh. "I'll take her out on a long walk during that time."

He grunts. That's probably his version of crying tears of joy.

In the upstairs hallway, he stops at an open doorway. The room is empty except for a handful of large boxes and a mattress wrapped in plastic.

"This will be my room?" I ask.

He frowns, and my stomach squirms.

"I mean, this will be the room where I sleep when you're away?" I clarify so he doesn't think I'm trying to move in full time or something. "When I'm taking care of the dog."

He folds his arms. "Yes."

The way he stares at me, it's making my stomach do tippy-taps like the dog's paws on the floor. My nervous reaction is to smile again, and his frown lines deepen.

"Great." My voice is practically a chirp.

He tilts his chin to the bathroom down the hall. "You can use that bathroom. I have my own en suite."

His eyes linger on me, and I try not to shift under the weight of his gaze. This guy does *not* like me, but I'm going to turn that around once he realizes how much easier I can make his life. Besides, he'll never even see me.

Losing this job is not an option.

Read *Behind the Net* or listen in duet audio!

Want a bonus spicy scene with Finn and Olivia?

Five years later, Finn still can't keep his hands off Liv. Part 1 of the bonus scene is spicy, part 2 is wholesome with the whole Rhodes gang.

To receive the bonus scene, sign up for my newsletter at www.stephaniearcherauthor.com/finn or scan the QR code below.

I send 1-2 emails a month with updates about what I'm working on, fun facts about the books, and chatty stuff about makeup, TV, and podcasts.

Author's Note

And that's a wrap on the Rhodes brothers' love stories! Thank you so much for picking up this book. Writing the Queen's Cove series has been the most creatively fulfilling, mind-bending, hilarious, challenging, life-altering experience. I promise I'm not obsessed with people getting married, I just had this idea for 'four brothers, four weddings,' and these books appeared in my head. I set out to write something for myself that was pure candy—funny, spicy, swoony, and heartwarming—and it turned in to… all of this. I'm forever grateful to my readers. You changed my life.

If you enjoyed this book, please consider leaving me a review. Reviews help other readers find books they love.

Even before I wrote That Kind of Guy, I knew this book was going to be my favorite. I *swoon* for the "guy falls first" trope (lol, can you tell?). I also wanted to do a contemporary take on fated mates, and Finn and Olivia appeared. Something about people finding their way back to each other at the right time makes my heart very happy.

Wrapping up this series makes me feel like my favorite TV show is ending, but I am *so* excited for what's next in Queen's Cove. Perhaps you noticed the anvil-sized hints I dropped about Beck and Cassidy. Ever since he walked into my head during *The Wrong Mr. Right*, I've been excited to write his book. I can't wait to ruin Beck's life. I'm not sure when that book will be out yet.

You know when you have to sign something, but you don't

have a flat surface so you need to use someone's back? That's how I wrote this book. Major thanks to Helen Camisa, who let me voice note most of the plot to her, and who always has hilarious, wild, swoony ideas. You have her to thank for Miri organizing the strippers. Thank you to Brittany Kelley, Grace Reilly, and Bruce for being the best virtual coworkers ever. Or maybe the worst, because we're sending each other gifs when we should be writing. You all rock. Thank you to Alana Schick for explaining how a PhD program works. Any errors in this book are my fault entirely. Thank you to my besties, Sarah Clarke, Alanna Goobie, Bryan Hansen, and Anthea Song, for cheering me on and telling me I can do anything. Huge props to my editor, Jessica Snyder, for gently leading me in the right direction.

And lastly, thank you to my guy, Tim, the inspiration behind Finn's list of injuries. You're the most accident-prone person I've ever met—the hospital is ready to give us our own parking spot—but you're everything to me.

In the meantime, I'm starting a new series! The first book in my hockey romance series will be out in the summer of 2023.

Until next time,
xo Stephanie

**Turn the page to discover more spicy,
laugh-out-loud romances from Stephanie Archer.**

THE VANCOUVER STORM SERIES

S T E P H A N I E   A R C H E R

He's the hot, grumpy goalie I had a crush on in high school ∴.. and now I'm his live-in assistant.

After my ex crushed my dreams in the music industry, I'm done with getting my heart broken. Working as an assistant for an NHL player was supposed to be a breeze, but nothing about Jamie Streicher is easy. He's intimidatingly hot, grumpy, and can't stand me. Keeping things professional will be no problem, even when he demands I move in with him.

Beneath his surliness, though, Jamie's surprisingly sweet and protective.

When he finds out my ex was terrible in bed, his competitive nature flares, and he encourages and spoils me in every way. The creative spark I used to feel about music? It's back, and I'm writing songs again. Between wearing his jersey at games, fun, rowdy parties with the team, and being brave on stage again, I'm falling for him.

He could break my heart, but maybe I'm willing to take that chance.

Behind the Net *is a grumpy-sunshine, pro hockey romance with lots of spice and an HEA. It's the first book in the Vancouver Storm series and can be read as a standalone.*

The best way to get back at my horrible ex? Fake date his rival.

Being the team physiotherapist for a bunch of pro hockey players is challenging enough without my ex joining the team. He's the reason I don't date hockey players.

Vancouver Storm's new captain and the top scorer in pro hockey, Rory Miller, is the arrogant, flirtatious hockey player I tutored in high school. And he's just agreed to be my fake boyfriend. I get sweet revenge. Rory gets to clean up his image. It's the perfect deal.

Faking with him is fun and addictive, though, and beneath the bad boy swagger, Rory's sweet, funny, and protective.

He teaches me to skate. He sleeps in my bed. He kisses me like it's real.

But is there anything fake about our feelings?

The Fake Out *is a pro hockey fake dating romance. It's the second book in the Vancouver Storm series but can be read as a standalone.*

My arrogant fake fiancé? I can't stand him.

Cocky and charismatic Emmett Rhodes isn't a relationship kind of guy, but now that he's running for mayor of our small town, his bachelor past is hurting the campaign.

Thankfully, I'm the last woman who would *ever* fall for him.

We're total opposites—he's a golden retriever and I'm sharp and snarky, but he'll co-sign on my restaurant loan if I play his devoted fiancée. Between romantic dates, a prom night re-do, and visits to a secret beach, things heat up, and the line between real and ruse is lit on fire. I'm starting to see another side of Mr Popular, and now I wonder if I was all wrong.

We can't keep our hands off each other, but it's all for show . . . right?

A hilarious, enemies-to-lovers, fake dating romantic comedy with lots of spice and an HEA. This is the first book in the Queen's Cove series and can be read as a standalone.

The hot, commitment-phobe surfer is the only one I can turn to . . .

In my small town bookstore, I'm surrounded by book boyfriends, but I've never had one in real life. At almost 30, I've never been in love, and my bookstore isn't breaking even. Something needs to change, and I know exactly who's going to help me: Wyatt Rhodes, the guy everyone wants.

He agrees to be my relationship coach, but his lessons aren't what I expected.

Between surfing, mortifying dates, and revamping my store, his lessons are more about drawing me out of my shell than changing me into someone new. But when we add praise-filled 'spice lessons' to the curriculum, it's clear he wants me. He's leaving town and I'm staying to run my store, so it can't work, but that doesn't seem to matter to him.

He's supposed to find me someone to fall for but instead, we're falling for each other.

A hilarious, small town, friends-to-lovers romantic comedy with lots of spice and an HEA. This is the second book in the Queen's Cove series but can be read as a standalone.

The deal is simple: the grumpy guy will pay off my debt if I find him a wife.

Holden Rhodes is grouchy, unfairly hot, and has hated me for years. He's the last person I'd choose to inherit an inn with. As we renovate the inn and put his dating skills to practice, though, I see a different side of him.

What if I was all wrong about Holden?

When we add 'friends with benefits' to the deal, our chemistry is so hot the sparks could burn down the inn. Holden's a secret romantic, and I'm secretly falling for him.
I'm terrible at bartending, a video of a bear stealing my *toy* went viral, and everyone in this small town knows my business, but Holden Rhodes is so much more than I expected.

I don't want him to find love with anyone but me.

A grumpy-sunshine, friends-with-benefits, small town romantic comedy with lots of spice and an HEA. This is the third book in the Queen's Cove series but can be read as a standalone.